HAPPY
Is the
BRIDE

Center Point
Large Print

Also by Janet Dailey and available from
Center Point Large Print:

Christmas in Cowboy Country
Long, Tall Christmas
Christmas on My Mind

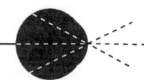

**This Large Print Book carries the
Seal of Approval of N.A.V.H.**

HAPPY
Is the
BRIDE

Janet Dailey
Lori Wilde
Cat Johnson
Kate Pearce

CENTER POINT LARGE PRINT
THORNDIKE, MAINE

This Center Point Large Print edition
is published in the year 2017 by arrangement with
Kensington Publishing Corp.

The text of this Large Print edition is unabridged.
In other aspects, this book may vary
from the original edition.
Printed in the United States of America
on permanent paper.
Set in 16-point Times New Roman type.

ISBN: 978-1-68324-465-3

Library of Congress Cataloging-in-Publication Data

Names: Wilde, Lori. Man of honor. | Johnson, Cat. Getting saddled. |
Pearce, Kate, 1963– Taming the sheriff. | Dailey, Janet. Wedding bet.
Title: Happy is the bride / Janet Dailey, Lori Wilde, Cat Johnson, Kate
Pearce.
Description: Large print edition. | Thorndike, Maine : Center Point
Large Print, 2017.
Identifiers: LCCN 2017019370 | ISBN 9781683244653
(hardcover : alk. paper)
Subjects: LCSH: Romance fiction, American. | Weddings—Fiction.
Classification: LCC PS648.L6 H35 2017 | DDC 813/.0850806—dc23
LC record available at https://lccn.loc.gov/2017019370

Contents

Man of Honor

Lori Wilde

Chapter One

"I'm getting married. Say you'll be my man of honor."

Air Force Major pilot Shane Freemont stared at his foster sister and best friend in the whole world, Ellie Carson, feeling a band of hot tension knot up his shoulder blades the same way it did at the end of a dangerous mission.

During the heat of the battle, he was fine. Cucumber cool. Ice in his veins. It was the aftermath that got him. The moment when everything fell silent. The sapping ebb of adrenaline and testosterone catching up to his muscles and bones.

They were standing in line at an Austin, Texas, vegan bakery at ten a.m. on a Sunday morning in late May. Ellie wore a lacy white maxi dress, her long curly blond hair braided at the temples and held back with daisy clips. With the powder-blue wall behind her and a radiant glow spilling from her pores, she looked like an angel.

"Married? To whom?"

"Why, Brady, of course. I told you all about him."

"That's impossible." Shane grunted. "You've only known the guy two months. You can't be serious."

"Don't give me that look."

"What look?"

"The I'm-the-big-brother-and-I-know-best look. Just be my friend, okay?"

"Can I be the rational friend who points out when you're about to make a big mistake?"

"No," she said solidly. "You must be the supportive, nonjudgmental friend today."

"I was afraid of that."

"Please listen. I knew from the first date that Brady was The One." Ellie folded her delicate palms over her heart, a honker of a diamond ring glittering on the third finger of her left hand.

The happiness shining from her dear face scared the crap out of him. He didn't trust it. Feared she was leaping right off a cliff without looking down to see if there was a net.

Shane clenched and unclenched his hands. "What if it falls apart?"

"Supportive friend," Ellie chirped.

"Um . . ." Shane cast around for something supportive to say. "No judgment. I just want to know if you've fully thought this through. Marriage is a big deal."

"I have faith." She said it as if that made perfect sense. That faith would solve everything. "You have to take risks to reap rewards."

Shane believed in taking risks. Calculated ones. Risks based on analysis and experience and preparation. Risks that left nothing to chance or affairs of the heart. That belief had kept him alive for thirty years and nothing was going to change his mind.

"But is the risk worth the reward?" he persisted.

"Without a doubt. I've never felt this way about anyone. This is happening. Get used to it."

"When is the wedding?" he asked, hoping for a date three years in the future.

"June eighteenth."

"Of next year?"

"*This* June eighteenth."

"As in three weeks from now?"

"As in." Ellie did a little happy dance right there in the bakery. "I wanted to do it while you were on leave. I can't get married without my best friend."

Shane felt like a shit heel for what he was going to say next, but supportive friend or not, it had to be said. He took her small hand in his, ran his thumb over the back of her knuckles. "You don't have to go through with this wedding. Even if you're pregnant. I'll help you. You won't have to go it alone. I'll be there for you, Ell. Always."

Ellie's dark eyes dimmed and her sweet smile evaporated. She tugged her hand from his, blinking at him as if he'd reached out and slapped her. She sucked in an audible breath. "I'm *not* pregnant."

He cocked his head, confused. "Then why the rush? You don't have to marry the guy, Ellie, just because you said yes. Think it through. You got caught up in the moment. A shiny ring. A declaration of love. Understandable. It's not too late to change your mind."

Her chin trembled slightly, and for a moment he thought she was going to cry, but she hardened her jaw and said, "What you're failing to understand is that I love him with all my heart and soul."

But how can you love him? He wanted to yell some sense into her, but instead he said in the softest voice he could muster, "You don't even know him."

"But that's the thing. I *do* know him. From our very first date when we saw into each other, soul to soul. Brady and I are soul mates."

Soul mates? Oh Lord. Shane jammed his fingers through his hair in frustration. "Ellie, I'm trying here, but that sounds wacky."

"Just because you've never experienced love at first sight doesn't mean it doesn't exist."

Okay, he wasn't getting through to her. Time to try another tactic. "Why can't you wait? What's the harm in waiting? It would give you time to plan the wedding of your dreams."

"I've been waiting for twenty-eight years for my Prince Charming. I don't want to wait a second longer. I want my life to start now. I don't have parents to pay for the wedding and I can't expect Brady to foot the bill for an elaborate shindig. A small, intimate wedding on a budget works fine."

"But if you waited until your friend Kelly's tour in Afghanistan is over, she could be here. And you would have a proper maid of honor."

"*You're* my best friend."

"Kelly's a woman."

Ellie straightened, ironed her mouth flat. Her bottom lip trembled again and this time she was unable to fortify it. "If you don't want to be my man of honor, just say so. I understand. You're a traditionalist. A macho pilot. Maid of honor duties are too girlie for you even with the name change."

Shane's heart stumbled. The last thing he wanted was to hurt her feelings. When he looked at her, he saw that scared, defenseless eight-year-old with thick glasses and a severe overbite who the other kids picked on. He'd come to her defense, punching out the bullies and getting in trouble for it. He felt that same surge of protectiveness for her now.

"Whoa there, Ell. Don't misunderstand. I'm humbled to be your man of honor if that's what you want."

All right, maybe not thrilled. That would be overstating. And yes, the thought of leading the bridal party and helping Ellie shop for a dress and planning the bachelorette party made him twitchy, but he was an Air Force pilot.

He thumbed his nose at death every week. He could handle that froufrou, estrogen stuff without feeling like he had to surrender his man card.

"If it's not the maid of honor thing, why are you so against me marrying Brady?"

"You really want to know?"

"I do."

"The two of you don't have anything in common. He's from old Texas ranching money and you and I are from the way wrong side of the tracks. He's country and you're city. He's a cattleman and you're a vegan."

"Big deal. He's handsome and kind and he loves me as much as I love him. We can work through anything else."

"Just because you're in love with someone doesn't mean they're right for you."

Ellie hitched in a stuttering breath and whispered, "You've never been in love, have you, Shane?"

"I love *you*," he said staunchly.

"It's not the same thing." She folded her arms and shook her head, and he couldn't help feeling he'd disappointed her in a hundred different ways. "And if you can't be happy for me, I don't know if you should come to the wedding at all."

A flood of heat flushed his body. "You don't mean that."

She tilted her head and studied him, her eyes

soft and sad. "I've known you since I was eight years old, and you're the only family I have. No biological brother could have been better to me than you. But Brady is about to become my husband and—" Her eyes rounded and her jaw dropped.

"Ell?" Alarm raised the hair on the back of his neck. "What is it?"

"I get it now. You're *jealous* of my relationship with Brady because you don't have someone to call your own."

"What?" Shane snorted, incensed. His pulse quickened and heat burned through his bloodstream. "No. That's not it."

He was not jealous that she'd found love and he hadn't.

Was he?

Shane gulped. Maybe he was.

Ellie placed a hand on his forearm. "You don't have to worry. No man could ever take your place in my heart. And we'll still talk on the phone and text as much as we ever did. Things will stay the same between us. You'll see."

"Things will change."

"For the better," she said. "You have a friend in Brady. He already respects the hell out of you and he appreciates all the ways you took care of me when we were growing up."

Shane exhaled on a loud chuff. He wasn't holding his breath on that one. He didn't let many people into his close circle of friends. "Your mind is made up."

She smiled gently at him like he was a deluded child who understood nothing and nodded. "I'm doing this with or without you."

He shrugged, offered up a half smile. "I had to take a shot at talking you out of it."

"I can appreciate that. But since you can't, I need to know. Are you with me?"

He chucked her lightly under the chin. "I'm always with you, kid. I have your back until the end of time, and if it all falls to pieces, I'll be there to put you back together again."

"It's not going to fall to pieces." Her face glowed with certainty.

And he realized he'd never been that certain about anything in his life. "I'm at your service. Tell me where to start."

"Help me pick out the wedding cake," she said.

"Done."

"Oh, and I want you to meet Brady." She turned as they reached the counter so she was looking out the bakery window.

"I'll have to meet him if you're going to marry him."

"That's good. Because here he comes." She waved over Shane's shoulder as the bell above the door chimed.

Ah, she'd planned a surprise attack all along. Damn. Ambushed by his best friend.

16

"Oh," she said. "And Brady's got his best woman with him."

"Best woman?"

"Yes." Ellie giggled. "Gender-bending wedding attendants on both sides of the aisle."

Shane grunted. He loved Ellie and he'd move heaven and earth to make her happy. If this was what she wanted, he was all in. Clenching his jaw and forcing a smile, he turned toward the door.

And came face-to-face with the most gorgeous woman he'd ever seen.

From the second Meg Stoddard laid eyes on Ellie Carson, she distrusted her.

Although, to be fair, Meg had distrusted her from the moment her best friend, Brady Cutwright, had told her how he'd met Ellie.

Through a matchmaking service that professed they could teach anyone how to fall in love with anybody.

Warning bells had sounded in Meg's head and she'd immediately thought, *gold digger.*

"Don't look so disapproving," Brady had said. "Ellie and I are so different and come from opposite worlds. We would never have met any other way."

Maybe you shouldn't have met, Meg couldn't help thinking.

Being in the hospitality business as the manager of her parents' dude ranch, Meg had honed her

17

ability to read people and situations quickly and to listen to her gut. And her gut was telling her that a starving graphic artist who'd grown up in an orphanage saw Brady as a shiny meal ticket.

Of course, she hadn't actually met Ellie yet, so yeah, she was being a bit judgy. She and Brady lived on adjoining ranches and they'd been best friends since they could walk. She couldn't feel more protective of him if he'd been her brother.

They'd seen each other through everything—college, career challenges, relationship potholes . . . They'd gone on trips together. Gotten drunk for the first time together. Shared laughter and tears.

Brady was the salt of the earth. Kind, loyal, generous. The one true constant in Meg's life, and she knew without a shadow of a doubt he would always be there for her, come what may.

Which was why she felt so protective of him.

What troubled Meg most was that she'd never seen Brady this smitten over a woman and she feared he was in for a big crash. Particularly because he was refusing to draw up a prenuptial agreement.

The woman they'd come to meet was standing at the bakery counter.

Ellie looked like an ethereal, big-eyed, hippy-chick waif. Meg recognized her from the photographs Brady had shown her and from Ellie's social media pages.

Yes, Meg had checked her out. What loyal friend wouldn't snoop under the circumstances? Brady seemed to go in for the damsel-in-distress type. One of the reasons why she'd never taken their relationship beyond friendship.

Keep an open mind. Tacking on a smile, she softened her face. *This is me. Being supportive.* Muttered a silent mantra: *reserve judgment, reserve judgment.*

"Angel!" Brady exclaimed and rushed into Ellie's embrace.

"Pookie!" she cried and strapped her slender arms around his waist as they melted into each other's mouths.

A collective "Aww!" went up from the bakery patrons.

For the life of her, Meg couldn't keep from rolling her eyes and she was grateful Brady's back was turned so he couldn't see her.

But the guy standing beside Ellie saw it, and an amused smile tipped up his lips. Meg's heart skipped a beat.

Six foot. Black hair, short military cut, wicked dark eyes, five-o'clock shadow, motorcycle boots. Great posture. Cheekbones straight from *Last of the Mohicans* casting call. Brown bomber jacket. Cocky jaw. An even cockier stance.

And just who might you be?

Meg sucked in air as every muscle in her body tightened and tingled. Heat filled her pelvis, flared up her spine, lodged in her brain. Her cells came alive, wriggling and tingling. It was instant. Electric. A throb of energy strong enough to buckle her knees and hijack her brain.

Quickly, she stiffened her legs and dropped her gaze before she burst into flames. Who cared who he was? That was just estrogen talking, and the fact that she hadn't had a date in oh . . . quickly, she mentally counted on her fingers and came up short. Thirteen months.

Neither was she the only one ogling Mr. I'm Too Sexy for This Earth. Half the women in the bakery were giving him come-hither glances. He was definitely blessed with a deep gene pool. Who could miss those broad shoulders, pearly whites, and proud nose?

Oh, the damage he could do to her.

Unsettled, Meg loudly cleared her throat. "Ahem."

Sheepishly, Brady and Ellie broke apart.

With her cheeks blushing pink, Ellie turned to the man behind the counter. "I called earlier. We have an appointment to sample wedding cakes."

"Jan will be right with you," the man said and motioned for them to step aside so he could wait on the next customer.

"Excuse me for being rude. I just had to have some Brady sugar first," Ellie said and extended a petite hand. "I'm Ellie."

"Hi." Meg upped the wattage on her smile,

giving it her best I-Run-a-Dude-Ranch welcome. "Megan Stoddard."

"Brady's told me so much about you." Ellie's dark eyes sparkled like rainbow obsidian in direct sunlight. "I just know we're going to be close. I've never had a sister."

The woman possessed an arresting combo of natural blond hair and ebony eyes. She was even more beautiful in person than in pictures, and Meg could see why Brady was attracted to her. Not only beautiful but intelligent, too.

Brady wrapped his arm around Ellie's shoulders, pulled her close, pressed his lips to the top of her head.

"He's told me a lot about you, too," Meg said, holding on to her skepticism in the face of Ellie's overwhelming optimism.

Yes, Ellie seemed really nice and genuine, but she might just be a truly gifted swindler. Meg noticed Mr. I'm Too Sexy for This Earth looked as dubious as she felt. At least they had something in common: mutual mistrust of their friends' marriage madness.

"This is my best friend, Shane Freemont," Ellie introduced. "He's my man of honor."

Shane stepped forward, an I'm-barely-civilized smile on his handsome face, a roguish glint in his blue eyes. He stuck out his hand. Big. Square. Neatly trimmed nails. Callused palm.

Meg took it.

And was totally unprepared for the jolt of skin-to-skin contact. Her heart flipped up into her throat. She gulped it back down. It flipped up again. Her palm was seared to his. She wanted to pull it away, pull it out of the fire.

But she was transfixed by his lush, full smile. Mesmerized. Awestruck.

Commanding, steely, and yet somehow totally genuine, he carried his Top Gun good looks like he had no idea he was a rare eagle.

"Good to meet you," he said, his words normal, pedestrian even, but his voice . . .

Oh my God, that voice! Low and deep and smooth. A charming voice, so warm and cozy it stoked images of crackling logs in a fireplace, snowbanks outside the window, and bare skin on plush rugs.

Hot sex, Meg thought and blinked at him vacantly, struggling to keep her breathing slow and easy. "You too."

He was still holding on to her hand, pumping it leisurely. His stare pinned on hers.

She should look away. A smart person would look away. She didn't look away. *Stupid.*

Meg hissed in air through her teeth. "You . . ."

"Yes?" His blues eyes were incandescent. Or maybe it was just the bakery lighting. And he smelled so good. Like sandalwood and leather and sage. A musky, manly scent that unraveled her.

"You can let go now," she murmured.

"Huh?" he said, as if he'd been so busy peering into her he'd gone momentarily deaf.

"My hand. May I have it back?"

"Oh." His face dissolved into a genuine smile. "Sure. Yes. Right."

But he didn't drop her hand. Instead, he leaned in, tugged her toward him slightly, and she thought, *Holy vegan cupcakes, he's going to kiss me.*

Chapter Two

Shane Freemont did not, in fact, kiss her.

Meg felt both desperately relieved and wildly disappointed. Her heart spun like a whirligig in a wind tunnel. What was the matter with her? She wasn't the kind of woman who wished for strangers' kisses.

Instead, he ducked his head close to her ear and whispered, "We need to talk."

What? Hmm. Yep. Sure. Anything for Mr. I'm Too Sexy for This Earth.

He let go of her hand then and, untethered, she floated dizzily. Before she could gather her thoughts to make a coherent reply, a side door opened and a plump woman with a cherubic smile and dangly Ewok earrings emerged.

"Hi." She motioned them to follow her into the back room. "I'm Jan. Are you ready to taste wedding cakes?"

Yes! Chocolate. Sugar. Butter. That was precisely what she needed to ground her. *Lead on, Jan.*

Brady took Ellie's hand and they went together, leaving Shane and Meg to bring up the rear. Meg purposely held back. She didn't want to walk abreast with the man who'd sent her ovaries into overdrive.

But Shane held back, too, flourishing his arm for her to proceed ahead of him. "Beauty first."

Oh, he was a charmer. "No, you go. I insist." She motioned him forward. She tried not to ogle him, but he was so damn gorgeous. Her eyes were magnetically drawn to him.

He didn't budge. "After you."

"Are you using this as an excuse to stare at my butt?"

That sly smile was back. "It *is* worth staring at."

Meg snorted, pointed. "You go."

"Seriously," Ellie called over her shoulder. "Is the entire wedding going to go like this with you two?"

"Get a move on," Brady added. "Who cares who goes first?"

A sheepish expression crawled across Shane's face. Meg felt dopey as well for making a big deal of it and she moved forward.

But so did Shane.

Their shoulders collided in the doorway, and for a moment they were momentarily stuck. Sandwiched by the doorframe and each other.

Instant heat fled across her shoulder, down her body, and flooded her pelvis. Embedded there. Swam around. Got comfy.

Good grief. What was this nonsense?

"You go forward," Shane said, his voice sandpaper gruff. "I'll step back."

Hmm, he sounded unsettled. Maybe more unsettled than she.

Who cares? Get away from him.

Away from the feelings that touching him provoked.

She gave a little hop, broke free of the doorway and his shoulder. But landed awkwardly on the kitten heels of her open-toed sandals and wobbled. What she wouldn't give to be wearing her cowgirl boots.

With spurs.

Shane grabbed her elbow to steady her.

For God's sake, stop touching me!

She wrenched away, but that upset her balance even more, and he snaked his arm around her waist to hold her in place.

Anchored. Secure.

Meg thought the shoulder-touching thing had been bad, but it didn't begin to compare with the hormonal explosion when his broad hand was splayed just under her right breast and his body was pressed against her and his face was so close to hers that if she turned her head, their lips would touch.

The nearer he got, the better he smelled. Good enough to lick.

Or eat.

He could seduce a woman with his scent alone. What was that aftershave? Versace? Paco Rabanne? Ralph Lauren? Except he hadn't shaved this morning, as evidenced by the scruffy jaw, so no aftershave.

Could it be his natural bouquet?

If this was his natural fragrance, he was the Lamborghini of pheromones, Meg decided, struggling to regain her equilibrium. You could never trust that kind of power. A man who smelled like that was bound to attract women far and wide. A cornucopia of women would fall at his feet, rendered helpless by such an enticing aroma.

Even ol' Jan, who was clearly married from the wedding ring on her finger, inhaled deeply when she walked by him.

Ah, crap!

Meg was toast the minute he'd wrapped his arm around her waist. A light-seeking moth scorched by his insanely good-smelling flame.

"You okay?" Shane asked.

"Fine. Thanks." Why did she have to sound so breathless?

She staggered away from him, blindly entering a room set up with slices of various cakes for sampling. Disoriented, she glanced around.

Ellie and Brady were already feeding each other bites of strawberry cake with fondant icing and grinning at each other like they knew the secrets of the universe and weren't about to enlighten anyone.

Why was she here? Oh yes, Brady. She'd agreed to be his best woman. Meet Ellie. Help the happy couple choose the perfect wedding cake.

She accepted the thin slice of strawberry cake Jan passed to her. It tasted like summer, red and sweet and ripe.

Jan extended a plate to Shane, but he waved it away.

"Shane doesn't like strawberries," Ellie said. "So this one's out."

"Shane's not the groom," Meg said, belatedly realizing how sharp she sounded. She wasn't a sharp person. Normally she was very upbeat and happy. But something about this guy knocked her off her game. "Um . . . I'm just saying, it's your day. You should have the cake you want."

"Agreed," Shane said. "If you want strawberry, Ell, get strawberry."

"There are many more cakes to taste." Jan cut off small chunks of another cake. "Banana with peanut butter cream cheese frosting."

Meg liked that one, too, but hey, it was cake. What's not to like?

"Too Elvisy," Ellie said. "Maybe in Vegas, but not for a dude ranch wedding."

"You're getting married at a dude ranch?" Shane grunted.

"Meg's dude ranch," Brady explained.

Shane shot her a look. "You own a dude ranch?"

She hot-potatoed his gaze, focused on tasting

the cake. "My parents own Hawk Creek Ranch. But they're retired now and live in town. I manage it."

"What's wrong with a dude ranch?" Ellie studied Shane as if his approval meant the world.

"Nothing's wrong with a dude ranch," Shane said. "It's just not you."

Ellie linked her arm through Brady's. "Brady's a cowboy."

Shane eyed Brady, who was wearing cowboy boots, starched jeans, and a Stetson. "No kidding. What's that got to do with anything?"

Tension ripped through the room, as thick and solid as royal icing.

"Something you want to say, Shane?" Brady asked, resting a hand on his hip as if there was an invisible holster strapped there.

"Ellie's not a cowgirl and it's her big day. Why can't she have someplace she'd enjoy?"

"The dude ranch venue is free," Meg said. "My wedding gift to them."

"Listen up," Ellie said in a voice so strong and firm that Shane's eyes widened. "I *want* to get married at the dude ranch. I'm in love with a cowboy. My life is changing. *I'm* changing."

"Yeah, bending yourself into a pretzel for a guy you barely know."

"Shane!" Ellie scolded. "This isn't the time or place."

Shane looked like he wanted to say a lot more but clamped his lips closed, nodded curtly.

Brady stepped closer to Shane. Meg's pulse accelerated and she held her breath, fought an impulse to start a wedding cake food fight to defuse the situation.

"Let's call a truce. Put our feelings aside and make this work. We both love Ellie and want the best for her." Brady extended his hand. "Deal?"

Shane glanced at Ellie, who had her hands clasped together in front of her heart, in a prayer pose, her bottom lip tucked up between her teeth in a disarmingly waifish gesture.

Saps.

Ellie had both men wrapped around her pinkie. But Meg was on to her. Ellie was one of those eyelash-batting women who made guys feel all strong and protective. She was manipulating them every which way but loose.

"Deal," Shane said and shook Brady's hand.

Everyone fake smiled and went back to tasting cake. Waters calmed. Fires doused. Crisis averted.

"Which one is your favorite?" Jan polled after they'd sampled all the offerings.

"Carrot cake," Shane said, which didn't surprise Meg. All that spice.

"Chocolate," Brady voted. Of course. The old standby. Brady was nothing if not steady and consistent.

"Meg?" Ellie asked. "Which one is your pick?"

"It's not my wedding."

"But you have an opinion."

"What was your favorite?" Meg asked Ellie.

"White chiffon cake with white chocolate icing, blackberry mousse, and fresh raspberries."

The most expensive cake on the printed price list, Meg noticed. The cheapest was the chocolate. "I vote with Brady."

Ellie reached over to stroke her finger down Brady's jaw. "We can get chocolate for the groom's cake. Or—" she turned to Jan. "Can we get a half-and-half groom's cake? Half carrot cake, half chocolate, to please the two men in my life?"

"Sure. Whatever you'd like," Jan said.

"There now." Ellie smiled sweetly, her face a moonbeam. "Everyone's happy."

"But it will cost double," Jan added.

"Money's no object when it comes to my beloved's happiness," Brady cooed, opened his wallet, and took out his American Express Black Card.

Beloved? Cooing? Flashing his credit card? This was her Brady?

Though his net worth was somewhere in the neighborhood of twenty million, Meg had never seen Brady be frivolous with money. She didn't like the changes she saw in him. Not one bit.

And she couldn't help wondering if her best friend was following his heart to ruin.

"Wait." Shane put a restraining hand on Meg's elbow to keep her from leaving the room as Brady and Ellie followed Jan to the front counter to settle up their order. Felt another shock of energy run up his arm the same way it had when they'd shaken hands and bumped shoulders in the doorway.

Meg tensed.

Did she feel it, too? The heat? The electricity? The sparks?

Forget about that. Get to the point. He had to talk to her about the wedding.

She turned to face him, her expression cool, unruffled. She possessed liquid green eyes, a cynical mouth, and slender, expressive hands.

His pulse galloped. What was it about her that threw him off-kilter?

"Yes?" Her cool, arid tone made him think of Salt Lake City.

He widened his smile, hoping to charm her, but her eyes turned frostier. "Could we go somewhere after this?"

She stared at him warily. "Why?"

"We need to talk."

"About what?" She narrowed her eyes at him suspiciously, as if she thought he had ulterior motives.

"Them." He gestured in the direction Brady and Ellie had gone. "May I buy you lunch?"

"No, thanks. I'm full of cake."

"I saw a park across the street. We could walk and talk."

She hesitated for so long he was sure she was going to say no, but then she nodded. "I'll leave first. You can meet me over there. I don't want them to think we're talking about them behind their backs."

"But we are."

"They don't need to know that." She turned, cut off the conversation, and hurried after the happy couple.

Shane canted his head and watched her walk away, smiling. She could put that swing in his backyard anytime.

"Stop staring at my butt," she called over her shoulder and disappeared around the corner.

When Shane got back into the bakery lobby area, Meg was already telling Brady and Ellie good-bye. They invited him to lunch with them, but he declined. Waited until they'd left the bakery parking lot before trotting over to the park across the street.

He stood feeling the warm sunshine on his face, searching for Meg. When he didn't immediately see her, he wondered if she'd blown him off.

"Ahem."

He turned to find her standing in line at a kiosk that sold snacks for humans as well as the park ducks. Sunglasses perched on her nose, she looked adorable, and a spontaneous smile broke across his face.

"There you are," he said, coming up beside her.

"Here I am," she said dryly. "What do you want?"

You. With whipped cream and a cherry on top.

Meg took her turn at the counter, ordered duck food. The gangly teenager in the kiosk gave her a paper cone filled with little pelts and change for a five. Before moving away from the spot, Meg counted her change.

"Do you always do that?" Shane asked.

"Do what?" She slipped the coins into her pocket and moved off.

He followed her. "Count your change."

"Doesn't everyone?"

"No."

"Well, that's just silly. What if a clerk shorted you?"

"It's change. What's the most you could lose? A few cents?"

"It's not the money," she said. "It's the principle."

"Being?"

"It's not fair to shortchange someone, whether it's due to thievery, incompetence, or laziness."

"Wow," he said. "You're idealistic."

"I believe in justice."

"Do you hand the money back if they give you too much change?"

"Absolutely. Fair's fair. It cuts both ways."

"At least you're not a hypocrite."

"Did you think I was?"

He studied her straight posture, the proud tilt of her head. "It hadn't occurred to me, no. You seem like a moral, upstanding citizen."

"Thank you." She slid her sunglasses down on her nose and assessed him over the top of the rims.

"Listen," he said and momentarily got sidetracked by the fine freckles sprinkled over the bridge of her nose. He had a thing for freckles. Freckles were friendly, even if Meg Stoddard hadn't been exactly welcoming.

She craned her neck, blinked. "I'm listening, but you're not talking."

"Listen," he said again, starting over. "You're not any happier about this wedding than I am."

She pushed her sunglasses back up and pursed her lips.

Shane held his breath, felt his smile disappear as he waited for her answer. A bump of uncertainty, the likes of which he hadn't felt since asking a girl out for the first time, knocked against his ribs. He did his best not to squirm.

"No," she said finally. "I'm not."

"Their relationship happened too fast."

"Yes." Carrying her paper cone of duck food pellets, she started walking toward the pond.

He went after her.

Kids played on the lawn. A guy threw a Frisbee to his Border collie. A group of elderly folks practiced Tai Chi. Moms pushed babies in strollers. Dads carried toddlers on shoulders. Family day at the park.

"I mean, why the rush to the altar?"

"Is she pregnant?" Meg arched a perfect brow that peeked over the top of her sunglasses.

Shane had an irrational urge to trace that brow. With his tongue. "No. Which is my point. What's wrong with a long engagement?"

"Brady says when you've met your soul mate there's no reason to wait."

Shane blew a raspberry. "Soul mate?"

"You don't believe in soul mates?" Meg asked, her voice even, and Shane couldn't help feeling the question was some kind of test.

"No." He paused. "Do you?"

Meg shook her head, as if it was the most ridiculous thing she'd ever heard, and Shane breathed a sigh of relief. Okay. They might not trust each other, but they were on the same page.

"Ellie believes in love at first sight." Shane noticed that Meg's lips, even while pressed into that disapproving line, were utterly kissable. Plush and pink and shiny.

"Deranged."

"I know."

"I mean, what can you tell about someone in a split second?"

"Precisely."

Although he could tell from the way Meg moved with that smooth, sensual grace, she'd be good in bed. An image of her in *his* bed popped into Shane's head and it was all he could do to fight off an erection. It had been a long time since he'd been this turned on.

Meg sat down on a park bench beside the pond. "I like ducks," she said. "They follow me wherever I go."

"That's because you feed them."

"No, really, long before I fed them, whenever I'm near water, a duck comes up to me or lands near me. It's weird."

"Maybe it's just coincidence."

"Ducks calm me."

"Why's that?"

"It's something about the way they glide on the water. So beautiful and graceful."

"They're dirty birds," Shane said.

"You'd think you'd have more respect for them. Ducks are symbols of freedom. They fly. Like you do."

"They eat mud from the same water where they go to the bathroom."

"I don't think about that part."

"Tend to look on the bright side, do you?"

"By nature I'm an optimist."

"But not in the case of Brady and Ellie's romance?"

"Did you know that they met through a dating service that coaches people on how to fall in love?" she asked.

"What do you mean?" Shane sat beside her, acutely aware of how close they were.

Apparently she was aware of it, too. She tucked her purse into the small space he'd left between them.

Keep your distance, buddy.

Message received.

Ducks spied the paper cone in Meg's hand and came waddling out of the water. She tossed the pellets with a deft hand. They squawked and gobbled it up. Soon quacking feathered creatures surrounded their park bench.

"I don't know the details," she said. "But basically this dating service is a proponent of some study undertaken by a famed psychologist who claims the intimacy between two strangers can be accelerated simply by their asking each other a series of questions designed to escalate vulnerability."

"Seriously?"

"For realz." She tossed more pellets. "Brady let me see the questions."

He liked watching her move. Easy. Casual.

The gold bracelet at her wrist caught the sun, glittered. "The dating service forced their relationship."

"My thoughts exactly. Except that they both willingly went to a dating service that advertised this method of falling in love. So clearly they were both looking for someone."

"But it's not real love. How can it be when it's clearly manufactured?" Shane snorted.

"If it's love at all."

"How can a series of questions cause someone to fall in love? That's not how you fall in love. Falling in love takes time. Lots of time. There's no such thing as accelerating love."

"Well," Meg said, "some studies have shown that people who go through challenging events together form bonds more quickly."

"Bonds, yes. Love?" Shane shook his head.

"Ellie's pretty. I'll give her that. Lust at first sight is a thing. Chemical reaction. Hormones. Pheromones."

Shane's body confirmed that theory. He couldn't stop looking at Meg, or thinking about her. He wanted to touch her skin, smell her hair, taste her lips.

"You've got to admit Ellie does know how to get her way."

"Wait, what?" Shane blinked, felt like he'd gotten whiplash. He'd been mentally kissing Meg and wasn't sure he'd heard correctly.

He'd thought they were on the same page here.

"Your best friend," Meg said. "She's a little manipulative."

Shane's blood heated. "Whoa. Hold on there. Ellie's not the least bit manipulative. She's the kindest, most honest person I've ever known. If anyone in that relationship is manipulative, it's Brady."

"How can you say that? He's the one with money. Ellie's taking advantage of his generosity."

Shane turned on the bench so that he was facing her. Meg didn't move except to dust the duck food crumbs from her hands.

"Excuse me? What are you saying?"

Finally, Meg swiveled around, met his eyes. If the purse hadn't been between them their knees would be touching. "I can't help but wonder if Ellie is more interested in Brady's money than she is in the man."

That went all over Shane. In fact, it pissed him off.

Who was Miss High and Mighty here to be passing judgment on the one person in the world Shane loved? He had to clamp his teeth down on his tongue to keep from saying something he would regret.

He chuffed out a breath. "Ellie's not after his money. She doesn't have a greedy bone in her body. All she wants is to be loved."

Meg pursed her lips. "For Brady's sake, I hope you're right."

"He'd better treat Ellie like a princess or he's going to have to answer to me. And you can tell him that verbatim." Shane jumped to his feet, fists knotted at his sides, heart racing. Shit. He was letting her get him worked up.

Calmly, coolly, fully in control, Meg gazed up at him. "Passionate, aren't you?"

"About the people and things I care about? You betcha."

"I admire your loyalty," she said. "Even if you do irritate me."

"Me? *I* irritate *you*? Listen, lady, if my best friend wasn't marrying your best friend, I wouldn't have two words to say to you."

With infuriating casualness, Meg picked up her purse and got to her feet. "You may be one sexy beast, Shane Freemont, but you are *not* God's gift to womankind."

"We don't have to like each other," he said, even at the very moment he was wanting to rip off her clothes and roll around on the ground with her. "But we do have to get through this wedding without causing problems. Because I'll be damned if I'll let you ruin the happiest day of Ellie's life."

Chapter Three

Meg regretted how she'd let things get out of hand with Shane. He was right. They both loved their friends and wanted the best for them. It was their loyalty that put them at odds with each other.

So she phoned him when she got home. Apologized. Called for a peace treaty.

Shane graciously told her she had nothing to apologize for. She was only looking out for Brady's best interests, and he respected that.

When she saw him the following Saturday at the cowboy-themed couples' wedding shower he was throwing for Ellie and Brady, she had to confess that she was impressed. He'd rented out the party room of an Austin hot spot that had cozy, rustic décor and overlooked the Colorado River.

The room was decorated in denim and red bandannas. The nubby brown material of the table runners accentuated the barnyard feel. The centerpiece crystal vases, filled with daisies and framed by white flickering candles, added a subtle touch of elegance.

Straw cowboy hats of different sizes, colors, and stages of wear, strategically hung on the back wall, continued the folksy Texas chic. A burlap banner hanging from the cedar rafters was adorned with Brady's and Ellie's names cut from scraps of denim, and Photoshopped pictures of the bride and groom-to-be as toddlers were juxtaposed against their engagement portrait.

Off to the side was a photo booth complete with props—wanted posters, more cowboy hats, hobbyhorses, Lone Ranger masks, toy cap guns. Along with paper signage on wooden sticks to hold up that read "Wild West," "Howdy," "Yee-Haw," and "Outlaw."

Country music played over the sound system. Currently, Jerry Jeff Walker was singing, "I Love You." Two buffets were set up, one for beef barbecue, the other vegan fare. A chalkboard, suspended over a metal trough packed with ice, beers, water, soda, and wine coolers, proclaimed "Waterin' Hole."

Wow. How had Shane put it all together so quickly? He must have been on it the entire week.

She searched the crowd of arriving guests and spied Shane glad-handing some of Brady's friends. He was dressed in starched jeans, a white button-down, Western-style shirt, and square-toed ostrich quill boots.

Their eyes met and that same one-two punch of breathless electricity passed between them again.

Except it was stronger this time. Darker, richer, more potent.

Her body wanted his something fierce. But that was a line she couldn't, wouldn't cross. Too fraught with complications. An affair with this package of walking dynamite could go wrong in more ways than she could count.

He lifted his head, made eye contact with her, and surrendered a big grin. Caught off guard by the genuineness of his smile, Meg ducked her head and pretended she hadn't seen him, struggling to sort out the fizzy effervescence in her stomach.

What was the matter with her? She wasn't shy. No retiring violet. And yet, under the heat of his blue-eyed gaze, she felt like a simpering debutante at her coming-out party.

He moved toward her, parting the people before him with nothing more than the strength of his personality. Folks just naturally moved out of his way. Many turned to give him a second glance.

Meg had to admit he was a man worth looking at. Hard-bodied, tight muscles, arresting eyes.

Were all fighter pilots born this way? Full of heat and swagger? Or were they made through reverence and the adulation of an adoring public?

Maybe it was a little of both.

Either way, he had more charisma in his little finger than Maverick from *Top Gun* had in his entire body.

"Well," he said when he drew close enough

for her to hear him. "If it isn't the best woman herself."

"Good job with the shower, Freemont," she said, keeping her tone and facial expression as light and even as possible.

"What?" The quirk of his mouth was disarming. "You expected me to screw up?"

"The thought did cross my mind. Who puts a fighter pilot in charge of a wedding shower?"

"I have hidden depths, babe," he said glibly.

Babe shouldn't have sent a shiver of anticipation skipping down her spine. But damn if it didn't. If she'd been in a mood to take offense, she could have pronounced the term demeaning. However, she could tell from his tone and his body language he was teasing and meant no harm.

She folded her arms over her chest, a feeble defense against his magnetism. "Who helped you?"

"You're looking at him."

Meg didn't buy that for a second. "You did this all by yourself?"

"The restaurant staff set up the room, but the design was mine."

"Hmm."

"You can say you're impressed. It won't kill you."

"I said you did a good job. Take it or leave it."

"Are you always so stingy with your praise?"

"When someone is fishing for compliments, yes."

His lively eyes danced with amusement. The man could seduce a nun with that grin. "Honestly, I could go on bantering with you all night. But I'm the host and the new arrivals need greeting. Mix and mingle," he invited. "Grab a beer. Enjoy the party."

It sounded like a good-enough idea, so she wandered over to the Waterin' Hole, grabbed a Corona, and twisted off the top.

"Hey there."

She looked up to see Brady coming toward her, smiled happily. "Hey, Braid."

"Shane did a nice job with the shower." Brady reached for a beer of his own and guided her off to one side.

"He did."

Brady took a sip of beer. Rubbed a hand over his lips. He shifted his weight. Cleared his throat.

Meg had known him long enough to know when he had something on his mind. "Is something wrong?"

"Ellie wants a prenup. Out of the blue." He shrugged. "She tells me she wants a prenup because she doesn't want anyone thinking she's after my money."

"Oh," Meg said. "Well, a prenup's not a bad idea."

"I don't want one," he said. "What's mine is hers. End of story. She's the other half of me."

"That's very romantic, but—"

Brady loomed over her, his eyes narrowed, mouth compressed. For the first time in the twenty-eight years she'd known him, she felt intimidated.

"Did you say something to Ellie?" he asked.

"Me? What? No!" she said, then guilt sloshed into her stomach. *Shane.* He must have told Ellie what she'd said in the park last week. The tattletale.

"I know you don't like her, Meg."

"I don't know Ellie," Meg protested. "But I certainly don't dislike her. It's just that you're rushing into this marriage and I'm worried about you."

Brady clenched his jaw. "You need to understand something. I love her with all my heart and soul, and if you and I are going to continue to be friends, you're going to have to respect that."

What? Meg flinched. She couldn't have been more shocked if Brady had physically struck her. "Of course. I love you and only want the best for you."

"I know." He offered up a half-flag smile.

Rusty, jagged guilt poked her. Her motives had been pure, but her suspicions about Ellie had hurt him. "I'm sorry. Please forgive me?"

His face softened. "This is the first time you and I have ever gotten crossways."

"It is." She stood there feeling like a jerk. "Let's not do it again."

"Agreed."

"Hug?" She opened her arms.

"Always." Brady enveloped her in a bear hug and she felt marginally better.

Ellie appeared, looking utterly guileless, eyes aglow. "Aww, you two are adorable. Meg, I'm so glad you're Brady's best friend. If a guy has a woman as his best friend, you know he's going to make a good husband."

It was a blanket statement and probably not generally true. But in Brady's case it was.

"He *is* a catch." Meg patted Brady's chest. "Be good to him."

"I plan on spending the rest of my life proving my love." Ellie's smile was so sweet and natural, Meg couldn't help liking her. And that made her feel even crappier for what she'd said about Ellie to Shane.

Speaking of Shane, she had a bone to pick with him for shooting off his big mouth.

"Tell her," Brady said to Meg as he slung his arm around Ellie's shoulder. "Tell my bride-to-be we don't need a prenup." He bent to nuzzle Ellie's neck and Meg heard him whisper, "What's mine is yours, angel."

The businessperson in her wanted to say,

everyone needs a prenup, but the friend in her couldn't be that blunt. Meg raised her hands. "That's between you guys. It's none of my business."

"Brady," Ellie said. "It's the smart thing to do."

"Do you ever foresee yourself divorcing me?" Brady asked.

Wake up! Meg wanted to say. Thing change. People change. The unforeseeable happens. Nothing is set in stone.

"Not if the polar ice caps melted, not if an asteroid hit the earth, not if a solar storm hit, not if . . . well, just face it, big guy, you're stuck with me." Ellie giggled again.

"Then there's no need for a prenup." Brady's tone brooked no argument.

"But—"

"End of discussion," he said. There was a look in Brady's eyes that caused a swamp of tenderness and a ping of envy inside Meg. He did love this woman. "Now, let's go open presents."

He ushered Ellie to a chair beside the table laden with gifts, called for everyone to direct their attention to the proceedings, and sat down beside his wife-to-be.

Meg went looking for Shane and found him in the corner of the room, where he'd ensconced himself to watch Ellie and Brady open their presents and jot down in a cell phone app what guest had given what gift.

49

"Got to hand it to you," she said. "You make a pretty great maid of honor."

"Man of honor," he corrected. "Did you see who gave them the Pappy Van Winkle?" He nodded at Brady, who was holding up a bottle of expensive Kentucky bourbon and cracking a joke about wedding-night shenanigans.

"I'm making a guess here, but I'm assuming it's from his cousin Lincoln, who's a horse breeder from Lexington."

"Thanks." Shane thumbed that into the cell phone.

"Listen," she said, trying not to notice what long fingers and strong tanned hands he had. "That wasn't very sporting of you to tell Ellie I thought she was after Brady for his money."

He raised his head and looked at her as if she'd disappointed him in some fundamental way. "I didn't tell her."

"So she came up with the prenup idea all on her own?"

"Yeah," he said. "She must have. Or she picked up on your vibe."

"You didn't suggest it?"

The look he gave her was hard and flat. "No. I didn't tell her you basically called her a gold digger because I didn't want to hurt her and I didn't want to color her perception of you."

Ouch!

"I suppose I deserved that," she said. "But

Brady's had women take advantage of him for his money before, and he's so trusting and this thing with Ellie happened so fast, I couldn't help worrying. It made me bitchy."

"Not bitchy," he said, his tone relaxing. "Just honest. You were expressing your opinion."

"I should have had more respect for your relationship with her. I sometimes have a bad habit of shooting off my mouth before I think."

He looked amused. "Are you under the impression I'm mad at you?"

"Well, I did dis your best friend."

"Wanna see the footprints in my mouth from all the times I've had my foot stuck up there? You're not the only one with strong opinions."

"Apparently not."

"We're passionate people," he said. "We don't have to apologize for that."

Passion.

Oh yeah. It oozed from his pores. The heat. The energy. The verve. He was a powerful guy and her womb whimpered, *I want.*

"We see something we don't agree with, we speak our minds."

"Uh-huh," she murmured because she was too busy staring at his gorgeous face to process what he was saying.

"But we're also strong and hardworking and we're going to pull off a damn fine wedding for Ellie and Brady."

"That might be why they asked us to be their attendants."

"Lucky them." His roughish grin unraveled her, leaving Meg feeling that he knew exactly what she looked like naked. "And lucky me that you're Brady's best friend."

Breathe, she reminded herself.

"I'm glad you didn't tell her what I said." Meg glanced over at Ellie, who was gazing at Brady as if he hung the moon. "I like her a lot and I was too hasty in my judgment."

"Brady's not bad either," Shane said. "Even if we don't believe in this love-at-first-sight, soul-mate bunk, doesn't mean they don't have a fighting chance."

"We suspend our disbelief." She carved up a smile, serving it on a platter for him like a willing servant girl. Good grief, what was she doing? "For their sake."

"I'll try if you will."

"Deal."

"Looks like they're finished opening gifts," he said. "Time for me to do my duties and announce food is served."

"Anything I can help with?"

"Naw. Just sit back, relax, and enjoy the evening." He headed over to Brady and Ellie.

Leaving Meg at loose ends. She grabbed a plate and joined the line queuing up at the buffet.

She'd cleared the air, apologized, made things right with Brady and Ellie and Shane. She should be feeling better and ready to embrace this wedding and her duties as best woman.

Instead, she couldn't shake the feeling there was something she'd missed. Something she wasn't addressing. Something that could get her in a lot of trouble and mess up this whole affair.

Then Shane turned and gave her another knee-melting stare, and Meg realized what that something was.

Insatiable, red-hot, sharp-tipped desire.

Three hours after the bridal shower, Shane finally tumbled into bed, exhausted. It had gone well, yeah, but in truth, being a man of honor was much harder than he had anticipated.

The pressure cooker of the tight timeline increased the stress load. Not that he minded stress. He was a fighter pilot, after all. He ate stress for breakfast and went back for seconds.

Rather, it was the überfeminine stuff, like shopping for Ellie's wedding dress, that triggered him. Sitting for hours, watching Ellie try on one fluffy white gown after another, drove Shane nuts. They all looked identical to him.

Ellie sensed his restlessness even though he thought he'd done a damn good job of not squirming, and apologized.

Unfortunately, there was no one else to help

her. Just like Shane, she had no parents, no siblings, no extended family she knew of. It was the two of them against the world, the way it had always been.

No. Not just the two of them. Not anymore. Brady was in the picture now.

And Megan.

Meg.

Of the long legs, sexy body, thick hair, and plush lips.

Thinking of her, his mouth watered and he started to get hard. Normally, when he wanted a woman this much, he simply went after her.

And he rarely struck out.

But Meg was off-limits for obvious reasons.

However, he couldn't deny that she'd been looking at him the same way he looked at her. With hungry eyes. Plus, she'd been sending all kinds of come-get-me signals. Leaning in close, licking her lips, laughing in a deep-throated way, blushing whenever their eyes met. Toying with her hair.

Oh, she was game all right.

Nope. Not gonna do it. Not this time.

He wasn't going to make a pass at Meg even though every masculine bone in his body spurred him to do exactly that. He wasn't going to do anything to jeopardize his best friend's happy day.

But he liked Meg's intensity. Whenever he was

around her he felt charged up, like he did in the cockpit. Excited. Powerful. Brave.

He appreciated her practical approach to life and he could tell she wasn't the kind of person who let people down. You could rely on Meg Stoddard. Of that he had no doubt.

She had style and flare. She didn't mince words. She spoke truthfully and from the heart and he respected her.

He admired the way she stood up to him. They could go toe to toe. He hadn't ever been in a romantic relationship with someone who would stiffen her spine, stare him right in the eye, and call *bullshit*.

He liked it. He liked it a lot.

You're not in a romantic relationship with her.

No. But he wanted to be. And Shane was accustomed to going after what he wanted. Balls to the wall.

And that was the danger.

New rule: no more fantasizing about Meg.

Easier said than accomplished.

Whenever he closed his eyes he saw her. He gritted his teeth, willed his thoughts to something else. But every time his mind wandered back to Meg. The way she'd looked at the party tonight. A knockout in a hot red tunic top, black leggings, and red cowgirl boots.

And her scent.

Even now, here in the dark, he could smell her.

An erotic aroma of magnolias, heat, and apricots. He loved apricots. Loved the sweet taste of the ripe flesh.

Did Meg taste as good as she smelled? His erection tightened.

Jesus, Freemont. Have some self-respect. Control. Get in control.

Excellent advice. But how?

Cold shower. The horny bachelor's old standby. It had worked for centuries for a reason.

Shane rolled out of bed. Bounced the painful distance to the bathroom. Grunted when the cold water hit his skin.

He heaved in a shocked breath of air, stuck his head under the flow, felt the icy water deflate his arousal and wondered just how many dunkings he was going to have to take between now and the wedding.

And just how long did it take for a guy to get frostbite from too many cold-assed showers?

Chapter Four

The wedding was four days away and the pressure was on. Meg was over at Brady's ranch daily, working with him and the wedding planner to finalize the details, helping him write his vows, reassuring him that everything was going to go smoothly on the most important day of his life.

And it was her job to make sure everything was perfect.

That included providing security, not just to keep out the wedding crashers but to chase away the paparazzi who'd gotten wind that Brady's second cousin, Travis Whitely—Austin's latest "it" guy country-and-western music star—was coming to the wedding.

Both Meg and Brady had gone to high school with Travis, back when his name was Brian Dobbs. Brian, aka Travis, had called Meg personally and convinced her a big security presence was necessary. He was paying for it, but Meg was the point person.

As another part of her best woman duties, she was in charge of the getaway vehicle Brady and Ellie would leave in after the wedding. Brady didn't want his brand-new Ford King Ranch pickup truck decorated, so they'd planned on using Ellie's Prius. But driving the low-slung Prius over the bumpy pasture roads out to the chapel on Meg's dude ranch presented problems for a quick departure.

Until Meg came up with an alternate proposal.

Let everyone think they were taking the Prius, so the couple's friends and attendants could have fun decorating it, but leave on horseback to Brady's ranch, where they would transfer to his pickup for their drive to the airport.

Ellie loved the romance of a horseback getaway and Brady liked the idea he wouldn't have to drive the highway in an attention-getting vehicle shoe-polished with JUST MARRIED and dragging streamers of tin cans.

To travel the escape route as rehearsed, Meg took out Jiggs, a high-spirited gelding that didn't get ridden as much as he should because the dude ranch guests generally wanted tamer horses, and headed for the cowboy chapel located at the back of the ranch.

The chapel was quite a distance from the main house, guest bunkhouses, and the other amenities because it had been built a hundred years earlier, when it had served the residents of a small town that no longer existed.

Meg's ancestors had bought the chapel land as part of their ranch deal, and they'd kept the chapel to hold church services for their ranch hands, with circuit riding preachers rotating

through. Nowadays, Meg rented it out for cowboy weddings.

It had started off as an insufferably hot June
morning, but the wind had changed direction,
bringing in clouds and cooling things off. Maybe
they'd get some rain out of it.

Jiggs was lively, living up to his name, pulling
at the bit to have his way. Dancing gracefully
along the dirt path. Meg could feel his need to
expend pent-up energy. She gave him his head,
allowing him to break into a canter.

No gallop, though. Not with this horse. Jiggs
leaned toward high-strung and required a strong
hand. If she let go of control, he'd run away with
her.

But man alive, could the horse move.

He was powerful, magnetic, compelling. His
personality reminded her of Shane. Fearless. A
warrior. Wild at heart.

Meg's own heart fluttered.

She'd only seen Shane once since the night
of the bridal shower, and that had been briefly,
when she'd gone with Brady for the tux fittings.
Shane was going to wear his Air Force dress
blues, but he'd come along to the fitting with
Ellie.

Afterward, they'd all gone out to eat. Shane and
Meg had sat on opposite sides of the table, but
they'd been unable to stop making eye contact.

And smiling.

They'd both been smiling a lot.

Yearning.

Or maybe she'd been yearning alone and reading something into his smile that wasn't really there.

Meg ducked her head, concentrated on slowing her breathing, realizing too late that Jiggs had taken advantage of her distracted mind and was galloping. His long legs eating up the ground that flowed beneath them. Hooves rasping against the earth.

What most of the guests who came to her ranch didn't know was that horseback riding was about bringing two beings into harmony though each had their own center of gravity. They didn't understand that in order to ride gracefully, smoothly, you had to re-center the horse's sense of gravity with the rider on his back.

With a start, it occurred to Meg that the same was true when two people had sex. That you had to re-center in a relationship as intimacy developed. Each person with their own center of gravity, trying to balance with the other.

She thought again of Shane, squelched it.

Focus.

Raising her head, she glanced around, saw that the clouds overhead had curdled, darkened. The wind blew stronger, cool air from the north mingling with the hot summer breeze from the south, sending dust eddies across the pasture.

Uneasiness raised the hairs on Meg's arms. She hadn't bothered to listen to the weather that morning, but she'd lived in Texas long enough to know tornado potential when she saw it.

Instinct told her to go back, but Jiggs was a bullet train, blasting over the prairie. She drew back firmly on the reins, urging him to slow down.

Jiggs didn't want to comply, but Meg persisted, and gradually, he slowed. By the time she had him under control again, they were at the chapel.

And the sky was malevolent.

She studied the dark thunderclouds, tried to gauge whether she had time to make it back to the stables or whether she should hightail it to the church's storm cellar.

But if she went inside, she'd have to abandon Jiggs to the weather. He was fast. At a gallop they had a chance to make it back to the stables before the storm hit.

Meg whirled the horse around, nudged him in the ribs, yelled, "H'ya."

At the same moment, a fork of yellow-blue lightning shot from the sky, fried a tall oak tree just a few yards away with a sizzling crack of hot heat and a thunderclap as loud as a Smith & Wesson .44 magnum going off at close range.

Jiggs let out a whinny of terror and reared up on his back legs.

Meg struggled to stay in the saddle, but it was a hopeless cause. Gravity took hold of her, and when Jiggs bolted in the direction of the ranch house, Meg's feet slipped from the stirrups and she fell to the hard-packed earth.

The impact knocked the air from her lungs. She stared at the sky, gasping for breath, watching the clouds swirl and churn above her, and thought, *Some best woman I am. If I get killed by a tornado, it's going to ruin the crap out of Brady's wedding.*

Shane had called ahead before arriving at Hawk Creek Dude Ranch. The woman who'd answered the phone told him Meg had ridden a horse out to the chapel. Perfect. As the man of honor, he needed to see the wedding venue in person, get the lay of the land.

By the time he arrived at the ranch, the sky was moody dark. He didn't like the looks of those clouds. The weather had come up fast, seemingly out of nowhere.

But he was a pilot, had seen severe storms merge in a matter of minutes. It was Texas after all, and they were in the southern tip of Tornado Alley. In the spring and early summer months, you had to expect the unexpected.

At the dude ranch check-in desk, he found a beleaguered-looking middle-aged woman with vibrant purple hair, ample cleavage, and a deep furrow between her eyebrows. She was on her cell phone, while at the same time the landline was ringing off the hook.

Her name tag identified her as Harrie. Short for Harriett?

"Hi, Harrie," he said, friendly as could be. "I'm Shane. I called ahead. I'm here to check out the chapel for the wedding. Is Meg around?"

"Just a sec." The woman held up a hand. Hung up the cell phone, answered the house phone, identified the caller, and asked if she could call the person back.

While he waited, Shane picked up a folded map of the ranch that showed the location of the chapel and tucked it into his back pocket. Finally, Harrie returned her attention to him.

"I don't like the looks of that sky," Harrie fretted. "You shouldn't go out there. In fact, I'm trying to get Meg to answer her cell phone so I can tell her to get her butt back here, but she's not picking up. I hope she didn't leave her phone behind. Sometimes she does that when she goes riding. Escaping technology, she calls it. I tell her God gave us cell phones for a reason. So we can always be in touch. I'll try her on the phone one more time. If I can't get hold of her—"

Shouts came from outside the window. A commotion of some sort.

Shane went to the door to see what was going on. Harrie followed him. A saddled gelding, his eyes wild, came tearing into the parking area, three cowboys in pursuit.

"That's the horse Meg was riding," Harrie exclaimed. "Jiggs is a handful and spooks easily. He must have thrown her."

"Because of the storm," Shane said grimly, stalking down the wooden porch toward his vehicle.

"Where are you going?" Harrie asked. One of the cowboys snagged the errant horse and tried to calm it.

"To find Meg," he threw over his shoulder.

"But you don't know where the church is," Harrie called.

"Gotta map." Shane patted his back pocket.

"You'll need a horse or an ATV."

"Gotta Jeep."

"Bring her back safe," Harrie yelled against the wind. "And hurry. That sky looks bad. I'm herding the guests to the storm shelter."

The sky did indeed look bad. It was the yellow-green color of an old bruise. The air was both cold and warm. Lightning flashed. Thunder crashed. The perfect stew for brewing tornados.

The cowboys seemed to know what he was up to and opened a double gate that led into the pasture. Shane briefly consulted the map, pinned the location in his mind, and pumped the gas pedal, sending the Jeep jolting over the one-lane dirt path toward the chapel.

The sky was pea green now. The pressure in the air building against Shane's eardrums. His head ached and his pulse thumped. And all he could think was, *Meg's alone out there and a tornado is coming.*

It only took him a few minutes to drive to the chapel, but it felt like two days. Wind buffeted the Jeep, howled around the doors. On either side of the road, twin dust devils rotated.

Shane coughed, cleared his throat. The steeple of the church come into view. He spied a big old oak split right in two, the center burned black and still smoking from a lightning strike.

He saw a person sprawled out on the ground.

Meg!

Get up, Meg told herself, *or you're going to make like Dorothy, fly over the rainbow and see Oz firsthand.*

She wasn't sure how long she'd been there. It certainly couldn't have been more than five minutes, but she was still having trouble drawing in air; muscle spasms gripped her belly and her back. And her lazy legs were saying, *Yo-ho, missy, not getting up until the lungs are back at work.*

She gasped, heaved, tried to haul in more air, but it was as if only the very top part of her lungs were capable of expanding. Panic set in. *I. Can't. Breathe.* A million butterflies batted fragile wings inside her rib cage.

This was no time to be losing it. Tornadoes waited for no woman.

Oh shit, oh shit, oh shit. She really was going to die.

And then Shane was there and she wasn't alone anymore. Wrapping his big, strong arms around her, carrying her toward the chapel just as big white stones of hail started falling from the sky.

She clung to him. Her lifeline.

He ran, bumping across the uneven ground. Hail smacking all around them, lightning illuminating the sky. Thunder roaring. But no rain. Bad sign.

He reached the door of the chapel and kicked it open with the toe of his boot. She was glad she hadn't yet replaced that door latch that didn't hold well.

They tumbled inside and Meg took her first deep breath since Jiggs had thrown her. Sweet, beautiful air.

"We need to get to a reinforced doorway," he said, desperately searching the one-room chapel.

"Storm cellar," she said, still too wobbly to speak in full sentences. "Out back."

He bent to pick her up again.

"I can walk." She grabbed his hand, tugged him with her out the back door to the cellar.

The wind was whipping so furiously she couldn't get the door open. And the hail was coming down hard. She worried about Jiggs. Hoped he'd made it back to the stables after dumping her off.

"Let me help." The storm was so loud that Shane had to yell even though he was standing right next to her. He took hold of the handle, their hands touching, and together they yanked it open.

The wind snagged the door, jerking it from their hands, flopping it open wide. The wind was all around them. A terrifying force. Gathering energy.

Meg stared into the gaping darkness of the cellar. Hesitated. She had no idea what was down there. Spiders. Snakes. Varmints. But she knew for certain what was up here. A badass tornado.

"In." Shane directed her.

She took a fortifying breath. Thank God for that. How beautiful it was to breathe. And plunged down the stairs into the unknown.

Inside, the cellar was dank, musty, inky. The only light coming from the tainted sky above them.

That bleak light was extinguished when Shane slammed the door closed behind them, dimming the sound of the storm.

The blackness was complete. Midnight in the wilderness wasn't this dark. Hail pinged against the tin door.

Meg shivered.

"Are you hurt?" Shane asked, low and concerned.

"I'm okay." She hugged herself in the tiny space, tried not to think about spiders and snakes.

"What happened? When I saw the oak tree and you lying on the ground, I thought you'd gotten hit by lightning. I thought you were . . ." His voice bogged down. "Dead."

"Jiggs threw me when lightning struck the oak tree," she said.

"I figured. The horse came running up when I was talking to Harrie. That's how I knew you were out here."

"So Jiggs is all right?" Thank heavens for that.

"Scared, but your ranch hands were taking good care of him. You're the one I'm worried about."

"I'm okay now. I landed hard. The fall knocked the breath out of me. I couldn't make my lungs or legs work."

"When I think about what could have happened if I hadn't come along when I did, I—" He broke off.

"But you did come along." She laughed, albeit shakily. "And rescued me like some knight in shining Jeep."

"You could have saved yourself. I didn't know there was a storm cellar nearby."

"I could have saved myself, yes, but knowing

I'm not in this alone makes me feel a whole lot better. What *are* you doing here, by the way?"

"Dropped by to check out the place. I should have done it already, but I've been so busy with all the other man-of-honor stuff, this is the first chance I've had."

"Your sense of timing is impeccable."

"Pilot's instinct."

She wasn't sure what he meant by that and they both fell silent. Outside, the storm railed. Inside, she heard a click, and the light of Shane's cell phone illuminated his face. He looked so gorgeous with wind-tousled hair.

Meg's heart skipped a beat. Or two.

"Damn," he said. "I'm on eight percent charge."

"Quick, shine it around. We're supposed to have alternative light sources stocked in here and you can save what little battery you have left."

He flashed the light around the room. The cellar was small, with dirt walls and floor. Thankfully, at first glance no snakes, and hopefully any spiders that might be lurking weren't the poisonous kind.

There was a wooden bench and a small shelf that held a flashlight, candles, matches, and a kerosene lantern. Shane turned on the flashlight and gave it to Meg to hold while he shut down his cell phone and lit the lantern.

He set the lantern in the middle of the dirt

floor, plopped down on the wooden bench. There was nowhere else to sit. Meg switched off the flashlight and sat down beside him.

It fully hit her, then. She was in a tiny storm shelter.

Alone.

With Shane.

The man who'd left her hot and bothered from the moment they'd shaken hands in the vegan bakery.

She could smell him. His sexy scent overriding the earthy smell of the cellar. He was breathtakingly handsome in the reflected glow of the lantern, shadows honing the lines and planes of his masculine face.

He leaned in and her breath stilled. She hoped, prayed he would kiss her even as she knew it was a stupid, stupid idea. She barely knew this guy, but she wanted him. Especially after he'd daringly rescued her.

Oh how she wanted him! More than she had ever wanted anyone.

Wind thrashed against the cellar door, demanding and relentless. Hail continued to batter, a sharp punctuation to her inner turbulence.

Meg bit her bottom lip, stared at his mouth, thought about how he might taste, felt her body flood with warmth and moisture and sensation. "A tornado could ruin this wedding."

"Yes," he said, his blue eyes murky in the duskiness.

"Do you think it's an omen?" she whispered. "A sign they shouldn't get hitched?"

"It's just a storm," he said.

"Storms can be destructive. They can maim and kill."

"They can also purify." He hooked her gaze and she saw something powerfully arousing in his eyes. "Purge."

That's when she knew they were no longer talking about storms. At least not the kind that came from the sky.

He touched her hand. A slight movement. His fingertips barely grazing the side of her palm.

It was a big hand. A callused hand. Full of experience and vitality. She could feel his life force throbbing from his skin into hers. Blasting through that thin thread of contact. Stirring her nerve endings. Singing through her blood. Surging sweet heat into her pelvis.

Spinning. Whirling. A storm all its own. Gathering speed. Growing. Accelerating. Annihilating any sense of reason or control.

Gone. She was absolutely gone. He lowered his head, mouth millimeters above hers. Meg licked her lips and parted her teeth, ready to let him in if he wanted to go.

Chapter Five

When Shane had woken up that morning, he couldn't have guessed he'd find himself in a dark, cramped storm cellar about to kiss Meg Stoddard.

She peered at him, eyes wide open, moist lips parted. On her beautiful face an expression of desire, delight, and surrender. Sending a clear message. *If you kiss me, I won't complain.*

He wanted this. Craved it. Had been aching for her from the moment they'd met.

Not smart, however. Not smart at all. His best friend was marrying her best friend. No two ways about it, they'd be seeing each other often. If they had a one-time fling, it would make for awkward moments at dinner parties, family celebrations, and holidays, when they were bound to run into each other.

And that would cause him to avoid going to events with Ellie and Brady that Meg might be attending and probably vice versa.

Think it through, Freemont. Calculate the risk. Is a few minutes of pleasure worth the damage that hot sex with Meg was bound to wreak on his relationship with Ellie?

Watching Meg moisten her lips with that sweet

pink tongue almost tugged a whimper from his throat.

No. No, it wasn't worth the risk.

In the nick of time, Shane reined in his self-control, lifted his head, straightened his spine, moved back.

Meg exhaled. Loudly. The sound signaling both relief and disappointment.

Me too, babe. Me too.

He cast around for something to say. Something that wouldn't call attention to the fact he'd nearly kissed her. "Wonder how long this storm is going to last."

"We could look it up on weather tracker. Where's your phone?"

He pulled his phone from his pocket, turned it on. A weak signal. One bar. Switched it back off. "Not enough power for internet service. But from the sound of things, we're here for a while."

"I hope it's only hail and a tornado doesn't touch down. Your poor Jeep."

He shrugged. "I have insurance. We're safe. That's the important thing."

"I suppose." She kept clasping and unclasping her hands.

"Something wrong?" he asked.

"Just worrying about the ranch."

"You've got a great staff. I'm sure they're taking care of it."

"I know, but I tend to be a worrier. It's in my DNA."

"You need a distraction."

Meg's eyes widened and she audibly sucked in air, and he knew she was thinking what he was thinking. Making out would be one mighty fine diversion.

"We could play twenty questions," she said quickly.

"I haven't played that in years."

"Me neither."

"Hey, what about those questions you were telling me about? The ones from that dating service Ellie and Brady went to?"

"Um . . ."

"Are they too racy?"

"No, surprisingly, they aren't racy at all," Meg said. "I found that confusing. I expected racy."

"Do you remember any of them?"

"There were three levels of questions, each level supposedly leading to greater and greater intimacy."

"Wanna try it?"

"Increase our intimacy?" Her words came out high and airy, scared.

"No. No," he rushed to say. "Bust the myth. Show it wasn't the questions that caused Brady and Ellie to fall in love but rather they fell in love because they were looking to fall in love.

It wouldn't happen to us because we're not interested in falling in love."

"No, we aren't."

"I mean, we do have chemistry. We can't deny that."

"We do," she admitted.

His pulse jumped and his body tensed involuntarily. "But that's just sexual attraction. It doesn't mean anything else."

"No siree."

"A few measly questions aren't going to make us suddenly fall in love." Shane rubbed his knee. Old football injury. Getting stiff from sitting too long.

She scoffed. "No way."

"Do you remember any of the first-level questions?" he asked, perplexed as to why he was steering the conversation in the direction of love and intimacy. Playing with fire he was, and no good reason why except as a way to distract her from worrying about the storm.

And to distract himself from thoughts of kissing her.

Meg tucked one side of her lip up between her teeth. The sight of that plush pink lip sucked up against her pearly whites tightened erotic muscles below Shane's belt and he was grateful for the camouflaging dimness.

"Let me see. I think there was a question along

the lines of tell your partner five things you like about them already."

"We're not partners."

"It's just you and me here," she said. "So yeah, we kind of are."

"Partners-in-storm." He chuckled, playing off partners in crime.

"Besides that, we're partners in a nontradiional wedding. Man of honor and best woman."

"Oh yeah. That too."

"Who goes first?" Meg asked.

"Goes?" Shane blinked, so lost in her eyes he'd dropped the conversational ball.

"I'll go first." She glanced away, mumbling. "I like the way you walk into a room as if you own it."

"Interesting." He raised his eyebrows, perplexed that something as simple as walking into a room impressed her.

"Your turn."

"I like how you stand up for yourself," he said. "You don't let anyone mow you down or take advantage of you."

"I have a strong-minded mother. She passed it on to me."

"Good genes."

Meg stretched out her legs in front of her, the tips of her boots almost touching the lantern in front of them. "I like your appetite for life. You're earthy. A paladin."

"A what-a-din?"

"Paladin. It means a champion."

"I like how you use big words," he said, deepening his smile. "You're smart. You would come in handy on *Jeopardy!*"

"I like how practical you are." She laughed. "Thinking of ways to make money off my smarts."

"I like the way you don't take offense at my practically."

"And I like the way you fill out a pair of jeans."

"Well, if we're going there, I like that you've got rockin' hot legs."

"Leg man, are you?"

He let his gaze linger on her breasts. "Among other things. Your turn."

"Hmm," she purred. "I like the way you make me feel sexy."

"Same here."

They stared at each other. Breathed in sync.

"Well, that was pretty painless," he said. "I don't feel increased intimacy. Do you?"

"If you don't count being jammed into a tiny storm cellar alone with you and talking about our sexy bodies, no."

"That's physical. Nothing mental or emotional for me. You?"

"Me neither," she denied.

"Good."

"Great."

"Terrific." Why did he feel so unsettled? "Do you remember any more questions?"

Meg tapped her chin with her index finger. "Oh. This one's easy. Given the choice of anyone in the world, whom would you want as a dinner guest?"

"Chuck Yeager."

"Why?"

"He's the Yeagermeister," Shane said.

"And that means . . . ?"

"He inspired me to become a pilot." Shane notched up his chin. "How about you? Who would you invite to this dinner party?"

She paused, reflected on that. "Living or dead?"

"You want a ghost at your party?" he asked.

Her giggle surprised him. He hadn't pegged her for the giggly type. "Let's assume because this is a fictional dinner party, the deceased guests can appear as they did when they were alive. No ghosts."

"I can roll with that. Who's your pick?"

"My grandmother."

"A sentimental choice. Maternal or paternal?"

"Maternal. Gram was amazing. A single mom after her husband took off and never came back. Raised my mom and uncle while working as a chuck wagon cook on this very dude ranch. She's *my* hero."

"She's the reason you're a cowgirl?"

Meg nodded. "Absolutely. If she hadn't started

78

working for the ranch, my mom wouldn't have met my dad. Hawk Creek's been in my dad's family for five generations."

"Now that's some deep family roots." The old emptiness he felt over his lack of family crept in, but he pushed it aside. He'd made peace with his orphaned status a long time ago. "How long has your grandmother been gone?"

"Five years. She died two days before I graduated from TCU with my degree in ranch management. Cancer. What I wouldn't give to hug her one more time." Meg sighed, sadness tugging her mouth down. Her hand strayed to her heart.

Watching her, a flick of something knifed Shane's gut. A feeling he had no name for. He'd never known his grandparents, but he missed the loss of something he'd never had.

"Let's take relatives off the table," he said, wanting to erase the sorrow from her eyes. "What prominent person would you most like to have as a dinner guest?"

"Hmm." She paused, thinking. "How about Margaret Thatcher?"

"The Iron Lady?"

"Yes."

"Any particular reason why?"

"She was tough."

"So are a lot of women."

"Honestly? I'd like to ask her about the quote:

'To wear your heart on your sleeve isn't a very good plan; you should wear it inside, where it functions best.' "

"Why?"

"I want to know if she really believed you can't be warm, caring, empathetic, and strong at the same time."

"Ah," he said.

"Ah what?"

"Nothing."

"It's something or you wouldn't be looking like a smug cat who got the last bit of cream."

He shrugged, almost too casually. "Nothing. It's just that you want to have your cake and eat it too."

"Huh?"

"You want to be soft and feminine but tough as nails at the same time. Sorry. You can't have both. Thatcher would tell you as much."

"Channel Margaret Thatcher's ghost, do you?"

"No. But I know leadership. You can't be a strong leader and also give in to your emotions."

"Ever?"

"Not if you want to win."

"And winning is everything?"

"What else is there?"

She shook her head, pursed her lips, clicked her tongue. "My grandmother was strong and loving."

"She wasn't Margaret Thatcher. She didn't run Great Britain."

"Thank God. Can you imagine the Iron Lady as your grandmother?" Meg asked.

"I can't imagine anyone as my grandmother because I never had one."

Silently, she reached over and took his hand, squeezed it. The gesture was kind, generous. It made him feel vulnerable. He moved his arm, pretended he needed to scratch his cheek. She settled her hands back in her lap. He couldn't tell if he'd bruised her feelings or not.

"What were some of the other questions?" he asked.

"Hmm." She tapped her chin. "Would you like to be famous? And if yes, in what way?"

"My goal is to be the best pilot I can be. If that brings me fame somehow, I'm good with it, but fame isn't something I chase." He studied her. "How about you?"

"Same thing. Fame seems more annoying than anything else. My main concern is doing my job well."

"Look at that." He smiled. "We have one thing in common. We put a high premium on our jobs and doing them well."

"We're both workaholics. I wonder if we have anything else in common."

"Do you want a mint?" he asked, pulling a tin of lemon mints from his pocket.

"Thank you," she said. "Don't mind if I do."

They sat sucking mints and listening to the storm rage. Taste buds buffeted by tangy sweet lemon. Eardrums pummeled by howling wind.

"We both like lemon mints," he said. "That's two things in common."

"Neither one of us is fond of short engagements and quick weddings," she said after a long moment. "So that makes three."

"Which means?"

"Absolutely nothing in the grand scheme of things."

She was right, but he found himself wishing the things they had in common held some kind of significance. "I doubt Ellie and Brady have three things in common."

"I would be surprised if they did."

"And yet they're crazy for each other."

"Lust," Meg said. "Lust at first sight is easy enough."

"You mentioned there were three levels of intimacy in the questions Ellie and Brady answered. What were some level-three questions?"

"I wish we had cell reception so I could look it up online. Let me think a minute." She glanced sideways, screwing up her mouth as if it would help her recall. "Oh, I've got one. What does friendship mean to you?"

"Ellie," he said succinctly.

"I'm not letting you get away with that. Elaborate."

"I'm taking on maid-of-honor duties for her. That should tell you something about our friendship."

"You love her."

"I'd lay down my life for her," he clarified.

"That's what friendship means to you? Loyalty? Protectiveness? Altruism?"

"All of the above."

"Wow."

"Wow?"

"That's a tall order for friendship. I'm impressed. Or maybe even jealous. You'd die for her?"

"I'd die for anyone I love. Brady wouldn't do the same for you?"

"Oh I'm sure he would, but I was going with a lighter definition. To me, friendship is when you feel safe enough to say anything to another person, knowing they won't judge you."

"Agreed," he said.

"We're lucky," she said. "To be able to have such great friends of the opposite sex."

"We are."

Silence stretched between them.

"Did you and Brady ever . . ." He trailed off.

"Ever what?"

Shane flapped a hand. "You know."

"Hook up?"

"Yeah."

"Brady's like a sibling. The way it is with Ellie and you."

"So no?"

"Well . . ." Meg swished her tongue around in her mouth. "We kissed once. In college. After a kegger. It felt too weird and we vowed never to do that again. Did you and Ellie ever—"

"God no!"

That brought another long silence, punctuated by the storm.

"I've got a question for you. It's not part of the quiz."

"What's that?"

"How come you've never been married?" Meg asked. "You're handsome, hot, and a military pilot. What's wrong with you?"

"Never found anyone who could hold my interest for long. How about you? Why aren't *you* married?"

"I was with a guy for five and half years," Meg confessed. "We broke up last year."

"What happened?"

"One night he made a reservation at the fanciest restaurant in Austin. I was certain he was going to pop the question. I spent two hundred dollars on a new dress. Waxed everywhere. Had my hair done."

"It didn't go as planned?"

"Instead of getting down on one knee, he

broke the news he'd snagged his dream job. Offered a position with CNN as a war correspondent in the Middle East. He decided he wanted the job more than he wanted me."

"Stupid man."

"No." She shook her head. "Not stupid. We had different priorities. That's all. Or maybe we had the same priorities. Our careers. I couldn't ask him to give up on his dream to stay here in Texas for me. And how could I leave the family business? I grew up on this dude ranch. My parents count on me to run it."

"Do you miss him?"

"I'm over him. I have a full life," she said simply. "Breaking up worked out for us both. I just sort of wish I hadn't wasted five and a half years waiting for him to commit."

"But you did love him."

"Apparently not enough to give up Texas and my family."

"You shouldn't have to cut off pieces of yourself in order to fit into someone else's life," Shane mused.

Meg looked startled. "That's precisely what I told him."

"What was his name?"

"Grant Portman."

"I've seen his reporting on CNN. You were with *that* guy?"

"Why do you say it that way?"

"He thinks a lot of himself. You can tell by the way he preens on camera. You could do much better."

"Oh," she said. "And who do you have in mind?"

He grinned and said, without thinking, "Me."

"I forgot to tell you," she said, blowing past that, but even in the muted light he could tell she was blushing.

"Tell me what?"

"There's one more step to the intimacy thing besides the questions."

"What's that? Getting naked? Now it's all starting to make sense."

Playfully, she swatted his shoulder. "No, it's not getting naked."

"What is it, then?"

"I doubt you'd be game."

"Never know until you ask."

"The final component . . ." She paused, teasing him, the vexing woman.

"Yes?"

"Stare deeply into each other's eyes for four minutes. And it has to be four minutes. No shorter."

"Piece of cake," he said, making a dismissive noise even as his gut torqued at the thought of staring into her eyes for four whole minutes without kissing the hell out of her.

"You're up for it?"

"Are you?"

"Bring it," she scoffed.

"I'll set the timer on my phone. Hopefully the battery will last that long."

"I'm in."

"Sit on the ground by the lantern."

"Let's do it."

Kindled with yearning, they scooted off the bench, settled cross-legged onto the ground opposite each other, started the timer on Shane's phone, and began the stare down.

Chapter Six

Ten seconds in, Meg realized that four minutes was a very long time to be staring into someone's eyes. Especially someone who revved your engines and made every sexual cell in your body vibrate with hammering need.

"So," he said, "we're really doing this."

"No talking," she shushed.

"Yes, ma'am." He smiled.

"Oh yeah," she added. "We're not supposed to look away, and try not to blink."

"Gotcha."

"Shh."

They sank into it. Face to face. Eye to eye. No talking, touching, blinking, or looking away. Fully engaged.

It was petrifying and exhilarating at the same time.

Meg had tamed wild horses and branded cattle. She'd water-skied the Colorado at breakneck speed and skydived with Brady once on a dare. Nothing compared to this.

Peering deeply and intensely into the eyes of another person for four minutes put all that other stuff into a big wicker basket labeled: EASY.

Her pulse skittered like the claws of a nervous

animal trying to get out of a tight spot. Sweat trickled between her breasts. She bit her lip. Shifted.

Shane grinned.

Meg huffed.

The lantern cast spooky shadows, causing Shane to look devilish. Did she look devilish, too?

She noticed the shape of his nose. Admired it. Saw, too, that his pupils dilated wider the longer they stared at each other. Were hers dilating as well?

Meg wanted to look at the phone to see how much time had passed, but she wasn't supposed to look away.

Finally, she gave up resisting the sheer terror of looking that closely at someone and having them look at you with the same intensity. She accepted it. The connection. The deepening bond. The total intimacy.

"Windows to the soul," Shane murmured.

This time she didn't shush him because she was thinking the same thing. If you stared at someone long enough, you stopped seeing the color and shape of their eyes and instead started to see *into* them.

See past the pretenses and defenses. The masks and walls. He was much more than a fighter pilot or a kid who grew up in an orphanage or Ellie's man of honor. He was more than his name. Or his gorgeous, hot body and handsome face.

He was simply a soul.

And so was she.

Two souls together in concert. United.

Looking at him, into him, through him, she felt . . . Well, what? Meg examined the feeling. Came up with one solid word. *Courageous.*

She felt courageous. Allowing herself to be this vulnerable felt extremely courageous. Facing a fear she didn't even know she had.

The fear of intimacy.

Was Shane experiencing the same thing? Questioning, she stared deeper. Fell further.

Me. You. You. Me. Was there any difference between the two?

Not at this moment. Not with their souls yoked by a singular smoldering gaze that lasted four limitless minutes.

Goose bumps rose on her arms, spread to her chest, over her heart. They rushed to the back of her neck, up her jaw, across her face, and embedded in her brain. And she realized the whole world was inside each of them.

Cosmic.

They were cosmic explorers, dipping into the lunar landscape of each other's inner being.

And in that landscape she was surprised to discover profound healing.

Their breathing slowed, grew shallower, until

they were barely breathing at all. Who needed air when they had each other?

In those four short minutes, they wove their own threads through the fabric of one another's lives, adding depth and texture, color and warmth. And formed their own unique world.

The long labyrinth of that look swept them on an odyssey through time and space. Creating a history of their unique world, filled with knowledge and experiences, suffering and sadness as well as exalted states of joy and happiness. Through that one extended stare they understood everything about each other and were transformed.

And when the timer went off, they both jumped, blinked, and finally took a deep breath.

Remembered who and where they were.

And Meg felt a deep and immediate sense of loss. "Wow."

"Yeah." His voice dropped, heavy, leaden. "Wow."

Where did they go from there?

Shane was studying her with bedroom eyes and Meg thought, *This time I'm going to kiss him if he doesn't kiss me.*

But she didn't have to.

He crooked two fingers underneath her chin, tilted her face up to his, dipped his head, and claimed her.

She surrendered. Willingly, enthusiastically his.

In fact, she already had her mouth open, inviting him to slip his hot, wet tongue between her lips. She slid her arms around his neck, guided his head down to deepen the kiss.

Sweet heaven, he tasted good! Better than anything she could have imagined. Better than rainbows and music and halos.

More. She needed more.

The man was a mind reader. He plumbed the depths of her mouth, stoking the flame with an experienced tongue, hot and searching.

Meg melted into him.

Shane enveloped her in his arms, drawing her to his chest. It had been eons since she'd felt the hard angles of a man's body pressed against her curves. They fit perfectly, as if they were made for each other.

Her brain tried to put up a protest. *Hang on. Too much, too fast. You're reading more into this than you should.*

But her heart won, shoving aside all doubts. Later. She could have regrets later. For now, she had nowhere else to go. Nowhere else to be but in Shane's strong arms.

The kiss deepened, turned languid, a silent tranquil lake within the stiff drag of erotic undercurrent rolling between them. His exquisite mouth tantalized, extracting impossible responses from her body.

She collapsed into both the inner and outer

storm. Submitted. Spinning, whirling, spiraling out of control. In the aftermath, she would be left ripped apart, wasted, but oh what a ride!

Meg ran her fingers through his hair, clutched his head between her palms, held on. The entire solar system was here in the space of their mouths, rich, mysterious, unfathomable. It was at once enthrallingly strange and persuasively familiar.

He increased the pressure. Their bodies were molded to each other. His was rock hard, hers soft and compliant. Being here with him set off sexy, dramatic sensations of want and need, desire and delight.

Thrilling!

But she had to ask herself some hard questions.

Was this merely chemistry or a false intimacy? Or was there more to it? It felt like so much more, but in trusting those hopes, was she setting herself up for heartache?

But in the upheaval of arousal, she couldn't answer such hefty questions. All she wanted was to kiss and hug and lick and taste. Everywhere. In every way a man and woman could join. She wanted it with Shane.

The light from the lantern waned, but they were so preoccupied they didn't realize the kerosene had run out until they were plunged into darkness.

Flustered, Meg pulled back.

"Blinded by the dark," Shane murmured, and his unerring radar found her lips again, giving her no time to think.

Who cared? Thinking was overrated.

Firm. His kiss was firm and so was his body. More than firm. He was hard all over.

Their breaths mixed. Heat plus heat equaled blazing. His palm cupped her cheek. Coarse calluses caressed her skin. He tilted her chin, giving him easier entrance to her mouth.

Meg gasped, hauling in his aroma. The smell of him enriched what she tasted—truffles, saltiness, the sweet muskiness of a rumpled bed after love-making on a hot summer afternoon.

He made a brusque masculine noise, half impatience, half desperation.

Her pulse raced a mad dash through her bloodstream until she was dizzy and steamy. Faint. She felt faint from the sheer joy of him.

Fully, she let go, allowed herself to be submersed. In the sensation, in Shane, in sheer splendor.

Keeping their mouths connected, Shane eased her into his lap. Her hands explored him, eager and enchanted by what she found. The strong tendons of his neck. The bulky muscles of his biceps. The lanky sharpness of his shoulder blades. The smooth shape of his head.

He was foreign terrain and she was an avid

tourist, visiting his breathtaking vistas for the very first time.

Her bottom was rooted against solid thighs, the denim of his jeans stretched taut over his erection.

Lightly, he nipped her bottom lip, and her entire being turned elastic. Pliable with heat and perspiration and need. Stark raving need.

Everywhere his fingers touched, her flesh caught fire.

The cellar was so dark, she couldn't tell if her eyes were open or closed. It didn't matter anyway. She was in deep.

He panted.

Surprise! So did she.

His hands keep sightseeing, his tongue conquering. He was powerful, commanding, confident. If he flew fighter planes the way he kissed, there was no war his side wouldn't win.

Her nipples hardened, tight flower buds inside her bra, a pitiful moan seeping from her lips.

He squeezed her tight, chuckled low in his throat. Was he tickled that he was driving her crazy?

A deep-seated, devastating ache throbbed between her legs. She needed him, oh how much she needed him, as all the fantasies she'd been having about him grew and bloomed.

But at the zenith of her fantasies came doubts.

They had to talk. Reluctantly, she wrenched her mouth from his.

"What's the matter?" he wheezed.

"Shane, I . . . you . . . we." Damn, she was wheezy, too.

"You wanna stop?"

"No . . ."

"But?"

"We're just having fun, right? This one time."

He hesitated a moment. "Of course. One time."

"We're not going to let this affect our relationship from here on out. I mean, as Ellie and Brady's best friends, we'll be seeing a lot of each other, and I don't want things to get weird."

"No weirdness," he promised.

She exhaled. Wondered if she was sad or glad.

"Something else on your mind?" he asked.

"Are you afraid of getting hurt?"

He touched her cheek in the darkness, sweetly, lightly. "Are you?"

"I guess. A little."

"We don't have to do this, Meg. Maybe we shouldn't do this if you're unsure."

"But I want you."

Shane groaned. "Meg, I want you so bad I can't breathe."

"This is a risk," she said. "What if the sex turns out to be so great, once isn't enough?"

"It's a calculated risk. We're banking on each other and our self-control. I can keep this in its place if you can."

But what if she couldn't? She almost asked him that but was afraid if she did, he would call the whole thing off, and that wasn't what she wanted.

"On a practical note," she said. "Do you have a condom?"

"I'm a fighter pilot, babe. I'm always prepared."

"Good to know."

He found her again in the dark. His mouth softer this time. More gentle. His hands skimmed over her body, his touch setting her skin ablaze. His hot fingertips as deadly as the lightning that had felled that oak tree.

They undressed each other. Bit by bit, taking their time. Forgetting the storm outside and why they were down there. The storm inside their bodies commanded their full attention.

When they were fully naked and Shane had the condom in place, he eased his hands between her thighs.

Meg parted her legs, letting him inside.

She abandoned herself. Merged with him. Left all her cares and worries behind. Reached for the ultimate expression of love.

Discovered it.

Touched it.

Became it.

Their joining was brilliant, a fierce celebration of life, vibrant sex fueled by the newness and dangerous circumstances.

"Megan," he whispered in a hushed tone. "Meg." A few more well placed kisses, then, "Meg, Meg, Meg, Meg."

Like a chant.

A prayer.

They dissolved into each other, any hint of separation vanishing. They were connected in the same way they'd connected when they stared into each other's eyes. On the most basic and primal of levels.

Her heart filled to bursting. Staggered. Overwhelmed. A dam ready to crack, spill over, drown everything.

He pitched into her and she made a bleat of satisfaction, adhered tightly to his waist, going where he took her. Happy for the ride.

His fingers tangled in her hair, his verve scorching as savagely as her own. With him inside her and at the controls, she felt like a plane, flying high in the sky. She was the vehicle of their ascent, sailing through the clouds, breathing through to the other side.

Shattering the sound barrier.

Shattering warp speed.

Shattering whatever intentions she'd had to keep this casual and light.

She was hooked. Snared. In love with the flight they'd taken together and aching to take it again and again and again.

They shuddered together. Giant rolling thunder crashing around them. They were one and it was the most blissful moment of her life.

As they lay spent, addled in each other's arms, struggling to catch their breath and make sense of the precious journey they'd just gone on, there was a knock at the cellar door.

And a distressed voice called out, "Meg? Shane? Are you in there?"

Chapter Seven

Because the battery was out on Shane's cell phone and the kerosene was gone, they had to dress hurriedly in the dark. Fumbling for garments, exchanging items when they found something that belonged to the other.

"Meg?" It was Brady's voice, filled with concern, followed by Ellie's higher-pitched timbre. "Shane?"

"Hang on!" Shane called. "We're coming out."

"Hurry, hurry." Meg jammed her arms through her blouse, did up the buttons as fast as she could.

"You decent?" Shane whispered.

"I thought I was pretty good," she quipped, "but it's hard to evaluate your own performance."

He laughed, touched her in the dark, connected with her shoulder, slid his hand down her arm to find her palm, and squeezed it.

Brady, however, did not hang on. He yanked opened the cellar door, letting in a flood of afternoon light, and peered down the stairs. Ellie peeped around his shoulder.

"Hi," Meg said breathlessly and wriggled her fingers at her best friend and his bride-to-be.

"Are you all right?" Brady asked, appraising

Meg as he descended a couple of steps into the cellar. "We were scared to death you got caught out in the storm."

"Fine. We're fine. Shane got me to the shelter in the nick of time."

Brady glared at Shane. With one glance at them, he had already put two and two together. "Is that so?" His tone was firm, challenging.

"Um . . . we're coming up if you'll back off," Meg said, knowing Brady had nothing but her best interests at heart.

Brady ducked his head, stepped back.

Feeling like a teenager who'd gotten caught doing the nasty on her parents' couch, Meg went up the steps ahead of Shane. She could feel the heat of his gaze on her bottom.

She climbed out, joined Brady and Ellie, saw chunks of hail melting on the ground littered with leaves, twigs, and broken limbs from nearby trees. "Did we get a tornado?"

"Formed right over us." Brady grunted. "But it didn't touch down. Hail damage, though."

"I can see that," Meg mused, threading a hand through her sex-tousled hair.

"Your Jeep is beat to hell," Brady told Shane as he came up behind Meg.

"How's Jiggs?" she asked.

"Fine." Brady nodded, still sending Meg and Shane disapproving looks.

"You . . . um . . ." Ellie pointed at Meg's

blouse. "Your buttons aren't done up right. And you . . ." She swung toward Shane. "Your shirt is on wrong-side out."

Simultaneously, Meg and Shane checked their clothing. Sheepishly, Meg hastily redid her buttons, while Shane stripped off his T-shirt and turned it right-side out, giving Meg a heart-stopping glimpse of his bare chest.

Oh the things she'd missed seeing in the dark. Next time she wanted all the lights blazing.

Ahem. There won't be a next time.

Why not? whined a petulant part of her.

Why not? Foolish question. This affair was bound to go nowhere. Shane was a military pilot stationed at Lackland Air Force Base in San Antonio. Long-distance relationships didn't work. She'd already figured that out with Grant.

Who's talking long-term here? What was wrong with enjoying what she had while she had it? Shane was on leave and in Austin until after the wedding. Four more days. They had four more days.

Four days filled with frantic wedding prep and the main event. There was no time for another rendezvous. She had to be happy with what she'd gotten. A soul-stirring afternoon of splendid sex in a storm shelter. It was a story to tell her grand-daughters when they were over eighteen.

"I'll call Harrie and the ranch hands and let

them know you're safe and sound," Brady said, pulling out his cell phone.

Shane leaned in close to Meg, murmured, "You okay?"

"Sure." She smiled bright as fresh-perked coffee. "Why wouldn't I be?"

"We didn't have time to discuss what happened down there."

"Nothing to discuss."

"You sure you don't need to talk?" He touched her elbow.

"If I do, I've got Brady."

Shane's jaw dropped. "You're going to tell him what happened?"

"Don't look shocked. Not in graphic detail. He *is* my best friend. Weren't you planning to tell Ellie?"

"I don't kiss and tell."

"Then I won't either," she said and turned away before he could start quizzing her again.

If he kept pushing her, she didn't know how long she could hold out. How long before she cracked and told him she had strange and wondrous feelings for him. "I need to get back and assess the extent of the storm damage. A rancher's work is never done."

"You really are all right?"

"Never been better," she lied. "Never been better."

Ducking her head, she hurried around the side

of the church, hoping to get away from every-one long enough to catch her breath and make sense of her out-of-control emotions.

But no such luck.

Ellie followed her.

Meg kept up the forced smile, turning the wattage up for good measure. Hoping to convince Ellie everything was hunky-dory. "Can I grab a ride with you and Brady back to the ranch house?"

"You're not going back with Shane?"

"Nope."

"Not even after you two . . ."

"After we what?"

"Um . . . okay, if that's how you want to play it."

"There's nothing to play."

"I see the way Shane looks at you. The way you look at him. There's something going on." Ellie stared pointedly at Meg's blouse. "Obviously."

Was it still buttoned up wrong? She wasn't going to check, to confirm Ellie's suspicions.

"Look," Ellie said, "what you and Shane do is your own business, but I just wanted to let you know something about him."

Meg took the bait. "What's that?"

"The guy doesn't commit easily. It takes a lot to earn his loyalty, but once he does, he's committed for life."

"Is that a warning?"

Ellie stepped closer, leveled her a cool stare. "I couldn't love him more if he were my own brother. So don't . . ." She pointed a finger under Meg's nose. "Toy with his heart."

"Noted," Meg said and squelched the question on the tip of her tongue. *But what if he's toying with mine?*

With Ellie and Meg out of earshot, Shane braced himself for what Brady was going to say. He didn't blame the other man for the dark, overprotective, big-brother expression in his eyes. He would have been just as territorial of Ellie if he'd caught her with Brady under similar circumstances before they'd gotten engaged.

They were standing in front of Shane's Jeep, and sure enough, it was beat to hell. Pockmarks were everywhere and the windshield was cracked. Shane stuffed his hands into his front pockets, shifted his gaze away from the other man.

"Sorry about your ride," Brady said.

"Worse things have happened."

"Harrie told me you came out here to save Meg."

Shane nodded, playing it cool. From where he was standing, he could just see the back of one of Meg's legs and her red boots. He wished they'd had time to talk before Brady and Ellie barged in on them.

Then again, what would he have said?

What had happened in the storm cellar had left him speechless. He felt as if he'd been picked up by a cyclone, spun around until he was squeezed inside out, and had not only managed to live through it but had enjoyed the experience immensely.

Crazy.

No explanation for it. Other than forced intimacy. Chemistry + danger + proximity = the kind of excitement a fella could mistake for deeper, mushier feelings. Throw in graduated questions designed to increase familiarity and four minutes of eye-gazing, and, well, that same fella might even begin to think he was falling in love.

But he wasn't. You couldn't fall in love in an instant. Not even after great sex. Love took time. How did that Bible verse go? Love is patient, love is kind . . .

There was nothing patient about what he and Meg had done. It might not even have been kind, seeing as how he was feeling raw and achy and blown wide open.

"Meg's been hurt before. I don't want to see her hurt again," Brady said.

"By Grant Portman?"

"She told you about that?"

"She did."

"She was with him a long time," Brady said.

"More than five years. She's in a good place now. I'm confident she's over him, but when Meg loves, she loves hard. She loves with all her heart and soul."

"From what I can tell, she does everything that way."

"So you can see why I worry."

"I can."

Brady pushed against Shane's shoulder with the tip of his finger. Hard. "And you aren't going to break her heart."

"I won't," Shane vowed, but he couldn't help wondering if he already had.

Meg, Shane, Ellie, Brady, Harrie, and the ranch hands worked cleaning up the storm damage until the sun disappeared. By the time Meg rolled into bed, she was tired all the way through the marrow of her bones.

Tomorrow would be even busier as cleanup from the storm continued amid wedding preparations. They were coming down to the wire. Several members of the wedding party were arriving in the morning, and they would also be busy with departing dude ranch guests. Meg had cleared her calendar of reservations for Wednesday through Saturday to accommodate the wedding guests.

But even though she was absolutely exhausted, Meg couldn't sleep. She kept thinking about

Shane and what had happened down in that storm cellar.

She wasn't imagining it. Something monumental had occurred. But she had no name for it. She only knew how she felt.

Joyous, melancholy, eager, testy, bold, edgy, expanded, doomed. So many mixed-up emotions.

What could she do about them?

What was there to do about them?

Yes, they'd had spectacular sex, but that was all it had been. The more she tried to make something of it, the more likely she was to get hurt. They'd made a strong but brief connection. It was over. End of story.

But what if, whispered a small voice in the back of her mind. What if it was more for him, too? *Aren't you even going to try?*

And do what? Profess her undying love?

Meg flopped over onto her stomach, punching lumps from a pillow that wasn't lumpy. It wasn't love. It couldn't be love. They'd only known each other three weeks and had only met a few times.

Brady and Ellie fell in love on the day they met.

They were one in a million. How special for them.

But what if it was love? What then?

Well, you know what? She would be seeing more of Shane. A lot more over the years. If something was there, it would stand the test of time. If not, so be it. No reason to fret or grasp or chase.

Unless he meets someone else because he has no idea how you feel about him.

But what if he didn't feel that way about her?

You never know until you try.

Ridiculous. Even if he did feel the same way about her, it could never work. Not when Shane was a fighter pilot, deployed for months at a time. Not when he lived in San Antonio and she was dug in, managing the dude ranch. There was no give here. It was the same quandary she'd had with Grant.

But . . .

"Shut up," she scolded the voice that could get her into so much trouble. "Just shut up and let me sleep."

But yelling at herself didn't work. An hour later, the same arguments were still circling around in her head.

So she got right up and went to work.

Shane hadn't had the opportunity to corner Meg for a long talk. They were both so busy with wedding preparations, they barely had time to eat or sleep, much less have a heart-to-heart talk about their storm-cellar escapade.

He hoped to get her alone on Friday evening following the rehearsal dinner. He needed to kiss her again. To see if things between them were just as combustible as before.

The rehearsal dinner was held in the same place the wedding reception would be. A converted bar decorated in country chic. From the ceiling over the long, family-style chow tables hung a wagon-wheel chandelier with Mason jar light covers. Wildflowers arranged in old cowboy boots served as centerpieces. The backs of the chairs were decorated with lasso ropes. White twinkle lights ran down the main wall, creating a fairy-tale atmosphere.

"Oh, Shane," Ellie said when he escorted her inside the building following the wedding rehearsal at the chapel. "I feel like the cowgirl version of Cinderella."

"You're truly happy?" he asked.

She cupped his chin in her palm, looking him squarely in the eye. "I have never been happier. Do you remember when we were kids and dreamed of having a forever family?"

He nodded. They'd created elaborate fantasies about the people who would adopt them—billionaires with yachts, famous actors, their favorite sports heroes.

"Well, I've finally found that with Brady."

"Yeah," he said, studying her beaming face. "I can see that."

"Don't worry," she said. "You'll always be part of my life. That's never going to change."

Tenderly, he kissed her cheek and wished that were true, but it wasn't something he could take to the bank. Things changed. Brady was in the picture now and Ellie wouldn't need him as much.

And that was as it should be.

He was happy for her, but yes, a little sad for himself. For so long they had been each other's soft place to land. Now that was Brady's job. He would miss spending so much time with Ellie.

As if on cue, Brady appeared to slip his arm through Ellie's and spirit her off to their places sitting side by side at the head of the long, wide table. Feeling a little lonely, Shane cast around for Meg, intending to ask her if she was free for a conversation once dinner was over.

He spied her talking to a man who'd come into the barn on Brady's heels. A jolt of jealousy shook through him. Confused him. He had nothing to be jealous about. But jealous he was.

The man looked vaguely familiar. Who was he? Curious, Shane stepped closer.

The guy tilted his head, his face earnest in the light as he spoke to Meg in urgent, hushed words Shane couldn't hear.

He recognized the guy from TV news.

Grant Portman.

Meg's ex. The guy she'd been with for five years.

Fresh waves of jealousy washed over Shane. A whole ocean of it.

And when the guy went down on one knee in front of Meg, a small black jeweler's box held in his hand, it was all he could do not to yell, *No!*

But he had no claim on Meg. None at all. He was in no position to go down on one knee and pour his heart out.

Primarily because he couldn't even begin to put words to what was in his heart. For so long he'd avoided romantic entanglements and now he was caught in one he didn't know how to get out of unscathed.

Chapter Eight

Three hours later, Meg's heart was still in her throat after Grant's unexpected marriage proposal.

He'd shown up out of nowhere, told her how desperately he'd missed her, what a terrible mistake he'd made, gone down on one knee, cracked open a jeweler's box with a marquise-cut diamond ring big enough to choke Jiggs, and asked her to marry him.

Grand gesture. Grant was full of them.

And it seemed he was more full of himself than ever. Having the audacity to do this here and now, and expecting her to fall at his feet without any recent contact or preamble. As if she'd just been sitting waiting for him to return.

People were staring. *Shane* was staring. She hadn't known what to do. She'd told Grant it wasn't the time or place for a marriage proposal. Did the polite thing and invited him to dinner.

Which, unfortunately, he accepted, promptly taking over the rehearsal dinner, regaling guests with stories of his Middle East adventures, how he'd been embedded in Afghanistan with an elite army team.

People around the table lauded him as a hero, which Grant soaked up with a boastful grin.

Shane stared at him through heavily lidded eyes, his mouth pressed into a grim line.

It was easy for Meg to see who was the real hero here. The fighter pilot who controlled himself, as opposed to the grandstanding journalist. The one who did his job to protect his country. The one who didn't brag or romanticize war.

Being away from Grant for a year had cleared her vision. Given her perspective. Even though he was handsomer than ever, Meg was glad he'd thrown her over for his career. She'd dodged a missile.

Ellie said, "I heard a news report about a gonzo journalist who was so intent on getting a story that he refused to follow the rules and almost got the team he was embedded with killed. Was that you?"

Meg had heard the same news report, even though the journalist hadn't been identified. She'd wondered at the time if it was Grant. He'd never been much of a rule follower.

Grant's eyes widened, then narrowed. He guffawed. Quickly sidestepped Ellie's question with a quip to Brady. "Your bride-to-be is a sharp tack. Better be careful where you sit."

Shane was grinding his teeth so hard that Meg could see his jaw muscles clenching beneath his tanned skin.

Meg eased the tension by proposing a toast to the happy couple and things went smoothly from there, until the party broke up and Grant waylaid her again, dragging her into the shadows. She glanced around for Shane, but he'd already left. So much for a rescue.

"You didn't answer my question," Grant said, pulling her into his arms.

Meg pushed back, ducking under his arm, slipping away. "Do you really expect me to take you seriously? I haven't heard from you in a year and you show up here with an engagement ring? What gives?"

"I missed you." Grant leaned in for a kiss.

Meg ducked his lips. "And?"

"I'm moving back to Austin."

"You got fired because of that stunt you pulled in Afghanistan," she said flatly.

"CNN and I weren't a good fit." His smile was glossy glib.

"So you thought you'd just come home and take up where you left off?"

"It's not like that, Meggers. I missed you. Being away made me realize just how much."

"Your being away made me realize some things, too."

"Such as?"

"I'm really glad you didn't ask me to marry you last year. It would have been a huge mistake."

"Does that mean you're turning down my marriage proposal?"

"It does."

"You've met someone else," he said flatly.

"That's not why I'm saying no."

"The fighter pilot."

"What makes you say that?"

"I saw how you looked at him and I saw how he wanted to pound my face in."

"Yes, it's the fighter pilot."

"He's not right for you."

"I know that. But neither are you."

"You're going to end up with a broken heart."

"Most likely."

"You're breaking mine," Grant said.

"No, I'm not. You still have your greatest love."

"Who's that?"

"Yourself."

Grant laughed at that. "Maybe you're right."

"We had some good times. Made some nice memories, but we were each other's starter relationships. There's no going back. Move forward. You'll land on your feet, Grant. Of that I am one hundred percent convinced."

"You sure?" He threaded his thumbs through his belt loops, took on a cocky stance. "I won't ask a second time."

She'd once taken his swagger as self-confidence; she now saw it for what it was. Arrogance. Had he gotten worse or had she always been so blind?

"I'm counting on it," she said and walked away.

· · ·

She left Grant, went in search of Shane. She'd planned on telling him how she felt about him once the wedding was over and Brady and Ellie were safely off on their honeymoon in Cabo, but she couldn't put it off any longer.

Grant had forced her hand.

She had to admit it. She had feelings for Shane. Feelings that weren't going to go away anytime soon. She was going out on a limb, taking a risk. But she was going to do it anyway. If she didn't tell him how she felt, she'd spend the rest of her life wondering *what if.*

No regrets. If he turned her away, painful as it might be, she could live with that. What she couldn't live with was not knowing.

She went to the bunkhouse bungalow where he was staying through the weekend, knocked softly on the door. "Shane? It's me, Meg. Are you still awake?"

A few seconds ticked by. It felt like an eternity.

She knocked again. "Shane?"

No answer.

She sighed, sank against the wall. She'd worked up her courage to walk over here and now she had all this unused adrenaline coursing through her body.

Forget about tonight. You've got the wedding in the morning. Go to bed. Get a good night's sleep. You can talk to him after the wedding.

Smart advice. She turned to head back to the main house, started at a movement in the shadows behind her.

Her heart sped up. Had Grant returned?

Shane stepped from the darkness.

Her pulse quickened even more. "Hi."

"Hello." His voice was even, noncommittal. "Were you here to see me?"

"I was." The light summer breeze drifted over them, along with the smell of the honeysuckle that grew along the fencerow.

They moved toward each other simultaneously, searching each other's faces.

"We never got a chance to talk after . . ." Meg said.

"I know."

"That thing with the questions and the four-minute eye gazing."

"Potent."

"It made me consider whether Brady and Ellie were on to something. They seem so happy."

"Could just be a self-fulfilling prophesy."

"Could be." She bobbed ahead. "But . . ." She gulped, gathered her courage. "I felt something, too. Something powerful. For you."

He stared at her. Into her. The same way he had in the cellar.

Meg held her breath. She loved him because he was so much larger than life. Whenever he walked into a room heads turned. He was big and commanding and proud. Being with him expanded her; she felt less constricted, more open to possibilities.

The way he took the initiative gave her a thrill, even if it meant she sometimes had to buck him to get what she wanted. Nothing wrong with a spirited debate. It spiced things up. His enthusiasm was infectious, and together they were dynamic.

Electric. She thought of their afternoon together, felt heat rush to her cheeks. She wanted to do that again and again and again.

Forever.

"What?" He said it so softly she barely heard him.

"I think I might be . . . I could be . . ." Did she dare say the words?

Head cocked, he watched her intently.

Meg moistened her lips, splayed a palm against her chest. *Do it. You're here. Now or never.* "I think I'm falling in love with you."

He said nothing. Not a word. No smile. No frown. No facial expression at all. Blank. Unreadable. Emotionless. A warrior's stare.

Meg shivered, regretted starting this, but she'd come too far to back out now. Silence stretched out for millennia. Finally, when she could stand it no longer, she whispered his name. "Shane?"

"I have strong feelings for you, too, Meg," he said. "But it's not something I can trust."

A thick lump of emotion squatted in her throat. "I see."

"I'm not saying this to hurt you." Shane's eyes darkened. "But the truth is you can't fall in love with someone in a matter of weeks."

"Why not?"

"Lust, sure. I lusted after you the first day we met. But love? Love is something that takes time. Lots of time."

Meg rolled her fingernails into her palms, squeezed hard. "So you don't really believe Ellie and Brady are in love? They've only known each other a few months. How long is long enough?"

"I don't have an answer for that."

"I see."

"You've got history with Grant. He wants you back. I saw him ask you to marry him. I won't get in the way of that."

"I told him no. I don't want Grant. I want you."

"You don't even know me," he said harshly.

His words were a punch to the gut. She took it, absorbed it. "I know you're afraid of what you're feeling. Ellie told me you'd never been in love."

"Yeah, well, maybe I can't fall in love. Maybe I'm not genetically built to fall in love."

"That's bullshit and you know it. For a brave

guy, Shane Freemont, you sure are scared of me."

"You're right," he said. "I am."

"You know the definition of courage? Feeling the fear and doing it anyway. Jump with me, Shane. Let's take a chance on us. What's wrong with exploring this? Taking our time. See where it goes."

He shook his head. "It would be a long-distance relationship. Those are hard to maintain."

"So you're telling me in your book it's better to have never loved at all than take a risk on loving and losing?"

"Meg, I don't believe your feelings are real. We were in a forced situation. We played some silly game . . ."

"And by damn if we didn't fall for each other."

"That's what I'm saying. It's a parlor trick. It's not something we can trust."

"Maybe you can't trust your feelings, Shane, but I can trust mine. I love you. There. I said it." Her heart was thumping so loud and hard it sounded like a rock band was inside her head, pounding out a fierce drum solo. "Deal with it."

"You're not," he said. "You just think you are."

"Don't you dare tell me what I feel." She blinked hard. "Don't you dare." Then Meg ran away before she broke down and started crying in front of him.

Well, hell, he'd screwed that up royally.

Watching Meg flee, he felt like an utter shit heel. He'd bludgeoned her with his truth and she'd said, *I love you.*

Those three terrifying words he'd only said to one person in his entire life. Ellie. And that was a different flavor of love from what Meg was talking about.

Her departure left him hollow and alone, wanting to protect her and run after her and confess that he loved her too. But how could that possibly be so? How could he trust that these feelings were the kind that could last a lifetime?

God, how he wanted her. In his arms. In his bed. But forever? How could he make such a promise and make it stick? The only thing he knew for sure was that whenever he was around her, need for her drove him wild.

Every cell in his body yelled at him to stop being a fool and go after her, but his feet were rooted into the dirt. If he went after her, he'd make love to her, and if he made love to her again . . . well, he didn't know what would happen.

And from a practical standpoint, he had to be up at dawn to help Ellie get ready for her big day.

Man of honor. He was the man of honor.

So why, then, did he feel so damned dishonorable?

Meg marinated in misery all night. Woke on Brady and Ellie's wedding day feeling worse than the night before.

She tried to fight the blues. Posted an I'm-the-best-woman smile on her face. Faked it. Fooled people. But deep inside she couldn't run from her despair. She felt lost to herself, to every-thing she had ever known. To the familiar sights and sounds and smells and textures and tastes of home, even as she was in the midst of them.

Everything she'd once believed about herself felt false. Every comfort she'd ever turned to failed her. Every conversation seemed empty. Every hope a sham.

Who was she? Where was she going? Nothing held meaning. Nothing felt real.

Put one foot in front of the other. You'll get through this. The hurt will go away eventually.

At noon she went to help Brady dress for the 3 p.m. wedding. She found him standing in front of the mirror in his bedroom reciting his vows. "Have you eaten lunch?"

"Not hungry."

"Are you nervous?"

"Nope."

"Not in the least?"

"Meg," he said, "I've never been so sure of anything in my life."

"Okay."

"You got the ring?" he asked.

Meg held up her right hand with Ellie's ring on it. Shane was in charge of Brady's ring. "Do you have the license?"

Brady looked panicked. "I don't know. Where did I put it? Maybe it's in my desk."

"I'll check your desk—you finish getting dressed." She rummaged through his desk, found the license. Turned back to him with it held triumphantly in her hand.

"What do you think?" Brady stood there with his arms out.

"C'mere," she said and crooked a finger at him. "Your bow tie is crooked."

He came over and she fixed it for him. "I think Ellie is a very lucky woman."

"I'm the lucky one," he said.

"You're both lucky to have found someone willing to lay it all on the line for love." Meg suppressed a sigh.

"So," Brady said, "Grant asked you to marry him last night."

"He did," Meg said mildly, not wanting to get into it.

"You turned him down."

"I did."

"Because of Shane?"

124

"No. I wouldn't have said yes either way. I've grown beyond Grant. Thankfully."

"But you're in love with Shane."

"Is it that obvious?"

"Painfully." Brady's sympathetic smile turned her inside out. "I'm sorry things didn't work out for you two."

Meg shrugged. "I'll live."

"You're strong," he said. "It'll be all right."

"Until then," she said, "do you have a quick cure for a broken heart?"

He shook his head. "I'm sorry for the pain, sweetheart. You've just got to go through it."

"I was afraid you were going to say that."

"Shane's the broken one. If he can't make room in his heart for a wonderful woman like you."

"I'm sure it's because of his childhood. He just doesn't trust love."

"You'll let me know if there's anything I can do?" Brady rubbed a comforting hand over her shoulder.

"I will, thanks."

But Meg knew there was nothing Brady could do. It was her sorrow and the only way through it was to endure.

Sometimes it truly sucked being strong.

Chapter Nine

Nobody, not even Ellie, could help him. Shane could find no peace from his own mind. No matter where he looked.

He stared at himself in the mirror. Was it his imagination? Or did his eyes seem sunken deeper in his head? He'd never been a melancholy guy, or given to much reflection. This state of mind was new for him and he hated it.

Antidote.

He needed an antidote for the blues. Needed something to break this inner storm and let the light in.

He'd already tried several diversions. Cold shower at two a.m. It only made him shiver, did nothing to drive away the agony. He'd gone for a horseback ride to catch the sunrise, but that stirred romantic thoughts of Meg and he wished she were with him.

In his loneliness, he'd shuffled back to the ranch and ate breakfast in the mess hall, grateful for company. But the eggs had tasted like sawdust in his mouth, the conversations seemed banal. People were wondering what the bride's dress looked like and what would be her something blue. That reminded him he needed to ask Ellie if she had something blue.

He didn't want her to miss out on any of the traditions.

The sky was bright, but all he could see were clouds. He tried to shake off the gloom for Ellie's sake. This was her wedding day, but he could find no joy.

He had nowhere to turn. There was nothing to be done. Nothing to think. Nothing to do to fix it. He'd made his choice. He'd turned Meg away after she told him she loved him. It was done.

Torment. Torture. How was he going to get through this?

Acceptance. That's where he had to land. Accept that this was the way it would be. Should be. For Meg's sake. She deserved someone who could love her without a second of hesitation.

That's when he knew the truth of it. He wasn't worthy of her. She had the capacity for so much love. And he? He'd grown up an orphan. He didn't know the first thing about love.

Except for Ellie.

Ellie was his saving grace.

It would soon be time to head to the chapel. He hurried to the main house, where Ellie was staying in the bedroom next to Meg's. He knew Meg was over at Brady's ranch, but nonetheless his heart skittered when he passed by her door.

He knocked gently on Ellie's door.

"Well?" Ellie said. "How do I look?"

She twirled for him in fluffy white chiffon and sassy cowgirl boots.

"There's never been a more beautiful bride. There never will be a more beautiful bride," he said.

"You say that now," she chided. "But just wait until you have a bride of your own one day. You'll change your mind."

"Ellie, you know I'm not the marrying kind."

She sank her hands on her hips and glared at him. "Ask yourself if that's really true, Shane Freemont. Or just some story you've been telling yourself for thirty years."

"I don't think I'm capable of long-term commitment."

"You committed to the Air Force."

"That's different."

"Why?"

"I needed a job. A place to belong. Besides, the Air Force taught me how to fly. In the sky I'm free."

"What about Meg?"

"What about her?"

"You don't have to pretend with me. I know you." Ellie came near, put her palms on either side of his face, and shook his head around. "You're in love with her."

"Is this love? This horrible, miserable sick feeling?"

"No," she said. "That's your fear of love.

You love her and it happened in a heartbeat and that's why you're so scared."

"Let's say you're right and I take a chance on love and it doesn't work out? What then?"

"But what if it does?"

"I . . ." His jaw unhinged and he couldn't find the words to describe the depth of his fear—not that it wouldn't work out with Meg but that it would.

"I know what you're going through because I've been there. I experienced the same thing when the lightning bolt that is Brady Cutwright struck me."

"What? I thought you knew right away Brady was the one for you."

"My heart did. It was my contrary mind that resisted. I'm sure it's because of our childhood. Growing up without parents or family. Having no one to lean on but each other. We trusted ourselves, Shane, but we were the only ones we trusted. We didn't let other people in. We closed ourselves off to love."

She was right.

"When Brady told me he loved me, I had to do a lot of soul-searching. And I discovered that it wasn't so much loving him and losing him that I feared but getting him and failing him because I had no pattern for what love was supposed to look like. Or worse, that I was incapable of loving him the way he deserved to be loved. Do you think that could be true for you?"

Nailed it. To the cross.

"Look, even if what you're saying is true. Things between me and Meg . . ." He paused. "I'm an Air Force pilot stationed in San Antonio. She runs a ranch her family has owned for five generations outside Austin. I can't ask her to give up her home and her job for me."

"Maybe not, but your commission is up in six months. And I thought you always wanted to run your own charter airplane company. You know, lots of ranches in central Texas have their own airfields. Plenty of ranchers need pilots."

"Yeah," he said, but this was her day. Not his. They shouldn't be talking about his problems. "So how are you doing right now? Do you want me to start the Jeep so you can make a clean getaway? 'Cause I'll do it. Just say the word."

Her laugh was a little shaky and she put a hand to her stomach. "If I ran now, I would never stop running. Brady is the second-best thing that ever happened to me. I won't let a little fear cause me to throw that away."

"What was the first-best thing that happened to you?" he asked.

She smiled at him like he was as dense as a black hole. "You."

"Me?"

"If I hadn't met you, I doubt I would have the capacity to love at all. But I loved you, and that's what gave me hope that I could love Brady, too."

"Ah, Ell; ah, honey, don't cry. You'll ruin your pretty makeup." He grabbed a fistful of tissues from the box, thrust them at her.

"They're happy tears, Shane. Tears of joy that I have so much love to give and I'm not afraid to give it." Delicately, she dabbed at her eyes, laughing through the tears.

"Before I forget," he said, "I meant to ask, what's your something blue?"

Impishly, she grinned at him. "Why silly, you walking me down the aisle in your Air Force dress blues. That coupled with your blue mood should make for plenty of color."

The little one-room chapel in the pasture was packed, with more guests than seats. A long white carpet ran from the door, down the aisle to the altar.

Brady stood waiting for his bride, his forehead glistening with a sheen of sweat. Meg was beside him, along with his two former college roommates from UT serving as groomsmen. Discreetly as she could, she passed him a tissue. He swiped at his face, his breath coming in shallow gasps.

"Don't you dare faint," she whispered from the corner of her mouth.

Brady attempted a smile, fumbled it. "I think I'm gonna throw up."

"You're not going to throw up. And don't lock your knees."

"You're the best best woman ever," he said.

"Except for the one you're waiting for."

They stared at the back of the chapel, watching as Ellie's two bridesmaids started down the aisle an evenly spaced distance apart. Travis Whitely played a soulful rendition of Pachelbel's "Canon in D" on his acoustic guitar.

Once the bridesmaids reached the altar, the organist took over, playing "The Bridal Chorus."

And Ellie appeared on Shane's arm. Because she had no parents, Shane was going to walk her down the aisle as her man of honor. He wore his Air Force dress blues and looked so devastatingly handsome Meg forgot to breathe.

Every eye in the place was trained on the two of them. Ellie was stunningly beautiful, an angel in white cowboy boots and a cowgirl hat with a veil.

"I love that woman with all my heart and soul," Brady said.

Tears welled up in Meg. For the tender beauty of the moment. For the love in the room. And for herself. Because the man she wanted was walking straight toward her and she couldn't have him because he was too damn scared to let himself love her.

Ellie's smile met Brady's and their gazes connected and Meg could tell they were so into each other nothing else existed. She'd shared that look once with Shane for four incredible minutes.

They'd been the most life-changing four minutes she'd ever known and she would always remember them.

Then Ellie caught Meg's gaze, held it, and gave her a secret smile that said, *we're sisters now. Sisters of the heart.*

Shane and Ellie reached the altar. Shane transferred Ellie to Brady's arm and took his place on her left side, her man of honor.

The minister cleared her throat. "Brady and Ellie wrote their own vows. Although Brady confessed his best woman, Megan, helped with the big words."

A ripple of laughter went through the congregation, soft and cheerful. Nice day. Unusual wedding. Everything was working out fine.

"Take it away, Brady," the minister invited.

Brady took his bride's hands in his, peered deeply into her eyes, and began. "Some people say it's impossible to fall in love at first sight."

Meg hazarded a glance at Shane. He was looking right at her. She gulped. Bravely held his gaze.

"Some say those first-meeting stirrings are nothing but lust, chemistry, hormones."

Shane bit his bottom lip, but his eyes never strayed. They were locked on each other again the way they'd been that afternoon in the cellar. Was it really just four days ago? It seemed a century.

"Some say there's no way you can know if those first stirrings of love will last."

The church sat rapt. No murmurs, no rustling of clothes or programs. Not a sound.

"I say those people are just chickenshit," Brady said, and the entire congregation guffawed. Trust a cowboy to speak the raw-boned truth from the heart. "Scared of the unknown. Scared of losing control. Scared of letting themselves fall fully and completely in love."

People leaned forward in their seats, hanging on Brady's every word. Meg and Shane stood deadlocked. Not blinking. Not looking away. In the moment. Right there. Listening. Looking. As if the message in Brady's heartfelt words was meant just for them.

"When I first looked into your beautiful face, my angel Ellie, I knew I'd been made for you and you made for me. I had no doubt. Some fear, yes. But I knew the fear was holding me back from the best life had to offer."

People in the pews were crying. Meg felt

tears well up in her own eyes. But Shane stood stoic. An airman, a pilot. Holding on tight to his emotions.

"Wow," said the minister. "I think that's the first time anyone has ever said *chickenshit* in their wedding vows."

More laughter from the congregation.

Ellie said her vows, echoing much of what Brady had already said in a sweeter, gentler way.

When she finished, the minister turned to Meg, pantomiming for her to pass over the ring. She handed it to Brady. Shane gave Ellie Brady's ring.

"If there is anyone here who can show just cause for why this man and this woman should not be married, speak now or forever hold your peace."

Shane and Meg simultaneously cleared their throats. She smiled, happy that they'd been thinking along the same lines.

Brady and Ellie jumped, looked startled.

"Just kidding," she and Shane said in unison, as if they'd practiced it.

Brady reached for Ellie's hand, drew her closer to him. Put his ring on her finger, gazed at his wife. "I loved you at first sight and I promise to love you until I draw my last breath."

Ellie beamed an angelic smile, slipped the ring on his finger. "You are my soul mate. The other half of me. I vow to stay with you until death do us part."

Meg was getting choked up. *Don't cry, don't cry. You'll embarrass best women the world over.*

Brady and Ellie stood in the bright light of their love in that special delicate moment, and the entire congregation breathed as one. A splendid, beautiful capsule in time.

"Do you, Brady Eugene Cutwright, take this woman to be your lawfully wedded wife?"

"I do!"

"And do you, Eleanor Jayne Carson, take this man to be your lawfully wedded husband."

"I do!"

"Now you may kiss the bride."

Chapter Ten

In the hubbub of wedding pictures, receiving lines, and cocktail hour, Shane didn't get an opportunity to speak to Meg. He had so much to say to her that he didn't know where to begin.

But then he had an idea. An idea that meant he had to avoid her until he was ready to talk. So when she came looking for him, he dodged her and hoped she'd forgive him later when he explained everything.

At the reception, when the wedding party sat for their meal, he and Meg flanked their best friends, the bride and groom. Shane was so nervous he didn't know if he'd be able to eat. He hadn't been this nervous since his first solo flight.

Once everyone was seated and the wedding planner gave the cue, Shane stepped up to the microphone to deliver his speech. He glanced over at Ellie's shining face, saw she was holding hands with Brady. Then he slid his gaze over to Meg and his throat clogged.

Shane couldn't catch his breath. Meg was so damn beautiful it about broke his heart. Was this how Ellie felt about Brady?

Ellie touched his hand. "Take your time. Breathe."

Easier said than done. He smiled at her, forced himself to exhale, then breathe deep.

What he was about to do was a huge risk. The biggest risk of his life. Uncalculated. Based on nothing but gut instinct. Anyway, no amount of analysis, experience or preparation could save him if he failed.

Clearing his throat, he unfolded the piece of paper with his notes and began to read in the glow of the twinkle lights and lanterns. "I started working on this speech the day my best friend asked me to be her maid of honor."

This drew laughter from the audience.

"Except she was kind enough to change the name to man of honor. But I haven't acted as a man of honor." Shane looked down the table at Meg again.

She was looking at him, sitting quiet and self-contained. Listening.

It was a start.

"You see, even though I told Ellie I was on board with this marriage, that I would stand by her no matter what, I didn't believe in the love she'd found with Brady. I couldn't conceive how it was possible she could fall in love so quickly. I was one of those *some people* Brady spoke of in his vows. Frankly, that kind of love was beyond my comprehension. Secretly, I kept thinking eventually Ellie would wise up and figure out things were moving

138

too fast and she'd call the whole thing off."

The room was silent. No one spoke a word.

"But then it happened to me." He gazed out at the audience, studied the faces. He was about to announce his feelings for Meg to everyone. He'd thought he might falter but instead felt bolstered. "From the minute I laid eyes on her, I felt something I've never felt before. Something that scared the hell out of me because it was that powerful. That inexplicable. That mysterious. That wondrous."

Microphone in hand, he turned to the bride and groom, but his eyes were trained on Meg. "Brady and Ellie are the brave ones. It can be the most terrifying thing in the world to open yourself up, to be vulnerable and let someone love you and to love them back unconditionally. To take that dive because your hearts tell you it's right. To not listen to family and friends when they speak against what's right for you. I raise my glass to the happy couple." Shane raised his champagne flute. "Brady and Ellie, your love is a shining example. A beacon of hope to those of us lost in the wilderness. You two are my heroes."

"To Brady and Ellie," the crowd cheered in unison, clinking glasses. A few people sniffed. Some dabbed at their eyes.

Shane drained his glass, sat down, completely out of steam.

Meg gave a great toast to the couple but never looked at Shane. His heart was a snare drum, pounding hard and deep. Scared. So damn scared.

Somehow he made it through the meal. He couldn't have told anyone who asked what he had eaten. He'd put it in his mouth, chewed, swallowed it down. Waiting. Just waiting for it to be over so he could get to Meg.

When the meal was finally finished and the dancing began, he pushed back his chair, moved toward her, only to discover she'd slipped away from him.

Oh God, where had she gone?

He wanted to search for her, but Ellie was pulling him out on the dance floor for what would normally have been the father-daughter dance. He was the only family she had.

"I love you," Ellie said. "You have no idea how much."

"Yeah," he said. "I kind of do. I feel the same way about you."

They touched foreheads and slow danced for one song; then Shane passed her over to Brady and stepped to the sidelines.

"Dancing for the first time as a married couple," the DJ said. "I present to you Mr. and Mrs. Brady Cutwright." Strains of Eric Clapton's "Wonderful Tonight" spilled into the air.

"That was some speech," Meg said, stepping

up beside him. "Kind of makes you believe in love at first sight."

"Thanks." He held out his hand. "I meant every word."

Meg sank her palm into his and he spun her out onto the dance floor, joining the bride and groom. Their bodies fit perfectly as they glided together.

"What changed?" she asked.

"Ellie helped me figure something out," Shane said, pulling her close.

"What's that?"

"Love isn't something that happens to us. Love is a choice we make. Sure, biology matters. Chemistry stirs the soup. But love is more pliable, more deliberate than we pretend it is."

"You don't say," she murmured.

"That day in the storm cellar, when we asked those questions and stared into each other's eyes, we consciously added the most important ingredient to chemistry to turn it into love."

"And what was that?" Meg asked, her eyes fixed on his.

"Trust. It's something I've struggled with my whole life and I know it's because I was orphaned young and life kicked me around. I was afraid to trust. Afraid of getting left again."

"But you're no longer afraid?"

"No," he said. "Because of you." Shane swung

her around in an elaborate dip and kissed her neck.

"You know," she said, "I keep thinking about what Ellie said."

"Hmm?"

"If a guy has a woman as his best friend, you know he's going to make a good husband."

"That does speak well of his ability to have a stable relationship with a member of the opposite sex."

They smiled deeply at each other, their dancing flowing effortlessly. "Does that mean I'll be seeing more of you?"

"Count on it."

"What about the long-distance logistics?"

"You know," he said, "I've always dreamed of having my own charter business, and my Air Force commission is up in six months."

"You'd give up being a fighter pilot for me?"

"For us," he corrected. "I'd have to give it up eventually."

"What would the Yeagermeister say about that?"

"Probably 'never wait for trouble.' "

"Ah," she said. "Wise man."

"I've got something for you."

"Oh?"

"A present."

"The man of honor doesn't get the best woman a gift."

"Who's to say? This was a nontraditional wedding anyway." He took her hand, led her off the dance floor. Headed over to his suit jacket, took out a jewelry box.

"This isn't . . . Shane, you're not about to—"

"It's not an engagement ring," he said. "Not yet. I want us to date. I want to have the full experience. Intimate dinners. Sunset cruises. Horseback rides. Plane rides. I want more intimate questions. And more four-minute eye gazing."

"Yes," she said. "Oh yes."

"Open it."

She undid the wrapping, opened the box, laughed with joy at the duck charm bracelet nestled there. "Oh, oh!"

"Now you'll always have your ducks in row," he said.

"I love it." She flung her arms around him. "And I love you."

"I love you, Meg. With every breath in my body. And when the time is right for us both, I'll ask you to be my bride. But for now, there's something I've always wanted to do."

"What's that?" she asked as he attached the charm bracelet to her wrist.

"You know," he said, "I've always wanted to have sex in a hayloft."

"Follow me." She giggled. "You've come to the right place."

And as they walked away together in the dark, headed for a secluded hayloft hand in hand, it happened.

A holy presence came over the night—sweetly, softly. They felt it filling their bodies. Their minds bathed in mellow bright light. Their hearts, their full, full hearts, permeated with peace. A deep, abiding peace moving through them like warm ocean water, flowing through their spines, their brains, under their skin. Everywhere. Peace generated from joy.

And the sexual fires smoldered, joining them. One. No separation. There in the hayloft, when they came together, all their old fears and doubts and distrust fell away and they stood in the light of pure love—new beings, free beings—totally transformed.

Getting Saddled

Cat Johnson

Chapter One

"I now pronounce you husband and wife. You may kiss the bride."

In response to the preacher's directive, the groom dipped the bride into a dramatic kiss worthy of any classic Hollywood romance film.

As the wedding guests cheered and whistled, Erin surreptitiously wiped the moisture from her eyes.

Next to Erin, her assistant Jessica shook her head, sending her blond hair bouncing. "How do you still get choked up at every ceremony? We're doing two, sometimes three weddings a weekend and it's only May. June will be even busier. I would think you'd be immune to all this sappy stuff by now."

Even after years in this business every ceremony still touched her heart. Erin gathered her composure and turned to her already jaded assistant to set the girl straight. "Of course not. Each wedding is special. The day I don't get choked up will be the day I know I should consider hanging up my wedding planner hat."

Jessica rolled her eyes. "You're such a romantic. That's why I don't understand why you aren't married at your age."

At your age?

The words reverberated like thunder in Erin's head, making her want to tear out her own locks.

How old did Jessica think she was anyway? She was sure the younger woman hadn't meant the words to be an insult, but she still couldn't help feeling she'd just been called old.

Jeez. They were barely fifteen years apart in age. Erin would turn forty in December and that was still over half a year away. She had plenty of time to find the perfect man and settle down. Later. When she could slow down at work and not risk the competition taking over the Austin wedding planning market.

One day Erin would have a steady man in her life. A house with a yard. Kids even. Until then, she was perfectly happy sharing her apartment with Maurice. Yes, Maurice was a cat who wanted nothing to do with her if she wasn't filling his food bowl, but he was still a companion. She wasn't completely alone.

"I'm not dating because I'm concentrating on my job." And with that, Erin was putting an end to the absurd conversation.

The starry-eyed bride and groom were slowly working their way down the long aisle of the church. They looked so young, so eager, so ready to begin their life together. The maid of honor and best man followed, arm in arm, and then two more pairs of bridesmaids and groomsmen fell in behind.

The wedding party would be followed by the one hundred and fifty guests who were already getting on their feet and waiting for their turn to exit. Erin's short break to watch the vows was over.

It was time to get back to work. She had a wedding to run. The bride and groom might be the stars of this production, but it was Erin, acting in the dual roles of stage manager and director, who would make sure it went off without a hitch.

"Let's get these doors open and these people on their way." Like a quarterback dismissing the team huddle, Erin clapped her hands together and spun toward the doors nearby.

Jessica secured one side of the double doors as Erin handled the other while she reviewed the plan. "I need you to organize the receiving line. The wedding party should line up on the lawn where we discussed so the guests have room to go all the way down the stairs and start a queue on level ground rather than waiting on the steps. But make sure the bride and groom are facing away from the sun. We don't want them squinting for the photographs because of the glare."

Jessica let out a laugh. "Okay, will do."

Frowning, Erin glanced at her assistant. "What's so funny?"

"It just never ceases to amaze me how you can go from teary-eyed romantic to a tyrannical general in seconds." With a smirk and without waiting for a response, Jessica headed outside.

Tyrant. Humph. Sentiment was one thing; work was work.

After a brief moment of wonder as to how today's twentysomethings seemed to have no problem speaking their minds to their bosses, Erin followed Jessica outside while pulling her cell phone from her jacket pocket.

She placed a call to the banquet manager at the catering hall and confirmed things were running on schedule and the first guests would likely arrive for cocktails within the half hour. She also needed to make sure there was some-one waiting outside the venue to help push the bride's grandmother in her wheelchair up the ramp.

That done, she disconnected the call and glanced at the line forming on the lawn. Jessica might have more opinions than Erin would like, but the girl followed directions to the letter. That was all that really mattered.

So many details went into the successful planning of a wedding and Erin loved every minute of it.

Speaking of details . . . she was worried about the swan ice sculpture. That bird and its skinny neck was just too delicate for Erin's comfort, yet it seemed as if every bride who wanted an ice sculpture at the cocktail hour chose a swan.

Before she had a chance to put the cell away and move on to one of those many details she needed to attend to, the phone vibrated in her hand.

The number on the display was unfamiliar, but that was nothing new. Except for her mother and sister, the only calls she got were business-related. "Hello, this is Erin."

"Hi. Um, is this the wedding planner?" The girl on the phone sounded painfully young. That alone wouldn't preclude Erin from taking the time to speak with her. Brides seemed to get younger and younger every year. Of course, that could be because Erin was getting older.

"That's right. I'm Erin Saddler, owner of Happy Is the Bride Event Planning. How can I help you?"

"Oh good. Jan from the vegan bakery in Austin gave me your number. She said she's worked with you in the past."

"Yes. Many times. I just love Jan. She's such a sweetheart, and those cakes they make there are to die for. Are you a bride?"

To save time, Erin began the walk toward her car. Jessica was handling things here at the church, so Erin was free to drive over to the catering hall to see for herself that everything was in order. Erin caught her assistant's gaze and motioned toward the parking lot.

As Jessica acknowledged Erin with a nod, the girl on the phone continued, "Yes. My fiancé and I just got engaged. I'm sorry, I'm so excited I'm forgetting myself—I'm Ellie."

"Ellie, congratulations. No need to apologize. It's an exciting time for you. That's perfectly understandable and the reason I'm in business actually. To take the extra work off the already busy bride and groom's shoulders so they can relax and enjoy the time." Erin slid into her car and switched the cell to speakerphone.

"That sounds pretty amazing . . . and impossible." Ellie's tinkling laugh had Erin picturing a young sprite living in the forest. "There seems like so much to do. And we have a unique challenge I hope won't be a problem."

"I'm sure it's nothing we can't work around if you choose to go with our company."

How bad could it be? Erin had orchestrated events for everyone from rock stars to dogs—literally. Some heiress had had a wedding for her and her neighbor's dog. Erin was fairly confident she could handle most anything at this point.

"Well, for one thing my fiancé—Brady—his family owns a cattle ranch."

This was Texas. Even in the city of Austin, running into cattle ranchers from the surrounding areas was common.

"All right . . ." Erin waited for the problem.

"I'm a vegan, so I'm a little concerned about keeping both sides happy with the food at the reception."

"Ah, okay. I don't see a problem with that." The venue schematic was already forming in Erin's head. She pictured two buffet tables. One vegan-friendly. The other beef-centric, perhaps with a barbecue theme. And Erin knew the vegan bakery could fill any of their dessert needs.

"That's good to hear. But there's one other thing that might be an issue . . . the wedding's June eighteenth."

Again, Erin didn't see an issue, but brides tended to worry. "Not a problem. That gives us a year—"

"I meant *this* June."

Erin quickly did the math in her head. "That's only—"

"Less than a month away. I know it's soon." The bride-to-be completed Erin's sentence, confirming the bad news.

Ellie had sounded so sad, almost miserable with her fear that she wouldn't have the wedding she wanted on the date she'd chosen, that Erin hated to disappoint her. Even so, three weeks was tight. "Um, I don't know—"

The bride rushed to add, "We already have the place for the reception and there's a chapel there for the ceremony. Will that make it easier?"

That last bit of information saved Erin from having heart palpitations. She blew out a breath of relief. "Yes. That'll definitely help."

"So . . . do you think you can do it? Will you take the job?" A bit of hope crept into Ellie's voice.

Erin couldn't let her down. She lived to make brides' dreams come true and that wasn't going to change just because there were a few obstacles in the way.

Drawing in a bracing breath, Erin said with more conviction than she felt, "Yes. Definitely."

"Really?" In a complete one-eighty, the bride's tone changed to elated. Almost bubbly.

"Yes. We'll get it done." Somehow. Erin didn't quite know exactly how just yet, but she'd figure it out. Come hell or high water.

She hadn't built her reputation as one of the premier event planners in Austin by shying away from a challenge. And this certainly would be that—challenging.

Wait until Jessica heard she'd accepted a wedding that had to be put together in three weeks. Erin's assistant was never going to let her hear the end of it.

Chapter Two

It was hot as hell. But then again, that shouldn't be a surprise. This was Texas after all, but today was hotter than usual for a day in late May.

Tanner should be able to handle the heat. He'd been working a ranch most of his adult life. He didn't let that stop him from bitching about it now.

"Damn, it's hot as blazes out here today." Letting out a huff, Tanner ran his handkerchief across his forehead.

The thin cotton was so damp with sweat and smeared with the dust he'd been working in, the red paisley pattern was barely visible any longer.

Knowing it would only get worse before he was done for the day, Tanner shoved it dirty into the rear pocket of his jeans.

"Eh, the heat won't last. Supposed to cool off a bit next week." Randy, the young ranch hand working with him, didn't look particularly disturbed by the heat kicking Tanner's ass.

That made Tanner feel old, which only annoyed him more.

Was he just getting old? He considered the possibility.

Nah.

He quickly dismissed the thought. At forty-one he was still in his prime. But that didn't mean he had to like sweating under the noonday sun. Oh he'd do it, but he sure as hell didn't have to enjoy it.

Taking the tool in hand again, Tanner went back to work.

The steady sound of the post-hole digger—the chomp of the metal blade hitting the dirt and the swoosh as Tanner pulled it out again—became hypnotic. Combined with the warmth of the sun and the touch of the wind, it lulled him into a relaxed rhythm.

After today's work he'd sleep good tonight.

City folk wouldn't need yoga or meditation or pills to sleep at night—and more pills to get through the day—if they'd just pick up a tool and work up a good sweat every day.

Planting his tool in the ground, Randy leaned on the long wooden handles and let out a long, low whistle. "Holy cow . . . *Who* is that?"

Frowning at Randy, Tanner wondered what had the kid ignoring his work this time.

Today's youth had a crap work ethic.

With that thought, Tanner realized he really was starting to act old. That was something his papaw would have said. In fact, Papaw might have actually said it, word for word.

He supposed he shouldn't be quite so cranky, but damn, was it hot. And it would be nice if the ranch hand helping him would actually, you know, *help*.

Tanner planted his own post-hole digger into the dirt and leaned on it as he tried to see what had Randy so distracted. He spotted the car parked in front of the Cutwrights' house.

Actually, it was less car and more mommy minivan, but either way it was nothing for Randy to be so excited about. People came and went all day around here, especially since Brady had gotten engaged. And as far as vehicles went, this one was pretty plain. Straightforward. White. Square. Probably useless in the mud.

Then a woman stepped from around the nose of the van and into Tanner's view and he had to give Randy a pass for staring.

She opened the passenger door and bent at the waist as she fiddled with something inside.

Holy cow was right. A few other exclamations, not quite as tame, flew into Tanner's mind.

"Don't know who that is." But Tanner would sure like to get to know her.

Mommy van or not, she certainly didn't look like any mother he'd ever seen. Though he wouldn't mind if she called him *daddy*.

Even at this distance he could see the glint of red as the sun hit her glossy chestnut hair while it bounced around her shoulders.

And that body . . . phew!

In spite of the length of the skirt that came

all the way down to her knees, he could tell she had legs that went on for days and hips he'd really enjoy getting his hands on.

Nope, he didn't know who she was or why she was here, but he'd have to make it his business to find out.

It was a rare occurrence that a female—and one that shapely to boot—showed up unexpectedly at the ranch. Brady Cutwright's wife-to-be, Ellie, was here a lot. And Brady's friend Meg Stoddard, who owned the adjacent ranch, visited all the time. But this woman . . . he was sure she'd never crossed his path before.

Maybe she was lost. If that was the case, it was up to him to investigate and help her out; she might need some direction. In fact, his being ranch boss meant it was Tanner's duty to be on top of what happened around here.

He pulled off his work gloves and shoved them into the belt on his jeans. "I'm gonna go check it out. See if she needs any help. You keep digging. I'll be right back."

"Hey, why do I have to stay and keep working and you get to go?"

Tanner glanced back and saw the kid's deep frown. " 'Cause I'm your boss, that's why."

Before Tanner took even a step toward the house, Randy scowled deep. The kid's reaction made Tanner grin, but it sure as hell didn't make him change his mind.

Someone had to get those holes dug. Lucky for Tanner, he had somebody to delegate to. Besides, from what he could see at this distance, the lady in question wasn't Randy's type. The kid liked them young and dumb, in painted-on jeans and showing enough cleavage to be illegal.

The twenty-two-year-old cowboy wouldn't know what to do with a real woman, and as far as Tanner could determine, that was what the mysterious lady was. A real woman who'd need a real man, and he was just the guy for the job.

The closer he got as he headed toward the house, the more details he could make out. Their mysterious visitor's tight skirt looked like it belonged on a naughty librarian or a sexy secretary . . . and maybe Tanner had watched too many dirty movies during his misspent youth.

Sometimes his current lack of a steady lady in his life made itself very apparent. Today's little fantasy about the Cutwright family's unexpected feminine company was proof of that.

Tanner sidelined his fantasies and got his head back to the business of being the ranch manager greeting a guest . . . before his hard-on greeted her for him.

Given she was still bent over, he would have to address her posterior, which was no problem for him. "Excuse me, ma'am. Can I help you?"

She bolted upright and turned, arms loaded. It

had been a long while since Tanner had been in school, but what she held looked like a couple of years' worth of schoolwork barely contained in a few large white binders. His fantasy immediately shifted from *naughty librarian* to *hot for teacher*.

"Hi." She frowned. "Um, any chance you're Brady?"

Tanner let out a snort. He respected his boss, the whole Cutwright family, but no way any one of them would be covered in sweat and dirt from digging holes the way he was now. "No, ma'am. I'm Tanner Black. Ranch manager. Brady's my boss."

"Oh good. At least I'm in the right place." She smiled until it reached her sky-blue eyes.

Up close he could appreciate the porcelain quality of her complexion. This woman would fry up in no time out in the sun, which would be a perfect reason to keep her inside—in his bedroom.

She still hadn't offered up who she was or why she was here, but upon further inspection the van provided his answer. The lettering on the side panel supplied him with a company name. He considered the other tidbit of information that the van's lettering supplied—the company's location.

Austin.

She was a city girl.

Pity. City folk made Tanner twitch.

"You the wedding planner?" he asked.

"I am. Erin Saddler, owner of Happy Is the Bride Event Planning. I'd shake your hand, but . . ." Her gaze dropped to the binders about to slip from her overloaded arms.

"That's a'ight." As dirty as he was, it was probably best she couldn't shake his hand. In fact, he thought twice before offering to take the notebooks from her for fear he'd ruin those pristine white binders. "Can I help you with some of those?"

"Thanks. There are actually a few more." She took a step back from the open door and he saw them on the floorboard.

"No problem. I'll get 'em." Tanner was reaching into the van for the books when he heard the screen door of the house slam.

"Erin?" The voice of Brady's fiancée came from the porch.

"That's me. And you must be Ellie, my bride-to-be." At Erin's reply, Tanner went from wondering what the hell she had in these binders that weighed so damn much to thinking no woman's voice had ever cut through him quite like Erin's did.

And she wasn't even talking sexy. They were talking about his boss's wedding, for cripes' sake. Nothing that should have every cell in him aware of her.

161

Tanner straightened up in time to see the bride-to-be trotting down the stairs, beaming with the biggest grin on her face. That was pretty much how Brady had looked lately, too.

Young love—they'd better enjoy it before they got cynical like him.

"I'm so glad you could meet with us so fast." Ellie reached out to take one of the books in Erin's hands.

"Not a problem. The sooner the better. It's going to be tight." Of course, Erin was talking about the timing of the wedding, but Tanner's mind went to bad places as he started to ponder everything that was tight on Erin's tempting little body.

Down, boy.

Tanner wrangled his libido into check and reminded himself that city girls and country boys didn't mix well. Been there, done that, and he had the scars on his heart to prove it.

"We realize the date we chose is coming up fast, but neither of us wanted to wait." As the bride turned toward the house, Brady appeared in the doorway. "Oh good. Here's Brady now."

Erin flashed first Brady and then Ellie a brilliant smile that showed off her perfect white teeth. "And now I can see why you don't want to wait."

Ellie giggled. "I know. Isn't he the cutest?"

Tanner rolled his eyes as he followed behind

the two women. He felt nothing but respect for the Cutwrights, but this shindig, which seemed to grow daily until it had taken on a life of its own, was bullshit in his opinion. Waste of time and money, if you asked him.

Then again, unlike Tanner, the Cutwrights had the money to waste. That was probably one reason for the wedding planner's warmth as she greeted Brady: dollar signs.

Thinking of Miss Erin Saddler, wedding planner extraordinaire, as just another money-hungry big-city business owner helped. Tanner needed something to balance out his other, baser feelings for the woman as she climbed the steps ahead of him and he got another eyeful of her shapely behind in that skirt.

Yeah, he needed to get out of there before he embarrassed himself.

Ellie led Erin into the house and Tanner could finally think again, now that her tinkling laugh and twinkling eyes were safely out of range.

"Here you go, boss. Have fun." Grinning, Tanner shoved the books toward Brady while thinking that whatever those binders contained was going to be anything but fun.

Brady was no dummy. He narrowed his eyes. "Oh no. You don't get out of here that easily."

Tanner frowned. "What's your wedding got to do with me?"

"Ellie and I have another appointment we have

to get to this afternoon, so I need you to take the wedding planner over to Meg's and show her where the reception's gonna be. And drive her out to the chapel so she can see where we're having the ceremony."

Oh no. No, no, no. Him alone in his truck with her was not gonna happen.

He'd been too long without his hands on a woman to be alone with Miss Sex on Heels inside the confines of the cab of his truck.

Tanner was into many things, but self-torture wasn't one of them. He had a bad feeling Miss Saddler was already going to invade his sleep tonight, just from this one brief encounter by the minivan.

He didn't need to fuel that fire with any more time spent with her—alone and in his own damn pickup truck to boot.

"Why don't you just give her the directions? Meg can show her around there."

"Meg is meeting us in the city for our appointment. It's wedding stuff and Ellie wants her there."

Tanner lifted one shoulder to concede Brady's point as he crafted another suggestion to get himself out of escorting Miss Tight Skirt. "The dude ranch has staff. They can take her around."

"Meg's crew has their own work to do. This time of year you know she's booked full up. It's nice enough of her to clear her reservations for the week of our wedding on top of letting us have the ceremony and the rehearsal dinner and the reception there. I'm not gonna take her crew away from their work."

"Fine. I'll do it." Tanner scowled, unhappy with the turn of events. To make sure his displeasure was fully known, he added, "It's not like I got a fence to put up or anything."

Brady shook his head. "I knew you were a confirmed bachelor, but I had no idea your aversion to marriage included other people's weddings, too."

"Maybe it's my aversion to city folk and not weddings. You ever think of that?" Tanner cocked a brow high.

The problem was, this particular city girl made him want to break his own rule. Made him want to run his hands through her hair to see if it felt as soft as it looked. Made him want to lean in and get a better whiff of whatever damn scent she wore, which still clung in the air long after she was gone.

"Well, you can get in that fancy air-conditioned truck of yours and chauffeur that city girl in there around for an hour or so while Randy works on the fence and finishes the afternoon chores in this heat. Or I could see if Randy wants to take her over to Meg's while you finish up work here for the day. You decide." Brady folded his arms and waited.

Given those options, there was no choice in Tanner's mind. "What time you figure she'll be ready for me to take her over to Meg's?"

Brady grinned. "Thought you'd say that. And I'd say in about an hour."

"A'ight." With a nod, Tanner spun on one boot heel and headed back out to the new paddock to break the news to Randy and then get himself and his truck cleaned up before either could mess up pretty Miss Erin and her skirt.

Chapter Three

A wedding on three weeks' notice.

The bride and groom must be crazy to plan such a thing.

No, she must be crazy to agree to put it together for them . . . and on a dude ranch no less!

But now that Erin realized who the groom's family was, it was a good thing she had said yes. The Cutwrights were an important family in this part of the country, with the money to match the status. Having their wedding on her résumé would boost her reputation and her business in a way that no amount of posting on social media could—no matter what Jessica said.

But in exchange for that coup, she was certainly being put through the wringer.

Erin drew in a breath as she bounced along in the passenger seat next to a cowboy who spent more time fiddling with the radio than he did keeping his eyes on the road. Though, actually, they'd left the road a few miles ago. Now they seemed to be driving in a field of some kind. Nothing roadlike about it.

He hit another pothole or gopher hole or whatever kind of hole was found out in the middle of nowhere and Erin's teeth clashed together.

She'd be lucky if she didn't end up biting her own tongue off during this ride from hell.

"Where exactly are we going?" she asked.

"Chapel."

Another one-word answer. Those were all she seemed to have gotten from him since they'd climbed into the truck. Oh, he was a perfect gentleman but not exactly a conversationalist.

She gripped the safety bar above her head a little tighter and shot him a sideways glance.

This man was all Texan and all cowboy, from the dirty boots and jeans right down to the can of chewing tobacco she'd noticed tucked away beneath the dashboard in the center console. Which was what made it even stranger that she couldn't stop looking at him.

Maybe it was the sun-kissed light brown hair. Or the green-blue eyes. Or just the fact that he was so completely the opposite of almost every guy she came across in Austin.

Austin was in Texas, but it seemed more like an artistic island set adrift in a sea of ranches.

The population of the city was probably made up of as many transplants as locals.

The cultural scene was unique unto itself. Austin was a Mecca for music lovers and musicians alike. It was the kind of city where you could not only find a vegan bakery but the business did so well they were thinking of expanding into a second location. And in Austin you were as likely to see a fuel-efficient hybrid as a good ol' boy diesel truck.

She suspected here, not too far outside of the city, Tanner Black's life was the complete opposite.

The top one hundred country songs played on the preset radio stations in his oversized, fuel-guzzling pickup truck. She'd bet he ate meat and potatoes for every meal. Accompanied by a good old American Budweiser. No micro brewed local beer for this man.

After having met him just an hour ago, Erin had a strong sense of who he was already. What she couldn't figure out was why she felt a tiny bit of disappointment every time he gave her one of his one-word answers.

"So Brady's friend owns the church as well as the dude ranch?" she asked in an attempt to spur conversation.

"Chapel. And, yup, she does."

At least that was more than one word, but the response hadn't given Erin any more satisfaction than his previous ones had.

He hit another bump that jostled her nearly out of her seat. She gripped the seat belt cutting into her chest with one hand and clung harder to the ceiling handle with the other.

"Have we considered how the guests are going to drive out here? It's kind of rough going." The way Tanner's truck was bouncing on this rough terrain, she didn't think a normal car would be able to navigate it.

"Don't know. That's not my responsibility."

This was a real issue, and that the bride and groom hadn't thought of it was a big problem for her. Make that another problem in an already challenging event.

With a huff of frustration, she asked, "What *is* your responsibility?"

For the first time during the drive, he turned to look directly at her. A crooked smile lifted one corner of his mouth. "Right now, babysitting you."

The cocky grin confused her. He slammed on the brakes and threw the truck into park before she could decide whether he was angry about his babysitting duty or not.

Erin frowned. "Why are we stopping?"

They appeared to be in the middle of nowhere.

"We're here." He tipped a chin in the direction of something past the passenger side of the truck. When she could wrestle her eyes off the dark shadow of the stubble covering his chin and stop wondering if it would feel as tantalizing against her skin as it looked, she twisted in the seat to follow his gaze.

There, in the middle of the field, was a building. Smaller than she'd envisioned, it was obviously the chapel.

He was right. It was definitely not a church

in the conventional sense. Nothing like the big, modern structures you'd find in a city. Nor like the imposing old churches modeled after Gothic cathedrals.

This was so quaint and so picturesque she wouldn't be at all surprised to find a row of artists lined up with easels and canvases attempting to capture its charm.

"It's beautiful."

"Yeah, it is."

Surprised, she swung her eyes to look at Tanner. That he had an opinion *and* had agreed with her was more than she'd expected.

"Does anyone use it?" she asked.

"You worried it's full of mice and spider-webs?"

She hadn't considered that before, but now . . . "A little. But I'm curious, too. It's so charming, but it really is off the beaten path."

"Meg uses it for the guests at the ranch. But nah, there's not a weekly Sunday service, if that's what you're asking."

"Can we go inside?"

"Sure. That's why we're here." He turned off the ignition and reached for the driver's side door handle.

Erin was just pulling her cell phone out of her bag so she could snap a few pictures when the passenger door opened, startling her. She spun to find Tanner standing with one hand out.

Damn him. Just when she'd made up her mind that he was a jerk, he was acting the perfect gentleman by opening her door and offering a hand to help her out of the high truck.

She turned in her seat and his gaze dropped to her shoes. "Those heels aren't gonna be your friend in this dirt."

"I'm afraid you're right." She cringed and glanced at how far down the ground looked from here. Climbing up had been challenging enough, but climbing—or maybe jumping down—was scary. Especially in four-inch spikes. She laughed. "Any suggestions for my dismount?"

He smiled. "Don't worry. I gotcha."

Before she knew what he had in mind, big, strong hands encompassed her waist and she was flying through the air only to land softly on the ground. He continued to hold her as she grabbed for his biceps when she felt her heels sink into the grass and soft dirt.

"You okay?" he asked.

Still gripping muscles that felt much harder beneath her hands than they'd looked peeking from beneath the short sleeves of his T-shirt, she managed to nod. "I think so. You're right. These are impractical shoes. Lesson learned."

"They're nice though."

A compliment from the man of few words threw her. "Thanks."

She realized she probably should let go of him now. Or at least soon.

The fact that his hands remained on her waist didn't help her nervous reaction to this man.

What was it about him? She'd met with powerful CEOs of Fortune 500 corporations, as well as demanding fathers of brides who wanted to dictate where every penny of their money was going. She'd never felt quite like this. Not like the way she was feeling in front of one working cowboy who'd already told her the only thing he was responsible for regarding this wedding was babysitting her.

But oh how good his hands felt on her.

Work. That would help her get her head back on straight and hopefully make her stop thinking about how good those big, strong hands would feel on the rest of her body.

While she was naked.

In bed.

With him.

Erin cleared her throat. "Impractical shoes or not, I guess I should try to make it to the building. If I can't do it, the guests certainly won't be able to."

"A'ight." He released his hold on her, forcing her to do the same. Dropping her hands from his massive arms, she reached back into the truck and grabbed her cell while he continued, "It's actually not as bad as it seems."

"It's not?" she asked, not quite believing him.

Her skepticism had him chuckling. "The grass is high now, but the crew will come out and brush hog it the day before the wedding."

What the hell was brush hogging? Whatever it was, he seemed to think it would help, and judging by the context of his comment it would make this nearly knee-high grass less of an obstacle.

"Ah. Good. Perfect. The brush hogging, I mean."

"You know what brush hogging is?" He cocked up one brow.

"Not really," she admitted.

He grinned and offered her his arm. "Come on. There's a path over here laid out with field-stones. I should be able to find it for you. It'll be easy to see once they knock down the grass for the ceremony."

"A path sounds good." A bit wobbly, she held on to his arm and tried not to fall down and embarrass herself.

Keeping a slow pace, he didn't rush her. Once they found the path, it was easier going but still challenging. "I hope the bride wears practical shoes."

"Cowboy boots." He let out a snort. "The fact I actually know what kind of shoes Ellie is gonna wear tells me this wedding has pretty much taken over everything at the Cutwright place."

"No doubt."

She cut him a sideways glance as she gripped his arm. She probably could have let go of him once they'd reached the path but better safe than sorry.

Yeah right.

Silently, she admitted she just liked holding on to him. And he was willing, so she certainly was.

"The good news for you is that it'll all be over soon."

"Which I'm guessing is bad news for you because you gotta plan it," he said.

"You're right. Not that I'd ever complain."

"No, I'm sure you wouldn't."

She was deciding whether that comment had been an insult or a compliment when he disengaged himself from her grasp.

"Here we are. Let me get the door." Tanner wrestled for a moment with the solid aged wooden door of the chapel until it finally gave way to his efforts.

A burst of cool air hit her in the face as she took a step inside, looking around her. It was beautiful, and Erin couldn't help but lose herself in admiration. "Wow."

"Old buildings like this were built well. Thick walls. Stone foundation. High ceilings. It all works to keep the heat out."

"It's perfect." She turned to see him smiling at her and asked, "What?"

"Just nice to see a city girl can appreciate something in the country."

Looking at Tanner, Erin knew she could appreciate more than just the chapel during her excursion away from the city.

Chapter Four

The lovely wedding planner walked through the chapel, oohing and aahing over every little thing from the architectural details to the seating capacity while jotting down notes on her cell phone. Of course, that was only when she wasn't taking pictures from every angle.

Tanner made his own to-do list.

First on the list was to remember not to touch her again. It was far too tempting. And he definitely had to stop looking at her butt.

In no specific order he added the rest of his list.

Stop laughing at her jokes. Stop being so affected by her smile. In short, stop enjoying being in her company altogether.

She was a city girl and he wasn't interested in a relationship with one of those again.

She was also his boss's wedding planner. An employee of Cutwright Ranch, if he wanted to stretch the facts a bit. That made a one-night stand with this woman out of the question. He would no more offend his boss than he would want to do that to this woman, who seemed nice, if a bit sheltered and clumsy.

But again, she was a city girl. They tended not to navigate the country too well. And there was no reason why they should have to. He was certain her impractical shoes worked just fine in what he imagined was her cushy, air-conditioned Austin office, where she conducted meetings with beautiful people in similarly beautiful outfits on a regular basis.

No need for her to be able to get in and out of a King Cab pickup in Austin. The backseat of a taxicab would be easy enough for her to navigate.

Even with the growing list of cons in his head, he jumped to listen when she turned to him and opened that rose-colored mouth of hers.

"I think I have everything I need."

Good. It was too quiet with just the two of them here. "All right. I'll bring you over to the barn."

"The barn? I thought we were going to see the hall being used for the reception and the rehearsal dinner."

Against his own self-imposed rule, he couldn't help his smile. "Well, I hate to break it to you, but—"

"The reception is going to be in the barn." She looked accepting, if a little worried about that.

"You got it." His smile broadened.

Okay, maybe it was all right that she amused him. Making fun of the silly things the folks from the city said was a long-standing tradition in private among the ranchers, particularly at

Meg's dude ranch, where the crew encountered more than their fair share.

But Tanner wasn't enjoying making fun of Erin. He was just plain enjoying her.

He sighed.

Good thing this wedding was going to come and go fast, like a summer storm. And like those storms that rolled through, wreaked havoc, and then disappeared as quickly as they'd come, she was probably going to leave him with nothing but a mess and memories.

He needed a distraction. Getting to the barn would help. At least there would be other people around the dude ranch. Maybe he'd bring her to the front office first. Introduce her to Harrie there.

It was not only a good idea, it would probably help Erin out, too. She'd need to know who was really in charge of that place for her planning. Meg might own and operate the dude ranch, but Tanner knew the business would fall apart without Harrie in that front office keeping things running smoothly.

But before he could get there, he had to get Erin back to where he'd parked and get her inside the truck. Maybe he should just drive it over to the chapel. He hadn't parked all that far away, but still those fifteen feet seemed more like a quarter mile to him while Erin was gripping tight on to his arm.

His hard-on sure liked it. His mind, totally torn between wanting her to never let go and wishing she'd disappear completely from his sight, not so much.

"You need me to pull the truck closer for you?" he asked, specifically not offering her his arm again.

She shook her head. "No, I think I can make it back."

His efforts to avoid contact were for naught as she grabbed on to him anyway.

Oh well.

He was a strong man. He'd survived way worse than having a pretty girl holding on to him. He'd live through this . . .

They'd barely taken one step toward the truck when she froze, nearly yanking his arm out of the socket as he continued forward and she stopped dead in her tracks.

Frowning, he turned to see what was wrong, figuring it was shoe-related. Probably her heel stuck in the dirt, or maybe she'd lost the damn thing entirely, like Cinderella at the ball, even though Tanner was certainly no Prince Charming.

What he saw was Erin, wide-eyed and pale, staring at something on the ground.

"What's wrong?" Even as he asked the question, he saw what she had. A snake in the grass. That explained her reaction. "Don't worry about him. It's just a rat snake."

"Rat snake?" She didn't look relieved as she repeated his words.

"Yeah, they're pretty common around here. They're harmless. Don't worry. They're actually good to have. They keep the rodent population down."

She opened her mouth and just shook her head, paralyzed in place and not looking like she was going to move anytime soon.

He began to fear she'd hyperventilate, and it was becoming apparent she wasn't about to walk past the snake in their path. He was starting to think she wouldn't be any happier about walking through the grass either.

His .22 was in the truck. He could kill the snake, but he'd rather not because they really were harmless and beneficial.

With a sigh of resignation, he did the last thing he wanted to do. He scooped her up in his arms and carried her toward the truck.

He didn't let himself notice how damn good she smelled. Or how her hair felt when the breeze blew it against his face. Or how cute the squeak she made was when he'd picked her up.

Tanner definitely didn't notice how blue her eyes were this close. Or how warm her body was against his. And he really, really didn't imagine tossing her onto a big bed and having his way with her. Nope. Didn't do it.

He'd go back to the ranch and tell Brady his job was done. He'd shown her around, and if there were any more tour guide duties, Randy would have to take over.

The thought of that rubbed Tanner so wrong it made his skin itch and he knew there was no way in hell he'd turn more time with Erin over to Randy or anyone else.

He might not want this city girl for himself, but he'd be damned if anyone else got the pleasure either.

Finally, he reached the truck. He went to set her down so he could open the door and help her inside and she clung tighter, staring at the ground below with fear in her eyes.

He made a show of kicking the grass with his boots. "It's clear. Promise."

She finally nodded and released her hold on him when he set her feet on the ground. Sad but true, he missed the contact the minute it was gone.

"Thank you for saving me."

He hadn't saved her from anything because there had never been any danger, but he was too busy worrying about saving himself from her at the moment that he said, "No problem."

Not want her? Yeah right. Even Tanner didn't believe his own bullshit.

Crap. It was going to be a long three weeks until the wedding.

Chapter Five

Standing against the wall, arms folded, amused look firmly in place, Tanner Black had to be the most infuriating man on earth.

So why did she keep trying to imagine what he'd look like without his shirt on, drenched in sweat?

Erin shoved that image out of her mind and turned to him. "You can stop now."

"Stop what?" He cocked one brow.

"Waiting for me to complain about the barn." She might have reacted like a typical city dweller when she nearly passed out at the prospect of having to turn the barn of a working dude ranch into the wedding venue for one of the richest families in Travis County on three weeks' notice, but she'd gotten over that as soon as she saw it.

Someone had already taken what had once been a utilitarian building, probably filled with all the ranch horrors she'd feared, and converted the large open and airy structure into a building perfect for large functions. It was clean and updated in the places it needed to be, while retaining the old charm and hallmarks of the past and its history.

Boy, had she lucked out because the clock was ticking and finding another available venue at this late date would have been difficult. Not impossible—she'd have found something some-where—but nothing this charming.

Meanwhile, her current challenge was still leveling an amused gaze in her direction. "Oh, I wasn't expecting you to complain. I knew once you saw the place you'd be fine. That's what makes this so enjoyable for me."

"I don't understand."

"Seeing you make a snap judgment based on nothing more than a single word and then getting to watch your assumption be completely turned upside down by the reality is very satisfying."

Erin's retort was cut short by the vibrating of her phone. She glanced down at the readout and saw a name that had her groaning.

"Disgruntled client?" he asked.

Erin frowned. "No. All my clients are very happy, thank you."

"Ah, then a boyfriend you're on the outs with." Tanner nodded knowingly.

"Nope. Don't have any of those either."

As the phone stopped vibrating and the missed call message appeared on her screen, he pushed himself off the far wall and ambled toward her. "You don't have which part? A boyfriend or one you're on the outs with?"

"Either. I work too hard to have any time for dating right now." Which was exactly why she was dodging her sister's calls.

Erin knew what Ashley wanted. An answer she didn't have.

Tanner had reached the spot where she stood. Even the slowest swagger covered ground when a man's legs were that long. Not to mention muscular.

"So why the long face and ignoring the phone call?"

"Why are you so interested?" she asked, genuinely curious. This man had done nothing but act like she was an amusing annoyance all afternoon and now he was interested in her personal life?

Her question elicited a laugh from the cowboy. "Hell if I know. I've asked myself that same question more than a few times today."

Not much of an excuse, but instinct told her it was the truth so she decided to answer him. "It's my sister. She's getting married this weekend. And months ago I told her I was bringing a date."

"And?"

"Now she wants his name for the calligrapher to put on the place cards."

"And you don't have a date." He guessed her problem in one try, which only pissed her off.

Hating to admit it, she had no recourse but to 'fess up to the truth. "No, I don't. Okay?"

He lifted one shoulder. "So just tell her that. What's the big deal? Not everything works out. Plans fall through."

"Not for her." Everything worked out perfectly for Ashley.

Ten years Erin's junior, Ashley had done everything she'd set out to do. She'd laid out her life plan while still in high school and damned if she hadn't accomplished each and everything on her list.

College. Grad school. Husband. Good job in corporate America. All before she turned thirty.

Tanner rolled his eyes. "Women."

"What does that mean?"

"You make simple things hard."

"How's that?" She planted her hands on her hips and waited for an explanation.

"From what I see, you could just tell her you don't have a date and be done with it, but since you don't want to do that, why not just invite someone to go with you? See? Men are good at solving problems. We're more logical. Less emotional." His grin told her he was baiting her with that last comment.

Determined not to rise to his verbal sparring, she still couldn't help saying, "Easy? How in the world is your solution easy?"

"Don't you have any friends?"

"Yes, of course I have friends."

"Then just ask one of them." He made it sound so simple, she almost believed he could be right.

Erin racked her brain for someone.

The truth was, she spent most of her waking hours with her assistant.

The more Erin thought, the more she realized she'd let many of her friendships slip over the years. Even the group of girlfriends she'd go on getaway weekends with, she rarely saw anymore. Erin worked weekends now, and even if she did make time to go away midweek, they had families and normal Monday-through-Friday jobs.

Yes, she'd still make time for a call or maybe lunch on their birthdays, but otherwise she'd really drifted away.

None of that mattered right now anyway because all those friends were women. For her current situation she needed a man.

The few men she saw on a regular basis were also work-related acquaintances. Florists. Musicians. Catering hall staff and management.

Besides the fact that she shouldn't muddy the waters between business and personal life, she couldn't waltz into her sister's wedding with her gay floral designer or the married drummer from the band.

Erin sighed. Where did a girl find a real man? One big and strong and handsome, who'd look impressive walking into the reception on her arm?

She dared to look at Tanner, who stood by silently waiting for her with an amused smirk.

"You wouldn't happen to be single and available this Sunday afternoon, would you?"

"Actually, I am. Both."

She'd been joking, but seriously, could this work? She shook her head, dismissing the idea. "You wouldn't want to go with me."

He lifted a shoulder. "Sure. Why not?"

Now that he'd said what amounted to yes, Erin questioned the wisdom of asking him. "But you said you don't even like the city or city people. The wedding's in Austin."

"Just because I don't choose to live there or date someone from there doesn't mean I refuse to ever step foot there. Hell, I go to Rodeo Austin every year, but that's set out a ways from the city limits. Now, if you'd invited me into the middle of the city during that damn music festival they have when the place is packed full of tourists and weirdos, I'd have to say no. Hell no, over my dead body, to be exact."

Still considering whether this was the craziest thing she'd ever done, Erin looked him up and down. "Do you have anything to wear?"

"You mean this won't do?" He leveled a look of disappointment at her. "Damn, you're a snob. Just because I work all day in torn jeans and old boots doesn't mean I don't own other clothes."

Overlooking the snob comment, she asked,

188

"So that's a yes? You have a suit? Or at least clean jeans and a sports jacket?"

It wasn't a black tie event, thank goodness. Given it was a Sunday afternoon, he could get away with more casual attire, just not as casual as he was now, or the way she suspected he preferred to be dressed.

"I've got something that won't embarrass you, don't you worry." He laughed and shook his head.

"What's so funny?"

"Me, that's what. Here I am trying to convince you to take me when you asked me in the first place. You do realize I'd be the one doing you a favor by going, right?"

Gruff as he was, he was also correct. He would be doing her a favor by going as her last-minute date, but given what little she knew of the man, she had a feeling she'd be better off dealing with her sister's gloating and going alone.

That would be preferable to taking someone who could embarrass her.

Tanner was as handsome as he was cocky. He'd probably clean up nicely in the right clothes, but when it came right down to it, he was first and foremost a cowboy. He worked in the dirt and crap all day—literally.

How had she ever thought she could clean him up and pass him off as her actual date in front of all the white-collar city dwellers her sister would have at this wedding?

Erin shook her head. "Maybe this is a bad idea. You don't have to—"

"Oh my God! You really don't trust me not to embarrass you." He opened his eyes wide at the realization before scowling. "Typical. Looks like I was one hundred percent right about you city folk."

"Stop. No." In spite of her protest, Erin had to admit, at least to herself, that he was right. She was being a snob. Ashamed by her own prejudices, she said, "I'm sorry. You're right. I was being ignorant and closed-minded."

When she finally brought herself to raise her gaze to his face, she didn't see what she'd expected. He wasn't angry. He appeared almost intrigued. "Thank you for admitting that. I appreciate your honesty."

Something in her shifted. Maybe it was his easy acceptance and forgiveness of her faults. She didn't know. Whatever it was, she didn't want to be the person he had assumed she was. She wanted to be better.

Never one to throw caution to the wind in the past, she decided to do just that now, with him. "Prove me wrong."

Tanner cocked a brow high. "Excuse me?"

"Be my date to the wedding on Sunday and prove me wrong. I want you to."

"Why?" he laughed.

"Hell if I know." She turned his own words back on him.

In reality, she did know why. Her comfort zone had become a prison of her own making. It was time to blow the walls off this box she'd gotten so used to living in.

A date with Tanner Black was about as far outside that box as she could get.

Chapter Six

A wedding date. What the hell did Tanner know about being anyone's date at a family member's wedding?

Not much, that's what. Yet he'd volunteered anyway. Not just volunteered but talked her into taking him when she'd hesitated.

He obviously had heat stroke.

Pausing in his work long enough to wipe the sweat from his forehead, Tanner glanced up. He spotted his boss heading from his truck toward the house.

Besides having to be Erin's date, Tanner also had to clear cutting out of work early with his boss.

"Hey, Brady! Got a second?"

Brady paused at the sound of Tanner's voice and turned. "Sure."

The younger man wandered toward where Tanner and Randy were working. Not wanting this to be a public discussion, Tanner strode to meet him halfway. The last thing he needed was to have Randy overhear he had a date on Sunday.

"How's that fence coming along?" Brady scanned the line of posts that was going to form a new paddock for the horses.

"Good. We'll finish this section of posts today."

Brady nodded. "Sounds good. So what's up?"

"I need to get out of here a couple hours earlier than usual on Sunday. I figure if we start afternoon chores early, we can get them done before I have to leave, so Randy doesn't have to handle it on his own. If it's okay with you, that is."

Tanner never took time off. Not sick days. Not personal days.

He didn't think Brady would have an issue with the request. Even so, he wanted to be respectful and ask. The Cutwrights had always been generous bosses. They treated him good. It was only right to show them the same courtesy.

"Sure. No problem." Brady's mouth formed a grin. "Got a hot date?"

"Actually . . ." This part wasn't as easy as asking for the time off. "That's something else I guess I should probably run by you."

"Now I'm really intrigued." Widening his stance, Brady folded his arms and looked like he was settling in for a good story.

Just what Tanner didn't want—this becoming a big deal.

It wasn't. Not at all . . . and maybe if he kept telling himself that, he'd start to believe it.

"So, um, you know your wedding planner?"

"Erin?" Brady's eyes flew wide. "Holy shit. You don't have a date with Erin, do you?"

"It's not a date. She just needed someone to

take to her sister's wedding, but if it's a problem for you, I'll tell her I can't go." And why did that offer leave a feeling of disappointment in Tanner's gut? It wasn't a date and he wasn't really sure he wanted to go in the first place.

"No, it's not a problem. I think it's great you're getting out there. Good for you, man." Brady slapped him on the back while a stupid grin beamed on his face.

This was what Tanner got for getting drunk one night after the big implosion of his relationship with Jill and confiding in Brady. "I'm not getting back out there. It's just a favor."

"A favor for a smart, successful woman who also happens to be gorgeous. A favor that involves spending a whole evening together, dining and dancing and who knows what." Brady's sug-gestion hung temptingly in the air.

Damned if Tanner hadn't thought the same thing himself. He couldn't even laugh off Brady's insinuation.

He drew in a deep breath.

Maybe there was one last hope that would save him from himself and this ill-conceived plan. "Is Ellie going to have an issue with it, you think? If she does, I'm fine with backing out. Don't want to mix business with pleasure and mess up your wedding."

Brady let out a chuckle. "Don't worry. Ellie doesn't have a problem with it either."

"How do you know? You should ask her."

"I don't have to ask her. She already commented on how she hoped you and Erin hit it off during the wedding because you would make a cute couple."

Tanner felt the frown settle on his brow. "Cute?"

Tough. Rugged. Stubborn. Yes to all, but the last thing a hardworking Texas ranch boss was, or wanted to be considered, was cute.

Holding up one hand, Brady laughed. "That was Ellie's word, not mine. You are coming to the bridal shower, right? Ellie asked. Erin should be there."

"Bridal shower? Me?" Tanner nearly choked on the words.

"Why not? It's coed."

That other men would be forced to be there, too, didn't make the idea any more appealing. "Uh, no. I'm busy that day."

"Do you even know what day it is?" Brady asked.

"Whatever day it is, I'm busy."

Brady laughed. "Okay. I'll tell Ellie no. But as for leaving early on Sunday, it's not a problem. Go. Have fun."

"Thanks."

Happy this painful conversation was done, Tanner was about to take his leave when Brady added, "Come in late Monday if you need to."

"I won't need to. I'll be here on time. Early, even, to make up the hours." But damn, now his mind had gone to bad places and his body had followed. Tanner's displeasure deepened. Time to cut this conversation short. "I gotta get back to work."

"Sure." Still smiling, Brady nodded.

Just like that, one little date that wasn't even really a date had snowballed into a big deal. Grumpy, Tanner stalked back to where Randy was working and grabbed the tool he'd left leaning on the post.

"What did you have to talk to Brady about?" Randy asked.

Not looking up as he pounded the blades of the post-hole digger into the ground, Tanner said, "None of your business, that's what."

"Hey. No need to be rude about it." Randy actually sounded hurt.

"Not being rude. Just stating a fact." He was having enough issues with his knee-jerk decision to go to this wedding with the sexy wedding planner in the temptingly tight skirt as it was. He definitely didn't need to share his doubts or—God forbid—his feelings with a kid.

Pride. It had to have been his damn stubborn pride that had made him argue to convince her he could pull off stepping in as her wedding date.

Yup. That was the only explanation. *Pride goeth before a fall.*

He might not be a poet or a philosopher or even a churchgoer nowadays, but he'd been dragged to enough Sunday services by his mama to remember that quote from the Good Book. He was certainly paying for being prideful.

Now he'd have to break out his Sunday-best clothes, which he hadn't worn in a very long time, and go to some highfalutin wedding in the city he usually avoided. And be on his best behavior, all to prove to Erin that he could clean up good and not embarrass her in front of her city-folk family.

Yup, definitely heat stroke, because he sure as hell hadn't been thinking clearly when he'd thought this was a good idea.

But even as he sweated and dug and beat himself up over the decision, in the back of his mind he couldn't help wondering what Erin would be like when she wasn't working. Among friends. After a celebratory champagne or two.

Did she dance? Slow or fast? Did she expect him to dance? He could hold his own on the dance floor when necessary, but he was nothing to look at out there, especially if the DJ played some of that new dance stuff.

Now, holding Erin close and swaying to an old country standard would be another thing entirely. Which led back to what he suspected was the real reason he was going to this wedding

Sunday. He wanted to spend more time with her.

Why? He hadn't forgotten about the disaster his one and only relationship with a city girl had been. He should know better than to expect different results with a different city girl, yet he was going anyway.

Tanner decided to give himself a break about being weak.

Erin was a looker, despite how snooty and silly she was when it came to the country. Tanner smiled at the memory of Erin in his arms that day after the snake incident.

He was an adult. He could be strong and resist her obvious charms. He could enjoy a beautiful woman's company for a night and then walk away. It wasn't like she was going to invite him home with her.

That thought caused enough disappointment to worry him. Maybe he wasn't as strong as he thought he was.

Chapter Seven

Erin parked the car and strode toward the office that evening looking and feeling a whole lot different from when she'd left that morning to go to the Cutwright ranch.

Her heels might possibly be ruined from the trek through the country. She was sweaty and her hair had started to frizz. And the biggest change—for better or worse—she had a date to her sister's wedding.

She didn't quite know how to feel about that. Part of her was on high alert, waiting for the disaster that could come. The other part—a part she was trying to ignore, not quite successfully—was aflutter with a combination of excitement and nerves at the prospect of a date with the hot cowboy.

Erin shook her head and tried to clear it of his presence and focus on work as she pushed through the front door and into the air-conditioned air.

Jessica glanced up from the desk. "How did the meeting go?"

"Good, actually. I got a lot accomplished. I'll fill you in as soon as I get something to drink. It's so hot out there, I finished my bottle of water long ago."

"Did you get back to your sister? She left like five messages on the office line." Jessica's voice followed Erin to the back room of the office, where she reached into the fridge for a cold bottle of water.

Though Jessica had a tendency to exaggerate, Erin didn't doubt Ashley had been blowing up the phone lines.

"Yes." Erin cracked open the bottle and took a long sip before wandering back to the front. "I texted her from the car."

She'd texted there'd be two names for the place cards. Hers and Tanner's. Then Erin had summarily ignored the following calls from Ashley, as well as the text demanding to know who Tanner Black was.

This was just the beginning. She was in for an inquisition live and in person, she was sure. At the rehearsal dinner. Before the ceremony. Definitely during the reception while he was there with her.

She hadn't really thought this through. How in the world would she explain Tanner? Just a friend? A stranger who was kind enough to take pity on her and be her date on just days' notice? The only man she knew who wasn't gay or married? All of that made her sound like a lonely loser.

True or not, she didn't want anyone to think that.

She should call Tanner to cancel. But then she'd have to tell her sister her date wasn't coming, and that seemed worse.

Erin sighed.

Jessica must have heard. She pinned Erin with a piercing stare. "I thought you said today went well?"

"Workwise it did. This wedding might not be a disaster. In fact, I think I can make it great. It's my personal life that's the problem."

"Personal life." Jessica's eyes widened. She went so far as to get up and move around to sit on the edge of her desk, closer to where Erin stood. "Do tell."

"It's just I invited this guy to be my date to Ash's wedding and now I'm second guessing myself."

Jessica's brow creased. "Why? A date with a man sounds good to me. Do I know him?"

When Jessica looked a bit too excited, Erin decided she'd better knock any romantic notions out of her assistant's head. "He works on the ranch where I went for the meeting today."

"Ooh, a cowboy." Jessica's whole face lit up.

"How is his being a cowboy a good thing?"

"How is it a bad thing?" Jessica seemed honestly baffled by Erin's doubts.

"You've met my sister and her fiancé. You know the kind of jobs they have and the people they hang out with. That's who's going to be at this wedding when I arrive with a man who, if I'm lucky, will show up in jeans and boots that don't have cow manure on them."

"I think you're being a little narrow-minded."

"That's what he said." Erin scowled at being censured by a twenty-five-year-old.

"I dated a cowboy once. They clean up real nice when they need to."

"Really?" Erin was afraid to hope.

Jessica rolled her eyes toward the ceiling dramatically. "Oh my God, don't look so surprised. Trust me, clothes look mighty good on a man who works with his body all day. It'll be worth it, even if he does arrive in jeans and boots. A man like that will put all those guys with desk jobs to shame."

When Jessica put it like that, Erin was a little tempted to see for herself. But still concerned. "But what—"

"Stop! Erin, do you hear yourself?"

"I guess not. What am I saying that's so wrong?"

"We did a whole unit about this in my psych class. You always come from a place of *no* when a decision involves men and relationships. You need to reset your default and start from a place of *yes*."

"What exactly does all that mean?"

"Trust everything will work out. Trust him. Go to the wedding. Say yes to having a great time."

When Erin didn't immediately agree to blindly trust a man she'd known for mere hours, Jessica let out a huff. "Okay, how about this? If you're that worried, tell him to meet you here early. That way if he shows up in something inappropriate, you have time to dress him."

"Dress him in what?" It wasn't as if Erin had a closet full of men's clothing. What was she supposed to do? Drag him to a mall on a Sunday afternoon and hope to find a jacket that would fit his bulging arm muscles?

Memories of those muscles and how they'd felt beneath her hands, how he'd scooped her up so easily and carried her to the truck, momentarily distracted Erin until Jessica continued, "Call Andre. You've given him enough business. He owes you. With Andre's stock of men's suit rentals and his eye for fashion, he'll fix up your cowboy in no time."

As much as Erin hated to give in and admit it, Jessica's idea wasn't horrible.

This could actually work. That meant, like it or not, she was going to the wedding with a man who made her mouth go dry and her knees weaken. It didn't really matter that it was a fake date. It felt real enough.

Fear made Erin want to say no to the whole thing, which only proved Jessica's amateur analysis of her. What else might she end up saying yes to?

When it came to Tanner Black, Erin was afraid to ponder that question.

Her cell phone rang, just when Erin didn't have the time to deal with calls. With one eye on her computer screen, she grabbed it without looking at the caller ID.

"Hello, this is Erin."

"Hello, this is your sister." The attitude was clear in Ashley's voice as she mocked Erin's greeting. "Nice of you to finally answer a call."

"I'm sorry. I've been busy." And she was sorry she hadn't checked the name on the cell's screen first.

"So have I. I'm getting married Sunday, in case you've forgotten."

"I haven't forgotten. I put it in my calendar so I wouldn't."

Ashley countered Erin's teasing with a *humph.* "Brat."

"Bridezilla." Erin smiled at her clever retort. Once the wedding was over she wouldn't be able to use it anymore, so she had to get it in now.

"Whatever. So who is this mysterious man you're bringing?"

This was why Erin needed to learn not to answer the phone without checking the caller ID. She didn't have an explanation for who Tanner was.

Well, she did, but not one she liked.

Erin sighed and realized she had yet to answer Ashley's question. "If I told you, he wouldn't be a mystery now would he?"

"Fine. I'll just ask him when I see him. Will you be bringing him to the rehearsal dinner, too?"

"No. He's, uh, busy that night." Not that she'd asked.

"You're seriously not going to tell me anything about him?"

"Nope."

"Ugh, you are so annoying."

Erin smiled. She was beginning to like having a mystery man to torture Ashley with. And keeping him a mystery cut down considerably on having to come up with excuses. The fact that it annoyed her sister was a bonus.

As much as she was enjoying that, it was time to get back to work. Reaching for her notebook, Erin said, "If you're done interrogating me now, I have a million things to do."

"You always have a million things to do."

"Tell me about it, so let me go and I'll see you Saturday."

Ashley sighed. "All right. And let me know if Tanner decides he can make it for the rehearsal dinner."

"He won't." Because Erin had no intention of asking him. "Now I really gotta go. Love you. 'Bye."

"Love you, too."

Relieved to finally be free of the questions she didn't want to answer, Erin disconnected the call and sagged against the back of her chair.

Relationships were exhausting. Apparently, even fake ones.

Chapter Eight

Tanner straightened his tie and fought the urge to tear it off.

He hadn't worn a tie in years. Hell, he hadn't worn a jacket that wasn't meant to ward off the rain or cold in just as long. But he had put on both today, in addition to a brand-new button-down shirt and a new pair of dark denim jeans he'd actually gone shopping to buy.

Good thing he already owned a decent pair of boots he never wore for work or this little shindig really would have cost him a fortune. He'd only had to polish his good boots to make them presentable. He'd shined up his buckle, too, while he was at it. His black Stetson, after a thorough brushing, topped it all off.

It was all a lot of effort, but looking in the mirror, he figured it had been worth it. He looked good if he did say so himself.

Damn good. Good enough to impress even the woman who was expecting him to fail, which had made it doubly worth the effort because no matter what she thought, there was no way he was going to screw up today.

Not even close.

When was the last time he'd gone to so much trouble to impress a woman? And a woman he wasn't even planning on sleeping with to boot. He couldn't remember, which probably meant the answer was never.

But he'd done it for Erin Saddler, just to prove she was wrong about him. Tanner had decided not to examine his motives any further than that. He figured he might not like the answer he came up with.

Hell, he'd even washed and vacuumed out his truck. Why, he had no clue. It wasn't like he was actually expecting her to travel with him. Chances were slim to none she'd be willing to climb up into his passenger seat and ride shotgun to her sister's wedding.

More likely she'd take her own car so she wasn't dependent on him any more than she had to be. He shook his head at the thought.

Women. Always having to assert their independence nowadays, instead of letting a man handle things.

She'd texted him an address and asked him if he could meet her there in the early afternoon. In spite of himself, he enjoyed the fact he now had her number in his cell phone, even if it was only to nail down the details. It made up for the fact that he'd had to hustle to get the chores done early . . . all while fighting off Randy's questions.

It had been a challenge. Tanner had managed it, though. Finished his work, showered, dressed, and gotten away from Randy without revealing anything.

And he'd done it all in time to arrive early.

He swung his truck into the parking lot of the Austin address she'd given him and stared at the commercial building. The lettering on the door read *Happy Is the Bride*, and Tanner knew immediately where he was.

This was Erin's office. She'd had him meet her at her place of business instead of her home.

He didn't know how to feel about that.

Actually, yes, he did. It was kind of insulting. Like she didn't want him to have her home address.

Feeling the slight keenly, he climbed out of the truck and slammed the door behind him.

Jaw set, he strode directly to the door. He didn't knock. Why should he? This wasn't a private residence. Instead, he pushed right through.

As he stepped into the office, he was struck by the feminine feel of it. Classical music played from hidden speakers. The scent of rose and something else—lavender maybe—struck him full in the sinuses.

And amid it all was Erin.

When the door set a tiny bell to tinkling, she twisted toward him. At her feet, facing away from him, a blonde sat on the floor and fussed at the full skirt of Erin's strapless and sexy-as-hell gown.

Looking panicked, Erin said, "Tanner. Oh my God, is it that late already?"

The blonde slapped at Erin's leg with one hand while holding on to the hem of the dress with the other. "Erin, stand still."

He'd expected to find her in her usual business mode. All serious and stiff, organized and punctual. Finding her flustered and unprepared was surprising . . . and endearing.

"Um, hey there. Don't worry about the time. I'm a few minutes early."

She glanced down at the girl on the floor, still working on her dress, and then back up at him. "I'm sorry. It's just going to be another minute, I hope. My heel got caught in the hem and tore it."

"No problem." His piss-poor mood and the insult that had caused it forgotten, he was entranced by what she was wearing. "I, uh, didn't realize the wedding was so formal."

"It's not. Don't worry. I'm the maid of honor, so . . ."

"A fancy gown you'll never have reason to wear again is a requirement?" he suggested.

"Exactly." She actually smiled, a genuine smile that transformed her already good looks into a face that was breathtaking.

It had him thinking she should do it more often. Then hoping she wouldn't as he forced himself to tear his gaze away.

"Okay. You're done." The girl dropped the hem of the skirt.

"Oh, thank God." Erin blew out a breath with visible relief. "Ashley would kill me if I were late."

"Just be careful so you don't tear it again." The blonde stood and turned to face him so he finally got a chance to see her and she him. Her eyes widened. "Are you Erin's cowboy?"

Erin shot a glare at the girl as she said out of the side of her mouth, "Jessica."

Tanner couldn't help but smile, both at the fact that Erin had obviously told this Jessica at least something about him but also at being called *Erin's cowboy*. Especially after seeing Erin's reaction to hearing it.

"I guess I am." Hat in hand and still grinning, Tanner took a step forward. "Tanner Black."

"Jessica. Erin's assistant. You look really amazing."

He laughed and glanced down at himself. "Do I?"

"Yes, you do." Jessica shot Erin a glare. "We couldn't have done better if we'd dressed you ourselves. Right, Erin?"

Looking unhappy, Erin nodded.

"Well, thank you. That's quite a compliment . . . considering."

"Considering I'm a city snob?" Erin asked.

"No. I was going to say because you're wedding professionals."

"Oh." At least Erin had the decency to look ashamed at her assumption before she spun to face Jessica. "Speaking of being wedding professionals . . . You still need to get to the church and make sure the flowers for the Mahoney ceremony arrived and got put in the proper places."

Jessica cocked a brow high. "I'm aware. I was on my way out the door when you tripped on your skirt. Remember?"

Erin sighed. "I know. Thank you for fixing it. I'm good now, so you can go."

"I'm going." Jessica grabbed a tote bag from the back of a desk chair as she whirled past it. She reached to pull open the front door, but not without one more amused glance back at both of them. "You two have fun."

Tanner's mouth twitched with a smile. This Jessica would make a good match with Randy. It seemed both of their coworkers were busybodies when it came to other people's personal lives.

When the whirlwind that was Erin's assistant was finally gone, an uncomfortable silence fell between them.

Finally, Erin said, "You really do look nice, Tanner."

"I thought so, too, until I got a look at you." He let his gaze drop down her formal gown.

"I'm sorry. I should have warned you I was in the wedding party." She pursed her lips and paused a second. "You know what? I've got something that would be perfect for you. Hang on. I'll be right back."

"A'ight." He didn't have anywhere else to be. He leaned back against a desk and folded his arms, settling in to wait.

She didn't keep him waiting long. Shortly, Erin and her gown were whirling back toward him. In her hand, she held a scrap of cloth in the same color as her dress.

Erin stopped within touching distance and raised her hands before pausing. "Do you mind if I . . . ?" She gestured toward his chest.

A beautiful woman wanted to touch him. Who was he to object? "Not at all."

She took another step closer and reached toward the single breast pocket in his sports jacket. He frowned and watched as she did some sort of creative folding with the material. A minute later he glanced down and found he had a perfect pocket square that matched her dress.

"I'm impressed." He raised his gaze to hers.

"It's just some of the leftover fabric from when the seamstress hemmed my gown. I always keep the scraps. You never know when you'll need them." She pulled her gaze away from his and glanced down at the pocke square. "Anyway, at least we match. I hope you don't mind the color."

He lifted one shoulder and joked, "Eh, it's okay. I'm man enough to wear pink."

"Actually, officially it's rose quartz, the hot wedding color last spring when we ordered the dresses. But yeah, you are man enough . . . to wear pink, I mean." She blushed in a color not much different from the rose hue of his new pocket square.

Erin blushing was as unexpected as her being flustered. Both warmed him to her and had him rethinking his initial opinion of her as a cold, hard, snooty businesswoman.

This evening might be more interesting than he expected. Tanner smiled at that.

Chapter Nine

"You're seriously not going to tell me who he is?" Ashley still looked shocked, even though she had been obsessing over the same thing since they'd entered the bridal room.

"I told you who he is. His name is Tanner Black and he's my plus one. That's all there is to know." Erin had answered this same question in various forms so many times over the past few days, she didn't even have to think about it anymore.

Ashley scowled—an expression that was not an attractive accessory to a bridal gown. "There's definitely more to it than that."

"No, there really isn't." Erin laughed, partially because of how frustrated her sister had become simply because Erin wouldn't tell her anything else about Tanner, but mostly because there really was no more to tell.

"I don't believe you. I'm searching him online."

Confident, Erin shook her head. "Go ahead."

Her sister wasn't going to find any pictures of them together or any status messages that said *Tanner Black is in a relationship with Erin Saddler,* so what harm would it do to let Ashley search? At least it would keep her quiet for a few minutes.

"Fine. I will." Ashley whipped her cell phone out of the bodice of her dress, where Erin hadn't even noticed it was stashed.

Erin's eyes popped wide. "You're *not* keeping your cell phone in your cleavage during the ceremony."

"Why not?" Ashley frowned.

Besides its being an insult to the preacher and probably breaking some sort of rule of the church, there was a chance the thing could go off during the ceremony. A vibrating cleavage would be bad enough, but the idea of a bride with ringtone music blaring out of her boobs while she was standing at the altar was enough to make Erin's wedding planner head explode.

Sadly, Erin had a feeling neither argument would sway her technologically addicted sister, so instead she said, "Because it ruins the line of the dress and it will definitely show up in the pictures."

Pouting, Ashley let out a humph but didn't argue, and Erin scored one point for herself.

Enjoying Ashley being quiet and busy on her cell phone for a few minutes, even if it was to spy on Tanner, Erin went ahead and checked her reflection in the mirror. Her hair, at Ashley's request, had been left down and natural-looking, which was fine with Erin. She hadn't had the time or the patience to sit at the salon this morning to get a fancy updo.

She fluffed her hair a bit and then reached for her purse to grab her lipstick. She swiped on a final coat of color. They had less than half an hour until the ceremony and she didn't want to get caught short on time and have to walk down the aisle with faded lips.

"Now I know you aren't telling me the truth."

Nervous, Erin spun to her sister. When faced with Ashley's raised brow and pinched mouth, Erin's stress level shot up.

What did Tanner have online? She should have thought to search him herself before telling her sister his name. Cripes! Who knew what could be on there? Her sister knew, that's who, and Erin needed to know as well.

"Ashley, tell me. What did you find?"

"Nothing, that's what! Not one thing. Who doesn't have an online presence these days? Even serial killers and terrorists have social media accounts." As Ashley ranted, Erin let herself breathe again.

Erin couldn't help but laugh at her sister's expression of horror as Ashley tried to wrap her millennial head around the reality that someone might not have a Facebook account.

"Tanner's not a serial killer or a terrorist." As far as Erin knew anyway.

She trusted the Cutwright family to vet their employees appropriately. Brady wouldn't have assigned Tanner the duty of showing her around the ranch if he was some fly-by-night hired hand with an unknown reputation, right?

Wide-eyed, Ashley finally sucked in a breath. "Oh my God. Is he ancient? That would explain it."

Frowning, Ashley—firmly and proudly a member of the internet generation—was obviously still trying to reason out how any human could survive without visually recording his or her daily life on Instagram for all their "friends" to "like."

Not a surprise, given Ashley and Chad's wedding had its own hashtag and Pinterest board. There wasn't even a professional video crew because now there was an "app" for that. All the guests' posted wedding photos were going to be converted into one big video.

It wasn't just Ashley. It was the whole younger generation. That was one reason Erin had hired Jessica. She had a grasp on what was happening on the wedding scene for younger brides. But it seemed every time Erin wrapped her head around one new trend in millennial weddings, another new thing hit.

There might only be a decade separating Erin and Ashley, but the generation gap seemed huge. Sometimes Erin felt like she lived in a completely different world from her sister.

"No, he's not ancient. He's probably just a few years older than I am."

Although, to Ashley's generation, over forty probably was considered ancient. Because she would hit that milestone herself later that year, Erin tried to push that thought aside.

Ashley planted one perfectly manicured hand on her hip. "Then you explain why he isn't online."

Lifting one shoulder in a shrug, Erin said, "Maybe you spelled his name wrong."

"If I spelled it wrong then you spelled it wrong when you texted it to me, and that means the calligrapher spelled it wrong on the table place card." Ashley's eyes were wide with agitation.

"Relax. I texted it to you correctly." Remembering she was dealing with a bride here, Erin put herself into work mode.

It wouldn't be the end of the world if Tanner's place card were misspelled, but stress ran high on the big day. She needed to calm Ashley. It was her duty as both a sister and the maid of honor.

"Ash, he's a cowboy. Like on a real ranch. It's not that big of a shocker he doesn't have a bunch of social media accounts. There's probably no cell signal when he's . . ." Erin realized she didn't really know what Tanner's job entailed, but she'd seen enough cowboys on television and in movies to venture a guess. "When he's out riding the range or brush hogging or whatever he does."

"*You're* dating a cowboy?" Now Ashley widened her eyes for a different reason. Shock.

"We're not dating." Erin had a feeling she'd be saying that a lot today.

Ashley leveled a glare on her. "I don't believe you."

"Why not?" Erin laughed at the ridiculousness of the entire debate. She was actually telling the God's honest truth, but it seemed her own sister didn't believe her.

"Because my sister, the city apartment dweller, just said *brush hogging*. I don't even know what that is and I'm guessing neither did you before this Tanner came into your life. Now you're dropping the term into everyday conversation, so go on and try to deny you haven't been spending time with this cowboy. That there's nothing between you. I dare you."

Erin drew in a deep breath and let it out. There was no winning this fight. "You know what, ask him yourself."

Maybe Ashley would believe Tanner.

"I think I will ask him," Ashley said, as if it were a threat.

"Go ahead." Erin laughed but then began to rethink things.

What did she really know about Tanner? He just might lie to Ashley—to all her friends and relatives—to liven up the evening.

Oh, well. Too late now. Erin had a bride to prepare and they had a ceremony to get through. Time to get the bride's focus where it belonged. Off Erin's date and back on to something important, such as looking perfect. "Are you going to sit still and let me put your headpiece on? Or are you going to walk down the aisle without it?"

Chapter Ten

Tanner was enjoying people watching from the corner he'd staked out when a swirl of pink moving fast toward him caught his eye.

Looking breathless, Erin stumbled to a stop in front of him. "I'm so sorry I've been so busy. Are you doing okay on your own?"

Because this was the first time he'd really had time to speak with her, she wasn't kidding about being busy. Erin had been more than busy, going from being with the bride before the vows to taking pictures after. But the beer was cold and free and plentiful and the food—what he'd gotten so far—wasn't bad either.

"Sure. I'm good. I've never been to a wedding in a library before. It's . . . interesting." He smiled before raising the bottle to his lips.

"It's part of the Public Library System, but officially this is the Austin History Center."

"Ah, well. That explains it all." He grinned.

Erin smiled. "Ashley and Chad met here while they were both in college, doing research. She wanted to have it here badly enough, she was even willing to keep the guest list small so they could accommodate her."

He nodded. It was better than some cold banquet room at a hotel. As Erin had said, it wasn't a typical library. The building was historic and the architecture impressive. It had an open room that must be used for meetings or rented out for events like this, so it wasn't as if they'd be eating between aisles of bookshelves.

Brady and Ellie were getting hitched at a dude ranch, so Tanner had to think a library wasn't much crazier. Unconventional places for weddings must be the new thing, not that he knew about that stuff.

Erin shot him a sideways glance. "If you think the reception is interesting, you should have seen the proposal. In fact, you can see it if you'd like. It's on Facebook."

"No way."

"Yup." Erin let out a laugh when he shook his head, appalled at this generation. She eyed his beer. "You're not having the bride and groom's signature cocktail?"

Tanner laughed at even the suggestion. "Yeah no."

Erin glanced into her own glass, which contained the blue drink in question. "I have to pretend to like it, or at least pretend to drink it for the cocktail hour, but as soon as Ash isn't looking, I'm ditching it. Thank God they put bottles of wine on the tables for dinner. I'm switching the minute we sit."

"Good call." The concoction was a color that looked more like window cleaner than anything a man should put in his body. "I like this flowered head thing though."

Erin reached up and gently touched the ring of wildflowers circling her head like a crown.

"Thanks. Ashley and I made the headpieces ourselves." Erin leaned in close and said softly, "Do-it-yourself is the new trend for weddings."

"Oh, is it? I didn't know." With any luck, Brady wouldn't send him and Randy out picking flowers in the field for Ellie's bridal adornments. That would be too much to ask of any self-respecting cowboy. "It looks good, though. You did a nice job."

Erin blew out a huff. "You should have seen the first three I made and threw away. This is attempt number four . . . and after I brought it to my florist friend and had him fix it. And if you tell my sister that, I'll deny it and throw my blue drink at you."

Tanner let out a laugh. Erin was funny and warm and all the things he'd never expected of her.

"You know what?" She cocked her head and took him in from head to toe. "You're not so bad as a wedding date."

Shocked at the compliment, he had to work to swallow his beer instead of spitting it out. "Thanks. I was thinking the same thing about you."

"Thank you." She raised her glass and clinked it against his bottle before taking a swallow. She wrinkled her nose but then went back and took another sip, and Tanner had to wonder what was in it . . . and how tipsy Erin was going to get, because she already seemed on her way.

"So, do you have any more duties to fulfill? And why aren't there more of you? You know, bridesmaids?"

"Well, it seems one of the new wedding philosophies for the younger generation is not burdening their friends with the time and expense it takes to be in a wedding party. So I'm the only one who got the pleasure, but I think there isn't much more for me to do tonight. Ashley is forgoing most of the traditional stuff. No garter toss. No cake cutting because the wedding cake is actually cupcakes."

He hadn't been to all that many weddings, but of those he'd attended, not a one of them was anything like this. He glanced around the place one more time. There was a line of guests waiting for something.

He'd been to the bar, and knew it was on the other side of the room, so he asked, "What's going on over there?"

Erin turned to follow his gaze. "You mean the selfie photo booth or the charging station?"

Tanner lifted a brow. He truly was out of

touch. "Never mind. That's nothing I need to see."

She laughed. "Are you feeling as old as I am at this wedding?"

"Probably more. You should be used to all this kid stuff from your job."

"You're right. You'd think I would be." She turned back to face Tanner and surprised him when she reached out and straightened his tie. "You know, you can take your jacket off if you want. The groom and best man aren't wearing theirs."

Tanner had noticed that himself. Apparently suspenders were the thing to wear for a wedding party nowadays instead of jackets.

He shrugged. "It's okay. I kind of like my pocket square because it matches your dress. That way people know we're together." A smile lifted the corners of his mouth as he expected some sort of retort from Erin.

Instead, she sighed. "About that . . . My apologies in advance, but expect my sister to interrogate you any moment."

"About what?"

"Why you have no Facebook profile. Apparently that makes you suspect."

Tanner cocked a brow. "Does it? Well, then, she should be really appalled that I only recently got this fancy thing." He held up his cell phone. "Brady made me get it. He even paid for it. I was perfectly happy with the free flip phone I got with my service when I first signed up. I could make and get calls. That's all I needed. All I wanted. Not this *smart* crap."

Erin smiled. "You should say that to my sister. Just like that. But make sure I'm there so I can see her head explode."

"She a tech geek?" he asked.

"That's putting it mildly. Most people attend South by Southwest for the music. She goes to shop the trade show floor for new technology."

Tanner tipped his head in a nod. "Good to know. I probably shouldn't tell her I don't own a computer either, huh?"

Her eyes danced with a playful light of mischief. "Oh please, definitely tell her that."

Erin's evil side had Tanner liking her even more than before.

He was about to comment on it when her eyes widened and she turned toward him. Ducking her head until her forehead was nearly touching his chest she said, "Oh my God."

He reached out and put one hand on her shoulder. "What's wrong?"

"It's my ex." She said it so low he had to strain to hear her over the music.

Her ex. Wasn't that an interesting turn of events? He wanted to know more. "Ex what? Boyfriend? Husband?"

She glared up at him. "No, not husband. Boy-friend. We dated for three years during college until he broke up with me for some girl he'd been cheating on me with for the last year we were together. Though the bastard never admitted that."

"So what's he doing here at your sister's wedding?"

"His parents are friends with my parents. The whole family must have been invited. My sister could have at least told me."

The entire time Erin talked, Tanner was scanning the crowd, trying to figure out which guest it was she'd seen before turning away. His choices narrowed considerably when he saw some skinny dude's gaze land on Erin.

His hunch was confirmed when the guy's focus moved to Tanner, whose hand was still on her shoulder. "Any chance your ex is wearing a blue suit with a red tie?"

She yanked her head up to stare at Tanner. "Yes. Why?"

"Don't look now, but he's heading our way." Luckily, there were quite a few obstacles in his path. Waiters. Guests. Friends who waylaid him to say hello.

Erin glanced around them. If she was looking for an exit, she was out of luck. They were backed up against a wall and the door was behind her ex.

"You interested in talking to him?" Tanner asked.

"No!"

"You want him to leave you alone?" He really didn't have to ask, judging by her strong reaction to his first question, but he did anyway.

"Yes."

"Then follow my lead." He planted his empty bottle, as well as the blue drink he plucked out of her hand, on a nearby tray.

Tanner knew one surefire way to keep another man away from a woman—lay claim to her himself. Publicly. Visibly. It was the best way to leave no doubt about which man Erin was there with, and it would do a hell of a lot better job of conveying the message than his little pink pocket square.

He moved his hand to the nape of her neck while slipping the other around her waist. Pressing his hand against the small of her back to bring her closer, he dipped his head low and captured her mouth with his.

She stiffened with surprise before her lips softened.

It took mere seconds for him to forget the reason for the kiss and get sucked into the feel of it.

It felt good. Too good.

Drawing in a deep breath, he broke away from

her mouth, pulling back just enough so he could see her face. "Was that a'ight?"

"Yeah." Erin's reply was a little breathy.

Tanner tried to ignore the fact that he was breathing a bit heavily himself. He dared to raise his gaze and glance past Erin. The ex was still talking to some people across the room, but judging by the look on his face, he'd seen the kiss.

"Did it work?" she asked.

"Not sure. He's talking to someone right now."

"Then maybe we need to keep up the ruse. You know, to make it believable. Only if you want to, that is. If you don't mind . . ."

Erin's suggestion that they keep pretending to be more involved than they were was enough to get Tanner's complete attention.

Her ex nearly forgotten, all Tanner could think of now was kissing her again . . . and that she wanted him to.

Letting himself get another taste of this woman after he'd enjoyed the first one so much was definitely not good for him. But Tanner never had known what was best for him when it came to women.

Getting involved with her could set him up for failure and pain the likes of which he hadn't felt since things had ended with his own ex.

None of that stopped him as he said, "Nope. I don't mind at all."

The band stopped playing as the leader said into the microphone, "Please welcome for the first time ever, Mr. and Mrs. Chad Jackson."

Erin pulled out of his arms and turned to face the small wooden dance floor. Tanner did the same, finally able to breathe freely again without the feel and the sweet scent of her so close to h   i   m   .

"The bride and groom ask everyone to join them on the dance floor for their first dance."

Drawing in a deep breath that had her breasts rising and his gaze dropping to take in the move, Erin said, "You up for a dance?"

Erin, held close in his arms, swaying to the music. Tanner swallowed as his mouth went dry. "Of course. It's my duty as your date."

She smiled and held out one hand to him. "Lead the way."

Chapter Eleven

The slow music and being in Tanner's arms didn't help her get over that kiss. It had thrown Erin completely off-kilter.

She tried to write off her reaction as surprise. Unfortunately, she had a feeling it was more than that. It had been a really great kiss.

In fact, as far as first kisses went, it had been pretty spectacular. No awkward pauses. No clashing of teeth or bumping of noses.

It figured Tanner knew how to kiss well. He'd probably practiced quite a bit with plenty of women. She wondered how many and why one hadn't finally locked him down into a relationship.

At his age he should be attached, or at least have a failed marriage behind him. Shouldn't he? Maybe he did and just hadn't told her. After considering that, she couldn't stand not knowing more about him.

Curiosity got the better of her. As they swayed to the song Ashley had chosen for the first dance, Erin pulled back and glanced up at him. "Can I ask you something?"

With his big, strong hands firmly wrapped around her waist so she couldn't ignore the feel of them, Tanner nodded. "Sure."

"Why aren't you in a relationship?" She hadn't meant to ask that specifically, but somehow the question had slipped out.

More importantly, she shouldn't care about his relationship status considering this was a one-time thing. He was doing her this one favor by being her wedding date. Nothing more. She needed to remember that.

Apparently the slow dance, the blue drinks, and the hard-bodied cowboy holding her a bit too close had made Erin lose her mind.

"Why aren't you?" Tanner asked without missing a beat.

Erin frowned at how he'd dodged the question, but she wasn't going to be deterred. Now that she'd ventured down this path, she intended to keep going. "I asked you first."

He rolled his eyes. "Fine. I was in a serious relationship. It ended."

"Why did you break up?" she asked.

Tanner lifted one shoulder. "Jill wanted to change me. I didn't want to be changed."

"Oh." Erin chewed on that answer for a bit. She really couldn't argue with it, though she'd like more information. For instance, what did she want to change about him?

She'd opened her mouth to ask when he said, "Your turn, Miss Curious. I answered you, now you have to answer me. Why are you still single? I certainly hope it's not because that one ass cheated on you back while you were in college."

He looked far more interested in her answer than it warranted. He was going to be disappointed.

"No, it's not because of Jared. When I first started the business, I wanted to concentrate on building my clientele and my reputation. That didn't leave much time for dating. Especially given all the night and weekend hours. So I kept my head down and worked as hard as I could to make my company a success. When I looked up again, ten years had passed." She mirrored him and lifted one shoulder, pretending it didn't matter. That it didn't bother her to be dancing at her little sister's wedding when she hadn't even been able to come up with a real date. Although Tanner had turned out to be surprisingly good in the wedding-date department . . . so far anyway.

"Hmm." Tanner looked as if he was digesting her answer just as she had pondered his.

"Am I allowed a follow-up question?" she asked.

Glancing down at her as they moved slowly around the dance floor, he said, "Sure."

She braced herself and got up the nerve to ask what she'd wondered about. "What did she want to change about you?"

He cocked a brow. "Because I'm so perfect as I am, you mean?"

"Exactly." Erin laughed at his joking.

Single, age-appropriate men with a sense of humor, good looks, and muscles like Tanner's didn't exactly grow on trees. And she shouldn't be thinking things like that.

She and Tanner were so different it was ridiculous. There was no way they'd be compatible for more than a few hours. Sitcoms were written about couples with fewer differences than she and Tanner had.

"It wasn't a big deal. I'm a ranch hand. Always will be. She didn't want that, so I guess she didn't want me." Tanner lifted one shoulder in a halfhearted shrug. "When I realized she loved the city more than she could ever love me, staying together was pointless."

His answer echoed her own thoughts about opposites attracting for a while but not for the long term.

Oh well. She'd enjoy tonight and that would be that.

Tanner's mouth tipped up in a smile. He pulled her closer and rested his chin on the top of her head. "Blue suit is eyeballing us. Gotta make this convincing."

Resting her head against his chest, she said, "Good idea."

They rocked to the final strains of the love song and Erin tried to ignore the disappointment she felt when the dance ended and a fast number began to play.

Tanner dropped his hold on her and took a step back. "Another drink? A nonblue one this time?"

"Sure." She smiled until a flash of white behind Tanner caught her eye. "Uh-oh."

"What?" he asked.

"Determined-looking, nosy bride coming up on your six."

Tanner let out a snort. "Bring it on. I've faced worse."

"We'll see if you still think so afterward." Drawing in a bracing breath, Erin stepped around Tanner to face her sister. "Ash. Hey. Do you need me for something?"

"Yes. I need you to introduce me to your mysterious date here." Ashley's gaze landed square on Tanner, and Erin knew there was no avoiding the encounter now.

This had become quite a tangled web she'd woven by telling Ashley there was nothing between her and Tanner and then proceeding to pretend for Jared's benefit that there was. And beneath it all was the fact that she was still a little shaky, first from that kiss and then from the slow dance. What was that about?

Maybe she could keep this interrogation short at least. "Tanner, this is my sister, Ashley."

"Nice to meet you and congratulations. Beautiful wedding. I'm enjoying it. Thanks for inviting me."

Ashley's brow rose. "Actually, Erin invited you, which leads me to wonder where you two met and why I haven't met you before."

As Erin cringed at the attitude in her sister's question and braced for Tanner's answer, a savior appeared in the form of the catering manager, waving from across the room. "Ash, the caterer is trying to get your attention. He must have a question."

Without even turning to look, Ashley pinned Erin with a glare. "Can't you answer him? You insisted you could be my on-site coordinator today in addition to being the maid of honor. That's the only reason I didn't hire someone else to do it."

Erin opened her mouth to protest, but it was the truth. Ashley had offered to hire someone to run the event today so they could both just enjoy themselves and not be bothered with details and Erin had talked her out of it.

It had seemed like a waste of money when Erin could run this party with her eyes closed. She'd successfully worked with both the caterer and the band before.

"All right, I'll handle it." Erin sighed. She caught Tanner's gaze. "I'm sorry. I have to deal with this."

"Don't worry. I'll be fine. I'm looking forward to getting to know your sister." Tanner even looked like he meant it. He focused his attention on Ashley. "Can I get you something? I bet you haven't had time to grab anything to eat or drink."

As Erin begrudgingly left them alone, she had to admit that Tanner might be able to handle this on his own, maybe better than if she'd been there.

Fingers crossed that was true.

She made a beeline for the manager, planning to handle whatever he needed as quickly as possible so she could get back to Ashley and the pending disaster with Tanner.

Erin tried to keep one eye on her date and her sister while fielding the caterer's questions but lost sight of the duo behind a cluster of guests near the bar. Not being able to see them fueled her unease.

"Erin?"

"Um, yeah?" She'd been so distracted by searching the room for them, she must have missed a question.

"No cake ceremony at all? We just put the cupcakes out on the buffet and let the guests have at it?" he asked.

"That's what she wants." Erin shrugged.

Her sister had wanted a lot of things for this wedding that Erin didn't approve of, but Ashley was the bride and Erin's job was to keep her happy, so she hadn't argued.

"All right." The caterer looked unhappy but accepting.

"Anything else?" she asked, itching to get across the room to see how badly things had degraded while she'd been gone.

"Nope. That's it."

"Great. Thanks." She spun and nearly smacked head-on into Ashley.

"Ash." Glancing around, Erin didn't see Tanner. That didn't bode well. Had he left? The combination of concern and curiosity was killing her, but Erin was afraid to outright ask if Tanner had ditched her, so instead she said, "What's up?"

Ashley looked every bit the millennial bride with her signature drink poised in one hand and her cell phone at the ready to post pictures in the other as she said, "I just wanted to tell you that I get it."

Confused and a little afraid, Erin asked, "You get what?"

"You and Tanner. I get it now."

"Okay . . . what exactly do you get?"

"He's hot. He's charming." Ashley looked a bit devilish. "And the way he moves on a horse, I can only imagine how well he moves . . . you know . . . in bed."

Erin nearly choked at that comment. After glancing around to make sure no one else had heard—particularly not their parents or worse, the preacher, Erin focused on setting things straight. "Ashley, it's not like that."

Ashley rolled her eyes. "Whatever you say. I'm not going to judge you. I can totally see the appeal. Hot muscles. Hot sex."

Again, Erin cringed at the conversation they were having in a roomful of relatives.

"We're not having sex." She leaned in close and kept her voice down to barely a whisper, hoping Ashley would follow suit because her sister kept talking about inappropriate, not to mention untrue, things regarding Tanner.

Ashley frowned at her. "Wait. You're serious? You're really not doing it with him?"

"No, I'm not. Tanner and I aren't . . . you know."

Ashley's eyes widened. "Why the heck not? Have you looked at him?"

"Yes, of course I have." Erin really didn't need advice on men from her little sister.

"Then what's the problem?"

Erin searched for a reason but couldn't narrow it down to one—there were so many.

Ashley shook her head when Erin couldn't come up with an answer. "Well, as far as I'm concerned, you should go for it. Just, you know, don't hurt him when you're done with him. He seems like a nice guy."

Frowning, Erin knew she should end this ridiculous conversation, but once again her curiosity wouldn't let it go. "What do you mean? What makes you think I could hurt him?"

"Come on, Erin. There's no way it could be more than a fling. You two couldn't be more different, but that doesn't mean you can't have a little fun, right? As long as you both know going in that's all it can be."

This discussion was so frustrating on so many levels, it made Erin want to tear her hair out. Or possibly Ashley's hair. Luckily, they were both saved by their mother waving them down from across the room.

"Looks like Mom is trying to get your attention. You'd better go over." Without waiting, for fear Ashley would drag her over there with her, Erin spun in the opposite direction.

She was determined to get Tanner's report on what must have been one hell of an encounter between him and Ashley.

In a rush to find him, Erin took off across the room at the top speed she could manage given the crowd and the shoes pinching her feet. She nearly tripped on her dress again in the process and was forced to stop and inspect for damage.

Cursing her dress, the shoes, and the seamstress who'd obviously measured wrong, Erin lifted her skirt a tad to check the hem.

"Hey. All done with your duties for now?" A male voice that was becoming all too familiar to her had her whipping her gaze back up. Tanner, alone and smiling and looking completely unscathed by the encounter with her sister, stood in front of her.

"What happened with you and Ashley?" Erin demanded.

"We went to the bar, where I ordered her a blue drink. Do you know it's called the Something Blue? As in something old, something new. It still looks horrible, but at least it makes sense now."

"Yes, I know." Erin had helped her sister come up with the name. She should have tasted it first before approving the idea for the sickeningly sweet drink, however. "Go on. What did you two talk about?"

"We talked a little about the ranch. I showed her some pictures of it on her phone." He lifted a shoulder. "That's it. Then she left. Why? What did she say to you?"

"Not much." Just that Erin should have sex with him. She remembered what Ashley had said about Tanner's skill in riding and . . . other things, which raised another question. "How would she have seen you ride a horse?"

"I don't know." He frowned. "Oh wait, there's a video Ellie posted on the ranch's Facebook page. I'm in it, riding and roping some calves. Your sister must have found it and watched."

"Yeah, she must have." And Erin intended to do the same the moment she got the privacy to do so.

The rest of the conversation with her sister echoed in her head.

Don't hurt him when you're done with him.

You two couldn't be more different.

Erin didn't want a fling with Tanner. She hadn't really been the type for that when she was younger and she sure wasn't now, at almost forty. But Ashley was right that a relationship with him would be doomed to fail, just like his last one had.

Erin didn't want that either.

The one thing she feared she did want was Tanner, and what the heck was she going to do about that?

Erin shook her head to rid it of those dizzying thoughts. She glanced up and had a moment to observe Tanner unnoticed as he watched the dancers nearby. She realized for the first time how gorgeous his eyes were. And how strong his jawline was. And his cheekbones . . . wow.

She swallowed hard. "I think I need another blue drink."

"Coming right up." He smiled until it reached all the way to those eyes a woman could get lost in.

Oh boy, was she in trouble.

Chapter Twelve

Erin paused on the sidewalk in front of her office and turned back to face Tanner. "You didn't have to walk me all the way to the door."

"Sure I did. Believe it or not, I'm a gentleman. Sometimes." He grinned.

He'd ridden with her to the wedding in her vehicle, while his truck had been parked at her office. He might have had to ride shotgun while she drove, but he still had his man card and he was walking her to the door whether she liked it or not.

"Well, thank you." She broke eye contact before saying, "I had a really nice time."

"Me too." *Nice* seemed like a poor description for the surprisingly enjoyable time they'd spent together, but Tanner wasn't prepared to offer a better word. Remembering his new fashion accessory, he reached for the pink fabric in his jacket pocket. "I should give you this—"

She dismissed his offer with the wave of her hand. "Keep it. I mean, if you want to."

"I think I will. Thanks." Why, he didn't know. He'd never have need of a pink pocket square again, but for some reason he didn't want to give it up. "So, I guess I should get going."

"Early day in the morning, roping and riding and brush hogging?" She smiled.

"Yeah, something like that." He returned her smile and then realized she had her keys out, as if she was about to go into the office. "You're not going inside to work now, are you?"

"No. I'm just going to grab my laptop from my desk."

"So you can work at home," he guessed.

"No . . . maybe. I'll see." She laughed. "Well, I should let you go. Long way back to the ranch."

"Yeah." And not just in miles. The city and the ranch were worlds apart. He should keep reminding himself of that.

"Thank you for agreeing to go with me today. I appreciate it so much. And I really did have a nice time."

Nice. There was that word again. Tonight had been many things for Tanner, including nice, but most of all confusing.

"You're welcome. Anytime. Just give me a call next time you need a stand-in for a date and I'm there." Yeah, that sounded real smooth.

Loser. He nearly rolled his eyes at himself.

"Okay, thanks." She smiled but remained standing with her keys in hand. Waiting for him to leave, he supposed.

He needed to take the hint and go. "Um, so, good night."

"Good night, Tanner."

Before he could stop himself, he leaned in. It felt like a natural end to the night. He meant it to be a friendly peck. The equivalent of a handshake. Nothing more. Certainly nothing like the heated lip-lock he'd planted on her during the reception to make her ex jealous.

Only his mouth didn't hit her cheek. Instead, he pressed it to hers and the results weren't casual or friendly. It made him want to back her into that office, lift up that pretty pink dress, and take her on the desk.

He realized his mistake only after it was too late. Having her lips against his made him want more than he could safely have with Erin, which was exactly why he pulled back.

"Good night." Allowing for no more small talk, no more awkward pauses, he turned and strode fast toward his truck before he changed his mind.

Tanner's mind spun the whole drive back to the ranch.

She was a city girl. They were complete opposites. He'd been down this road before. He might have downplayed it for Erin when she'd asked, but the end of the relationship with Jill had been a wreck he feared he was still recovering from.

So why couldn't he stop thinking about Erin? About how the thought of seeing her again had his heart speeding. About how much it was going to suck when Brady's wedding was over and Tanner wouldn't see Erin again.

He'd given himself a headache by the time he pulled onto the ranch, where the fact that he had incredibly bad luck and worse timing was confirmed. Brady was pulling out just as Tanner was pulling in.

His boss flashed his lights and slowed to a stop. Tanner had no choice but to stop as well.

Brady leaned his arm on the open window. "You're home early. How was the wedding?"

"Free food. Free booze. It was good." Tanner kept his description short, hoping Brady would let it go at that.

"So, you going to see her again?" Brady asked.

"Yup, reckon I will. At your wedding."

Brady chuckled. "Stubborn as ever, you are."

"Nope." Tanner swung his head from side to side. "Just smart enough to know what's what."

"And what is what? Eh?"

"You don't put a plow horse in the pasture with a Thoroughbred."

Brady drew back. "Wow. That sentence could have come right out of my daddy's mouth."

"It did. Doesn't make it any less true." Tanner should have the sentiment burned into the wall above his bed so he wouldn't forget it. One night and a couple of kisses with Erin already had him forgetting things he shouldn't. "See you in the morning, boss."

After saying good night, Tanner hit the gas, heading for the bunkhouse before he had to answer any more questions.

The moment he walked in, he realized the questions weren't over yet. It was early on a Sunday night, so Randy was there and still awake . . . and curious.

"Where were you?"

"Out."

The kid frowned at Tanner's jacket. "What's that pink thing in your pocket?"

Crap. Tanner had forgotten about that.

"Nothing." He whipped out the offending swath of fabric and shoved it out of sight into the back pocket of his jeans. "Don't stay up too late. We need to finish that fencing in the morning."

"I know. We gotta get all our work done here because we'll be gone moving the herd in a couple of days. I know you don't believe it, but I do listen."

"Sometimes." With that last word, Tanner made a beeline for his bedroom to be alone. Women made life too complicated. Even a woman he wasn't dating.

Yet.

That thought had him stumbling on his booted feet. Did he want to date Erin?

Deep down, beneath the hard-earned knowledge and logic, in the place where raw feelings and desires lived, it seemed he did.

Not liking the conclusion he'd just come to, Tanner blew out a breath.

Thank goodness he'd be heading out in a few days. He could use the time away moving the herd to the summer pasture. A couple of long days in the saddle and short nights spent sleeping on the ground were exactly what he needed to get his head back on straight.

There was no danger he'd run into Erin on the trail the way there was here on the ranch. That would give him the time and space he needed to think.

If he came back and still felt this way—and he hoped to God he wouldn't—he'd worry about it then.

Chapter Thirteen

"So . . . have you been talking to your cowboy?"
Jessica asked.

"No. I've been a little busy. You know, planning the rehearsal dinner and the wedding that
are both *this weekend.*"

But Jessica's nosy inquiry raised a good point
that Erin had been wondering about herself.
Why hadn't she heard from Tanner since her
sister's wedding?

Not that she'd expected a lot, but she figured
she'd get at least a text. But nope. Nothing.
Nada. Zip.

That was the difference between men and
women. Whether you called it protocol or simply
good manners, a woman would have sent a
follow-up. Something simple like *had a great
time, thanks again.*

Although she was just as guilty as he was.
She hadn't sent a text to him either and she
really should have. She'd wanted to. Heck,
she'd had her cell in her hand a couple of
times, contemplating whether she should text
him and say thanks again. She hadn't.

Erin hated to admit why.

That evening with Tanner had stopped feeling
like a favor and started feeling like a date the

moment he'd kissed her. And she'd liked the feeling. Too much.

Way too much, considering even her sister saw how different she and Tanner were. How impossible a relationship between them would be.

"And he's not my cowboy," Erin added, as much for her own benefit as for her assistant's.

Jessica raised one brow. "Okay. If you say so."

Erin realized her denial had come a bit late to be completely believable, but she did have a lot on her mind. Like the wedding this weekend, where she'd definitely be seeing Tanner again. She'd seen his name on the guest list.

Then there was the meeting today with Brady and Ellie at the ranch—she could possibly run into him there, too.

Speaking of the meeting, she needed to get going. "I have to run. I might not be back before you leave for the day."

"That's fine. It's pretty quiet here at the beginning of the week. It's closer to the weekend things start to get crazy."

Wasn't that the truth? Weekends, when the rest of the normal working world rested, party planners were busier than ever. There was a whole weekend world of leisure activities Erin was missing out on.

Funny. She'd never craved a normal schedule or a normal life before.

Erin refused to ponder why she was now. It definitely had nothing to do with a certain sexy cowboy who had her walking a bit faster toward her car just at the thought of running into him.

She might have driven a tad bit faster than usual, or maybe it was just that traffic was light this time of day, but she made it to the ranch in record time. She had to slow on the gravel drive, but that was okay. It gave her the opportunity to look around her to see who might be working nearby.

A man in a cowboy hat walking toward the house caught her eye.

Gravel be damned. Erin hit the accelerator. That sent a spray of rocks shooting out behind her.

Cringing, she eased off the gas pedal a bit and navigated toward the house.

Closer inspection told her this cowboy wasn't the one she'd been hoping to see, and her soaring mood came back to earth.

Unaware of her disappointment, he strode over. He even opened the driver's side door and tipped his hat. "Ma'am, g'afternoon."

"Good afternoon to you, too."

"Anything I can help you carry in?" he asked.

"No, not today, but thank you." Was politeness bred into these men genetically? Not to mention good looks.

"Sure. Anytime." He grinned. "I'm Randy, by the way."

"Erin."

Randy nodded. "The wedding planner."

"That's me. Why, what have you heard?" She was only half-joking, but his eyes widened as her jest obviously fell flat.

"Nothing. I swear."

She smiled to ease his discomfort. "I was just kidding."

"Oh. Okay. Gotcha." He returned her smile. "So, I guess I'll be seeing you Saturday. At the wedding."

"You guess right." Erin remembered seeing a Randy on the guest list, and that he had been assigned to sit at the table with Tanner when she'd gone over the place cards. Hoping to sound casual and smooth, Erin took the opportunity to say, "I'll see you and Tanner both on Saturday. So, where is he today anyway?"

Randy's eyes brightened. "Well, he don't tell me nothing usually about where he goes, but I can guess. I think he's got himself a girl in town."

She felt her stomach drop. "Really. Why do you say that?"

"Well a coupla Sundays ago, he took off early and got all dressed up in a jacket with his good boots and hat on. Even had a little pink hankie in his pocket. No man is doing that except for a girl."

Erin's lips twitched. Randy was talking about

Tanner's date with her. "You're probably right about that."

Randy continued, "And today he asked to get off early and he was wearing his good clothes again. He even washed his truck. Gotta be that he's seeing her."

That information didn't sit so well with Erin. Unless Tanner had driven in to Austin to surprise her—which she really didn't think he would do, given they hadn't spoken or texted since the wedding—he had to be seeing someone else.

That information hit her harder than it should. He wasn't her cowboy, even if Jessica did call him that. He was free to see whomever he liked.

None of that changed the sick feeling in her stomach.

"Um, I have a meeting . . . inside." Beyond distracted, or maybe just distraught, Erin gestured in the general direction of the house.

"Oh, sure. Let me get the door for you." Randy took the front steps two at a time, reaching the door long before Erin did on her wobbly legs.

She managed to say, "Thanks."

"My pleasure." Randy delivered another tip of his hat and a grin, the charm of both lost on Erin in her current state.

In just a blink of an eye everything had changed. Tanner was dating someone. And Erin felt like she could no longer breathe.

Chapter Fourteen

"We need to go out to check on the bulls. The big guy has taken to ramming the fence. I'm afraid he's gonna bust it and they'll all get out. We might have to put him on his own and see if that helps."

Dropping the bale of hay he'd been carrying into the truck bed to be driven out to the horses in the field, Randy spun toward Tanner.

"Fine. I'll go out and do it now." The kid had delivered that response with more than his usual dose of attitude and Tanner wanted to know why.

As Randy stalked past him, Tanner grabbed his arm. "Hey. What's up with you? Something wrong?"

"No."

That figured. The one day Tanner was in a particularly good mood, Randy was acting pissy. Tanner cocked a brow and waited.

Finally, Randy realized he wasn't getting away without explaining and said, "I'm just getting tired of you disappearing all the time, and then when I ask where you've been, you're rude to me. We work together every day. We live together in the bunkhouse. But you treat me like some kinda . . . nuisance."

Maybe the kid was right. Tanner could have

handled things better. "You're not a nuisance. I just like my privacy."

"You can still have your privacy without being a dick about it . . . no offense."

Even in the middle of an argument, Randy was polite. He really was a good kid. He worked hard at the ranch and didn't go out with his friends much at night, which left Tanner in the position of being the kid's only companion for long stretches.

"I'm sorry. I'll try to do better."

Randy nodded. "Thanks. That's all I'm asking. I mean, I don't need details about whatever you and your new girl did on your date yesterday. Just don't bite my head off if I ask where you've been when you leave work in the middle of the day. You know?"

Tanner laughed. That's what the kid thought? That he'd been out with a woman? "I wasn't on a date yesterday. What would make you think that?"

"You got all dressed up again, just like you did that Sunday you took off and came home with a pink hankie in your pocket."

Tanner rolled his eyes. He was never going to hear the end of that pink hankie. "I had a meeting in the city yesterday. I wanted to look decent for it."

"A meeting? What kind of meeting?" Randy frowned.

"Don't push it, a'ight? I told you why I was dressed up and where I was."

No way in hell was Tanner going to tell Randy that he'd spent most of the cattle drive contemplating his life—or, more specifically, the pros and cons of having Erin in his life. When he finally stopped fighting the fact that he couldn't get her out of his head, the only thing left to do was make a plan to try to avoid a train wreck.

Maybe that was why his first relationship had gone off the rails—a lack of planning.

He wasn't going to let that happen this time. When he'd heard the hired hands on the cattle drive with them talking about a nice spread of land just outside the city being up for sale, the wheels in Tanner's brain had started to turn.

Now all he needed was the approval from the bank for the loan application he'd put in.

Well, that and Erin.

Nope, Tanner wasn't about to tell Randy any of that, even as the kid scowled when he said, "Fine. Thanks for telling me."

"No problem." Time to get this day back on track. "And as for checking on the bulls, how about we drop the hay for the horses and then drive out together?"

Randy looked a bit happier at that prospect as he nodded. "Okay. But we might want to hurry. I don't like the looks of that sky."

He turned to follow Randy's gaze and saw what the kid meant. There was a storm coming. Even the kid had worked the land long enough to recognize the signs.

Tanner's cell phone began blaring in his pocket with a noise he'd never heard in the half a year he'd had it. Seconds later, Randy's cell did the same. Tanner didn't like technology on a good day, but especially not when it was screeching at him.

"What is that?" he asked.

"Emergency alert." Randy pulled his cell out of his pocket and checked the display. Eyes wide, he looked up. "Tornado."

Tanner blew out a breath. Things were about to get real hairy, real fast.

The rest of the week passed in a rushed blur for not only Tanner but also everyone connected with the Cutwright family's place and the neighboring dude ranch.

The storm had hit Meg's ranch, catching her out in it. Luckily, she was close enough to take shelter in the storm cellar under the chapel and came out of it unscathed. Unfortunately, the chapel and the surrounding property didn't fare so well.

It took both Meg and Brady's crews, Tanner among them, working overtime to get the place back into shape. Come hell or high water—or tornado—Brady was intent on marrying Ellie as planned. The man was in love and he wasn't about to disappoint his bride.

They'd gotten everything fixed and ready not only for the wedding but in time for the rehearsal dinner.

As a thank you, Brady had invited the crews from both ranches to attend the dinner, so Tanner once again donned his best. His good boots and jacket hadn't gotten as much use in all the years he'd owned them as they had these past couple of weeks.

That was okay. He'd get all gussied up without complaint because tonight he was sure to see Erin and could put his plan into motion.

If all went well, it would be as easy as one, two, three.

Step one—ask her out on a real date, just the two of them. No relatives.

Step two—give her a nice, long good night kiss. The kind he'd always wanted to.

Step three—hope she agreed that his working his own place not far outside the city was the perfect compromise. They could have the best of both worlds. His and hers.

Thanks to the loan approval that had just come through today and the decision to go for it with Erin, Tanner was practically walking on air.

When he got a look at Erin directing a waiter

who was setting up the buffet inside Meg's barn, Tanner's spirits rose even higher . . . until she caught sight of him and her eyes narrowed.

Frowning, he moved toward her. That look on her face couldn't be for him. He hadn't seen or talked to her since her sister's wedding and that had ended pretty well, in his opinion.

Hell, he'd been too busy moving the herd and cleaning up the storm damage to do much of anything, let alone piss off a woman he hadn't seen.

There must be some issue with the dinner she was dealing with.

Confident, he closed the distance between them and smiled. "Hey. Fancy seeing you here."

Her glare told him he might have misjudged his innocence in causing her foul mood.

"Yeah. What a surprise. Are you here alone?" She lifted a brow.

"Uh, no. Actually, Randy drove over with me." Was she mad he wasn't technically on the guest list? The groom had invited them, but maybe nobody had told Erin. He should be able to straighten out the mix-up easily enough. "Brady said we should come over to eat, but if there's not enough—"

"That's fine. There's plenty of food."

There was also plenty of chill in the air and all of it radiated off Erin and directly at him. Why, he didn't know.

Frowning, Tanner took a step closer. "Um, is everything a'ight?"

"Fine. Perfectly fine."

Three *fines* in as many sentences. Tanner might be a confirmed bachelor—as Brady had dubbed him—but he knew enough about the opposite sex to realize the word *fine* rarely meant what the dictionary said it did when it came out of an angry woman's mouth.

Grasping at one more straw with the hope there was something wrong with the event and not between them, Tanner said, "Well, if there's anything I can do to help with this shindig—"

"Nope. I'm good. Got it covered all on my own."

"Okay. That's good. I'll let you get back to it then."

"Yup. Thanks."

With his head still spinning from her complete turnaround, Tanner watched Erin stalk off and blew out a long, low whistle.

"What has her looking so angry?"

Tanner turned at the question and saw Erin's assistant, Jessica, standing next to him, watching the departure.

"No idea. I was hoping you knew. Is something going on behind the scenes here with the dinner? Did you guys run out of ice or something?"

Jessica laughed. "Um, no. Everything is running

smoothly, as usual. And if we did run out of ice, we could just run out and buy some."

What did Tanner know about throwing a party? He lifted one shoulder. "Then I got nothing to explain it."

"Me either, but I suppose it's my job to find out." Jessica shot him a pretty smile. "See ya, cowboy."

"Yeah. See ya." At least Erin's assistant still liked him. That was something, he supposed.

Meanwhile, he had an offer in on a ranch and a loan pending, all for a woman who for some unknown reason wouldn't give him the time of day.

Tanner felt like that twister had come back around again, only this time instead of knocking down trees and taking out fences, it had turned his whole life upside down.

Chapter Fifteen

Erin was more than happy when she noticed the guests begin to thin. It was time for this night to be over.

Keeping the event running smoothly was job enough, especially after Brady had magnanimously invited all the workers who'd saved the wedding by clearing the storm damage. But to have to manage it under Tanner's close scrutiny made the night even more difficult.

Not to mention the twinge of pain she felt in the vicinity of her heart every time she caught him watching her.

She had been a fool to even think twice about him. He was a player, juggling as many women as his week would allow, apparently. And he did it while wearing the same outfit on all his dates, according to Randy.

If she found out he'd used her pocket square on his other date, she might blow her top. Erin's jaw clenched at that thought as her gaze swept the converted barn and searched for the tall, dark, womanizing cowboy.

When she didn't see him, she was hit with a strange sensation. Disappointment. Bad taste in men was par for the course for her, sadly. She always had gravitated toward the wrong sort.

Tanner was just one more in that line of bad choices.

"Erin."

She turned at the sound of her name and saw Brady striding toward her. She forced a smile. "Here's the groom-to-be. I think everyone really enjoyed the dinner, don't you?"

"I know they did. You got a lot of compliments."

"Me? All I did was oversee." Erin laughed. "Meg and the caterers deserve the compliments. It's a beautiful venue and the food was excellent."

"Yes, but you tied it all together. I guess we'll have to agree to disagree." Brady glanced around the room. "Hey, this thing is wrapping up. Why don't you head out?"

It was a tempting offer. She was exhausted, and tomorrow was going to be a big day. But she'd wanted to start some of the setup for the reception before she called it quits for the night. "I don't know."

"Meg's crew can handle things. I promise. She's set you up in one of the guest rooms, right?"

"Yes."

"Good. Then you can get back at it bright and early if you really want to." When she hesitated, Brady took her by both shoulders and turned her toward the main building. "Go get some rest. These guys could be here drinking half the night. There's no use in your waiting up for them to leave."

Erin glanced over her shoulder. "Okay, but you should get some rest yourself, you know."

"Oh, I plan to. Believe me. I'm right behind you. Don't want to be hung over for my big day."

For lack of energy to argue, Erin nodded. "Okay. 'Night, Brady."

" 'Night. And great job."

"Thanks." Relieved to have the decision taken out of her hands, Erin headed for the house.

Meg had given her a small but charming room. After the day she'd had, that four-poster bed would feel like heaven.

Considering how many guests were staying at the ranch, Erin had been surprised when Meg had offered her accommodations at all. She hadn't thought there'd be room.

Being on-site would help enormously. Brady was right. Erin could be up and at 'em at the crack of dawn without having to worry about the drive from the city. And she could do the setup in casual clothes with the convenience of having her own room where she could clean up and change into her wedding outfit.

The stone walkway to the house was lit but not brightly. Erin was concentrating so hard on trying to walk on her toes so her heels didn't sink into the gravel, she didn't notice she wasn't alone until a shadow fell across her path.

She managed to squelch her scream in time. She pressed her hand to her chest over her racing heart. "Tanner. You scared me."

"Sorry. Can we talk?"

"About what?" Her heart sped, partly from fright but mostly from being so near Tanner.

"About why you've been giving me the cold shoulder all night."

Erin didn't have the energy to fight both him and her feelings. "I'm not—"

"Cut the bull, Erin. You are and you know it. So how about you tell me what I did to piss you off so we can talk about it like adults."

Like adults? Was he calling her childish? She pressed her lips together as her anger rose. Suddenly no longer weary, Erin narrowed her gaze. "Okay, fine. Let's talk about it. Let's talk about how after what I thought was a pretty nice night together, I hear nothing from you. Not a call. Not a text. Nothing."

He opened his mouth, but she held up her hand to stop him.

"I'm not done. You wanted me to talk, I'm talking. Let's also talk about how you kissed me not once but twice and then I found out from Randy that you're off on a date, probably kissing who knows how many other women, too. Huh? How about that?"

Tanner mouthed a foul curse. "Randy told you I was dating other women?"

"Yes. When I was there on Tuesday to meet with Brady and Ellie. You left work early all dressed up in your date clothes, according to him."

"I wasn't on a date." He shook his head. "Those are my only clothes that don't have stains and holes in 'em. I wore them on Tuesday because I had a meeting at a bank about getting a loan to buy a property closer to the city."

Erin was confused. "I thought you hate the city."

"I do. But I like you and you like the city." He took a step closer and planted his hands on her shoulders. "And I didn't call or text after your sister's wedding because I was on a cattle drive and pretty occupied trying to talk myself out of the idea of you and me."

She understood without asking him why he'd try to talk himself out of liking her because she'd done the same with him. It was funny how much the same they were, considering they were complete opposites. The two of them together didn't make any sense.

Sometimes making sense was overrated.

Erin took a step closer and pressed her palms against his chest, intensely relieved he'd been meeting a banker and not a date. "So it didn't work, then? You talking yourself out of the idea of us."

Us. The word sent a thrill through her.

"Nope." He tipped her head back with a thumb and forefinger under her chin. "You think you could maybe give being with a cowboy a shot?"

"Hmm. I don't know. It depends." Erin pursed her lips. "Is this cowboy in question a good kisser?"

"He sure is, but maybe you need a reminder?" Tanner asked in a husky voice.

"Maybe I do."

He wasted no time. His lips were on hers immediately. Erin didn't hesitate either. She leaned into him and relished the feel of his hard body pressed tight to hers.

She couldn't stop her groan of satisfaction.

Tanner's lips tipped up at the sound before he plunged his tongue against hers. Then she was really a goner. She was breathless by the time he pulled back and leaned his forehead against hers.

He let out a sigh. "We probably shouldn't be doing this right here."

"Definitely not." Erin considered for barely a second before she said, "We should be doing this in my room."

Tanner leaned back and gazed down at her. "You're inviting me to your room?"

Erin's heart thundered. Tanner was a virile, adult man. She knew if they went to her room, it wouldn't be to talk or for a make-out session like a couple of teenagers.

If they went to her room, this relationship they'd both tried to talk themselves out of would take a giant, irreversible leap forward. Even so, she said, "Yes. Unless you don't want to—"

"Oh, I want to." He pressed a hard, quick kiss to her mouth before grabbing her hand. "Come on."

She laughed as he pulled her inside the guest entrance and stood in the hallway, unsure of which way to turn. She helped them both get there sooner by saying, "To the right. Last room. Past the laundry."

"Good. Far away from all the other guests." He grinned.

Knowing exactly why he'd said that, Erin felt her cheeks heat. Given her reaction to just Tanner's kisses, things could get loud.

He reached the door with a few long, fast strides. "Key?"

Erin pulled it out of her pocket and held it out for him, noticing her hand shook just a bit.

Was taking this step with Tanner so monumental it was enough to have her trembling?

Maybe.

Or maybe she just really wanted him.

As he bent his knees slightly to see the lock better, she noticed how incredibly thick and strong his thighs were. The jeans fit him like a glove and she didn't need much imagination to create a vivid mental image of how good he'd look stripped of them.

When he grabbed the knob in one big, strong hand and slipped the key into the lock with the other her mouth went dry.

The door swung in. He flipped the switch on the wall and the room lit behind him. He took off the cowboy hat and put it on the dresser inside before he turned back to face her and waited.

Erin didn't make him wait long. She strode inside, closing and locking the door behind her, and then stepped close to Tanner. Slipping her hands beneath his jacket, she felt the bulging hardness of his chest.

No doubt about it, he was all man. He worked hard for a living, relying on his strength and his muscles.

Why had she never realized the appeal of the working cowboy before? Instead, she'd spent years surrounded by cookie-cutter guys, not looking beyond the Austin city limits to where there was a whole other world.

Yes, she and Tanner were very different, but that was exactly what made him irresistible.

As the realization hit Erin, she noticed he was staring at her. Not moving, just watching.

His tightly held control was evident in his grip around her waist, the rapid beat of his heart beneath her hands, the quick rise and fall of his chest . . . yet he was being a gentleman and waiting.

She knew instinctively that with one signal from her—a word, a move—he'd unleash the need he held in check. Tanner, wild and uncontrolled, was exactly what she wanted. What she needed.

Reaching down, Erin grabbed the bottom of her cotton dress. The stretch of the material and the style made it easy to slip over her head.

She tossed the garment onto the chair. His nostrils flared while his gaze dropped. He took all of her in as she stood before him in nothing but lacy lingerie and heels.

Seeing the heat in his eyes ramped up Erin's own need for this man. Her lips parted as she found it hard to breathe. He jumped on the opportunity.

Tanner crashed his mouth into hers. Their tongues performed an erotic dance as he stole what little breath she had remaining.

He broke the kiss and began backing her toward the bed. "I've wanted you from the first day I saw you carrying all those books into Brady's."

His words sent a tingle down her spine. Her body vibrated from within, overwhelmed by the combination of nerves and anticipation and long-ignored physical need.

Goose bumps rose on her skin, following the

path of his hands as he ran them over her. He lifted her easily and tossed her onto the bed, following her down.

As much as Erin loved the weight of Tanner pressing over her, he had entirely too many clothes on. She pushed at him with both hands.

When he lifted himself off her, she reached between them and started to tug at his belt buckle, making little headway against it.

He stood and kicked off his boots. "It'll be faster if I do it myself."

"Fast is good." As far as she was concerned, the quicker he got naked, the better.

"Not always." He let out a breathy laugh as the belt gave way and the heavy buckle swung.

"I've got nowhere to be until the morning." Her announcement had him fumbling with his clothes in an attempt to get out of them.

"Me neither." He tugged his shirt over his head and her gaze dropped to his torso, a washboard of ridged, hard muscles.

The rest of the clothing quickly followed until a pile of his abandoned things lay on the floor and Tanner was crawling onto the bed gloriously naked.

He looked like a starving man, and what he was hungry for was her. Erin felt pretty starved in that department herself.

The distraction of Tanner, naked and braced over her, held all her attention, until he rocked back on his knees and tore into a condom wrapper with his teeth. She hadn't even noticed it in his hand until then. She'd been too busy enjoying the rest of the view. One particular part especially as it bobbed between them while he gripped it and rolled the latex down.

"You always travel prepared?" Erin was only half-joking as she tried not to be jealous of every other woman who'd ever had the pleasure of Tanner's preparedness.

"No." He leaned lower. "I knew I'd be seeing you. Wishful thinking on my part, I guess."

It was a good answer. She rewarded it by reaching up and pulling him to her for a kiss she got lost in until he slid one knee between her thighs and nudged her legs apart. Her body surrendered to his with the first thrust.

She cried out with the pure relief of finally being joined with him. Of getting what she craved.

Her tension broke and fled with every stroke until the thought that she'd ever been nervous with him seemed ridiculous. As did the notion that this man whose breath brushed her ear as he held her tight and made love to her had ever been a stranger.

It felt so natural, so right being with him.

Her muscles gripped him tighter and he groaned. As the orgasm rocked her, he lifted up enough that she could see his face. She saw in his expression the effect that watching her come had on him.

As her body pulsed around his, his breath came faster. His eyes lost focus until he finally lost control. Tanner slid his hands beneath her hips, clutched her close, and pounded them both to an explosive conclusion.

He collapsed on top of her, panting, not moving.

Finally, when both of their breathing had slowed, he pushed off.

Lying on his side, he pulled her to him with one arm he left draped over her.

He shook his head and opened his mouth. All that came out at first was a short laugh. Finally, he said, "That was . . ."

She understood his lack of words. "Indescribable?"

"Yeah. That about covers it." Tanner nodded before rolling over and swinging his feet to the floor.

Erin's heart fell. "Are you leaving?"

He glanced back as he reached for his jeans on the floor. "Hell no. I'm texting Randy and telling him to get a ride back to the ranch. I you don't mind me spending the night."

Erin smiled. "I don't mind."

"Good." He punched in a text and then tossed the phone to the nightstand before climbing back onto the bed. He gathered her close to him again. "You know what this means, don't you?"

The idea that they should repeat what had just happened came to mind. The thought that Tanner should be naked as often as possible did, too. Erin kept those thoughts to herself . . . for now . . . and said, "No. What?"

"For one, I'm now 'Erin's cowboy,' just like Jessica says."

"All right. I can handle that."

"Can you?"

"Mm hmm." Erin bobbed her head. "And what else?"

"That after I close on my place, the first thing I'm getting is a nice big bed . . . and Wi-Fi."

"That's an interesting combination. The bed I get, but why the Wi-Fi?"

"I'm hoping I can entice you to spend a whole lot of time there with me if I give you the tools. That way you can work nights from my place instead of your own." Tanner smoothed a finger down her cheek. "Do you think you could do that? Be okay staying outside of the city? Maybe even permanently one day, if it's not too far and you can still drive in to the office?"

Erin had never considered it before, but now it seemed so logical. Perfect really. "Yes."

"You really think you could ever see yourself with a cowboy for the long haul?" There was a small spark of hope inside him that began to show through.

She nodded. "Yeah. I think I can."

His eyes brightened further. "Even with how different we are?"

"I think it's *because* of how different we are. Being the same is boring."

Tanner donned a mischievous expression as he leaned lower. "Oh, I promise that you and me together will be anything but boring."

They'd already proven his point, but that didn't matter. Erin felt the hard length of him pressing against her and said, "Show me."

He rolled on top of her again. "Gladly."

They were both going to be tired for tomorrow's wedding, but it would be worth it.

Taming the Sheriff

Kate Pearce

Chapter One

"Still not married then, Nate? I thought you'd be the first man down." Brady Cutwright gave Nate a manly slap on the back. "Thanks for coming to my wedding."

"It's my pleasure. Couldn't let you go to your happy fate alone, now could I?"

Nate Turner grinned at his old college friend, who looked remarkably relaxed for a man who was getting married in two days. Nate had decided to make the long trip from home in California to Austin, Texas, into a vacation and planned to do some tourist stuff when the wedding was over. Being the deputy sheriff of a small northern Californian town wasn't exactly a stressful job, but he'd grown up there and everyone knew where he lived, so he was never really off duty.

"Come meet some of the guys." Brady steered him toward the bar. "Did you get booked into the hotel yet? Sorry there wasn't room up at the ranch for everyone."

"Not yet; I'm . . ." Nate studied the large guy in a suit who appeared to be guarding the entrance to the bar. "Are you expecting trouble?"

"Jeez no." Brady lowered his voice. "Do you remember Brian Dobbs?"

"The weedy guy who wrote poetry and stuff the girls loved?"

"Yeah, him. He changed his name to Travis Whitely." Brady looked at him expectantly. "The country and western singer?"

"Er . . . no?" Nate frowned. His musical tastes ran somewhere between the '80s pop his mom had forced into his brain during car rides to school, rap, and heavy rock. "It's not really my thing."

"Well, he's a big deal around here and, as he's my second cousin or something, he was invited to the wedding. He doesn't want the paparazzi hanging around, so he's keeping a low profile."

"That's low-key?" Nate glanced over his shoulder at the security guard who was checking each incoming guest against a list. "So that guy is protecting him from crazy fans?"

"Apparently." Brady grimaced. "And he hasn't even come down from his room yet."

"I can't wait to meet him," Nate said dryly.

"You probably won't recognize him."

"Is he singing at the wedding?"

"I hope not." Brady made a face. "You know me, Nate. I'm a simple guy."

At that moment they were hailed by a group of people, some of whom looked vaguely familiar. Nate took the seat offered to him as Brady went to get them a couple of beers and attempted to put names to faces he hadn't seen for about ten years. Luckily, in his job he'd honed that skill to perfection.

"Onsk!" One of the guys leaned forward to shake his hand. "Nate Turner, right? How are you doing?"

"Good, thanks, Steve." It was weird hearing the distinctive Texan drawl again. When he'd chosen to go to college outside California, he'd struggled to understand anyone during his first year.

"Onsk?" The woman beside Steve, whom he introduced as his wife, Bonnie, said with a polite smile. "Are you Polish or something?"

"Not exactly."

Steve grinned. "Honey, Nate's not Polish. He just has a great nickname: the One-Night Stand King."

Nate winced. "Yeah, as to that—"

Steve carried on talking. "Dated all the time but never took anyone out twice."

The lady didn't look very impressed. "It's weird how men think that's funny when other men do it but not when it's a woman."

"Um." Nate cleared his throat. "It's not quite what you're thinking, ma'am. I just had a lot of first dates."

Luckily, at that moment Brady rejoined them, giving Nate a chance to stop talking and take a look around the bar. The actual wedding was taking place at the Hawk Creek Ranch, which was owned by a friend of Brady's. The rest of the wedding party was camping out here.

He always tried to forget that stupid nickname, which made him sound like some kind of Lothario. It was so far from the truth it was ridiculous. But, in fairness, he couldn't say he'd changed his policy on dating much in the ten years since he'd left college. The only woman he'd taken out more than once was the local veterinarian, Jenna McDonald, and that had only been to annoy his old friend Blue.

Time was ticking on and he was beginning to wonder whether he was ever going to meet his match. In his family you were supposed to just *know* when you met *The One*. Due to his occupation, he'd developed a cynical streak a mile wild that made buying into the family legend somewhat difficult. All these years, something had stopped him from settling and he'd remained a bachelor. Standing up, he offered to get another round of drinks and made his way over to the bar, glad to escape the frosty glare of Steve's wife.

A commotion at the entrance caught his attention, and his hand automatically went to his nonexistent holster. The big guy was blocking the entrance and vehemently shaking his head. Nate's gaze narrowed as the man put his hand on the diminutive woman in front of him and shoved her backward.

"Hey." Setting down the tray of drinks, he walked over. "What's the problem here?"

Big guy ignored him, which was a new experience for Nate, seeing as where he lived he represented the entire force of the law.

"I said, what's going on?"

"There's nothing to worry about, sir. This . . . person was trying to get into the bar without an invitation."

Nate looked down at the flushed face of the woman the security guard still had his hand on and encountered a pair of furious brown eyes, a bow-shaped mouth, and a riot of black, curling hair tied back with a pink scarf.

"Honeybun, where have you been?" She blinked as he inserted himself between her and the guy, forcing him to drop his hold. "I told you to text me when you were coming down so I could meet you outside."

"Um, I . . . I thought you said meet in the bar."

He gave her his best reassuring smile and took her hand. "Maybe I'm the one who got it wrong. It wouldn't be the first time, now would it, honeykins?" He turned to the guard. "Check under my name—Nate Turner plus one. This is my plus one. Give him your name, darlin', and he can put it next to mine right where it belongs."

Della gave the man holding her hand one last incredulous look and turned to the security jerk. "It's Della Forbes."

She watched as he took a long time writing

it on his stupid list. Who would've thought the Cutwrights would hire security to keep people out of the wedding? They were known as a fine, upstanding family who usually welcomed all the locals to any event at their place. It hadn't occurred to her that she'd need help just to get into the only hotel in town.

She risked another glance at the guy beside her. Brown hair cut military short, gray eyes, and a lazy smile that made her want to smile back. She'd never seen him before in her life. He must have come for the wedding. He took hold of her elbow and gently steered her into the bar.

"Sorry about that. That security guy was way out of line putting his hands on you."

"It was really sweet of you to come to my rescue." She fluttered her eyelashes at him. "I had no idea they'd shut down the whole place just for a wedding."

"Apparently, one of the guests hired his own security." He tipped his Stetson to her. He wore the usual cowboy uniform of cotton shirt, jeans, and cowboy boots, but his accent definitely wasn't from Texas. "I'm Nate Turner. I'm a friend of Brady's from college."

"Della Forbes." She shook his outstretched hand and then hesitated. The security guy was still watching her. "Can I buy you a drink for being such a hero?"

"I just bought a round, so I'd rather get you

one." He picked up a tray of drinks and gestured at the table full of people toward the rear of the bar. "Let me just take these over and then we can get comfortable."

Unwilling to lose his protection while the security guy was still eyeing her, she followed him, staying at his shoulder as he distributed the drinks around the table.

"Hey, Onsk, is that your date? Did you just meet her?"

Fearing discovery, Della froze to the spot. Beside her, Nate looped a casual arm around her shoulders.

"This is Della, everyone. She's with me."

The group all acknowledged her. The man who'd first called out kept talking, his face flushed from too much sun and alcohol too early in the day.

"It's a three-day celebration, Onsky. Have you got a girl lined up for every event?"

"Nope, this is my one and only." Nate smiled down at her. "She's stuck with me for the whole weekend."

"How much did you have to pay her to hang around that long?" Steve demanded and laughed uproariously. The woman sitting next to him elbowed him in the ribs.

"I apologize for my husband. He's an idiot."

Steve belched behind his hand. "No offense to the little lady."

"None taken," Della answered, her smile so sweet he blinked. "Nate doesn't need to pay for dates. He's one of the good guys."

She turned on her heel and Nate followed her.

"Sorry about that," Nate murmured. "Steve was a jackass at college and obviously nothing's changed." He steered her over to the bar. "Now, what can I get you to drink?"

"Just some white wine, please."

He found her a seat and took the one next to it, chatting amiably with the bartender about the upcoming wedding. It gave her the opportunity to study him more carefully. He didn't look like the kind of guy who picked up women in bars and expected them to put out immediately. He looked like a nice, quiet, responsible guy. Did they really exist anymore? After her recent online dating experiences, she'd come to the conclusion most men weren't worth the effort.

"Here you go. Sorry again about Steve." He handed her a glass of white wine and picked up his bottled beer. "Are you meeting someone here?"

"No. I came on my own." She tried to think how to phrase her next comment without actually lying. "I'm visiting family and wanted some space of my own. I thought I could stay here but found out it's booked solid."

"You don't live in town?"

"My sister still lives here with my mother,

but there isn't much room in their house, so I usually stay here."

"Where do you live now?"

"The Bay Area. California."

"Cool. I live way up in northern California myself." He studied her carefully. "How long are you in town?"

"For a couple of weeks. Why?"

"Because I was wondering whether you'd be willing to do me a huge favor?"

She set down the wineglass on the bar with a deliberate thump. Sure, she was desperate to be close to the Cutwright wedding, but how far was she prepared to go to get what she wanted?

"What kind of favor?" she heard herself ask.

He held up his hands. "Not that kind, I promise. It's to do with what happened back there. When I was at college, I had this stupid nickname and—"

"Omsk or something, right?" Della interjected.

"Yeah. Onsk. The One-Night Stand King."

"*You* did?" She studied his friendly face. "Are you sure?"

"Yup. As you might imagine, it causes me some problems these days. I asked a friend of mine to accompany me to the wedding so we could put that nickname to rest."

"And where is she?"

"She bailed on me at the last minute." He grimaced. "Not her fault, but it left me in a tight spot."

She snapped her fingers. "*That's* why the goon let me in the bar because you said I was your date. There were supposed to be two of you at this wedding."

"Got it in one." He hesitated. "The thing is— if you're willing to help me out, you could *pretend* to be my plus one for the entire wedding. You could stay here with me—separate beds, of course—enjoy the weekend, and have a place to stay at no cost to you until we all clear out and the rooms become available again."

Della just stared at him. Was he for real? He was basically offering her 100 percent access to the Cutwright wedding and their guests, which was exactly what she'd been praying for.

"Why would you do that for me?"

"Because I'm sick of that nickname and you need a place to stay."

"You make it sound so simple."

"It is." He shrugged. "We help each other out. I doubt I'll be seeing any of these people except Brady again, so they'll never know that we're not together anymore. What do you say?"

Nate held his breath as she considered him; her dark brown eyes were like melted chocolate and her skin held warm tints of sunshine and olives. Her mouth . . . he had to stop staring at her luscious red lips because the urge to lean in and taste them threatened to overcome him.

He cleared his throat and tried to look as dependable as possible.

She blinked slowly and bit down hard on her lip, making his dress pants tighten in all the wrong places. *This one,* his mind whispered. *This is the one*. He pushed that ridiculous thought away and focused on her.

"You don't know anything about me, Nate. I could be a thief or something."

"I have good instincts." Actually, he didn't care whether she robbed him blind as long as she gave him the opportunity to get to know her over the next three days. "And you don't know much about me either."

"I know you're kind and honorable."

"Because I stopped that security guard from pushing you around? Anyone would've done that."

"No, they wouldn't." She pressed her hand to her spectacular bosom. "I won't steal from you."

"I have nothing for you to steal anyway." *Except my heart, and you can take that anytime you want*. He held out his hand. "Do we have a deal?"

She shook his hand, her grip surprisingly firm and businesslike. He didn't want to let go, but if he held on much longer she was going to think he was some kind of weirdo. He had to rein himself back. He'd achieved his first objective, which was to get her to hang around with him for a few days; now all he had to do was hang in there and convince her never to be apart from him again.

Easy.

Brady came up behind him. "You okay, Nate? I hear Steve was being obnoxious."

"He certainly hasn't changed much." Nate turned to Della. "Darlin', have you met Brady Cutwright?"

Della smiled. "Not for about ten years. He probably won't remember me."

"Sure I do. Your mom lives in town and you have one sister and a couple of nieces." He shook her hand. "How did you meet this old reprobate?"

She glanced up at Nate. "I'm living in San Jose California now—we met there."

"Lucky guy." Brady winked and patted Nate's shoulder. "Enjoy the wedding."

"We'd better go get checked in," Nate murmured. "There's a rehearsal dinner scheduled at six and we have to drive out to the ranch."

"Okay. I left my luggage in the car."

"We'll fetch that first and then go up." He took her hand again, which already seemed the right thing to do.

They'd just reached the exit when there was a commotion ahead. Two large guys in too-tight suits and dark shades were striding out the hotel exit, literally clearing the path ahead of them with a combination of size and the fear of being run down. Nate tensed, his keen gaze searching for the threat.

"Stay put."

He wished he had his uniform on and his gun at his hip. He drew Della against him, his arm protectively around her shoulders. She fitted neatly against his side.

The two men moved toward the one guarding the entrance to the bar, who stood back to let them pass and then fell in behind.

"Travis Whitely," Della whispered. "He looks different, but oh my goodness! He *is* here!"

Nate strained to see what she was talking about and finally noticed the short, skinny guy hiding behind the guards. His hair was bleached almost white, his sunglasses were fancy, and he had a soul patch on his pointed chin.

Nate fought down a chuckle. Brian Dobbs had certainly come a long way. In college his jeans had always fallen low down on his hips, exposing his ratty underwear, his stringy brown hair had needed a good wash, and he'd smelled like a cross between a cow barn and a pot factory.

"Excuse me, sir."

Nate instinctively stepped back, shielding Della as one of the men pushed by him. He glanced at Brian as he passed, but the country-western star was too busy waving at a group of women who were shrieking his new name. A diamond glinted in his ear as he nodded at the crowd.

"Way to make an entrance and make sure everyone notices you," Nate murmured.

"He's a star," Della said. "What do you expect?"

Her tone wasn't exactly rapturous. Nate looked down at her. "You don't like him?"

"I don't know him."

"He's a guest at the wedding, so you might get the chance to get to know him way better than you thought." Nate took one last look around as everything settled down. "Okay, let's go while the coast is clear."

They collected her luggage and walked back into the hotel. It was already hot. Nate wasn't used to the intense heat anymore and was already sweating as he hauled her bags up to the reception desk. His companion looked remarkably cool and composed.

"Hi." He smiled at the receptionist. "We're here for the Cutwright wedding. I'm Nate Turner. I left my bags with the concierge earlier."

Within minutes he and Della were escorted up the stairs to the second floor and let into a corner room, which had a great view over the town. There was only one bed. Nate halted in the doorway.

"Any chance we could get two beds? I'm a terrible sleeper."

The bellboy scratched his head. "I'll ask, but what with the wedding going on and everything, we're full."

"Thanks." Nate tipped the guy and he left, closing the door behind him.

Della stood in front of the four-poster bed, which was draped in filmy netting and bows like in a historical movie.

"It's beautiful." She half-turned toward him. "It's also huge, so if we can't swap rooms, I think we could both sleep in there and never see each other."

Except that Nate feared he would be easing over to her side the moment he got the chance . . .

"Or I can sleep on the floor," Della added.

He held up his hand. "If there's any sleeping on the floor, I'll be doing it."

"It's your room and you're paying for it."

"And you're a lady."

Her smile turned mischievous. "You don't know that."

Unbidden, a thought came into his head of her straddling him and taking away his control—

"You okay?"

"Yeah." He gestured at the bathroom. "Do you want to go first? I need a shower before the rehearsal dinner. I'd forgotten how hot it gets here."

"When were you last in Texas?"

"Graduation. I can't say I've been back since."

"Ah, that's right. You said you met Brady at college."

"Yeah, and the rest of them." He picked at his damp T-shirt, which was sticking to his skin. "I'm practically melting."

"Then go shower. It'll take a while for me to get dressed properly."

He studied her. "You look pretty perfect to me."

"And you're a sweetheart. I'm as sweaty as you are."

He was still smiling as he went into the bathroom. He liked her already. She was unflappable and had a sense of humor. Just his kind of woman.

Della waited until she heard the shower turn on and took out her cell phone, punching in the number with unnecessary force.

"Wade? It's Della. I'm here in Texas and I've seen Travis Whitely. I'll get your pictures, okay?"

"You'd better or I'm going to make sure you lose your job."

She tried desperately to reason with him. "It doesn't have to be like this. We're supposed to be a team."

"Yeah right, says the token pretty girl in the organization. After I'm done spreading the word, everyone will know how you really got your job."

She set her jaw. "I got it by merit."

"That's not how I'm going to sell it to the big man. You know how he hates scandal, and I'm going to dump you in so much shit you'll never survive. A gal with no talent who tries to sleep her way to the top won't last long in our business."

"But that's a total lie! Why are you doing this to me?"

"Because I can, baby. Suck it up, or better still, suck—"

She cut across him. "If I get the pictures and you get the credit, we're even."

"Sure, baby. I've been following Travis for years and something's going on in his life that he's not sharing with his fans. He's been seen in some weird places recently, so he's probably got some hot girl on the side, or else he's messing around with a married woman or he's into drugs and alcohol. I want to know what it is and you've got plenty of contacts in your hometown. Get pictures of him with any female he so much as *looks* at, okay? Or guy. That would be even better . . ."

She listened to his rambling, ignoring his crude innuendoes, and focused on the big picture. She needed to keep her job and he wanted exclusive pictures. No one would get hurt and no one would be able to pin anything on her. For once in her life, surely everything would work out just the way she wanted it to.

Except she'd be losing her self-respect. Maybe she should just quit; tell Wade exactly where he could shove his job. It was awful working for a man who hated her just because she'd refused to sleep with him.

But her family was counting on the financial help she was able to provide thanks to her career. Wade had threatened to bad-mouth her to his whole network of contacts in the Bay Area if she didn't cooperate. If that happened, it would be next to impossible for her to get any job in her field.

The thought of all that uncertainty and upheaval just because he'd hit on *her* made her feel sick. It seemed as if she couldn't win either way.

After concluding the call, she texted her sister, Adrianna.

Am staying up at hotel working. Call me if you need me or there is any change. x.

Will do. Love u sis x

She organized her side of the bed and plugged in her charger. She'd brought her good camera equipment, but she hadn't bargained on bodyguards. If things got hairy or anyone got suspicious, she'd do her best with her cell phone. Everyone would be using theirs so she wouldn't look out of place, and she had a good app that worked wonders with the most basic material. She preferred using a proper camera, though. Just the feel of it in her hands made her more confident and creative.

She could hear Nate Turner whistling as he showered. After a day spent with her stressed-out sister and mother, she appreciated his calm, relaxed way of dealing with things. Whatever he did for a living, his blood pressure must be nice and low. What did people do out in the wilds of Northern California? Hike? He certainly looked fit. She'd have to ask him a few basic questions and maybe answer some if they were to look like an established couple at the wedding.

She unpacked her bags, glad she'd brought some nice resort clothes with her. From what she knew of the Cutwrights, she guessed the wedding would be relatively low-key. She loved dresses and had something totally suitable for the actual event. Opening the closet door, she hung up her clothes and set her shoes on the rack. She spent a few minutes searching for an iron and found it hanging in a bag from the pole.

"Got it!"

"Got what?"

Turning triumphantly around, she was treated to the sight of a practically naked Nate Turner with a towel around his hips. As he rubbed at his wet hair, water rolled down over his excellent abs and muscled chest, making his skin glisten.

Della swallowed back the temptation to stick out her tongue and help him with the cleanup.

Instead she grinned like an idiot. "I found the iron."

"Awesome; my favorite kind of woman." He pretended to duck as she brandished it close to his head. "Just kidding."

"Too bad I hate ironing."

"Yeah?" He took the iron from her. "I love it."

She gaped at him. "You . . . *iron?*"

"Sometimes. I live alone, so someone has to do it. I find it soothing."

"You're still kidding me, right?"

"Nope." He placed the iron on the desk and turned to his suitcases. "Most of my stuff is going to need pressing after the trip from California, and seeing as you hate ironing, I guess I'm going to be busy."

"You could always ask the hotel to do it for you."

"I will if I make a mess of it." He hung a few shirts in the closet, three pairs of pants, and a sports jacket. "I'm planning on buying myself a new Stetson while I'm in cowboy country. Is there a good place to shop around here?"

"There's a great feed and grain store in town that stocks practically everything a cowboy could ever need, but you'd do better going into Austin. I'll take you tomorrow morning if you like."

"Awesome."

Della sat on the bed as he methodically unpacked the rest of his stuff, ironed a shirt, and pressed out the creases in her dress skirt. She supposed she should tell him to put some clothes on, but it was so long since she'd seen such a fine example of a man that she was enjoying the view rather too much. And hey, he was *ironing,* which somehow made it even hotter.

He reached for his cell and texted someone, a small smile hovering around his lips.

"My sister's checking up on me. She still worries about her baby brother."

"Sounds just like mine." Della finally gathered her things together. "I'll get changed. When are we supposed to be there?"

"You've got plenty of time."

She paused at the bathroom door. "For a Californian, you're remarkably laid-back."

"I live in a very small town." He winked. "We do have them out there. The pace is pretty slow. As long as there's some food left at the dinner, I'm good."

She escaped into the bathroom. Seeing as he'd chosen to go to college in Texas, maybe his daytime job had something to do with ranching, livestock, or agriculture, which might account for the laid-back attitude and his fit body. Riding a horse really worked those internal core muscles.

It was a shame he was putting clothes on again. She'd liked the way he hadn't tried to flex his muscles or, even worse, drop his towel to impress her. Mind you, she had been holding an iron in her hand . . .

She jumped into the shower and focused her attention on the evening to come. If she was lucky, Travis Whitely would turn up at the dinner, she'd get the pictures, and that would be that. She'd have the money she needed and no one would be the wiser. Perhaps then she could just enjoy the actual event with Nate Turner; get to know him a little, see if he really was as nice as he seemed.

She stepped out of the shower and toweled herself dry. But would he want to know her if he found out she'd deliberately planned on crashing the wedding just to get those pictures? The thought of disappointing him was surprisingly disturbing, but she had no choice. She had to go through with this. Any chance of a relationship had to take second place to her family's current needs.

Chapter Two

Nate surveyed the crowd gathering in the dining area and gently steered Della away from the group around Steve and his wife. He didn't want her to have to deal with that jackass again. If he were being truthful, he just wanted to talk to her, see if his first impressions were correct. From what he could tell, she was not only beautiful but also smart and funny. He couldn't quite believe his luck.

At the Stoddard dude ranch, a converted barn had been transformed into what his interior-design-obsessed sister would probably call *cowboy country chic*. There were long informal tables where everyone could sit together under wagon-wheel light fixtures and fairy lights wrapped around all the beams. It was a refreshing change from some of the hipster weddings he'd attended in the Bay Area.

Brady had told him that two days earlier they'd been visited by a tornado that had, luckily, not wrecked the chapel, the ranch, or disrupted the wedding preparations. People thought earthquakes were scary, but he'd rather risk the off chance of a shake than the certainty of a tornado season every year.

Della smiled up at him as he returned from the

bar with a glass of wine for her and a beer for himself.

"Thanks, Nate."

"You're welcome."

She wore a silky dress in pink, with white trim and buttons on the bodice, and had a matching flower tucked behind her ear. She looked like one of the retro pinup girl posters his friend Ted Baker collected and used as artwork in his mechanic shop. She wasn't that tall, which suited him fine because he was around six feet, but she obviously liked high heels, which made him very happy.

"Food's good," she remarked as she dabbed at her perfect red lips with her napkin.

"Yeah, it's excellent." He attacked his steak and baked potato like a starving man. "I've never been to a wedding where the beef was stacked right next to the vegan burgers. I guess Brady's bride doesn't eat meat. Seeing as he's a rancher, it must be true love." He drank some beer and his stomach gurgled. "The time difference is really screwing with my appetite."

"Mine too." She touched the wild flowers spilling out of an old cowboy boot that served as a centerpiece. "This décor is really cute."

"Yeah, I kind of like it myself." Nate took a swig of beer. "What do you do in San Jose?"

"I work for a digital arts company, specializing in photographic imagery for the media."

"So basically you take pictures?"

"Kind of, but my job is to take the image and manipulate it into something that can be used on many different digital platforms."

He looked at her. "Like . . . ?"

"Like the difference between how a social media post on your laptop compares to how something might look on your cell phone. They all have different requirements if they're going to look right."

"Ah, I get it now. Being in San Jose, with all those start-ups, I bet you're busy."

"Yeah, sometimes too busy." She sipped her wine. "I love being in the thick of things, but I also wish I could get away from it sometimes."

"There are great places to visit in the Bay Area."

"If you have time and money." She sighed. "Living costs alone eat up more than half my salary, and public transport sucks."

Nate grinned. "You should live out in the sticks. Our town gets one bus a week coming through from Sacramento."

"You're kidding." She put down her glass. "How do you all get around?"

"On horseback or in a truck, mostly."

"But what about folks who don't have those things?"

"There are only a handful." He shrugged. "We take care of them. The Hayes family, who owns the hotel, keeps a list of anyone who needs a ride anywhere and someone always signs up to take them."

She shook her head.

"What?"

"There are still places like that?"

"We just look out for one another, that's all."

"And I suppose there's no crime or anything either?"

"I didn't quite say that." Nate suppressed a chuckle. "We have our fair share, just like any other place. For example, there are always people coming in trying to grow pot. That needs weeding out for sure."

She pulled a face. "You're so funny."

"I try. Can I get you another drink or are you ready for dessert?"

"Definitely dessert." He helped her down off her stool. "I bet we're the only two Californians who still eat dessert."

"Probably." She glanced down at her bosom. "I can't stand all that kale and spinach juice."

"Me neither." He fake shuddered. "In Morgantown we have a bakery and coffee shop run by someone who trained in France. I stop in there at least once a day to get something sweet to eat."

Her gaze drifted over him. "You look pretty fit to me."

He patted his flat stomach. "Thanks."

"Must be all that horseback riding and fresh air. Why did you go to college in Texas?"

"Three reasons. I got an athletic scholarship from UT, I had family out here, and I wanted to get as far away from my parents as possible."

"A typical teenager, then."

"Yup. Not that I ever intended to be any kind of athlete. It just helped with the fees." Nate grinned at Brady and his fiancée, Ellie, as they strolled past them. "I spend more time in my truck these days, although I try to get out to the ranch and ride as often as I can."

"Your parents own a ranch?"

"Nope, but they do live on one. My dad and younger sister work there."

"So your sister's the cowgirl in the family?"

"I think she prefers to be called a cowperson," he said solemnly. "It's more PC."

"You—"

Her gurgle of laughter felt like a punch in the stomach, but in a good way. He couldn't stop staring at her lips. He brought his hand to her cheek and cupped her chin.

"Sorry, couldn't resist it."

Her smile died and her eyes locked on his. For a second he hesitated, the desire to kiss her at war with his fear of rushing her. Even as he made up his mind to go for it, her gaze shifted and moved past him to the doorway. Travis Whitely had arrived with one bodyguard, which he probably thought meant he was being *low-key*. Della might say she wasn't interested in the country-western star, but she sure wasn't ignoring him either.

He took her hand. "Do you want to meet him?"

She looked up at him, her brown eyes huge. "You know him?"

"He went to college with me, Brady, and some of the other guys. He didn't look quite like *that* back in the day, but the girls sure loved him even then." He tugged on her hand. "Come on; let's get our dessert and then we'll see if he remembers me."

Just as Della finished her third and final plate of dessert, the band struck up a tune and Nate drew her into a dance. It soon became obvious both of them had been out of Texas for far too long and had forgotten how to line dance. Not that anyone seemed to mind their lack of coordination and inability to turn the right way at any given moment.

Eventually, when he finished laughing, Nate took her hand and stepped back to the edge of the dance floor.

"Let's just watch and learn, shall we?" he suggested.

Della leaned back against him, enjoying the rare sense of being protected and appreciated. She'd always been the strong one in her family—

the one everyone else depended on to make things right—and nothing had changed. In fact, her mother and sister needed her more than ever right now. She just couldn't let Wade destroy her career when her whole family counted so much on her income.

Having been welcomed so warmly by the Cutwrights and given access to the reclusive star made her feel like a traitor; like she didn't deserve to be standing by Nate's side. Would he ever understand what drove her? He obviously loved his family, but would he be willing to compromise his beliefs to get what he wanted?

"Hey, you okay?"

She looked up into his concerned face and found a smile from somewhere.

"I'm good, thanks. How about you?"

As he smiled, his gray eyes narrowed and focused even more intently on her. "I'm also good. Are you ready to try dancing again?"

Even as she hesitated, he took her in his arms and eased her into the slow rhythm of a country ballad.

"We can do this. Just hang on to me."

The temptation to rest her cheek against the soft cotton of his shirt overwhelmed her. For a few precious moments she allowed herself to forget she wasn't as sweet and innocent as he thought she was and just enjoyed the sensation of being held like a precious object.

"Della . . ."

She took in the scent of his aftershave, the manly warmth of his body, and opened her eyes.

"Yes?"

"May I kiss you?"

In reply, she stood on her tiptoes and lightly brushed her mouth against his, making him inhale sharply and wrap his arm tighter around her hips. He made a soft groaning sound as he lifted his head.

"Way too nice," Nate murmured.

She grinned at him. "I hardly touched you."

"I know."

The song ended and he released his grip on her with obvious reluctance.

"Maybe we can try to do better next time," Della whispered. When was the last time she'd flirted with a man? When had she even wanted to? Nate Turner was making her break all her own rules.

"There'll be a next time?" He raised an eyebrow. "Now you're just playing with me."

"We are sharing a bed, you know."

"And I promised to keep my hands to myself."

She patted his sleeve. "I didn't."

With a laugh, he followed her off the dance floor. "You're going to kill me, you know that?"

"But at least you'll die happy." Della grabbed his hand. "Come on; let's get some coffee."

• • •

Later, as if in a daze, Della allowed herself to be brought closer and closer into Travis Whitley's orbit. There were a few people attempting to chat with him, but Nate seemed determined to stick around until he got the chance to renew his acquaintance with his old college friend. Della surreptitiously removed her cell phone from her purse and clutched it in her hand. Maybe if she were lucky, she could get a couple of really close-up pictures of the reclusive star and be done with it.

"Hey, are you Nate Turner?"

"Yeah. How are you doing, Bri, I mean, um, Travis?" Nate grinned at the star.

Della fixed a smile on her face as Nate drew her closer before reaching out to shake Travis's hand.

"This is Della. I think she's a big fan of yours."

Della was treated to Travis's famous panty-melting grin. "Nice to meet you, Della." He gestured at the empty seats around him. "Would you two like to keep me company for a while?"

Nate glanced down at Della, his eyebrows raised, and she nodded.

"That would be awesome," Nate answered for both of them. Travis was probably used to fans going gaga around him, so her lack of the ability to speak didn't seem to be a problem.

Nate's mouth brushed her ear as he whispered,

"We don't have to stay long if you have other things you'd rather do, okay?"

She wished she could just ask Travis if she could take his picture, but Nate's knowing him personally somehow made that more difficult, even more crass than she'd anticipated. Maybe after a while she could use the restroom and sneak a picture on the way back.

"What are you doing with yourself these days, Nate?"

Travis swirled the ice in his water; the way his cheeks hollowed with every suck on his straw made him look even more angelic than usual. He'd dyed his hair blond, probably in an attempt to look different, and abandoned his trademark cowboy hat, but he was instantly recognizable to anyone who bothered to look twice. Della's fingers itched to get that picture, but she put her phone away and accepted a glass of water from one of the bodyguards.

"I went home to California," Nate said. "And tried my hand as a cowboy. It didn't suit me, so I went back to school and eventually joined the sheriff's department."

Della double gulped her drink and ice water threatened to spill out of her nose. Nate was a *cop?* Was this how it felt to be some creep with a telephoto lens? Oh dear Lord, what was she supposed to do now?

Travis nodded. "I can kind of see you in law

enforcement. You were always something of a Dudley Do-Right."

"True." Nate chuckled and then turned to her. "You okay, Della?"

He patted her gently between the shoulder blades and she shot to her feet, spilling even more water over herself. Great, now everyone was staring at her as if she were nuts.

"I just need to use the restroom. I'll be back in a sec."

Smiling brightly at no one in particular, she made a run for the bathroom, only slowing to a more respectable pace when she was away from Nate's piercing gaze.

For once the restroom was empty. She took a few deep breaths, used the facilities, and then sat in front of one of the well-lit mirrors in the powder room. Part of her wanted to run all the way back to California, but Nate knew where she lived and he was a cop, so he would have no trouble finding her if he wanted to.

"Get real, girl," she muttered. "You're not that hot. This isn't a cop show."

And why would he bother? She was getting so ahead of herself. It wasn't like she'd done anything *illegal*. Or had she? Was being a paparazzi creeper at a wedding allowed? Were there privacy laws against that in Texas? She was so out of her element. Her boss wouldn't care either way, but she did. She hadn't seen the wedding invitation. Would the Cutwrights have insisted on no outside photography because they knew Travis was going to be there?

Della slowly exhaled. She'd just slightly bent the truth as to why she wanted to be at the hotel. She straightened her spine. All she had to do was play nice for a few days, not make Nate suspicious, get her pictures of Travis, and leave. But Nate was a cop, trained to notice things like her taking a million pictures of everything—especially Travis Whitley.

She groaned and buried her face in her hands. Why did her plan feel like such a betrayal? Nate was a nice guy, but she'd just met him, and in her experience four hours of enjoying a guy's company didn't make a relationship. But the potential was there . . . she could *sense* it.

She slowly raised her head and stared at her startled image in the mirror. Where the heck had that come from? He hadn't come on to her in any way. In fact, he'd been totally respectful toward her—apart from that certain look in his eyes that said he *knew* her, got her, wanted to know more . . . and that almost kiss.

She drew in another shaky breath. Family had to come first. They were counting on her more than ever now. She couldn't walk away from her career and she knew Wade would make good on his threats to ruin her professional reputation if she didn't go along with his scheme. She would get her first shots of Travis on the way back from the ladies' room. And if she had to give up the chance to get to know Nate Turner better, so be it.

Nate kept a lookout for Della's return even as he listened to Travis going on about his mansions and cars and his fulfilling life as a much-loved star. Nate couldn't imagine a less-fulfilling life if he tried, but then, Travis probably thought Nate was the most boring man in the world—living in his hometown, earning a pittance, and working odd shifts. They were like two different species.

"You should bring Della and come visit," Travis concluded in his soft drawl.

"That's really kind of you," Nate replied. "Where are you based now?"

"Nashville."

"Makes sense." Nate saw a flash of pink as Della emerged from the restroom. He tried to catch her eye. "I've never been there myself."

To his relief, she came right over to him and, with an apologetic smile, sat down. He immediately reached for her hand.

"Everything okay?"

"Just a bit of water damage to repair. I think I wedged an ice cube up my nose." Her smile was a little too bright for his liking, but that might just be because she'd been embarrassed.

"Travis was suggesting we come visit him in Nashville."

She looked startled. "At his home?"

Nate grinned. "Yeah. I've never been to Nashville before, have you?"

"Yes," Della answered. "It's beautiful."

"It sure is," Travis confirmed. "If you've never visited, Nate, there's even more reason to come." Travis's confident smile slipped a little. "I have an estate out there that's well-guarded and relatively fan proof."

"Relatively?" The cop in Nate had to ask the question.

Travis grimaced. "You'd be amazed at the lengths some people will go to just to see little ol' me."

"I bet that's quite scary." Della's brown eyes were full of sympathy.

"Yeah. Nothing like waking up in the morning and finding some strange woman sitting on the side of your bed watching you sleep."

Della shivered, and Nate put a protective arm around her. "Maybe you need better security."

"As I said, I've already got the best, and we've added twenty-four-hour cameras." Travis sighed. "It's all part of being famous these days. You can't do anything without being spied on, commented about, or criticized. Which is why it's so nice to be here with family and no press." He forced a smile. "But, hey, it's still a great life and I wouldn't change it for the world. What do you do, Della?"

She fidgeted with her purse. "I work in digital media at the Cassidy Corporation."

"Interesting." Travis looked at Nate. "Beautiful and smart. You're a lucky man."

"Tell me about it," Nate murmured, kissing the top of Della's head. "She's a keeper."

Travis grinned, making him look more like the boy Nate had known at college. "Let me know when you tie the knot and I'll come and sing at your wedding. For free."

Nate winked at him. "I'll hold you to that." He glanced around and realized there were several other people hovering around, hoping for the chance to speak with the star. "We'd better give you some space. Great to see you again, Travis, and congratulations on your success."

Della rose with him and smiled at Travis. "It was a pleasure."

Travis blew her a kiss. "The pleasure was all mine. If you weren't hanging out with one of the nicest guys I've ever met, I'd be asking for your number myself."

Della brought her hand to her cheek, and Nate laughed and hugged her hard. "*So* not happening."

He was still grinning as he walked her toward the bar.

"Would you like another drink, Della?"

"Yes, please. Something strong." She flapped her hand in front of her face. "I'm way too hot."

"I hear Travis Whitley has that effect on a lot of women."

"He's not really my type." She found an empty table and sat down. "His life sounded quite sad, actually. Imagine being stuck behind high fences, unable to go out when you feel like it."

"Imagine all those fans screaming your name and all those millions of dollars," Nate countered.

She considered him, her head tilted to one side like an inquisitive bird. "But it's almost as if the more famous he is, the smaller his personal space and ability to live like a normal person become." She sighed. "I actually felt sorry for him."

"So did I." Nate took hold of her hand. "I'm glad I'm not him—even though he probably thinks my life is as boring as it gets."

She studied their joined hands. "Are you really a cop?"

"Technically, I'm a deputy sheriff, but seeing as I'm the entire force of the law in Morgantown, California, I often get mistaken for a cop." He hesitated. "Do you have a problem with that?"

"Um, no, why should I?" Her voice was a little high and breathy.

He tried to make a joke of it. "Not planning a bank heist or anything, are you?"

"No." She wouldn't quite look at him, and every cop instinct he possessed screamed at him to sit up and take notice.

"Or do you just not like cops? I know a lot of people have issues with us."

"I'm perfectly fine with officers of the law." She eased her hand free from his. "The bar looks clear now—shall I go get some drinks?"

He watched her make her way to the bar, his smile dimming as he considered the not-so-good vibe he was getting from her. Did she just *not like cops* but was too polite to say so, or was something else going on? Nate finished his beer. Now his instincts were at war. His heart was insisting Della was *The One* and his head was worried she was up to something.

There was a sudden commotion over by the entrance as Meg Stoddard, Brady's best woman, came into the barn accompanied by a guy who looked way too familiar. Nate narrowed his eyes as he considered the man's perfect features and look-at-me smile. He'd definitely seen him on TV. From the expression on Meg's face, she wasn't enjoying the moment half as much as her companion was.

Della came back holding two beers. "What's up?"

"Look who's here." Nate pointed at the man

who'd taken a seat at the top table between Meg and the bride's man of honor.

"That's Grant Portman. He's on CNN."

Nate snapped his fingers. "I knew I'd seen him somewhere. I wonder what he's doing here? I don't think Brady mentioned he was coming."

Della laughed. "Who next? The Pope?" She gave Nate his beer. "This wedding is getting more exciting by the minute."

Chapter Three

Della woke up and slowly opened her eyes to find herself snuggled up against Nate's back. Her arm was around his waist and she was basically spooning him. So much for staying on her own side of the bed. When they'd returned to the hotel, she'd pretended she was supertired and he hadn't pressed her for anything. She'd been torn between disappointment and relief that he hadn't asked for more because part of her knew that if he did kiss her again, she wouldn't hesitate to kiss him back.

Not that she hadn't lain awake for at least an hour *imagining* that kiss . . .

She sighed and contemplated the creases in his white T-shirt. It was three o'clock in the morning. From what she could tell, he was sound asleep, so she could probably just ease backward and he'd never know she'd been wrapped around him like a limpet.

The trouble was, he smelled so good that she didn't want to move. And being this close to him felt right even though he was a cop who could bust her ass in a heartbeat. She was exaggerating, but her guilt wouldn't leave her alone.

"You okay?"

She jumped at his quiet question.

"Yup. I was just wondering how I ended up wrapped around you and how to extricate myself."

He chuckled, the sound low in his throat. "Stay put if you like. I'm not complaining. It's been a while since I've snuggled up to anything except my dog, Birdy."

"Your dog sleeps on your bed?"

"Hard to keep him off when he weighs over a hundred pounds and thinks he's still a puppy."

Della smiled against his back as the air-conditioning whirred and the faint sounds of night creatures permeated the thick glass of the balcony door.

"You don't date much, then?"

"Nope. Too busy. I cover Morgantown and a lot of the county around it, so I'm always on the move. I share the job with another deputy in Bridgeport, but because I live on-site and everyone knows me, I kind of get all the calls regardless of whether I'm on duty or not."

"That must be tough." Della *really* didn't want to get into a conversation about what he did. "I'm in the same boat—too busy to seriously date anyone."

He eased onto his back and she stayed on her side. It was dark enough that she couldn't see his face clearly, which was kind of comforting. He slid one hand behind his neck and the other arm around her shoulders, drawing her close.

"Is that okay?"

"I'll let you know if I get a crick in my neck." Della resisted the temptation to climb all over him but allowed her free hand to skim over his chest.

"Did you have a good time at the dinner?" Nate asked, his fingers rubbing small circles on her shoulder.

"Yes, thank you. I can't believe I met Travis Whitley *and* saw that pompous reporter guy trying to make the wedding all about him. I don't think Meg was happy about him being there."

"Yeah, dinner and a show. Way more exciting out here than in California."

"Do you really think Travis meant his invitation for us to visit him in Nashville?"

He sighed. "Probably not. From what he told me when you were in the bathroom, he's basically never there. Not a life I'd want, although he did make me feel like a boring homebody who's never done anything."

"Hey, you went to college in Texas. That was brave."

"And you moved all the way to California."

It was Della's turn to sigh. "I just wanted to get away. It was kind of selfish. My mom still hasn't forgiven me."

"Sometimes we have to do stuff to become the person we're meant to be, and sometimes it's hard to do that when you're stuck in a place where everyone thinks they know you." He hesitated. "My dad had this dream of owning his own ranch and expected me to come back from college with all the most up-to-date information to make it happen. But I soon realized I didn't want to be a rancher. Telling him that, and watching the dream fade from his eyes as he struggled to accept my choices, was one of the lowest points in my life."

Now she wanted to hold him and make everything better . . . she was *so* screwed.

"My mom wanted me to settle down, get married, and have babies like my sister did."

"Your mom sounds a lot like mine. She and my dad have the best marriage ever, but it's not easy to find the right person and I refuse to settle."

She patted his chest. "Why should you? You're young, good-looking, and have a steady job. I bet women swarm all over you every time you leave the house."

"Thanks for the encouragement, but the only woman I've met recently who I'd *like* to get to know seems to have a problem with cops."

Della stayed quiet for at least a minute before daring to reply. "Are you talking about me?"

"You're the only woman I'm currently sharing a bed with."

"But that was just for our mutual convenience."

He dropped a kiss on the top of her head. "It's okay, Della. I'm sticking to our agreement.

I'm not suddenly going to pounce on you."

Not being able to see his face clearly gave her a courage she normally lacked. "Not even if I was okay with it?"

He tilted his head up toward the ceiling as if seeking divine inspiration. "I'd still feel like I was taking advantage of you."

"But aren't you the one-night stand king?"

He groaned. "One date. Not one sleepover."

"So you've never had sex?"

"I didn't quite say that, but I certainly haven't racked up high numbers."

Della tried not to smile at his indignant tone. "Like, how high?"

Suddenly he shifted his weight, picked her up, and dumped her on his lap on top of the covers. Now she had to look at him and was relieved to see he was grinning at her.

"Two?" Nate said.

She held out her hand, palm up. "Snap."

He raised his eyebrows. "Man, those guys in San Jose must be slow and blind."

"Or I'm like you and just have high standards."

"I wouldn't have expected anything less." He cleared his throat. "I really want to kiss you."

Leaning in, she brushed her lips against his. "Then do it."

Nate took full advantage of her permission, coaxing her into opening her mouth and settling in for a slow exploration that made her grab hold of his shoulder and thread her fingers through his hair.

Yeah . . .

The One.

This was definitely the best kiss ever.

She shifted even closer, the tips of her breasts brushing up against his T-shirt, making him shudder with the need to uncover more, to claim more, to *take*. His fingers slid up her spine beneath her shirt to touch bare skin. He rocked his hips, drawing her even tighter against him, his palm pressed to her lower back.

It was way outside his normal experience, and some grain of sense, some hard-won caution from years of police work made him reluctantly ease back. She didn't like cops. She was hiding something from him.

Even as he thought that, he imagined his father's horrified expression—that a Turner would put anything ahead of discovering and keeping *The One* woman for him. But his cautious nature had saved his life more than once, and he had to be certain.

"Nate?"

He gathered his scattered senses and met her gaze head-on. "I'm sorry. That kiss went way too far."

She blinked at him. "For you or for me?"

"Probably for both of us."

He still couldn't quite bear to release her, but she settled that problem by moving off his lap, making him wince as her knee connected with his groin. Resisting the urge to whimper or drag her back and settle some things, he took an unsteady breath.

"Della, we just met and—"

She folded her arms over her luscious breasts. "So you think I'm being too forward?"

"No!" Now she looked hurt and he wanted to slap himself silly. "I think we should slow down, get to know each other over the next couple of days, and take it from there."

"Fine."

He wasn't dumb. He knew that when a woman said *fine,* things rarely were. "I like you a lot."

"So you keep saying." She studied him for a long moment and then released a slow breath. "But you're right. Give me two days."

"To do what?"

Guilt flashed in her eyes and he tensed. "To get to know you, of course. What else?" She crawled back over to her side of the bed. " 'Night, Nate."

He lay back down on his side and stared into the darkness. Why did he still have a sense that she was up to something? And if she was—what the heck was he going to do about it?

After a decent breakfast at the hotel and with several hours to spare before the actual wedding,

Della checked her cell for messages and then turned to Nate, who sat beside her in the booth.

"Do you still want to go look for a new hat?"

He put down his coffee cup and smoothed a hand over his unshaven chin. To her secret relief, he'd been his usual charming self all morning, hadn't once referred to their smoldering kiss of the night before.

"Yeah. I want to look good at the wedding. Do you know a place?"

"As I said, this is Texas, land of the cowboy hat. We could try Cavender's, for a start." She hesitated, unsure of how he felt about hanging out with her. "I can drive you there or give you directions."

He reached for her hand. "I'd love for you to come with me. Perhaps we can work on your aversion to cops on the way."

"What aversion?"

He didn't reply, turning his attention to signing the check.

Della touched his shoulder. "Let me know how much I owe you for the food and the room, okay?"

He looked up. "Hey, you're the one doing me a favor. I don't expect you to pay for anything."

"I'd like to pay." Then maybe she wouldn't feel so guilty. "If you hadn't offered to share your space, I would've slept in my car for three days."

"I've got this. You can pay for lunch, okay?"

He slid the signed receipt under his coffee cup and stood up, stretching the kinks out of his spine and making her all too aware of his lean, muscular physique.

"I probably need to shave."

She couldn't resist cupping his chin. "I kind of like it. You look like an old-time sheriff now."

"You like that idea?" His smile flashed. "You should come to our Historic Morgantown Day, when we all dress up like our forebears and parade around town."

"I think I'd enjoy seeing you swaggering around with your gun belt hanging low and your battered gold star on your leather vest. Do you have a mustache as well?"

"Nope, that's reserved for the villain—usually played by one of the Morgan brothers, the wildest guys in town." He took her hand again. "You really should come. I'd love to see you again."

Della thought about that as they walked back up to the room to retrieve their stuff. If she could get the pictures of Travis without anyone noticing, turn them over to Wade, and move on, why shouldn't she go see Nate Turner in his natural element, chasing down the bad guys? The idea appealed to her more strongly than she'd anticipated. Maybe it was fate.

Her sense of anticipation faded. What if the situation at home got even worse than it was now and she *had* to come back for good? Her mom had already made some pointed comments about her lack of loyalty to her sister. But if she didn't earn money, she wouldn't be able to send so much of it home to *support* her family. Unfortunately, her little niece Perry needed every penny she sent home more than ever now. And what about her sister's rat of a husband, who'd disappeared the moment things got difficult? No one seemed to be chasing after him. Just because she was the older sibling, was she doomed to be responsible for everyone forever?

Even thinking like that made her feel ashamed. They needed her. She hated what she had to do and already knew that all the money in the world might not fix her family's problems. But she had to try.

By the time Nate had acquired two new hats and a pair of boots, Della had to rush back to the hotel to get ready for the wedding at three. He was no closer to discovering what in particular she didn't like about his profession and even more certain that despite everything, she was the closest to *The One* he'd ever met or was likely to meet again. His romantic self remained at war with his cop self, his certainty that she was a good person at odds with his sense of something not sitting quite right.

It was both magical and infuriating.

He knew his dad and younger brother would be yelling at him to just tell her how he felt and take it from there, but he couldn't do it. He checked his cell. There was nothing from his sister or the rest of his community, which made a nice change. He loved them all dearly, but sometimes he yearned for some space.

Moving Della's discarded T-shirt to one side, he noticed she'd been doodling on the hotel notepaper by the phone. Well, not really doodling but writing Travis's name and underlining it about fifty times with a ton of question marks. Nate frowned. For someone who claimed not to like the man, she sure spent a lot of time thinking about him. At least she hadn't written Della Whitley in a heart . . .

He buttoned the pearl snaps on his newly ironed blue shirt and put on his best jeans. His grandfather's cuff links made from Morgansville gold and his father's rodeo buckle on his belt added a familiar touch to his new clothes. He'd thought about wearing his fancy new Lucchese boots but figured with all the standing and sitting at the wedding he'd do better to rely on his now second-best pair.

Checking his watch, he knocked on the bathroom door. "You doing okay in there, Della?"

"I'm just coming out now."

The door opened and she emerged in a rush of warm air and a subtle flowery fragrance. He barely managed to keep his mouth closed as he stared at her, doubts forgotten. She wore a red dress with white roses on the skirt and real roses in her hair, which was gathered up into a fancy topknot on her head. A couple of curls brushed her cheeks when she moved. She looked good enough to eat. His gaze dropped to her impossibly high-heeled shoes and he growled deep in his throat.

She blinked at him. "Do I look okay?"

She sounded anxious, her hands smoothing her skirt, which covered a net petticoat that made her dress kick out even more.

He took her hand and kissed it. "You look beautiful. Like a summer rose garden."

"You look pretty good yourself." Her appreciative gaze swept over him. "Are you going to wear your new hat?"

"Damn straight I am." He reverently lifted it from its box and set it on his head.

Della sighed and clasped her hands to her chest. "Oh my. You look like you stepped off the cover of a romance novel."

Nate snorted. "I've seen those books. My sister loves them, but for some reason those guys never keep their shirts on."

She gathered her wrap, large purse, and sunglasses as he located his sports jacket. Since the tornado had blown through, the good weather was supposed to hold up, but you never knew in

Texas. He opened the door with a flourish and bowed her through it.

"Ma'am."

The glance she gave him over her shoulder as she sashayed past made him feel hot and cold all over. Maybe his dad was right and he should just blurt it out—tell her that she was *The One* . . .

Even as he formed the thought, she was walking away from him, her gaze fixed on her cell phone. Nate let out his breath. They had all afternoon to spend together at a wedding; there was plenty of time to declare himself, if that's what he decided to do.

Della sighed with pleasure as they were escorted into the tiny wedding chapel at the Hawk Creek Ranch. Nate had told her it no longer served a real congregation but was available for special weddings. Meg Stoddard, whom she'd gone to school with, was Brady Cutwright's best woman and the Stoddard family owned the land, making it the perfect place for the celebration.

A long white carpet had been laid from the back of the chapel to the front and a country band off to one side played something soothing. There was no sign of Travis Whitley yet. Nate carefully took off his hat and placed it on the bench behind him as Brady and Meg walked up the aisle to await the bride.

Nate leaned down to whisper in her ear, "Brady looks calm enough."

"Did you think he'd bolt like a wild horse?"

"Nope. He loves that woman. I could see it in his eyes."

Della wondered what it would feel like to be loved that way—to have a man who put you first, loved you to distraction, and respected the heck out of you. Maybe a man like Nate Turner.

The music changed and the packed congregation stood as the bride, accompanied by her man of honor, Air Force Major Shane Freemont in full-dress uniform, walked down the aisle. Ellie wore a white chiffon dress with cowboy boots and a hat with a veil that made Della smile. The expression on Ellie's face as she reached Brady brought a lump to Della's throat and she fumbled for her handkerchief.

Nate took her hand and gave her his handkerchief. "You're a crier? I should have guessed."

She dabbed at the corner of her eyes with the starched cotton. "Don't say anything. You'll just make me worse. I have to get through this."

He chuckled and brought her hand to his mouth for a kiss. "You'll be fine. Concentrate."

It was hard to concentrate with him standing beside her, holding her hand and rubbing little circles on her skin. She turned her attention to the vows being exchanged by the couple and almost lost it again. *This* was what love meant. This was what she wanted.

It didn't take long for the service to end, and the happy couple progressed down the aisle grinning from ear to ear. Everyone followed them out for the pictures, which seemed to take forever. Still feeling guilty about gatecrashing the wedding, Della tried to avoid being in the group pictures, but Nate kept a firm hold of her hand and coaxed her into joining him. The only other person who was as reluctant to be photographed as she was Travis, which made her feel terrible about surreptitiously snapping pictures of him every chance she got.

Just as they'd left the hotel, Wade had sent her a text saying he could get double the money if she scored a photo of Travis drunk or misbehaving, which had made her feel physically sick.

The wedding reception was being held in the same converted barn as the rehearsal dinner except there were twice as many people, which made the place much louder. She spied Travis sitting in the quietest corner of the room, his hat low down, shielding his face. She almost wished he hadn't come so she could just tell her stinking boss what to do with his assignment and his threats—except she couldn't do that with her sister depending on her.

Nate went off to congratulate the groom,

leaving Della free to ease toward Travis, her cell phone at the ready. She'd taken a million pictures of him already, but none of them were great. If he would just look up, she could get some decent shots of his face and hope they would be good enough for Wade. Travis certainly hadn't brought a woman with him, gotten drunk, or misbehaved. Hopefully when she gave Wade the pictures, he'd stop threatening her and then not use them after all.

She had time to take a few shots before realizing the light probably wasn't good enough. If she came in from the other side, she could use her proper camera . . .

"You okay?"

She jumped as Nate came up behind her, two glasses of champagne in his hands.

"Yes. I was just thinking about taking some pictures." She patted her purse. "I brought my digital camera with me just in case. It's so beautiful in this part of Texas."

He handed her the glass of champagne, his gaze sweeping the area and the distinct lack of wedding guests.

"I bet Ellie and Brady would love more pictures to choose from. Brides and grooms can't seem to get enough of them these days. The last wedding I went to they even had those disposable digital cameras on each guest's plate."

She sipped at her champagne, her throat

suddenly dry. "Did you work out where we're sitting?"

He nodded to where Travis was already seated. "Over there, at the back with a group of Brady's old college friends, including the obnoxious Steve, I'm afraid."

"We'll just ignore him and talk to Travis." Della pocketed her phone and took Nate's arm. "We might as well go sit down. I think Meg's about to call us all to order anyway."

The food was good, but Nate hardly tasted it. He wasn't stupid and by his count, the only pictures Della had been taking for the past two days were of Travis. Sure, she was trying to be subtle about it, but he wasn't fooled. But why was she so interested in the country-western star? She'd insisted he wasn't her type, so why all the pictures?

When she left the table to powder her nose, she left her phone behind but took her purse. She was away long enough for Nate to start to get worried, but just then Travis spoke up.

"Nate, have you ever thought about going into private security?"

"In what way?"

Travis smiled. "As in head of my security team. I bet I could pay you a lot more than you're making now."

"I bet you could, but I love my job, and you

335

probably need someone with way more experience than me."

"True, but he still wouldn't be a friend. This is the first time I've been out of my house without being pursued for almost a year. It's awesome." A muscle twitched in Travis's cheek. "I've had security teams that have taken payment to let women into my house, called select paparazzi when I'm at the *dentist,* and generally screwed with my life."

"I wouldn't do that."

"Hell, I know. That's why I'm asking you." Travis hesitated, leaning in closer. "It's crushing me, this business. It's taken away all the joy I had from performing, and made me a prisoner in my own house."

"I'm sorry that's happening to you, but I still don't want the job."

"I'll pay you half a million bucks a year."

For a second Nate forgot how to breathe. "You're kidding, right?"

Travis winked as he stood up. "Nope. Think about it, okay?"

Holy cow . . . Nate stared down at his cell, his fingers sliding across the screen even as he realized he still held Della's phone and that he was flipping through endless pictures of a totally unaware Travis Whitley. *Hundreds* of pictures . . .

He put the cell in his pocket and headed out to

find Della, his good mood rapidly deteriorating as he found her snapping away at the interior of the barn with her digital camera.

Her warm smile stopped him in his tracks.

"I'm sorry, Nate. I got distracted. Were you worried about me?"

He tried to compare her apparently genuine pleasure at seeing him with what he'd seen on her phone. When he didn't reply, she put her camera away, her smile disappearing.

"Are you okay?"

He held out her cell. "You left this on the table."

"Oh, thanks, I meant to put it in my purse and forgot." She held out her hand but he didn't turn it over. "What's up?"

"Why all the pictures of Travis?"

She went still, the color rushing into her cheeks. "What?"

"I didn't mean to pry, but you must have taken hundreds of snaps of him and only one of the bride and groom."

She snatched the phone from his grasp. "Why wouldn't I want to take his picture? He's famous."

"And he asked to be left alone at this private, family wedding." He considered her carefully. "What's going on, Della?"

Her chin came up and she looked him right in the eye. "Maybe I'm just a . . . a little obsessed with him, *okay?*"

"Like you're a professional *stalker?*" He thought of the way she'd written Travis's name again and again on the notepad and her initial reluctance to meet the star. Nothing added up and he hated that.

"Yeah, why not? Everyone needs a hobby." She waved her arms around. "I can't help myself. He just does something to me that makes me want to hang around him all the time, read every scrap of information I can find about him on the internet, and one day, if God is willing, *marry* the man!"

Nate let out a slow breath. She was either being sarcastic or was totally off-the-charts nuts. "Is that why you agreed to spend time with me? Just to get close to *Travis?*"

"Yes! No! That's—" She bit down hard on her lip. "Dammit! Why did you have to put it like that?"

"Because I thought you liked *me.* I thought—" He shoved a hand into his pocket and took a step back, his heart banging in his chest. "But it's all good. Maybe if you ask him nicely, Travis will give you his room number and you won't have to waste your time shacking up with me. Hey, maybe I'll go ask him for you. How's that sound?"

He turned his back on her.

"Nate, I don't want to spend time with Travis. I—"

But he was beyond listening. Sometimes it really paid to ignore his softer side and focus on the reality of a situation. At least he'd learned to do that. The fact that it still hurt made no difference. He'd survive. He'd toughen up until one day the stupid Turner tradition that there was a perfect woman out there just waiting for him would die a natural death and he'd move on. Willing himself not to weaken, he headed for the bar and ordered a beer. The wedding went on around him, but he pretended not to care.

Chapter Four

The ride back to the hotel was made in complete silence. Della tried twice to talk to Nate, but he was having none of it. She might as well have been some kind of suspect he'd picked up in his patrol car. And heck, she felt like one. After a few minutes she subsided into a miserable guilty stillness as tears threatened to overwhelm her. She'd hurt him. She'd seen it in his eyes before he'd walked away from her.

She briefly closed her eyes as the glare of another car's headlights passed them on the other side of the road. Why had she panicked and said all that stupid stuff? Why hadn't she told Nate the truth? Why had she agreed that she was a *stalker* of all things? But she knew why. Better he thought she was a weirdo than a temporary member of the paparazzi intruding on Travis Whitley's personal space.

He held open the door into the hotel and walked her up to the room, key card in hand. She immediately made a dash for the bathroom, hoping a few moments alone might inspire her about how to talk to him, how to take that stubborn look off his face . . . but nothing occurred to her and she reluctantly walked back into the bedroom, only to find him packing his things.

"What are you doing?" Della croaked.

He spared her only a brief glance. "Giving you some space. Don't worry; the room's paid for until tomorrow."

"But where are you going to sleep?"

"I've got somewhere to go."

A tear trickled down her cheek and then another one. "Please don't do this. If anyone should leave, it should be me."

He carried on stuffing his belongings into his case as if he hadn't heard her.

"*Please,* Nate. It's not what you think—"

"Don't say that." He slammed the case shut and zipped it up. "I'm a cop. I've heard every excuse in the book and I really don't want to hear them from you."

"That's not fair," she whispered.

"Life's not fair." He swallowed hard. "Good luck with Travis and it was nice knowing you."

The next minute he was leaving, closing the door with a definite click behind him.

Della started to shake and then her knees gave way and she sank to the floor and just let it all out. Nate was the best thing that had happened to her in years and she couldn't have him because her life was a tangled mess of lies and obligations and . . .

"It's not fair!" she repeated as she hugged her knees and rocked back and forth.

Nate halted in the hotel lobby and took another deep breath. She'd been crying when he'd left and now he felt like a complete heel. But what was the point of staying? He'd dealt with a few stalkers in his day job. If she were obsessed with Travis, she'd *never* have time for him. He might as well accept that his Turner intuition was wrong, wish her well, and move on.

Except that he didn't want to. Except that he felt like his heart was being ripped in two . . .

"Hey, Nate."

He looked past the reception desk into the dark recesses of the small bar and saw Travis sitting in one of the booths.

"Hey." Grabbing his case, he walked toward his old friend.

"Trouble in paradise?" Travis pointed at his luggage.

"You could say that." Nate slid into the seat opposite. "Can I still get a drink around here?"

"Sure you can; I'm Travis Whitley. Everything stays open for me." Travis clicked his fingers and one of his bodyguards appeared. "Dec, get Mr. Turner whatever he needs from the bar."

"A beer will do fine."

"Yes, sir."

Nate took off his hat and ran his fingers through his flattened hair. "Thanks, Travis."

"You're welcome." When his drink arrived, Travis clinked glasses with him. "It was a great wedding, wasn't it?"

"Yeah. Although I never thought I'd see Brady Cutwright marrying a vegan."

"But he loves her. You can see it." Travis sipped his drink. "She's the perfect woman for him."

"Yeah."

"So, what's up between you and the darling Miss Della?"

"You don't want to know."

"Hell, I'm *dying* to know what made you abandon ship at midnight. You two seemed *right* together somehow."

"That's what I thought."

"And she didn't?"

"She's obsessed with someone else."

Travis shook his head. "Wow; women . . ." He hesitated. "Can't you talk her out of it?"

"I didn't even try."

"Why not?"

"Because . . ." Nate paused as the beer soured in his stomach. "I don't know why. There I was, thinking we had a future together, and then I found out she was just using me to get to someone else."

"That sucks."

Nate abandoned his beer. "Yeah."

Della spent a long while taking off her makeup and changing into her pajamas, but nothing could stop her constantly rerunning that last awful conversation with Nate in her head. Where was he now? The town was still full of wedding guests, so where was he going to sleep? She didn't want him out there alone, but if she went looking for him, she'd have to tell him the truth, and then she'd have to watch him walk away from her all over again.

She grabbed her cell and skimmed through the hundreds of pictures of Travis she'd taken, ruthlessly deleting almost all of them. She paused to study the superstar's face and felt another stab of guilt at the shadows in his eyes and the sense of vulnerability in his gaze. Whatever was going on in Travis Whitley's private life was hurting him. If she gave Wade these pictures, that made her as bad as he was . . .

But if she didn't, she'd lose her job, her promising career, and her income, which meant her family would be more desperate than ever. Even as she stared at Travis, her cell vibrated and she flipped through to text.

COME HOME RIGHT NOW! NEED TO GET PERRY TO ER!!!

With a gasp, Della slipped on her shoes, grabbed her purse, and ran toward the door. Her family only owned one car, and if her mom was out, then Adrianna was alone with the kids.

She didn't bother to wait for the elevator, running down the stairs to the lobby hardly aware of who or what was around her. Reaching her car, she unlocked it, threw her purse on the seat, and started the engine. Except it wouldn't start. She tried again and then again, her heart pounding so hard in her chest that she could hear it.

"Start, dammit!" She thumped the steering wheel. The battery had probably died. It had a habit of doing that, especially after a long trip like the drive from California.

"Della?"

She jumped as Nate's face appeared at the open window with Travis behind him.

"What's up?"

She gripped the wheel and stared straight ahead. "The battery's dead. I need to get to my mother's house."

He reached in and patted her shoulder. "Then I'll take you."

Nate glanced at Della as he drove through the center of town. Her hands were clenched into fists and her face was a waxen image of her normally vibrant self. She still wore her pink pajamas and her hair was braided down her back; she looked as vulnerable as hell. He'd managed to persuade Travis to stay at the hotel and had promised to call if they needed anything.

"What's going on, Della?"

"I need to get to my mother's house."

"So you said." He turned off the road into a residential area and used his calm-the-civilian-down voice. "Is she sick?"

"She's not there."

"Is it your sister, then?"

She still wouldn't look at him. "No. Can you pull up here?"

All the lights were on in the small row house. As he followed her up to the door, which stood ajar, all his senses were on high alert.

"Della! We're in here. Come *on!*"

"Adrianna."

The door at the end of the hallway stood open. Nate paused at the entrance as Della ran forward to embrace the woman seated on the couch. At first he wasn't sure what she was holding until he realized it was a small child wrapped in a cheerful patchwork quilt.

Della turned to him. "We need to take Perry to the ER."

"Got it." He helped Adrianna stand up. "Do you want me to carry your daughter?"

"No, I've got her."

Della grabbed his arm. "I can drive. You don't need to come with us."

"I'm coming." *What kind of a guy did she think he was?*

He marched back to the car, opening all the passenger doors, and waited patiently as Adrianna maneuvered herself and her daughter inside.

"Where's the hospital?"

"The one we need is about ten miles away," Della answered as she buckled up her seat belt.

He lowered his voice as they pulled away. "Wouldn't it have been quicker to call an ambulance?"

"Sometimes they can take forever to get here, so my sister doesn't trust them anymore."

"I'll go as fast as I can, then."

He concentrated on the route, testing the speed limits. The roads were empty at this time of night so there was no need to be stupid.

He pulled up right outside the ER and let Della and her sister out. "I'll look for somewhere to park and come and find you, okay?"

Della looked as if she was going to tell him to leave, but instead she nodded and briefly touched his hand. "Thanks, Nate."

"You're welcome."

It took him a while to find a parking spot. By the time he entered the waiting room, there was no sign of Della or her sister. He made himself known to the nursing staff, sat down in one of the hard chairs, and took out his cell.

He quickly texted Travis and Della and then sat quietly, letting the adrenaline stream out of him. It was weird not just walking through to the back and finding out everything he needed to know. He'd spent way too many hours in hospitals waiting for information he'd had to pass on to distraught families. He'd always hated that part of his job, but it had been necessary. He could only hope Della's little niece would be okay . . .

A long time later, when he'd almost nodded off, he felt a touch on his shoulder and Della sank into the chair next to him. She looked as if she'd been crying.

"Hey." He fought off a yawn. "How's Perry holding up?"

"She's stabilized, which is the most important thing."

A huge sigh shuddered through Della. He instinctively put his arm around her shoulders, and she leaned into him.

Her hair still smelled of roses and he inhaled her warmth and sweetness. Time ticked by, but he didn't care. Holding her, looking out for her, just felt right.

"Perry has hemophilia A."

"That's a blood disorder, right?"

"Yes. It's genetic. Usually it's under control, but she gets the occasional breakout bleeding and it has to be stopped."

"That sucks."

"Yeah, I know, and it's incurable, so she's going to be stuck on medication for the rest of her life." She swallowed hard. "I called my mom. She shouted at me for not being there for Adrianna immediately, and for abandoning my family and my home."

Nate kissed the top of her head. "People say all kinds of bull when they're in shock. She probably didn't mean it."

"I think she did." Della rubbed her cheek against his shirt. "But if I don't work, I won't be able to send money home, and then we'd all be in trouble."

"Your mom probably won't even remember what she said when she's feeling better. I'm sure she knows in her heart that you're doing your best."

She didn't answer him, but she didn't pull away either, so he held her close, smoothing a hand over her hair and down her back in an endless soothing caress. Eventually she stirred and straightened up, wisps of her hair stuck to her cheek.

"Thanks for being here for me—especially after what happened today."

Nate held her suddenly shy gaze. "Della, I'll

always be there for you. Don't you know that yet?"

She cupped his chin. "Don't say that. We hardly know each other and I'm—"

"Not available," Nate finished for her. "I know."

"*No!* That's not it at all." She blinked away the suggestion of tears. "I'm not stalking Travis Whitley either. It's . . . complicated."

He contemplated her for a long moment, aware of the honesty in her eyes as hope reignited within him.

"I'm here for you, Della. Just tell me what you need and I'll do it."

She stood up, one hand on his shoulder. "I need you to be patient with me, okay? I need you to . . . wait." She shook her head. "Oh Lord, that's not right either, is it? Why would you bother to do that? We hardly know each other."

"Yeah, we do." He grabbed her hand and pressed it to his heart. "We know how we feel *in here.* So I'll wait for you, Della, but at some point you'll have to be honest with me, okay?"

"I will." She bent to kiss his mouth. "Now let me go and check on Adrianna and Perry. When my mom gets here, we'll be able to leave."

She couldn't do it.

Della opened her eyes as the car drew into the parking lot of the hotel and Nate turned the engine off. She was dog-tired and Perry still hadn't been given the all clear. Her mom had decided to stay at the hospital with Adrianna, so after checking in with the neighbor who was watching Josie, her other niece, Della was free to leave.

"I'll walk you up to your room."

She jumped as Nate opened the car door and offered her his hand. It was funny how important and necessary his strength had become to her. He was as solid and reliable as a rock. She'd never had someone to lean on before. It was both thrilling and scary at the same time.

"Thanks."

It was quiet in the hotel lobby, the lights dim, and no one was manning the desk. Within moments they were standing outside the room, and Nate used his card to open the door.

"Sleep tight, Della. Call me if you need anything and I'll be right here."

She gathered her courage and faced him. "If you *stayed* right here, you'd be much easier to find."

"I need to go check in with Travis." Nate took off his hat and smoothed a hand through his brown hair. "He offered me a bed in his suite."

"So you'd rather be with him than me?"

"You told me you wanted me to wait, and hell, I don't *feel* like waiting with you standing there, all lush and rumpled and . . ." He took an unsteady step backward. "When we make love, I want it to be honest and true and . . ." He groaned. "*Special,* okay?"

"Okay." Now that she knew what she wanted, she could wait another day if he could. Rising up on tiptoe, she kissed the firm line of his mouth. "Good night, Nate, and thanks a million."

She closed the door behind him and contemplated what she had to do. Grabbing a pen and her notebook, she sat down and wrote a list of all the people she needed to contact before she lost her nerve. She was done with being scared. Seeing her niece fighting for her life again had reignited her desire to make the best of her time in this world, not to allow others to steal her joy.

It came down to something very simple. What was more important? Maintaining her self-respect or running scared from Wade's threats? She'd been looking at it from the wrong angle, allowing fear to dictate her responses. Now she'd met Travis, she couldn't imagine sharing her photos with the loathsome Wade, who would surely sell them to some celebrity site and make a fortune.

She was *good* at her job. She'd rather find an honest way to help Adrianna and Perry with the crippling costs of her ongoing treatment than give in to blackmail.

Opening her laptop, she pulled up her email

and started at the top with the CEO of her company, cc'ing Wade.

To whom it may concern . . .

"Her niece has hemophilia?"

"Yeah."

"Which type?"

"A, I think she said. I don't know much about it myself."

Nate sat across from Travis in the suite, where they were sharing a lavish breakfast. It was still early in the morning. He'd hardly slept and hadn't yet shaved.

Travis put down his fork. "Do you know you pay for the prophylactic doses by *weight?* So the bigger the kid gets, the more it costs?"

"That's like the blood transfusions, right?"

"Yeah, and guess how much that runs to a month? *Thirty thousand bucks.*" Travis whistled. "Can you believe that? And sure, insurance covers most of it, but there are always extra costs, like visits to the ER and days lost for working parents and all kinds of shit."

"Which probably means Della is helping to support her family," Nate said. "That's a heck of a burden on everyone."

Travis finished his coffee in one gulp. "It's not a burden if you love someone. I bet Della would tell you that."

"How come you know so much about hemophilia?" Nate asked slowly.

Travis studied the bottom of his mug. "Because I have a son. He's the same age as Perry and has the same condition."

"You have a *kid?*"

"Yeah. No one knows, okay? His mother didn't want anything to do with me or my fame or any of it, and I . . . let her go. But I pay for my son and I see him as much as I can. He's not doing too good at the moment, but I keep praying."

Nate reached across the table and briefly squeezed Travis's shoulder. "I'm sorry. I promise I won't tell a soul."

"Thanks, because if this got out, my ex would kill me. I slipped up last week and was seen near her house, and now everyone wants to know who my 'mystery lover' is." Travis managed a faint smile. "So did you and Della *really* fall out over her family obligations?"

Nate gladly accepted the change of subject. "Nope. I had no idea Perry was sick until Della needed a ride to the ER." Seeing as Travis had shared something so intensely personal with him, it only seemed fair to reciprocate. "Della was taking pictures at the wedding."

"So was everyone."

"She was just taking pictures of you."

Travis let out a breath. "Shit."

"I asked her whether she had some kind of thing going on with you and she got mad and insisted she was stalking you."

"She's not one of my regulars, and trust me, I know them all." Travis grimaced. "They follow me everywhere. In fact, I've never seen Della before in my life."

"She could be a secret stalker."

Travis raised an eyebrow. "Right. Or maybe she wanted the pictures for another reason. She said she worked in digital marketing or something? Maybe she was going to sell them to someone."

Nate felt like someone had stabbed him in the chest. "Della wouldn't do that."

"She might if she needed the money for Perry."

Nate sat back. "Damn. I need to talk to her."

Travis reached for the coffeepot. "You go do that, and let me know what she says."

After the mechanic fixed her car, Della packed up her stuff and attempted to pay the extras on the bill at the desk, only to find that all the charges had already been taken care of. Considering everything that was about to go down, it was the least of her problems and could wait. She walked back up the stairs and found Nate knocking on her door.

"Hey," she called out to him. "I was just going to text you. Where's Travis?"

He turned toward her, his expression grave, and her heart gave a little jump. Would she lose him now? Had everything she'd just done been for nothing?

"Why do you want to talk to Travis?"

"Not for the reason you think." She stopped walking and stared him down. *"Please?* I want you to be there as well."

"Okay, but—"

"Just let me get my purse."

She went into the room, leaving him leaning against the opposite wall, and picked up her bag from the bed. One part of her was terrified; the other felt strangely at peace. A last check around to make sure she hadn't missed anything and she returned to find Nate.

"How's Perry doing?"

"A lot better." Della was glad to be able to give him some good news. "She'll be coming home today."

"Awesome." He picked up her bag and pointed at the elevators. "We need to go up to the top floor."

There was a bodyguard stationed outside Travis's door, but he waved them both through.

Travis was sitting by the window drinking coffee. It was weird how the lack of the right cowboy hat made him almost unrecognizable. He gestured toward a seat, but Della was too uptight to sit.

"Morning, Miss Della, and what can I do for you today? Did my old friend mess up his apology?"

"Apology for what?" Della asked, looking over at Nate.

"Thinking you were a stalker when all you were doing was taking my picture for reasons of your own."

Her knees wobbled and she dropped into the chair behind her. "You . . . *knew?*"

"Honey, I've been in this business long enough to spot paparazzi fifty miles away. You were an amateur."

She took a deep breath. "I want you to personally erase all the pictures I took of you on my phone and my camera." She rummaged in her purse and put both items on the coffee table between them.

"Why?" Travis considered her as Nate took the seat beside him.

"Because I couldn't use them."

"Why not? You could've earned big money for every picture."

"I know." She met his calm gaze. "But it would've been a gross invasion of your privacy, and to be honest, I wouldn't have made any money. It was my boss who ordered me to get the pictures."

Travis just looked at her encouragingly, so she kept talking.

"He was mad when I wouldn't sleep with him and said he'd get me fired if I didn't do what he said." She pressed a hand to her chest. "I was afraid to say no because my family needs the money I earn to pay the extra medical bills. My mom's close to losing her house. It's no excuse, but at first I thought, it's just a few pictures, it's not hurting anyone, and my sister needs that money, but then I met you and *liked* you, and I didn't like myself very much at all."

She forgot how to breathe during her long and complicated explanation and took a big gulp of air to compensate.

"So what did you do?" The question came from Nate.

"I refused to send the images."

"Which means you'll probably be fired."

"No, I beat them to it. I quit." She shrugged. "It's just a job. I'm fairly certain I can find another one." *At least she hoped she could.*

"Della . . ." Nate reached for her hand just as Travis started talking.

"Let's do this. Sell the images yourself, Della."
"What?"

Travis shrugged. "I'd rather you got the money than anyone else. At least I know you'll use it for a good cause."

Della and Nate exchanged startled glances.

"Are you *serious?*"

"Hell yeah. I can even get my publicist to

358

tell you where you'll get the best price. Do you want to take a selfie of us together? Because then the public might think *we're* together and leave my ex in peace." He winked. "Sometimes we have to play ball with the bad guys if we want to be left alone."

"My old boss would be *furious*." Della imagined Wade's face if the pictures came out. "Actually, that might be awesome payback." She got to her feet, her gaze going from Nate to Travis and back again. "Thank you for the offer. But I still can't do it."

"You sure about that?" Travis asked.

"Yes. One hundred percent sure."

Travis rose and tipped his imaginary hat to her. "You're a woman of integrity, Miss Della, and I appreciate that."

"Thank you." She knew she'd done the right thing and had no regrets, but she could only wonder what her sister and mother might say.

Travis opened the outside door and beckoned to his bodyguard. "Get my bags, please."

"Yes, sir."

Nate walked over and took Della's shaking hand.

"You okay?"

She managed to nod as Travis turned back to them.

"The suite's paid up until the end of the week and I've ordered you dinner at eight. So I suggest you make good use of your time together." He winked. "From what I can tell, you two have a lot in common."

"How's that?" Della had to ask.

"You both turned down big-money deals with me. And in a weird way I appreciate your honesty enormously." Travis gave them one last killer smile. "Let me know the date of your wedding, okay? I'm singing."

"Thanks, Travis," Nate said, his attention still on Della. "Thanks for everything."

"You're welcome, buddy. Keep in touch."

Chapter Five

Nate smiled down at Della as the door closed behind Travis and his bodyguard.

"You okay?"

She looked up at him and he caught his breath at the conflicting emotions in her brown eyes.

"I'm just about holding things together. Considering that I've quit my job, refused to sell candid shots of one of the world's biggest country-western stars to the gossip rags, and pretended to be a stalker all in a twenty-four-hour period."

"Pretty impressive."

She placed her palm against his chest. "And I hurt you."

"I kind of understand why you did what you did."

"I thought, what's worse? Nate thinking I'm some kind of pathetic stalker person or that I'm getting pictures of his old college friend for the gossip sites."

"Tough choice." He stroked his thumb along the curve of her jaw. "I think I prefer the third option myself."

"Which is what?"

He kissed her nose. "The one where you try to

do your best to help your family even when the odds are stacked against you."

Her eyes filled with tears. "I don't deserve your understanding."

"Yeah you do. I get why you were reluctant to confide in me. I'm a cop and a well-known Dudley Do-Right."

"I wanted to tell you the truth, but I was afraid."

"Afraid that I'd arrest you?"

She knew he was kidding, but she wanted to tell him the truth. "No, that you'd look at me with contempt and walk away." She forced out a breath. "I couldn't bear to think you'd despise me."

He sighed. "I should've made you tell me what was up. I tried, but I really didn't want to hear your answers in case you actually were doing something illegal. My heart was at war with my stupid head."

"Your heart?"

"Yeah." He gathered his courage. "I'm all yours if you want me, Della. One hundred percent all in."

"But you hardly know me and—"

He kissed her on the lips. "I'm a Turner. I *know* you."

With a soft sound she kissed him back, her arms going around him as if they were meant to be there.

"I knew you were *The One* the moment I saw you that first night at the bar," Nate murmured. "And I fought that feeling every step of the way."

She drew back slightly to look at him. "You're kidding, right?"

"Nope. It's the family curse—or blessing, depending on which way you look at it. A Turner knows when he's found *The One* and that's it. Game over."

"Seriously?"

"Seriously. Why do you think my nickname was the one-night stand king?"

She shook her head. "Tell me."

"Because it only took five minutes for me to work out whether the woman I was dating was *The One* or not. After that I just stayed to eat my dinner and enjoy her company as a friend."

"But you had sex with at least two of them."

He made a face. "After I'd been the local sheriff for a couple of years, I got . . . cynical about the whole Turner legend thing and thought I'd try to prove it wrong. It didn't work, so I focused on my job and stopped looking."

"Until you met me."

"Exactly."

She regarded him steadily and he tried to look as resolute and responsible as possible.

"You know this is crazy, Nate?"

"All I know is how I feel."

"As of this morning I have no job and no future back in California."

"Then I'll move to wherever you find a job."

The thought of leaving Morgantown wasn't as much of a wrench as he'd expected. He'd do anything for her. If Della was okay with it, he might even talk to Travis about his ridiculous offer and live the high life for a year or so.

"You'd do that for me?"

"Sure. Or you could move to Morgantown and revive our local newspaper. Once a Turner man finds *The One,* you'll do anything to keep her and make her happy."

"Nate . . ." She bit down on her lip.

"I know it sounds crazy and the last thing I want to do is make you run for the hills." He kissed her again, capturing her face between his hands. "But it's okay. I can wait for you to get used to the idea of me hanging around."

"You sound so sure."

"I am. And seeing as Travis was nice enough to gift us his suite for the next day and a half, how about we put that bed to good use?"

"Wow, that was smooth."

"Well, I thought so." He hesitated. "Do you want me?"

He held still as her gaze went from him to the bed and back again. "You're sure about this?"

"More than anything in my life, but I'm not

going to push you into doing anything you don't like—although not taking me to bed will probably haunt you for the rest of your life."

"You're that good, are you?"

He winked. "Why don't you find out?"

She gave one more uncertain look at the bed. His heart stuttered in his chest as she faced him and slowly let her hair fall down around her shoulders.

He wanted to drop to his knees and kiss her feet—wanted to give her the world—and they hadn't even gotten naked yet.

"You start." She pointed at his chest.

"Yes, ma'am." He unsnapped his shirt and then unbuckled his belt. "Now you."

"I've got half as many clothes on as you do, so keep going."

He pretended to sigh as he toed off his boots and sat on the side of the bed to remove his socks. She was dressed for travel in leggings and a T-shirt, so she did have a point. Standing up, he finished unbuttoning his shirt. She licked her lips, making him want to throw caution to the wind and rip everything off as fast as possible. But then again, the anticipation in her gaze made him want to slow down, make her wait.

"Faster," she commanded.

He raised an eyebrow. "Only if you take something off as well."

She raised her arms and pulled off her T-shirt in one easy motion, exposing a pink lace bra that made his mouth go dry. He tried to get rid of his shirt and only succeeded in getting into a tangled mess that made Della snort with laughter.

"Don't ever try to be a stripper, Nate."

He grinned back at her as he undid his top button and eased down his zipper. Now she was the one who wasn't smiling, but he wasn't complaining, considering what she was staring at.

"Take off your pants, Della. I want to see you."

She did as he asked, giving him a moment to free himself from his jeans. His heart was thumping so loudly she could probably hear it. Jeez, her panties matched her bra. He was going to die of lust before they even got started.

She walked toward him. "Can I touch?"

"Anything you like. I'm all yours."

Her hands came to rest on his shoulders, shaping him, learning him, sliding up and down his arms and then his chest, making him shiver with delight.

"What's this?"

He looked down to where her fingers rested just above the jut of his hip. "Got caught by a knife when I was breaking up a bar fight."

"And this?" Her fingers traced the top of his tight white boxers, making him break out in a sweat.

"Gunshot wound."

Her sharp intake of breath was followed by her bending down and kissing the faint scar on his abs. Her hair brushed against the hardness of his arousal and he barely resisted the urge to wrap a hand around her neck to keep her there, or maybe a bit lower, for a long, *long* time.

Instead, he urged her upward to meet his mouth, locking their bodies together in an embrace that felt so damn right he wanted to weep.

"Della . . ." He kissed her luscious mouth, losing himself in her taste and warmth. "I want you so bad."

"Me too," she breathed against his lips. "Take me to bed, Sheriff."

Della squeaked as Nate picked her up and walked over to the bed, where he deposited her in the center of the silken quilt. He smiled as he lowered himself over her, his strong thighs parted around hers and his hands braced on either side of her head.

She cupped the back of his head, drawing him closer so she could kiss him, felt his body yield slightly and brush against hers. He was being so gentle she felt like a precious object. But she didn't want to be worshipped right now. She wanted to be loved. She scraped her nails over his scalp and he shuddered, his teeth catching at her lower lip, making her arch helplessly against him.

"Della . . . I don't think I can be slow this time."

"Okay." She smiled against the curve of his neck. "Then get to it."

He groaned as he captured her hands above her head and used his teeth to unlock the front clasp of her bra. His worshipful sigh as her breasts were revealed made her feel like a goddess. He bent to kiss her there and she closed her eyes as he explored her with such thorough determination that she wanted to scream his name.

She whimpered instead, but he didn't stop. Wriggling beneath him, she freed one of her legs and dug her heel into his ass, bringing all their important places into alignment. His hips bucked and she hung on tighter, aware of the hard, throbbing length of him rubbing against her panties and the rising need for more.

"Now," she ordered. *"Please."*

He eased away from her, shucking his boxers and removing her now-damp panties with the speed of a magician. She barely got a good look at him before he was protecting himself and covering her and—oh God. There he was, surging into her, making her come within seconds.

She clung onto him as he froze in place over her, a thick, solid presence while she clenched and rocked and rode him to the best orgasm of her life.

When she opened her eyes again, he was watching her, his expression strained, his biceps quivering with the effort to stay still, and not crush her with his weight.

"Thank you," she murmured.

"You're welcome." He licked the seam of her lips. "Can I have a turn now?"

"Of course."

"Thank God."

Then she forgot how to breath as he rocked against her, gathering her closer and closer, his fingers seeking out her pleasure as he took his, binding them together in the heat of a passion she had never imagined existed. When she finally came back down from the clouds, Nate was slumped over her, his head resting on the pillow beside hers. She turned to look at him and he groaned.

"Yeah, I know. Too fast. I'll do better next time."

"Foreplay and everything?"

"Whatever you want."

Della pretended to consider her options. "Can I tie you up?"

His brow furrowed. "You into all that *Fifty Shades* stuff?"

"Nope, just messing with your head. And how do you know about that anyway?"

"My sister gave me the lowdown. That was enough." With a growl, he rolled on top of her again. "I have handcuffs back at home, you know."

"You do? I can't wait to try them out." She kissed his nose. "On you, of course."

He eased away from her. "Let me clean up and I'll think about your suggestions."

She gave him a couple of moments and then followed him into the massive bathroom. He'd already turned on the shower, which gave her plenty of time to admire him naked.

He gathered up some towels and held out his hand. "Shower with me?"

"I'd love to."

And it was the truth. She loved everything about this hardworking, decent man. She even liked him, and he certainly seemed to like her.

"What's so funny?" He maneuvered her into the shower.

"You are."

"Don't tell anyone else that." His eyes crinkled at the corners as he soaped his hands and advanced toward her. "I have a reputation to maintain."

"As the one-night stand king?"

His soapy palms slicked over her back and ass. "Nope, as an officer of the law."

"With handcuffs and everything."

It was getting harder to come up with witty banter when his hands were all over her and his mouth . . .

"We'll have to make this quick." She managed to speak but only barely. "I need to go check in on Adrianna and Perry."

"Sure. I'll come with you." He dropped to his knees. "Don't worry. I'm a fast learner and an even quicker worker."

And then she forgot words as he loved her and just went with the feeling.

Della knocked on the door and stood back listening as her mother called for her to come right in. She still had a key, but after ten years away she no longer felt right about using it. She'd grown up in this house and in this friendly neighborhood. Everyone knew her family and her history, which was great, but it could also be stifling. She loved her family, but she didn't want to move back here. Of course if her sister needed her, she'd do it. That was a given. Family had to come first.

If she'd taken up Travis's offer to sell the pictures, she could've given her sister financial security for years . . .

What would Adrianna think if she knew?

Della paused in the dark hallway and grabbed hold of Nate's arm.

"Should I tell Adrianna what I did?"

"About the money?" Nate patted her shoulder. "It's up to you. How do you think she'd react?"

"I don't know. I'd hope she'd agree that I did the right thing, but then, I don't have kids and I know she'd do anything for them."

"Della, come on through! We have news!" Adrianna sounded more excited than she had for years.

Still holding Nate's hand, Della went through to the family room, where Perry was curled up on the couch watching something on her tablet while her mother and grandmother made lunch.

Della's mother went straight to Nate and held out her hands.

"*Gracias*. Thank you for helping my grand-daughter."

Nate held her hands and kissed her cheek. "I just provided the vehicle. Della and her sister did all the hard lifting." He turned to Adrianna. "How's Perry doing?"

"Much better now." Adrianna's smile was brilliant. "Guess what happened today?" She offered Della a piece of paper. "We had an email from someone at the Travis Whitley Charitable Foundation, offering to pay all the expenses incurred for Perry that aren't covered by insurance!"

"What?" Della grabbed the letter and started to read and then handed it to Nate. "Well bless his heart."

372

"Do you know this guy? Is he legit? Did you put him on to us? I have no idea how he found out about Perry."

Adrianna was babbling now, but Della didn't care. The sheer enormity and kindness shown by Travis was overwhelming her, too.

"I know Travis from way back and I can vouch that this is for real," Nate confirmed. "Della met him at the Cutwright wedding this weekend. That might be how he got to know about Perry."

"This is so amazing I can't quite take it in." Adrianna flapped the letter like a fan. "It means so much to our family." She grabbed Nate's hand. "Will you give him our thanks and our love when you see him?"

"Sure I will." Nate grinned. "Hopefully, one day you'll get the chance to thank him in person." He winked at Della and lowered his voice. "He did say he would sing at our wedding, right?"

She smiled foolishly back at him, aware that her mom was watching but not caring in the slightest. He was a good man and at some point she'd have to tell her family what he meant to her, but this was Perry and Adrianna's moment, not hers.

"Can I go say hi to Perry?" Nate asked.

"You can try," Adrianna mock groaned. "If you can persuade her to take her headphones off."

Nate walked over to crouch beside the sofa and offered his hand to Perry, who obligingly took out at least one of her earbuds.

Della watched his face as he talked, and something inside her, some little pocket of resistance, melted away, leaving her vulnerable but not scared. She'd let him in. They'd grow together and be better as a team. She knew it in her soul.

He looked up, as if conscious of the weight of her thoughts, and blew her a kiss. Her cell pinged, and to cover up her absurd desire to go kneel beside him and ruffle his hair, she checked her email.

An hour later, after Perry had gone to sleep, Della still hadn't mentioned her job loss to her sister or mother, but she was obviously ready to leave. Nate kissed everyone good-bye and accompanied her to the car.

"What's up?"

She glanced over at him as she settled into her seat. "I got an email."

"From your boss?" He turned the engine on for the air-conditioning but didn't release the parking brake. "Is he angry with you?" He quite fancied going to meet Della's dick of a boss and straightening out a few things with him.

"No, it wasn't from him."

She sounded . . . odd. "Then who was it?"

"Travis Whitley's publicity department."

"He has one all to himself?"

"Apparently." She cleared her throat. "They want me to work for them."

"That's good, right?" Nate said cautiously.

"Yeah . . . They're based in San Francisco and Nashville, but I can work from home." She suddenly covered her face with her hands. "This is like some kind of fairy tale."

He fought a chuckle. "With Travis as an unlikely fairy godmother? I suppose it is. Do you *want* to work for him?"

She sat back in her seat. "From the job description, I'd say it's a perfect fit for my skill set. And the salary is twice what I was earning before."

"Then what's stopping you?"

"Just that I tried to deceive him and yet he's done so much for my family and now—this!"

"Maybe the fact that you had the chance to do something underhanded and chose not to meant a lot to him. From what he told me, people he can trust are in very short supply."

"Then you think I should take it?"

"It's not up to me, but I do have an opinion if you want it." He smiled at her. "Take the job. Not that I'm biased at all, but then you could come live in Morgantown—we have great internet there, thanks to Chase Morgan—and maybe get to know me better, fall in love with me, and marry me?"

Her eyes filled with tears and he held his breath.

"Great internet, huh?"

He made a cross over his heart. "The best."

"*And* you?"

"If you want me."

"Happily ever after?"

"Why not?"

She slowly exhaled and reached for his hand. "Okay."

"That's it?"

The frown she gave him made him light up inside.

"It had better be."

The Wedding Bet

Janet Dailey

Chapter One

Packed in its open box, the bottle of twenty-three-year reserve Pappy Van Winkle bourbon stood on proud display among the coed bridal shower gifts. A short, stocky man in a plaid shirt, high-end jeans, and a silver longhorn bolo was staring at it as if it were the Holy Grail.

"Man, I'd kill for a shot of that!" he said to Linc, who was passing on his way to the buffet. "Whoever brought it, they must think a powerful lot of Ellie and Brady."

Linc stopped out of politeness. "Actually, I just met the bride. But Brady's my first cousin on his father's side. We go way back. In fact . . ." His mouth twitched in an ironic half smile. "It was Brady who introduced me to my ex-wife. So in a twisted sort of way, I owe him."

"Hot damn! So you're the one who brought the bourbon! Pleased to meet you!" He pumped Linc's hand. "Chet Bertelson. I'm Brady's cousin on his mama's side. That makes us practically kinfolk."

"Lincoln Cutwright. Pleased to meet you." Linc returned the handshake. He was about to ease away, but Chet wasn't finished.

"I've heard of you. You're the one who's got that big spread in Kentucky. Brady says you raise Thoroughbreds on it. Now that would be the life." He nodded toward the bourbon. "I bet you've got a few more of those bottles stashed away in your wine cellar."

"A few." There was actually just one left. Twenty-three-year reserve Pappy Van Winkle was liquid gold, as precious as it was scarce. A single bottle had recently fetched two thousand dollars at auction.

Chet was gazing at the bourbon, as if lost in thought. Linc was about to excuse himself and walk away when he spoke again. "Brady says you're a betting man."

This was getting personal. Linc shrugged. "What else does Brady say?"

"That you've got quite a way with the ladies."

"Maybe when I was younger. But I'm out of practice these days. Now, if you'll excuse me—"

"How would you like to make a little wager?"

Linc halted in his tracks, intrigued. Nobody could call him a compulsive gambler, but he loved the challenge of a sporting bet. Tracy, his ex, had claimed he'd wager his soul against the devil if given the chance. That was just one of the issues that had split them apart.

For all he knew, this mildly annoying fellow could be the devil in disguise.

"And the stakes?" he asked.

"My partners and I own the best rib house in

Austin. Ask anybody. Folks line up around the block every weekend to buy our ribs before the supply runs out. If you win, I'll put up all the ribs you want for a year, shipped anywhere in the country."

"And if I lose?"

"A bottle of Pappy Van Winkle, just like that one."

So far, so good. The stakes were just high enough to provide the rush Linc craved. "So what are we betting on?" he asked.

"That you can't bed a certain lady before the two lovebirds leave on their honeymoon."

Was this a joke? Linc shook his head. "Sorry. I like the stakes, but I don't make bets involving beds and women. Too many complications."

"Don't you even want to know the lady I have in mind?" Chet glanced toward the door with a wicked smile. "Right over there in the black shirt. She just walked in."

Linc followed the line of the man's gaze across the crowded room. He blinked, groaned, and swore.

He hadn't seen his ex-wife in five years. But damned if Tracy didn't look sexier than ever. Flame-colored hair, sea-green eyes, and a figure that rocked the tight jeans and silk blouse she wore. Tracy was, and always had been, a traffic stopper. And as far as Linc knew, she still couldn't stand the sight of him.

"So, do you want to change your mind?" Chet asked.

"Change my mind? Hell, I'd rather take on a man-eating tigress. Sorry, no bet."

"Too bad. Your loss." Chet raised his hand and gave her a friendly wave across the crowded room. Tracy waved back and turned away. Of course the two would know each other. Chet was Brady's cousin. Tracy was Brady's longtime friend. Their paths were bound to have crossed. But why would the little jerk have tried to set up that crazy bet—unless he knew for sure Tracy would never sleep with her ex?

He must've really wanted that bourbon.

Ignoring Chet for now, Linc watched his ex-wife weave her way among the crowd, stopping here and there to greet people she knew. She had a model's elegant stride and leggy figure—in fact, she'd been modeling when he met her. But Linc knew she'd used the divorce settlement to put herself through law school. Now, according to Brady, she was a trial lawyer with a kick-ass reputation. In her spare time she also did pro bono work for the under-privileged.

Saint Tracy. Some things never changed.

Was she coming this way? His pulse quickened, then slowed again as she veered off toward the sign that said "Waterin' Hole," where a big tub of ice held beer, water, sodas, and wine coolers. Either she hadn't noticed he was here or she'd chosen to ignore him.

Either way he would have to do something about that.

Linc hadn't planned to be here. But when Brady had mentioned over the phone that Tracy was on the guest list, he'd made a snap decision and caught a flight from Lexington. He and Tracy had unfinished business. Why not take this chance to settle it in person?

Tracy Duval fished a Mountain Dew from the tub, popped the tab, and took a long, deep swallow. She'd spent most of her Saturday doing legal assistance at a local women's shelter. At the end of the day she'd barely had time to run home to her condo, change, and make it to Brady's shower. Thank goodness she'd sent her gift early. One less thing to worry about.

Only now that she was here had Tracy realized how tired she was. The party looked like fun, but after a frenetic week, all she really wanted to do was go home and unwind. She would greet the wedding couple, say hello to a few friends, and sneak out early. Watching mindless TV in her pajamas struck her as a perfect way to end the evening.

Whoever was giving this party had done a great job. The folksy western theme was perfect for Brady and his bride. Tracy had barely met Ellie, but she seemed sweet and genuine. And the two appeared deeply in love.

Seeing them together, Tracy couldn't help remembering her own wedding eight years ago. She'd fallen head over heels in love with Brady's handsome Kentucky cousin. But after a dizzying courtship, her three-year marriage to Linc had ended with her leaving. She could only wish Brady and Ellie better luck.

The last time she'd spoken with Brady, he'd mentioned that Linc was sending a special gift, which implied that he wouldn't be there in person. Big relief. She wasn't up to dealing with her ex-husband tonight—or any other night.

She'd made her way to the vegan buffet table and was eyeing a veggie platter with hummus dip when a deep voice spoke behind her.

"Hello, Tracy."

The half-empty soda can slipped out of her hand and crashed to the floor, splattering her jeans and new boots with sticky Mountain Dew. Heart sinking, she forced herself to turn around and look up. Way up. Tracy wasn't a petite woman, but Linc, at six-foot-three, towered over her. Startled into silence, she took him in. At thirty-nine, he looked older than she remembered. There were creases at the corners of his hazel eyes and his rich chestnut hair had silvered at the temples. But the man was as flat-bellied and hot as ever, maybe hotter. Why couldn't he have gained thirty pounds and lost his hair?

"Let me get that." He grabbed a handful of paper napkins from the table, dropped to one knee, righted the can, and began sponging up the spilled soda. Looking up at her, he grinned. "As I remember, the last time I got down on one knee like this was when I proposed to you."

He was turning on the old charm, just like always. Everything came easy to Linc. All he had to do was flash that movie-star smile. She'd fallen for it back in the day. But now she knew better.

"What do you want, Linc?" she demanded.

"That can wait. Right now I could use a couple more napkins. Would you mind?"

She thrust more napkins at him. "Sorry I caught you off guard," he said. "I saw you come in. I thought maybe you'd seen me, too. I was over by the gift table with Chet Bertelson. He waved at you and you waved back."

"You know Chet?"

"I didn't until a few minutes ago. I take it he's a friend of yours." Linc finished sopping up the soda, gathered the napkins and the soda can, and dumped them in the trash barrel at the end of the table. Dipping into the ice tub, he rinsed his hands and shook them dry.

"He's not the kind of friend you mean," Tracy said. "And that soda can you tossed goes in the recycle bin, not the trash."

"So it begins." Linc raised an eyebrow, as if to say *fine, fish it out yourself.*

Same old problem, Tracy thought. She cared passionately about making the world a better place. And playboy Linc had never given a damn about anything—including her.

"About Chet," she said, changing the subject. "He's not really even a friend. Last year I represented a waitress who sued him for unlawful termination. He fired her because she was pregnant."

"I take it you won."

"I did. Now, for some reason, he seems to think that makes us buddies. I waved back at him to be civil. Then I headed the other way. If I hadn't, maybe I'd have seen you."

Strange that she hadn't seen him. Linc would've been hard to miss. The man attracted women like honey attracted bears. In fact, she'd noticed several ladies checking him out in the last couple of minutes.

That had been another flashpoint in their marriage. She'd never known Linc to be unfaithful. But in his fast-track world of horse racing, gambling, fast cars, and parties, he'd been surrounded by attractive, willing women. The worst of it was, he'd never understood how insecure that made her feel. Or maybe he hadn't cared.

It had taken her a long, rough time to get over Linc. She'd thought she'd made it all the way. But now, standing face-to-face with him, she felt a welling of those old hormonal urges. The memory of that great male body and the delicious things they'd done together was still enough to dampen her panties. But she was wise to him now. Whatever Linc wanted, if he thought he could still push her buttons, he was sadly mistaken.

She was looking up at Linc like a beautiful, defiant ginger cat, ready to spit and claw if he reached out to her. What had he done to make the woman so distrustful? He'd given her everything she wanted. He'd never cheated or laid a hand on her. And their sex life had been . . . *mind-blowing*. Just the thought of having her in bed—or anywhere else they'd done it—made him ache.

"We need to talk, Tracy," he said.

"So talk."

"Not here. Too noisy. What do you say we sneak out and get ourselves a nice, quiet dinner where we can have an intelligent conversation?"

"I just got here. Besides, what do we have to talk about? We've already said it all."

"Have we, Tracy?" Damn it, she was getting to him. "We never talked. You just walked out, without even saying good-bye. Next thing I knew, I was being served with divorce papers."

"And you didn't know why? I can't believe that. How could you be so dense? You were never there when I needed you. You were always off somewhere having a good time."

He reached out and caught her arm. The contact with her warm skin, through the thin silk sleeve of her blouse, sent a sensual jolt through his body. Linc willed himself to ignore it. "We're not having this conversation here," he growled, leaning close. "And I didn't come all this way to hash over the divorce. It's too late for that. This isn't personal. It's business."

"Business?" She pulled away from him. "Then why didn't you call me? We could've discussed it over the phone."

"Because I wanted to come for my cousin's wedding—and because I dislike doing business over the phone when I can do it in person."

"Is that why you didn't let me know you were coming?"

He shrugged. "Maybe if you'd known, you wouldn't have shown up."

The flicker in her eyes told Linc he'd hit home. But it was hard to believe she'd miss her friend's wedding just to avoid him. Damn it, things had been good between them once. She'd loved him—at least he thought she had—until he'd come home from a big race in Vegas and found her gone.

Up close she looked tired and stressed. Tracy had always taken life too seriously. Was she getting enough rest? Was she having any fun?

The urge to sweep her away to his hotel room and make crazy love to her until she lay limp and giggling in his arms was so strong it almost knocked him over. He wanted it to happen. Maybe under all that resistance, so did she.

"So what's the business about?" she asked. "I thought the prenuptial had settled everything between us."

"It did. Except for one thing—your horse."

"Oh." Her fierce expression softened. "Is Hero all right?"

"He's fine. But you need to make a decision about him. It's complicated. That's why we need to talk, and not here."

She sighed. "Fine. But I just got here. I need to make the rounds and at least say hello to a few people. I'll meet you at the entrance in, say, twenty minutes." She glanced at the Gucci watch he'd given her for the last birthday she was with him.

"Roger." Linc watched her walk away, admiring the sway of her hips and the taut contours of her lovely rump. *So damned proud*

389

and yet so vulnerable. She'd treated him like some kind of contagious disease. It would serve her right to be taken down a notch or two. But he'd sensed the need in her—a need that matched his.

Emotions warred as he watched her disappear into the crowd. Making moves on his ex-wife would be like stepping into quicksand. But the temptation was there, as well as the lure of the bet. Linc had always been a risk-taker. There was something about the rush of playing for high stakes—and winning—that made him feel alive. And getting Tracy in bed again would be the ultimate win. The ribs wouldn't be a bad payoff either.

He found Chet standing where he'd left him, still admiring the bourbon. Chet grinned at the sight of him.

"So, have you changed your mind about the bet?" he asked.

"Maybe," Linc said. "Make it three years' worth of free ribs and you're on."

Chapter Two

Pasting a smile on her face, Tracy wove her way through the crowd. She'd told Linc she needed twenty minutes to mingle and talk to the people she knew. The truth was, most of the people here were strangers. She'd greeted her casual friends on the way in. What she really needed was time to pull herself together.

What was wrong with her? How could she allow Linc to rock her world just by showing up?

She'd told herself she was over him. But facing him again had left her feeling as if she'd just slammed into a solid-glass wall.

In the restroom she let out her breath, wet her hands in the basin, and splashed her hot face. She was drying off when she heard a soft voice behind her.

"Are you all right, Tracy?" Meg Stoddard, Brady's best friend, had just walked in. Meg, who would be hosting the marriage ceremony on her family's guest ranch, was a stunning woman: smart, self-possessed, and genuinely nice. Tracy knew and liked her.

"It's been a long day, that's all," Tracy said. "I'm fine."

"You don't look fine. Can I get you something?"

"Thanks, I'll be okay. It's just that—" Tracy forced herself to laugh. "Sorry. I had a blast from the past a few minutes ago and I'm still in shock."

"You had—wait a minute." Meg stared at her. "I just put two and two together. Brady's cousin, that tall, heart-stopping hunk of man candy who sent the Pappy Van Winkle—he's your ex!"

"That's right. I hadn't seen him since the divorce. I didn't know he was going to be here until I walked in."

"Wow." Meg shook her head. "Brady introduced us when he arrived. I knew you'd been married to one of his cousins, but Brady's got a lot of relatives. I never made the connection until now. All I can say is, the two of you must've made a gorgeous couple."

"Thanks, but it takes a lot more than gorgeous to make a marriage—like the same values and the same priorities. Linc's not a bad person. He's kind and generous and he never mistreated me. But to him, life is all about fun and risk. He's nothing but a playboy and he'll never change."

"How do you know that?" Meg asked gently. "Maybe if you gave him a chance—"

"I gave him too many chances," Tracy said. "Linc is who he is—a man without a serious bone in his body."

"But, oh my God, what a body." Meg laughed.

"Let me tell you about the final straw, the one that sent me packing." Tracy didn't usually talk about her marriage, but now the words spilled out of her. "I'd signed up for this charity half marathon to raise money for a local homeless shelter. I'd never done anything like that before. I trained like crazy because I knew it would be tough. But all I really wanted was for Linc to be there at the finish line, to hug me and tell me he was proud. But of course he didn't show. Do you know where he was?"

"I won't even venture a guess."

"He was in Las Vegas, watching one of his damned *horses* run—and probably gambling to his heart's content. He chose that horse over his wife! I finished the race with a respectable time, came home, loaded the car, and was gone by the time his flight landed."

"And you've never had regrets?"

"Oh, I've had plenty of lonely nights. But then I reminded myself how much I wanted children—with the kind of father who'd show up for their soccer games and dance recitals and be there to counsel and support them. I knew Linc would never be that father. That was the real reason I left. I was hoping to find a man who'd put his family first. So far that hasn't happened." Tracy shook her head. "Sorry, Meg. I didn't mean to dump all this on you. I guess I just needed to talk."

"What are friends for? Don't worry, my lips are sealed." Meg gave her a reassuring smile. "Will you be spending time with Linc while he's here?"

"No more than I have to." Tracy glanced at her watch. "But I'm leaving here with him now. He wants to discuss some business over dinner—something about a horse."

"A horse? Really?" Meg raised a knowing eyebrow. "Well, whatever comes of it, I hope it's something good. If you need a friendly ear, I won't be far away."

"I'll remember that. And thanks for listening. It helped."

"Oh, I meant to ask," Meg said. "Brady and Ellie would love to have you at the rehearsal dinner. There'll be plenty of room and food, and they wanted to include some special friends and family. I know it's a last-minute invitation, but would you like to come?"

It was a surprise, but a nice one. "I'd be happy to come," Tracy said. Then, too late, she realized Linc would likely be there, too. Never mind. She was a big girl. And she wasn't about to let him spoil her enjoyment of the wedding.

Chin up, she made her way back through the room to where Linc waited for her. When she'd married him, she'd been young—just twenty. Eleven years older, Linc had treated her more like a toy than a wife. But now she was a mature woman of twenty-eight. She had built a life and a career on her own. She knew how to handle herself with men—even this man, who made her heart drop every time she looked at him.

"Let's get out of here." His hand brushed the small of her back as he guided her out to his rental car: a red Mercedes convertible. "I asked Brady to recommend a good restaurant. He gave me a couple of suggestions. I hope you like the one I chose."

"You could have asked me."

"I didn't want to waste time." He opened the door for her. Tracy sank into the buttery leather upholstery, fastened her seat belt, and closed her eyes.

"Tired?" He slipped into the driver's seat and closed the door.

"Mm-hmm." Tracy nodded. "It's been a long, rough week."

"Then you need to relax, have some fun." The engine purred to life as he started the car.

"Do you still drive like a maniac?"

He laughed. "Give me some credit. I don't want to lose my license—or my life. How've you been, Tracy? I hear you're a tigress in the courtroom."

"You make me sound like one of those TV lawyers in designer suits and four-inch heels.

Just so you'll know, every hour I spend in court demands hours of preparation behind the scenes. And the pro bono work I do, mostly for women, takes time, too. You want to know how I've been? I've been damned busy."

As the convertible pulled onto the expressway and sped up, the breeze caught her hair, raking it back to flutter behind her. It was getting dark, but she put her sunglasses on to shield her eyes from the wind.

Linc's hands rested on the steering wheel. Powerful hands, long-fingered and sensitive. He drove ten miles over the posted limit, with the confidence and skill of a man who enjoyed speed and the mastery of a beautiful machine. She could tell him to slow down, but she knew he'd only laugh. People didn't change.

With the rush of wind filling her ears, conversation wasn't worth the effort. It felt good to just sit back and feel the fresh air on her face. In the west, the last glow of sunset was darkening into night. A roiling cloud bank moved along the horizon. Sheet lightning danced in the distance. The thunder was too far away to hear, but Tracy could smell the coming rain.

When he took the freeway exit, Tracy guessed where he was going. In this part of town was an intimate and very expensive club that served prime steaks and vintage wines. But Linc drove right past the place, continued on another mile through a maze of streets, and pulled up to the curb in a neighborhood of low stuccoed buildings, graffiti-painted walls, and billboard ads with Spanish text. Young people dressed for a Saturday night strolled the sidewalks in couples and groups. A half-dozen teenage boys looking like something out of *West Side Story* loitered on a nearby corner. A police cruiser slowed as it passed them, then drove on.

The restaurant, which opened onto a cracked sidewalk, was dimly lit behind an arched doorway. A flickering neon sign above the door spelled out the name: *La Lagartija Roja*, The Red Lizard.

"Here we are." Linc parked the Mercedes and switched off the engine. "I remembered how much you liked Mexican food. According to Brady, this place has the best in town."

Tracy glanced around uneasily. "I love Mexican food. But aren't you worried about leaving the car?"

He laughed. "It's a rental. It's fully insured, and there are plenty of people out here. Relax; it'll be fine."

Tracy folded her sunglasses and put them in her purse. Now that the car had stopped, she could hear the muted sound of mariachi music coming from a radio somewhere. The aromas of pork carnitas, roasting chiles, and tobacco smoke mingled with the clean scent of rain. Thunder rumbled in the distance as the storm approached.

"You should at least put the top up," Tracy said.

"Not a bad idea." He punched a button and waited until the convertible's top had unfolded and clicked into place before climbing out of the car and coming around to open the door for Tracy. "Watch that broken curb," he cautioned as he helped her out. "It could give you a nasty stumble."

"Thanks." She took his hand and stepped up to the safety of the sidewalk. Her belly growled, a reminder that she'd barely eaten all day.

"Hungry, are you?" he teased.

"A gentleman would have ignored that," Tracy said.

"Sweetheart, I've never pretended to be a gentleman. You of all people should know that."

He opened the door, saving her the awkwardness of a reply. Inside, the restaurant was cozily decorated with adobe walls, Mexican pottery, and live green plants. A low blaze flickered in the Talavera-tiled fireplace on one wall. Candles in folk-art holders glowed on the tables. A trio of musicians was warming up on the stage.

The hostess ushered them to the quiet corner booth Linc had requested. Sliding into her seat, Tracy felt reality settling in. She was having dinner in a romantic restaurant with her ex-husband, a man she'd done everything possible to blot from her memory. And she couldn't take her eyes off him.

Back when they were married, an evening like this would have ended just one way—with a deliciously sensual romp in bed—or wherever they happened to be when the urge became too powerful to resist.

But if Linc was angling for a rematch—and she wouldn't put it past him—the man was in for a rude awakening. Her hormones might be screaming *yes!* but this time her cool, sensible head was calling the shots.

The server took their orders and brought two margaritas. Brady had been right about the restaurant. It was a perfect blend of folksiness and elegance, with its shadowed booths, flickering candles, and romantic music.

He reminded himself of the bet he'd made. He liked tangy barbecued ribs well enough. With an unlimited free supply, he could throw some great parties. But with Tracy sitting across from him, the candlelight mirrored in her emerald eyes, suddenly the bet didn't matter. It was the woman he wanted, in his arms and in his bed. He wanted to feel her long, silky legs wrapping his hips, hear her little gasping cries as he sent her spiraling out of control again and again.

This wasn't just about winning. It was about winning *her*.

"What about my horse?" Her question snapped him back to reality. "You said I needed to make a decision."

"That's right." Linc had given her the blooded bay gelding as a birthday gift. A few months later Hero, as she'd named him, had suffered a severe condylar fracture in his first race. The trainer had recommended putting him down, but Tracy wouldn't hear of it. After surgery and long, costly rehabilitation, Hero was sound enough for light riding, but he would never race again.

"Thank you for keeping him all this time," Tracy said. "I always meant to take him, but there's no way for me to keep him here. I live in a condo and can't afford full-time boarding."

"That's just it." Linc sipped his margarita, tasting the salt on the rim of the glass and thinking how beautiful she looked by candle-light. "Hero needs a better situation."

She sighed. "I understand. What Hero costs you in stable space, food, and care would be better spent on a horse who's out there on the track making money for you—or busy making babies."

Sadly, she'd nailed it. Raising Thoroughbreds was a business, and in cold, hard terms, Hero was a liability. Linc might have sold the horse sooner, but Tracy, as the registered owner, needed to sign the papers.

"I don't mean this to sound harsh," he said.

"Oh, but you do—and it is." A wistful smile teased her lips. Linc ached, remembering all the times he'd kissed her, and how intoxicating those lips had tasted.

"No, it's more than that. Hero needs a job. He's being fed and groomed and exercised some. But that isn't enough to keep him sharp. He needs work."

She nodded in rare agreement. "All I want for Hero is that he be valued and treated well," she said. "I can't take him myself; what other options do I have?"

"Here's what you're looking at," Linc said. "I've been putting the word out, and so far, you've got two offers. You can choose one—unless you have a better idea."

"I'm listening." She sipped her drink, her tongue flicking a grain of salt from her soft upper lip. Linc felt a stab of desire. He stifled a groan.

"Understand, Hero's not a youngster any-more, and that front leg could give him some trouble as he gets older. He's got champion bloodlines, but because he's gelded . . ."

"I know all that. But he's a beautiful horse and good-natured. Surely somebody would want to buy him."

"I have an offer of sixteen thousand cash from a spa and guest ranch in the Tennessee hills. Given his age and condition, that's about as much as you can expect."

She gazed down at her drink, as if weighing what he'd just told her. Linc knew she loved that fool horse. Hell, leaving Hero in Kentucky had probably been harder than leaving *him*.

"You said there were two offers." She was looking at him again, her eyes reflecting twin flames. "How much was the other one?"

"Zero."

Her eyebrows arched. "Tell me more."

"It's from a project that uses horses to rehabilitate disabled war veterans. They call it Horses for Heroes. If you chose them, you'd be donating your horse. All you'd get would be the tax write-off."

Her face lit in the first genuine smile he'd seen all evening. "And they'd take good care of him?" she asked.

"I'm certain they would. I could look into their facility to make sure, if you'd like."

"Would you? After I've heard back, I'll make a final decision. But that sounds like a good job for Hero."

"If it's a yes, I'll send you the paperwork." He returned her smile as the server appeared with their meals. "I had a hunch you'd make that choice. I guess I still know you pretty well."

"I'm surprised you'd say such a thing, Linc. You hardly took the time to know me at all."

I probably shouldn't have said that, Tracy thought as Linc's expression changed. The man had been so cocksure of himself. Now he looked as if he'd been doused with ice water. But the words were out and there could be no backing down.

Maybe he'd needed to hear them. Maybe it was time.

The plate of enchiladas in mole with rice, beans, sour cream, and fresh avocado slices looked delicious, but Tracy's appetite was fading. She'd thrown down the gauntlet. Sooner or later Linc was bound to pick it up and fling it back.

They ate in silence for a few moments, eyeing each other like two feral cats, hungry but distrustful. Tracy could feel the tension building. She was fully braced by the time Linc spoke.

"Is that why you walked out, Tracy? Because I didn't spend time with you?"

She met his wounded gaze. "You were never there for me. You were always off having fun—the races, the parties, the marathon poker games, the women . . ."

"The women were nothing but window dressing," Linc snapped. "The only woman I wanted was the one I had at home. As for the rest, you could have come with me, some of the time at least."

"I did at first, remember? But after the first few times I'd had enough of standing around in heels and a pretty dress, pretending to enjoy myself. I couldn't stand it—the people, the drinking and gambling, the whole empty, meaningless lifestyle. It was all about pleasure and the rush of winning—both races and bets."

"Pleasure?" Linc had put down his fork. "Let me tell you something you would have known if you'd cared enough to learn. I inherited the house, the stables, and the horses. Even in good times, when my Thoroughbreds are winning races and selling high at auction, the operation barely makes enough to keep it going. I support it with my business investments— the stocks, the franchises I've funded, the real estate properties, and more.

"Most of the people I meet at races and poker tournaments are in business, too. And while we're standing around, having what looks like a good time to you, we're exchanging tips and making deals. That weekend in Las Vegas when you left—while my horses were at the track, I was checking out the site for a new resort that was open to investors. I was *working, damn it!*"

"And spending every spare minute in the casinos, I'm sure. Whatever you were doing, it must've been more important than being there for me."

"And when were you there for me, Tracy? I should've known better than to marry a twenty-year-old child who'd never stopped believing that life should be a fairy tale—a child who expected to live happily ever after in a magical palace with Prince Charming at her beck and call."

As Linc's words cut into her, Tracy felt a rush of angry tears. Was that really what he'd thought of her? Had he treated her like a plaything because she was too needy and immature to be what he wanted in a wife?

Trembling, she rose to her feet and hooked her purse over her shoulder. "Whatever you thought of me then, I'm not a child anymore. I've grown up. And I don't have to sit here and listen while you talk down to me. Do you want to drive me back to my car now, or should I phone for a cab?"

A weary look crossed his face. "If you've really grown up, you'll calm down and finish your dinner."

"I *am* finished." Tears blurred Tracy's eyes. Opening her purse, she fumbled for her cell phone.

"Oh, what the hell!" He stood, fished a handful of bills out of his wallet, and laid them on the table. "Come on, let's go."

With a hand behind her elbow, he steered her toward the door and opened it to a deluge of windblown rain. Lightning sizzled across the sky. Thunder boomed like artillery fire. Rain fell in solid sheets, pouring off the edge of the restaurant's bar tile roof. Water poured down the narrow street, filling the gutters and flowing over the sidewalks.

"Are you sure you want to leave now?" Linc shouted over the din of the storm.

"We might as well. This storm could last for hours." Tracy was already regretting the argument she'd started. They could've finished their dinner on good terms and maybe even parted friends. But no, she'd had to go and open the old wounds—wounds that might never heal again.

"All right. On the count of three, we run for it. Ready?" He clicked the remote to unlock the car doors.

"Ready." Tracy knew they'd both be soaked to the skin in seconds. But that couldn't be helped.

Linc began the count. "One . . . two . . . three!" He grabbed her hand. Rain beat down on them as they plunged across the streaming sidewalk. Moving ahead, he opened the passenger door for her. Tracy took a long step to reach it and climb into the car.

At the last second something went wrong. Her high-heeled boot caught on the broken curb that was hidden by overflowing water. Her ankle twisted, throwing her off-balance. She stumbled to one side and went down.

Reflexively, she flung out an arm to break her fall. As her hand struck the hard cement under the water, something snapped and gave way. A stabbing pain shot up her arm.

Linc lunged for her, catching her waist and pulling her upright. "Are you all right?" His hands held her steady. Water streamed off his hair and clothes.

"I . . . don't know." She felt strangely weak, almost nauseous.

"Get in." He eased her into the car and closed the door. She sat huddled on the leather seat, shivering and in pain, while he went around to the driver's side, climbed in, and turned on the car's heated seats.

"What is it, Tracy? Are you hurt?" His eyes narrowed.

"It's my wrist." She held out her right arm, supporting it with the other hand. "It's killing me."

"Let me see." He felt her wrist with gentle fingers. She gasped with pain at the slight pressure.

"It could be a break, or at least a bad sprain." He reached around her, grabbed her seat belt, and fastened it. "Hang on. We're going straight to the nearest emergency room."

Chapter Three

Linc used the car's GPS to locate the closest hospital. The wheels raised geysers of water as he gunned the engine and sped along the rain-slicked streets. Beside him, Tracy huddled like a wounded bird, cradling her wrist and biting back the pain.

This was his fault, damn it. He should never have let go of her to open the car door. If he'd hung on to her arm a second longer she wouldn't have stumbled and gone down.

He'd had high hopes for the evening—a relaxing meal, some fence-mending conversation, one thing leading to another. Who could have predicted their informal date would end like this, with a fight, an accident, and a trip to the ER?

Chet Bertelson was going to enjoy that last precious bottle of Pappy Van Winkle. The little bastard would probably drink it all on a single bender. But right now that was the least of Linc's concerns.

Heated air blasted through the vents; not enough to dry their rain-soaked clothes, but at least it kept them from shivering. Tracy's black silk blouse clung to her skin. Her hair hung over her shoulders in wet strings. She looked miserable.

"How are you doing?" He reached past the console and patted her knee.

She managed a humorless laugh. "I've been better."

"According to the GPS, we should be there in a few blocks. Hang on."

"I don't have much choice, do I?" She sucked in her breath as the car jarred through a water-filled pothole.

"Sorry; I know that hurt," he said.

"It's all right."

"And I'm sorry I called you a child. You expected the love and attention a wife deserves and I wasn't there to give it to you."

"Do we have to talk about that now?" Tracy spoke with her teeth clenched against the pain.

"We can talk later—look, there's the hospital." Linc swung the car around to the emergency entrance, parked, and helped Tracy inside. Her face was pale and she was shivering again. Linc had dealt with plenty of horse injuries. A bad break, he knew, would be a shock to her whole body.

Luckily, the ER wasn't crowded. A middle-aged nurse got to Tracy in the first few minutes. Brisk and efficient, she wrapped her in a heated flannel blanket, put her arm in a supportive brace, and helped her into a wheelchair. "We'll get a quick X-ray and take it from there." She glanced at Linc. "You're her husband?"

Linc's eyes met Tracy's. She looked so help-less and scared that he was tempted to say yes, just to make sure he could stay with her.

"He's my ex," Tracy said, saving him from the lie. "But I don't have anybody else."

"Fine," the nurse said. "He can wait out here while we take the X-rays, then come back with you later. We'll need your insurance information."

"I left my purse in the car. Can you get it, Linc? The ID card is in my wallet."

"Sure." Linc hurried outside to where he'd left the car. He moved the vehicle out of emergency parking, found Tracy's purse on the floor, and carried it back to the ER.

I don't have anybody else. He remembered her words to the nurse. It was hard to believe a beautiful woman like Tracy hadn't found someone else by now. But then, neither had he.

Right now Tracy needed someone to be there for her. It felt surprisingly good to be that someone.

He found the insurance card in her wallet and took it to the registration window. It hadn't occurred to him that he could register for her, but her address was on the card and he knew enough about Tracy—date of birth, marital status, allergies, and general medical history— to give the needed information to the clerk.

He even remembered her cell phone number. Strange how those bits of trivia had stayed in his mind, long after he'd dismissed them as useless.

Too anxious to sit, he paced the waiting room. He was about to push through the swinging doors and demand to know what was going on when the nurse reappeared.

"We're waiting for the doctor," she said. "You can go back and wait with her, if you'd like."

He followed the nurse down the hallway to a closet-sized room with a curtained glass window in front. Tracy, dressed in oversized green scrubs, was sitting up on the bed. Her cold-packed arm lay in the support brace. Her wet clothes hung on the back of a chair. The ruined silk blouse was missing one sleeve.

She gave him a wan smile. "Sorry to be such a lousy dinner date."

"You're forgiven." He set her purse on the chair and walked to the side of the bed. He'd meant to brush a kiss onto her forehead, but when he bent down, it was her lips he found—ripe, satiny, and cool to the touch. For an instant she resisted. Then her mouth softened beneath his. Kissing her, even with gentle restraint, was still better than he remembered. It took an act of will to straighten and step back. When he did, he saw there were tears in her eyes.

"I don't think we'd better do that again," she said.

"Why not?" Linc's head was still pleasantly buzzing.

"Because things are already complicated enough. It took me a long time to get over you and get a life, Linc. I don't need to go back— not to any of it."

"Damn it, Tracy, I'm sorry," he said.

"For the kiss? Or for this whole crazy, stupid mess?"

Linc shook his head. "Not for the kiss. But the rest? Yeah, it pretty much sucks."

Lord, girl, how did we get from loving each other to here? Where did we go wrong?

He couldn't bring it up now and risk another battle—not when she needed him so much.

"What do you know about your wrist so far?" he asked, changing the subject.

"Just that it hurts—really hurts. The doctor has the X-rays. He'll bring them when he comes in." Tracy pushed back her damp hair with her left hand. "What am I going to do if it's broken? I'm right-handed. I live alone. My car has a stick shift. I don't know if I'll even be able to use my computer or text on my cell phone."

Linc gave her shoulder a gentle squeeze. "Let's worry about that when we know more, all right? Maybe it's just a sprain."

Tears welled in Tracy's eyes. "No, I can tell it's broken. Nothing less would hurt this much."

• • •

As if her words were a cue, the ER doctor, who hardly looked old enough to be out of high school, walked in carrying a manila folder.

Tracy faked a smile. "As Bugs Bunny would say, 'What's up, Doc?'" she asked, making a lame joke.

"Well . . ." The doctor spoke with a Texas drawl. "I've got bad news and good news. Take a look at this X-ray." He opened the folder and placed it where Tracy could see. Linc hovered, looking over her shoulder.

"This is your wrist. See the crack across this big bone?" The doctor pointed with his ball-point pen. "That's the bad news. It's called a distal fracture of the radius. In plain English, it's broken."

Tracy wasn't surprised. But she still felt sick inside. "And the good news?" she asked.

"The good news is you won't need surgery. It's a clean break, no displacement of the bone. With a cast to keep it stable, you should heal fine in about six weeks."

Six weeks! Tracy felt as if she'd been crushed by a cattle stampede. She had at least two trial dates scheduled, along with several depositions. Then there was her pro bono work. And there was Brady's wedding, less than a week away.

"Here's what to expect," the doctor said. "For

413

the first few days, until the swelling goes down, you'll be wearing a splint. You'll want to rest and ice the break as much as possible. You can take aspirin or ibuprofen for the pain. On the fourth day you'll come back to the hospital and get your cast. Understood?"

"Yes, but I need to be at work. And my friend is getting married next weekend. Will I be able to drive my car?"

The doctor shook his head. "No driving, period. You won't be able to manage a vehicle safely with the cast on your hand."

"Don't worry, Tracy," Linc said. "I'll be around until after the wedding. I can drive you where you need to go. After that, you can work something out."

But how can I ask you to drop everything and babysit me? We aren't married anymore. We're barely even friends!

Tracy knew better than to voice the thought. The cold, hard truth was, she needed Linc. Her ex-husband was the only help she had.

Linc watched while the nurse slipped a cotton sleeve over Tracy's hand and forearm, wrapped it in gauze and an elastic bandage, and fastened the splint—which looked something like a plastic sandal—around it. Tracy's lips were pressed tightly together. It had to hurt, but she didn't make a sound.

The nurse finished the job by strapping on a blue cotton sling to support the splinted arm. "Keep this on when you're up and around," she said. "Keep your arm elevated as much as possible and keep the wrapping dry. I'll make an appointment for the cast in four days—that would be Wednesday—and give you directions to where you'll have it done. It's in the ortho-pedic wing of the hospital."

"Can you make it any sooner?" Tracy asked. "I need to Skype into some important meetings that day—all day."

The nurse brought up the schedule on the computer installed in the room. "The schedule's full Tuesday morning. But if you want to chance it, you can come by that afternoon. There's an opening at two-fifteen."

Tracy glanced at Linc. "Does that sound all right? If you can't take me then, I can always call a cab."

"No, it's fine. I can take you," Linc said.

"Be aware that you're taking a chance. If the swelling hasn't gone down or the X-ray doesn't look good, you'll have to make another appointment," the nurse said. "But with no surgery and no bone displacement, you should be all right."

"I understand," Tracy said. "I'll take the appointment—and I'll bring back these scrubs I'm wearing then."

• • •

Linc drove Tracy back to her condo using the GPS. By then the storm had faded to a drizzle. The moon glimmered through thinning clouds. Tracy, in the scrubs and damp boots, huddled in silence beside him. Her left arm cradled her splinted wrist. "Still hurting?" he asked.

"Some. I've got ibuprofen at home. I'll take a couple of tablets when I get there." She glanced at him. "No need for you to come in. I can manage fine."

"Let me be the judge of that. Is there anything else I can do? What about your car? You left it at the party."

She sighed. "Yes, I was thinking about that. I hate to ask, but—"

"No problem. If you'll give me the keys, I'll get a cab and bring the car back for you."

"Thanks. It's a Mini Cooper. If I leave it there, somebody might be tempted to take it."

"Don't worry. You'll have it back tonight."

"Thanks again," she said. "I don't know what I would have done without you."

"Without me, you wouldn't have a broken wrist. So forget the thanks."

They arrived at her condo: a two-story town-house-style unit in a complex of similar buildings. When Linc came around the car to help Tracy out, she had her purse and the bag of wet clothes slung over her left arm. The keys were in her left hand. "I'll give you these after I let myself in," she said. "You can leave your car in visitor parking, over there." She pointed to a sign. "My parking space is number twenty-six, around to the side. If I'm asleep when you get back, just leave the keys on the kitchen counter."

After fumbling with the key, she unlocked the door and opened it. Linc hesitated, wondering whether he should follow her inside. "Will you be all right?"

"I'll be fine." She thrust the keys at him. "I'm just going to take something for the pain, brush my teeth, put on my pajamas, and go to bed. You're welcome to wait for your cab in the living room. There's cold beer and Diet Coke in the fridge."

"Fine. I'll move my car and be back."

After she'd closed the door, Linc called for a cab and parked his car in the visitor zone. By the time he returned to the condo and let himself in, Tracy had vanished upstairs.

From overhead, he could hear water running. He imagined her struggling to open a lid, brush her teeth, and get into her pajamas with a rigid splint halfway up her right hand. He was tempted to go upstairs to offer his help. But something told him he wouldn't be welcome. She'd had enough of him for one night.

She'd left a table lamp on downstairs. Its glow

revealed a room that was quietly tasteful, with overstuffed leather furniture, green plants, and framed art prints. A comfortable room, honest and orderly, like Tracy, who deserved better than to be injured on his account—and better than to be the object of a reckless bet.

Damn!

Linc glanced at his watch, opened a Diet Coke from the fridge, and settled into a chair to wait for the cab.

Ninety minutes later he pulled Tracy's Mini Cooper into the numbered parking place and unfolded his cramped body from the driver's seat. *Never again,* he vowed as he straightened to his full height and massaged the kinks out of his back. Another mile in that tiny car would have crippled him.

Leaving the car safely locked, he opened the door to Tracy's condo and stepped inside. The place was quiet, the table lamp still on. There was no light or sound from upstairs.

Was Tracy all right? She was probably asleep. But she'd taken a rough shock. If she'd passed out on the floor and he left her that way, he would never forgive himself.

He climbed the stairs on silent feet. In the semidarkness, the town house half-lit by the moon outside, he could make out an open bathroom with a high window and, across the hall, another door standing ajar. Stepping close, he eased the door open far enough to look into the room.

Tracy lay in a pool of moonlight that spilled through the window. Her eyes were closed, her hair a tangled fan on the pillow. The scrubs she'd worn home lay heaped on the floor next to the bed. Her right arm, wrapped and splinted from elbow to knuckles, lay flung to one side. Her bare shoulders, showing above the edge of the sheet, told him she'd been too tired to get into the pajamas she'd mentioned earlier.

The thought of her lying naked and vulnerable in her bed triggered a jab of desire, so powerful Linc had to bite back a groan. He recalled every detail of her beautiful body, the curves and hollows, the way she smelled, the way she tasted, the way her bare skin felt against his. Never in his life had he wanted a woman more than he wanted his ex-wife right then.

But decency and common sense won out. Releasing his breath, Linc moved the door back the way he'd found it and stole downstairs.

In the kitchen he found a cold Corona in the fridge, opened it, and tipped back the bottle for a long drink. He didn't feel up to driving back across town to his hotel—not yet, at least. And he didn't feel right about leaving Tracy alone after so much trauma, especially when she might need help getting herself together in the morning. It wouldn't be a bad idea to spend the night there.

The beige leather sofa looked well padded. With his height, he'd have to bend his knees or prop his feet over the end, but he was tired enough to sleep anywhere. His clothes were dry by now, so why not?

Linc finished the Corona and dropped the bottle in Tracy's recycle bin. Then he kicked off his boots, stretched out on the sofa, and covered himself with the knitted throw that hung over the back. Closing his eyes, he drifted into a restless sleep.

Tracy woke to the smell of coffee. She groaned and tried to push herself upright. Daggers of pain shot up her arm. Only then did she realize she'd put weight on her splinted wrist. She was going to have to be more careful.

But coffee . . . It smelled heavenly. Either somebody was brewing it next door with a window open or . . .

Linc! She'd given him her keys. Had he come back and spent the night?

Her robe hung on the back of the door. She pulled it down and slipped it on, right arm first. Fumbling with the fingers of her right hand, she managed to tie the sash. Until her wrist was healed, just getting dressed was going to be a full-time job.

Barefoot, she made her way down the stairs. Linc was in the kitchen, pouring a cup from the coffeemaker. Unshaven, uncombed, and dressed in his rumpled jeans and shirt, he looked sexy enough to trigger a warm tightening in the depths of her body. Beneath the blue silk robe, her nipples shrank to tingling nubs that showed through the fabric.

Easy, girl, she cautioned herself. Linc might be the hottest man she'd ever known, but she'd be crazy to go where her hormones were coaxing her. She'd been down that road before and she knew where it led.

He looked up and saw her on the stairs. "How's the wrist this morning?" His voice was muzzy with sleep. She remembered mornings, waking up to the sound of that voice in her ear, then rolling over and . . . *No, you can't go there!*

"My arm feels swollen," she said. "But I slept all right. You stayed here?"

"Right there on the couch. I've had better nights. But I wanted to stick around in case you needed me."

"I'd have been fine. I'm not a baby, Linc. I can take care of myself. You should have gone back to your hotel and had a comfortable night's sleep. If I'd been awake, I'd have told you to do just that."

"If I had, I'd have stayed awake wondering whether you were all right. Give me a break, Tracy. If you hadn't gone with me last night, you wouldn't have fallen. I feel responsible."

"Responsible or just plain guilty?"

"Take your pick." He gave her a disarming grin. "No sniping allowed until you've had some coffee. Come on down and join me."

Tracy sighed. Being contrary was the only way she knew to put distance between them—a distance she needed this morning. But Linc wasn't taking the bait. Taking care not to trip over the hem of her robe, she started down the stairs.

Linc knew he should avert his eyes. But the sight of Tracy moving down the stairs in a silky robe that floated around her bare legs, giving him glimpses of thigh, was enough to ignite his blood like a blowtorch touched to gasoline.

He tore his gaze away and focused on pouring the coffee into her mug, adding a little milk because that was how he remembered she liked it.

She perched on a stool next to the counter-top. "Thanks for getting my car, by the way. Was it all right?"

"Fine. Just a tight fit for me."

"Oh—sorry. I didn't think of that when I

asked you to go." She was being nice again. And the way the thin silk clung to her breasts was gloriously indecent. The strain against his jeans was getting painful.

"It wasn't that bad. Here you are." He handed her the mug. She took it awkwardly with her left hand and took a sip.

"Mind if I take a look at your splint?"

"Go ahead. You can pretend I'm one of your horses."

Linc ignored the jab as she extended her right arm on the counter. "I can tell you've got some swelling," he said. "You'll need to ice it today."

"Good luck with that. The icemaker in my fridge hasn't worked for six months."

"My mother always used bags of frozen peas and corn for ice packs. They worked fine. What's in your freezer?"

"Maybe one really old bag of frozen peas." She sipped her coffee. "I'm not much of a cook. Too busy with work."

"I already guessed that. I was going to make us breakfast, but you don't have much to work with around here."

"Sorry. Most mornings I just grab coffee and go. Because it's Sunday, I'd planned a grocery run. But that isn't going to happen. I guess if I get hungry, I can always order takeout."

She looked meltingly sexy sitting across the counter from him, sipping coffee in that next-to-nothing robe, with her hair tousled and her eyes still drowsy. Back when they were married, he would have swept her upstairs and spent the next hour finding ways to make her moan with pleasure. But that was then and times had changed.

"Tell you what," he said. "Let me run to the store for you. You can give me a list, or I'll just pick up whatever looks good. When I get back, I'll make us some breakfast."

"Linc, you don't need to—"

"Listen, we're both hungry and you can't cook left-handed. Besides, you'll need something to ice your wrist. I'll take the convertible."

"Fine. But take my keys, too." She shoved her key ring across the counter toward him. "I'm going upstairs to try to shower. If I'm not down here when you get back, you'll need to let yourself in."

He took the keys and put down his coffee cup. "On my way," he said. "Be careful not to get your splint wet."

"I'm not a baby, Linc."

Before she could escalate the comment into another argument, he was out the door. The woman was prickly this morning and he couldn't blame her. But even on edge, she was so sexy that it was all he could do to keep his hands off her.

The hell of it was, the woman was sending out

signals. Coming downstairs with nothing under that clingy silk robe, making eyes at him over her coffee . . . A splinted wrist wouldn't be enough to keep what he craved from happening. And if Tracy wanted it, too, how long could he resist her?

Driving to the nearby big-box store, he thought about the damned-fool bet and how he never should have made it. Sure, a good roll in the hay with his ex would win him a three-year supply of ribs. But that wasn't what he wanted. He wanted Tracy back in his life—for good. If she found out about the bet, she would never speak to him again.

He had to assume she *would* find out. Chet didn't strike him as a man to trust with a secret. If Chet told Brady, or anybody else who knew Tracy, it would all be over.

In the wagering game there was such a thing as honor. Linc had never backed out of a bet in his life. And he wasn't about to do it now.

As he saw it, he had a choice. He could win the bet, have one glorious romp with his ex, and lose her for good. Or he could keep hands off, lose the bet, and hope the truth would save him.

He had to take a chance.

He had to lose that bet.

Chapter Four

By the time Linc returned from shopping, Tracy had showered and dressed in a baby-blue T-shirt, yoga pants, and sneakers. Getting clean while hanging her right arm out of the shower had been a challenge. She'd splashed a lot of water on the floor. But she was learning to manage. Next time, she vowed, she would have this down, along with a lot of other things. For a long list of reasons, she couldn't depend on Linc to take care of her much longer. She didn't want to impose on him, she didn't want to feel obligated, and she could already sense the danger of falling under his spell.

She was in the kitchen, icing her wrist with the primordial bag of frozen peas when she heard the key turn in the lock. Linc walked in with two tall grocery sacks, which he set on the counter. "See, paper not plastic," he said.

He was wearing a new black T-shirt, jeans, and sneakers, which he'd evidently put on at the store. His unshaven jaw was shadowed with beard stubble. Hot. Sizzling hot. But then, the man would look sexy in anything. Or nothing, as she remembered well.

He tossed her two bags of frozen vegetables and put four more in the freezer. "Two bags at a time," he said. "When one pair starts to thaw, you can rotate them. Keep that up for the rest of the day and you should start seeing results. Don't plan to go anywhere until you get your cast on."

"Bossy old thing, aren't you?" she teased.

"Somebody's got to make sure you behave yourself." He began unpacking the bags, putting milk, eggs, and juice in the fridge. He'd included some frozen gourmet dinners she could microwave later on. Tracy got up to help him put some of the items away, but he stopped her with a stern look. "Stay put," he ordered. "Just keep icing that wrist."

Tracy had to admit it was fun watching Linc cook breakfast. He was surprisingly good at the job, frying bacon and scrambling eggs, mixing pancake batter, and setting the table. *I could get used to this,* she thought. But she knew better than to say so. She didn't want him to get the wrong idea.

So why did the wrong idea keep popping into her calm, rational head as she watched him?

"Breakfast is served." Pulling out her chair, he seated her before a plate heaped with bacon, eggs, and pancakes, with juice and coffee on the side. "Eat up," he ordered, taking his place across from her to eat his own breakfast.

"There's so much."

"What've you had to eat in the past twenty-four hours? By my recollection, half of a Mountain Dew, a margarita, and a few bites of an enchilada with mole sauce. Your body's had a shock. You need your strength."

Jockeying with her left hand, she managed to get a forkful of scrambled egg to her mouth. It was fluffy and perfectly seasoned. She ate a few more bites before speaking. "I appreciate all you've done, Linc, but you can't just walk in here and take over my life. I'm a big girl. I can take care of myself."

"Eat your breakfast." His tone was gruff, but his eyes twinkled. Tracy suspected he was enjoying himself. She poured some real maple syrup on her pancakes and took an awkward bite. Good. She took another. She really was hungry.

"You've got syrup on your chin." He reached across the table and, with a sexy smile, dabbed at her chin with his napkin. He was turning on the charm full blast. It was working, and so were her hormones. Linc knew how to push her buttons. If he kept pushing them, she wouldn't stand a chance.

Part of her wanted him to spend the day and longer. She imagined curling up with him on the couch, the tingling heat rising between them until urgency drove them upstairs to the bed. It would be wonderful, she knew. Sex with Linc had always been earth-shattering. But what then? Would he expect more, like a long-distance relationship, or would he just wave good-bye and walk out of her life? Either way, she wasn't ready to deal with the emotional avalanche that would follow.

If she didn't get him out of here, she would be brainless putty in his masterful hands.

"Listen, Linc," she said. "You've been a lot of help and I'm grateful. But I need you to leave after breakfast. I've got work to do—briefs to read, cases to research, notes to transcribe. I can do it on my computer, even one-handed, but in order to concentrate, I need to be alone."

He frowned. "Okay. But should you be working so soon?"

"I need to be working. I have meetings scheduled tomorrow, but I should be able to Skype into the office. I can keep the cold packs on my wrist the whole time. There's no need for you to show up again until the appointment to get my cast."

"Fine. I'll leave you my number in case you need anything. You'll have to take it easy for a few days before the wedding. I hope you'll be feeling up to the rehearsal dinner on Friday. Brady said I could bring a date and you're the only single girl I know well enough to ask."

"No need to ask. Meg already invited me. I wouldn't miss it."

"In that case, I'll be your ride. We can work out the details on Tuesday, when I pick you up for the cast. Now finish your breakfast. I'll clean up and load the dishwasher before I go—if you're sure you don't want me to stay. Last chance." He gave her a teasing look.

"No, I really need to work." That was true. So why was she disappointed that he was so willing to leave and stay away almost two days?

Linc stood, took the glass carafe from the coffeemaker, refilled both their mugs, and sat down again. "Tell me about your work. Brady says you're making quite a name for yourself."

Laughing, she shook her head. "That's Brady for you. Maybe someday I'll be a household word. But right now I'm just a junior partner in an up-and-coming law firm. There are five of us, all young, all hungry to get ahead. The adrenaline never stops rushing. We do both litigation and criminal cases. Not the big-money stuff yet, but issues like sexual harassment, business scams, petty crime, landlord versus tenant, divorce—you name it."

"So why do you do this, Tracy? You can't be making a lot of money or having a lot of fun. Why not go back to modeling? You were doing pretty well, as I remember. And you're as beautiful as ever—I mean that."

"Thanks, but I'm not twenty years old any-more. And it was never what I wanted to do with my life. I wanted to help people. I wanted to make a difference. I like to think I'm doing that now, or at least moving in the right direction."

"Brady says you're doing some pro bono work, too."

"I am," she said. "I spend part of every Saturday visiting women's shelters. That's where I really feel needed. I help with things like restraining orders, child custody, property and divorce issues, job applications, and any other legal concerns the women have. Most of them left home with nothing but the clothes on their backs. Most of them had been abused. Many of them have children to protect. They can't afford to pay me, but that doesn't matter. If I didn't need to make a living, I'd quit my job and do it full time—for nothing."

Linc stood and began clearing the table, leaving Tracy wondering if she'd said too much. He worked in silence, putting food in the fridge, rinsing the dishes, and slotting them in the dishwasher.

After what seemed like a long time, he spoke. "So, are you happy, Tracy? Is your life every-thing you hoped it would be?"

She paused before answering. "In most ways. Of course I'd like a family someday. But now doesn't seem to be the time." *A half truth. She'd always wanted a family. She'd wanted one with him until she realized he wasn't much of a family man.*

"How about you?" she asked.

431

"Work keeps me busy. I can't say I'm happy, but I'm not unhappy either. I guess I don't have time to give it much thought. Maybe if you'd stuck around, we'd both be happier."

He'd stepped onto dangerous ground and they both knew it. But maybe it was time to clear the air. They'd never talked over their separation; no counseling, no mediation. The prenup had already laid down the terms and the modest settlement Tracy would get if she stayed less than five years. Their lawyers had worked out the details, the papers were signed, and it was done.

"Remember what you told me about Hero? You said he needed to work. Well, so did I," Tracy said. "I had all the money I wanted to spend, a beautiful home, an expensive car, designer clothes, and hired help to do the housework. But I felt like a useless toy. I couldn't even be a partner to you because you were off working or playing or whatever you want to call it. The only way you seemed to want me was in bed. That part was great, but it wasn't enough.

"The volunteer work I did toward the end was a step in the right direction. But what I really wanted was a family with a man who'd be a good father to our children. You didn't seem to care about anything but your thrill-ride life-style. I couldn't see any way to change things. That's the real reason I left."

Linc's expression had gone rigid. Tracy braced

herself for a blistering defense—that she'd been selfish and immature, that she'd expected too much from the marriage. But the angry words she'd expected didn't come.

Instead, he exhaled, turned away, and hung up the towel he'd used to wipe off the countertop. "Something tells me we both need a break. Let's leave it there and I'll see you on Tuesday. Call me; you have my number. And keep icing that wrist." With that, he walked out the front door and closed it behind him.

Tracy sat at the table, fighting tears. She could already sense it: the hollow feeling that had always crept over her when Linc left. Her hand balled into a fist. *Blast it, just let him go!* She didn't want to feel this way. She didn't want to need him ever again.

Most of all, she didn't want to love him.

But her heart, it seemed, had a will of its own.

On Monday, after calling ahead, Linc drove out to the Cutwright ranch. As he pulled up to the rambling house with its broad, covered porch, Brady came out with two Coronas.

"Good timing." He grinned as Linc climbed out of the car. "With Ellie and her friends caught up in the wedding craziness, I've become a fifth wheel."

"You, a fifth wheel?" Linc laughed. "No way."

"Hey, I'm only the groom. All I really need to do is show up and stand in the right place."

Brady waved an arm toward the wicker chairs on the porch. "Come on up and have a seat. I was hoping we'd have time to visit."

Linc climbed the steps, took a seat, and accepted a Corona. Growing up as an only child, he'd thought of Brady as the closest thing he had to a younger brother. In recent years they'd seen too little of each other. It was nice, having a rare chance to catch up.

"You're looking good, Brady." Linc put a boot on the porch rail, opened the Corona, and took a long swig. "Getting married must agree with you. I've only just met Ellie, but she strikes me as a great girl."

"Thanks for not telling me it's too soon." Brady sank into a nearby chair. "Most of my friends have told me to give it more time. But, damn it, life is short. When you know you've found the right woman, why wait?"

As he looked at Linc, his expression changed. "Oh man, I stepped in that one, didn't I? You said the same thing when you married Tracy after knowing her just a few weeks."

"That doesn't mean it won't work for you and Ellie. Different people, different expectations . . ." As Linc sipped his Corona, he recalled his wedding to Tracy. He'd been head over heels in love with her. Truth be told, he still was— though he'd rather walk on a bed of cactus spines than show it.

"You two were so happy and so much in love," Brady said. "I looked at you and thought, *That's what I want for myself someday*. What the hell happened with you two anyway?"

Linc shrugged. "She was young and I was too involved in my crazy lifestyle to give her the attention she needed. I came home after a trip to Vegas and she was gone. End of story."

"You know you were an idiot, don't you?"

"The worst kind of idiot. I had a beautiful, intelligent, loving woman and I was too stupid to realize I needed to hold up my end of the relationship. It never occurred to me that I could lose her until she walked out."

"Maybe it isn't too late." Brady finished his Corona and set the empty bottle on the porch. "I saw you two leaving the shower together. Did you make it to that Mexican restaurant I told you about?"

Linc managed a rough laugh. "We did. We drove there in a downpour and got in a fight before the meal was half-finished. Coming out, Tracy fell and broke her wrist, and we spent a couple of hours getting her patched up in the ER. I drove her home, picked up her car, and spent the night on her couch. Not quite what you'd call a romantic date, was it?"

Brady shook his head. "You never can tell. At least she got to see a new side of you. That might be worth something. You and Tracy are

435

two of my favorite people. When I heard you'd be here, I was hoping you might reconnect."

"We reconnected all right. But not in the kind of way that leads to happy endings. I'm staying away now to give her some space."

"Are you sure that's what she wants? Tracy's never talked to me about the breakup. But in the years she's been back, I haven't seen her with another guy. It's been school, work, and the occasional dinner with friends. My guess is the lady's hiding a broken heart."

"A broken heart? Hell, she's the one who left."

"What if she left because she thought you didn't love her? Who knows? Maybe you've been given one last chance to change her mind."

"Maybe." Linc finished his beer. He knew better than to tell Brady about the stupid bet he'd made. The less said about that, the better. If Chet was going to be at the rehearsal dinner, it might be possible to get him off to one side to do some damage control. But if Chet opened his big mouth, any chance of a future with Tracy would be dust in the wind.

He made small talk with Brady a while longer—safe subjects like plans for the wedding and after, the ranching business, the future of horse racing, and updates on the family. Then he made his excuses and rose from the chair. "When you're in the mood for a trip, I'd enjoy hosting you and your bride in Lexington. I can show you the sights and there's plenty of room in my big house. Except for the help, I just rattle around alone."

"It sounds like you could use some company— the permanent female kind, with a ring on her finger. Think about it. Tracy's one hell of a woman. You'd be crazy to let her get away a second time."

"Message received loud and clear. I'll give it some thought. But Tracy's her own woman. She might not be inclined to come back."

Brady grinned. "Give it a try. The worst she can do is say no—or maybe punch you in the face. She does have a redhead's temper. See you at the rehearsal dinner."

Linc took his time driving back to town. The day had been long and slow. With no prospect of seeing Tracy, the hours until bedtime loomed even longer. More than once he'd reached for his phone to call to make sure she was all right. But he'd checked the impulse. Tracy wouldn't want to be babysat. And she had a broken wrist, not a life-threatening injury. She'd be fine— and if she wasn't fine, she could call him.

Besides, if he wanted to lose that fool bet, spending time alone with her could be a risk. Even now, the thought of making love to her was almost driving him crazy. He imagined bursting into her condo, bolting the door, and taking her where he found her—on the couch, on the table, on the rug, or even against a wall—thrusting into that hot, wet sweetness again and again until they both—

The wail of a siren behind him shattered his daydream. Glancing at the speedometer, he swore. He'd been going at least twenty miles over the speed limit.

Damn!

Ten minutes later he was on his way again with a costly ticket tucked in his wallet. He'd learned not to argue with Texas cops and this one had had him dead to rights.

Another thing he'd realized when that siren blasted him back to reality: fantasizing about Tracy wasn't going to help. If he really wanted her back, he needed to stop thinking like a hormone-crazed sixteen-year-old.

Her reasons for leaving him had nothing to do with sex. That part of their marriage had been spectacular. But when it came to responsibility and emotional support, he'd fallen far short.

Tracy had wanted children, but she hadn't seen him as father material. That hurt more than anything else she'd said, maybe because it was true. His own father had been away on business far more than he'd been home. And even when he was around, he'd spent more time with his horses and his gambling buddies than with his wife and son. Linc had grown up accepting his father's absence as natural; it was what a man did to provide for his family. And his mother had found ways to fill her time—things like luncheons, bridge games, shopping, and beauty treatments. His parents had rarely quarreled. But they'd slept in different bedrooms. Both of them had passed away in their sixties, ending their separate lives under the same roof.

Had his parents' marriage been the model for his own?

What a fool he'd been!

Tracy switched off her computer and closed her tired eyes. It was after eleven o'clock. She'd been reading briefs and researching legal precedents for hours. Her broken wrist was throbbing and her left hand was cramped from unaccustomed use. Time to call it a night.

Too wired to sleep, she found a beer in the fridge, popped the tab, and sank onto the couch. At this hour, with her basic cable package, there was nothing on TV but series reruns, pro wrestling, and infomercials. Settling for an old episode of *Law and Order*, she put her feet up and lay back against the cushions. Too bad her own job wasn't as exciting as this show.

Tomorrow morning she'd be Skyping in to two depositions and a partner meeting. Then, in the afternoon, Linc would be taking her to the hospital to get the cast on her wrist. She'd done her best to keep it iced and even worn the sling as much as she could stand to, but the break was still hurting. At least the cast would stabilize and protect it.

A smile teased her lips as she remembered how Linc had cooked breakfast for her yesterday, after spending the night on her couch. She'd missed that—waking up with him and sharing the morning. She'd missed other things, too: the sound of his voice, his laugh, the delicious roughness of his beard against her skin when he hadn't shaved.

And, heaven help her, she missed him in bed. She missed the warm tangle of their legs, the smell of his body, his masculine weight between her thighs as he moved inside her.

The beer had grown warm in her hand. She set the can on the coffee table, seized by a yearning so deep and poignant she moaned out loud. She wanted him. Not forever; there were too many unhealed wounds for that. But how could one night for old times' sake, with no strings attached, be so wrong?

The idea scared her a little. But what did she have to lose except her pride? With her left hand shaking slightly, she laid her phone on the table and punched in the number he'd given her.

The phone rang once, then again.

What if he wasn't alone? A man like Linc—all he'd have to do was smile at a woman and she'd follow him to his room. This was a bad idea.

She was about to hang up when he answered. "Hullo?" He sounded as if he'd been asleep. "Tracy, are you okay?"

"Yes . . . just checking in." She was already losing her nerve. "Did I wake you?"

"Yeah. But that's okay. How's your wrist?"

"Better. I've been icing it. It should be all right for tomorrow. Are you still coming to take me to the hospital?"

She felt tongue-tied. Why couldn't she just tell him what she wanted?

"How about I come early and take you to lunch first? Maybe something light. Then we can have a good dinner later on. I read about a great seafood place."

"Sure." At least he wanted to see her again. "What time for lunch?"

"Around twelve-thirty? That'll give us time to eat and get you to the hospital."

"Fine. I have to work tomorrow morning, but I'd planned to take the afternoon off."

"Maybe you're working too hard," he said. "Are you sure you're all right, Tracy? Is there something you need?"

I need you to come over here and make wild, crazy love to me. I need to fall asleep in your arms and wake up with your face next to mine on the pillow.

The words came to mind, but Tracy couldn't bring herself to say them. She'd only end up embarrassing them both.

"No, I'm fine," she lied. "Sorry I woke you up."

"It's all right," he said. "Get some rest. I'll see you tomorrow."

"Yes. Tomorrow." She ended the call.

Linc replaced the phone on the nightstand. The glowing digits on the bedside clock read 11:24. Wide awake now, he lay back on the pillow, staring up at the dark ceiling of his hotel room.

Strange, that late-night call from Tracy. She'd never really told him what she wanted, but he'd sensed the strain in her voice. Was something wrong?

Maybe he ought to get up, drive across town to her condo, and make sure she was all right. But he knew where that would lead. Resisting Tracy would be like resisting the warm, wet force of a tropical hurricane. And if he ended up spending the night, it wouldn't be on her sofa.

This was all his fault for making that idiot bet. He would give Chet a dozen bottles of Pappy Van Winkle just to have it over and done with. Too bad he didn't have the little bastard's phone number. He would call him right now to arrange a payoff in exchange for his silence.

As things stood, all he could do was control himself and hope for the best. He wanted Tracy back in his life, now and forever. He'd lost her once; he'd do anything to keep from losing her again.

Anything.

Chapter Five

Dressed in jeans and a black tank top, Tracy was waiting when Linc arrived to pick her up for lunch. When she opened the front door, his smile melted the last of the crumbling resistance inside her. Linc was a one-way ticket to heartbreak. But she was on the brink of falling for her ex all over again.

Not that it meant he felt anything for her. For all she knew, he was being kind because he felt guilty about her wrist. Or worse, he could be playing her for his own amusement. With Linc, she couldn't be sure of anything.

"What sounds good for lunch?" he asked.

"We agreed on something light. There's a good organic soup and salad place a few blocks from here. It faces a park with a pond. We can eat outside."

"That sounds fine." His eyes took her in as he helped her into the car. "You look pretty appetizing yourself."

"Same charming old Linc." She gave him a knowing smile. She was in a more sensible frame of mind today than she'd been last night. She'd given herself a good talking-to—a stern reminder to watch her own step—and guard her heart. But how long could she follow her own advice?

Adjusting the sling on her splinted arm, she settled into place. From the driver's seat, he reached past the console to help her with her seat belt. She'd gone braless because she couldn't work the fastenings one-handed. The brush of his arm against her breasts was enough to harden her nipples. She stifled a moan of response. She'd always been sensitive to his touch. Some things never changed.

"Point the way." He was clean-shaven today, dressed in a charcoal-gray polo and khakis. As always, he looked like a man in charge. He drove with the top down, the hot midday wind blowing Tracy's hair back from her face. The air seemed to crackle with electricity. Was a storm on its way or was she feeling the aura of power and excitement that seemed to surround Linc wherever he went?

Part of her wanted this to happen—the sense of risk, the giddy highs and lows that went along with loving him. But could she handle the letdown of finding out he hadn't changed? That was the question she needed to answer before it was too late.

The open-air café was one of Tracy's favorites. The outdoor patio, with a view of a wooded park, was relaxing, the food always fresh and tasty. They chose a quiet table and ordered iced tea to drink while they studied the menu.

She took a moment to decide on minestrone soup and a garden salad. Linc scowled at the menu.

"What is it?" Tracy asked.

"Where's the meat?"

"You said we should have something light. The menu is vegetarian."

"Oh." He shrugged. "Then I'll just have what you're having."

Tracy gave their orders to the server. "It'll be really good, I promise. And tonight we can try the seafood place you mentioned."

"About that . . ." he said.

"What?" Her bubble began to deflate.

"Sorry, Tracy; I got the call just an hour ago. I need to fly back to Lexington for a couple of days. A property I have shares in is about to be sold. I'll need to be there first thing tomorrow for the negotiations. My flight leaves at five today. I've already checked out of the hotel and put my bags in the car."

"Of course." Back when they were married, she'd lost track of the times she'd had to cancel plans because Linc had to be—or chose to be— somewhere else. She had no claim on him now, so she had no right to feel let down. But she did.

"Will you make it back in time for Brady's wedding?" she asked.

"I wouldn't miss it. My flight lands in Austin Friday afternoon, so I'll also be here to take you to the rehearsal dinner. You can count on it."

"I'll cross my fingers—and arrange a ride if you're not here. It never hurts to have a Plan B."

His hand closed over hers. "You won't need a Plan B, Tracy. I'll be here. I promise."

Their soups and salads arrived. Tracy had to eat slowly to keep from spilling, but they finished their meal in time for a walk around the park. The day was warm and sunny with a hint of a breeze. Children climbed on the playground equipment and threw bits of bread to the ducks in the pond. Couples and families picnicked on blankets under the trees.

"Sometimes when I look at families, I wonder how things would've turned out if we'd had a baby," Linc said. "Do you think it would've made a difference?"

The question opened a raw wound. "Only if you'd stuck around to be a father," Tracy said. "Otherwise, we'd just be passing the poor little thing back and forth between here and Lexington. Not a very happy thought, is it?"

He exhaled. "I really let you down, didn't I?"

"Never mind. I was the one who ended it." Closing the painful subject, Tracy glanced at her watch. "We'd better head out. We've got twenty minutes to get me to the hospital."

Linc let Tracy out at the entrance to the ortho-pedic wing. She hurried into the building, leaving him to look for a parking space in the crowded lot. By the time he tracked her down inside, a technician was wrapping her gauze-padded forearm in what looked like long strips of soggy neon orange tape, looping it around the base of her thumb to keep it stable. Tracy spotted Linc in the doorway and grinned. "It's fiberglass. The latest fashion. Comes in assorted colors. Dresses up any outfit. Every woman who sees it will want one."

She was damned adorable, Linc thought. Brave, too. If luck and fate allowed him to get her back, Tracy—and their children—would be his number-one priority. Whatever it took, he would rearrange his schedule, and his life, to be with them.

But first he had to convince her that he could be the husband and father she wanted. Whatever happened next, he couldn't let her down.

By the time Tracy's cast was finished, it was getting late. Linc would have to hurry to get her home and make it to the airport.

"I could take a cab home," she said as he helped her into the car. "It's not that far."

"No, sit tight. We'll be fine." He stomped on the gas pedal. The red convertible roared out of the parking lot and into the early rush-hour traffic.

Tracy checked her seat belt. Her right arm

was in a sling, which she didn't plan on wearing long. The fiberglass cast was light and strong. Once she got used to it, she should be able to manage fine. But right now, six weeks seemed like forever. The worst of it was not being able to drive her car.

Linc was weaving through traffic, making good time in spite of the crowded streets. Tracy would be counting the hours until he was back in Austin—*if* he came back. He'd made her a promise, but if something came up in Lexington, it would be no different from promises he'd made and broken in the past.

"Will you have time to check on that wounded veterans' place for my horse?" she asked him.

"I'll make time. If it looks right for Hero, I'll bring you the paperwork to sign."

"Thanks. I have a good feeling about it, but I need to be sure."

"I know you do." He reached across the console and squeezed the back of her hand. They were turning into the complex where she lived. Moments later they pulled up in front of her condo.

"I'll let myself out. You're in a rush." She struggled to open the passenger door with her left hand.

"Not that much of a rush." He came around, helped her out of the car, and walked her to the door of the town house. He used her key to unlock the door, then hesitated, as if waiting for her to go inside. She looked up, meeting his gaze.

Come back. Come back to me, Linc.

She knew better than to speak those words. She had no right to hold him to anything.

"I'll see you on Friday," he said, as if he'd read her thoughts. "That's a promise."

Gathering her into his arms, he kissed her, long, hard, and deep. It was a kiss that burned through her like summer lightning, a kiss poignant with need and bittersweet with remembered pain. A kiss made of promises and—perhaps—lies. Tracy felt it in every part of her body.

Their lips clung, lingered, then separated. "I'll call you," he said.

Then he was gone.

True to his word, Linc did call the next night. The phone rang just as Tracy was drifting off to sleep. She reached for it on the nightstand, almost knocking it to the floor with her clumsy left hand.

" 'Lo," she muttered.

"Did I wake you?" His deep voice was soothing, like a good shoulder rub. Tracy could feel the tension flowing out of her. She sank back against the pillows.

"Not really," she said. "I'm glad you called. How did your business meeting go?"

"Fine. But my mind wasn't on business. My thoughts kept wandering to a certain lady."

"That doesn't sound like you."

He laughed. "I checked out the horse place this afternoon. Nice people. They have professional degrees and really seem to believe in what they're doing. There's a clean stable with a paddock, an outdoor track, and an indoor arena where the veterans work with the horses. I watched for a while. The horses are gently treated and they look well cared for."

"So you think Hero would be all right there?"

"He'd get plenty of attention and he'd be doing valuable work. But the decision's up to you."

"Then it's a yes, I guess."

"Fine, I'll tell them. And I'll bring the paperwork when I come on Friday." He paused, as if stifling a sleepy yawn. "How's your wrist?"

"It doesn't hurt too much and the cast is keeping it stable, but it's going to be a long six weeks. The receptionist at work will be giving me a ride starting Monday."

"Should you be going back so soon?"

"It's a broken wrist, not open heart surgery, Linc. I'll be fine. You sound sleepy."

He laughed—a sound she'd always loved. "Maybe we both need some rest. I'll see you on Friday. My flight gets in at four. I'll call you when I'm on the ground. Sleep tight."

"You too." Tracy ended the call, pulled up the blanket, and closed her eyes. Loving Linc was like climbing onto a merry-go-round, wanting the magical whirl to go on forever, but knowing, somehow, that it would end. All she could do was hold her heart, enjoy the ride, and hope that maybe this time the ending would be different.

On Friday Tracy willed herself not to watch the clock, but as the afternoon wore on, she couldn't help checking the time. Linc had told her his flight was landing at 4:00. When he hadn't called by 4:30, she began to get anxious. She was imagining the worst when, at 4:55, the phone finally rang. Her heart skipped as she saw the caller ID. Was Linc back, or was he calling from Lexington to tell her he wasn't coming? Braced for disappointment, she picked up the call.

"Where are you?" she asked.

"At the airport. Our landing was delayed. But I told you I'd be back in time for the rehearsal dinner. I hope you're still planning to be my date."

"Well, nobody else has asked me, so . . ." She laughed, giddy with relief. "What time should I expect you to pick me up?"

"The dinner starts at seven. That'll just give me time to pick up my baggage and rental car, check in at the hotel, and change. What do you say I come by at about six-fifteen? That should get us there in plenty of time."

"Sounds fine. I'll be ready."

"And I'll drive you to the wedding tomorrow. June eighteenth. Does that date ring a bell?"

"No. I—oh, shoot!"

He chuckled. "Isn't it usually the man who forgets things like wedding anniversaries? Eight years tomorrow, if we'd made it that far."

"Well, all I can do is wish Brady and Ellie better luck with that date than we had."

"Something tells me there's more to it than luck."

"Maybe so." It was time to change the subject. "Anyway, I'm glad you made it back in time for the dinner. I'll see you later."

Tracy ended the call. She already knew what she was going to wear. Like the wedding shower, the rehearsal dinner would have a casual western theme. Most of the women would be in jeans. But she'd been dying to wear the new sundress she'd bought—deep blue and dotted with clusters of tiny red and yellow flowers. The bodice was cut low in front and the waist tightly fitted, with a flaring skirt that just covered her knees. With dangling silver earrings and red sandals, she would feel confident and sexy—even with a glow-orange fiberglass cast on her right arm.

She checked the time on her computer. She

had forty-five minutes to spend researching her current court case. That would give her half an hour to do her hair and makeup and change into the sundress. Everything took longer when she had to do it left-handed. She was learning to give herself extra time.

But right now she had work to do. Shifting her focus away from Linc and the evening ahead, she brought up a file on her computer and began to read.

Linc had paid to keep the red convertible on hold at the rental agency and it had been waiting for him when he walked out of the airport terminal. Now, after checking into his hotel and changing into jeans and a western shirt, he was on his way to pick up Tracy.

He had high hopes for the evening: a tasty meal, good company, and a leisurely drive home under the Texas stars with Tracy at his side. If he played his cards right, he wouldn't be kissing her good night at the door or sleeping on her couch. He'd be living the fantasy that had been torturing his libido all week.

Still, the thought of what could go wrong was enough to make him sweat. Everything depended on timing—and on the treasure that rested in its protective case, locked in the trunk of the car. His last bottle of Pappy Van Winkle had made the trip from Lexington. He would give it to Chet

Bertelson to pay off the bet and buy his freedom.

If his plan was to work, three things had to happen. First, Chet would have to be at the rehearsal dinner. Second, Linc would need a chance to get the little jerk alone to pay off the bet. Third, Tracy mustn't ever find out, or even suspect, what he'd done.

Wishing himself luck, he pulled up to Tracy's condo, pocketed the car keys, walked to the porch, and rang her doorbell.

No one came to the door.

Linc rang the bell again and waited. Maybe Tracy was in the bathroom and couldn't hear him.

He waited a little longer. What if she'd fallen and hurt herself? Or what if somebody had broken in? Prepared to smash the door down if necessary, he tried the knob.

The door was unlocked.

His pulse raced as he walked in and closed the door behind him. "Tracy!" he called at the foot of the stairs. "Are you all right?"

"More or less!" Her voice came from upstairs. She seemed to be laughing. "But I could use a little help. Come on up."

With a breath of relief, Linc hurried up the stairs and down the hall to her bedroom. In the doorway he stopped, as if he'd just been ambushed.

Tracy stood on the rug next to the bed, an

embarrassed smile on her face. She looked ready to leave for dinner, except for her dress. Held against her chest by her left hand, it hung loose from her shoulders and sagged at the waist. Only when she turned around, revealing the wide-open back, did Linc realize why she needed him.

"I can't zip my dress." Her voice was slightly breathless. "Could you give me a hand?"

"No problem." He walked over to where she stood. Her lovely back was one long, bare line, with no bra. At the base of the zipper opening, he glimpsed the edge of naughty little black lace panties. Except for the dress, she appeared to be wearing nothing else.

Close up, her sensual, womanly aroma dizzied his senses. Beneath his jeans, his erection was already rock hard. He took a deep breath and fumbled for the dress's zipper tab. Later tonight the dress would also need to be *un*zipped, Linc reminded himself. What followed would come naturally. He could wait that long, couldn't he?

As he inched the zipper tab upward, his hand brushed the satiny skin of her back. A little moan escaped her lips. She *wanted* him to touch her. The awareness slammed into him, sending him over the brink.

Abandoning the zipper, he ran his thumbs up the hollow of her spine. His splayed fingers moved around her ribs to cup her small, firm breasts. The nipples were swollen like summer raspberries. He stroked them, letting the wild sensations build. She arched her back, responding to his touch with little purring sounds.

"Oh, Linc . . ." Her voice was a lusty whisper. The dress fell around her hips and slid down her legs to the floor. He pulled her in against him, kissing the nape of her neck and the hollow of her shoulder. One hand moved down over her hip, fingers finding and lifting the lace band of her panties. She gasped as he found her wet cleft and stroked her—knowing exactly how she liked it—until she shuddered against his hand.

Even then, it might not have been too late to stop; but Linc was already yanking down his jeans and rolling on the condom he'd tucked in the pocket. Taking care to keep her cast out of the way, they fell across the bed. Aching with need, he peeled away the fragile panties, parted her willing legs, and came home—to where he'd wanted to be for five long years.

Their lovemaking was like a long-remembered dance. But they were different people now, older, stronger, and scarred with the pain of being apart. They knew who they were and what they wanted. Sex had always been good between them, but this time it was better than ever, ending in a climax that shook them to the depths of their souls.

Only when it was over and he was lying on top of her, kissing her laughing face, did the full implications hit home.

He had just won the bet.

And he was in big trouble.

Fifty-five minutes later, glowing and slightly rumpled, they walked into the converted barn where the rehearsal dinner was being held. The guests were still mingling, some sipping drinks and visiting, others filling their plates from the buffet and sitting down at the long family-style tables.

Linc's gaze scanned the room, searching for the stocky figure of Chet Bertelson. He spotted the man halfway across the large room, standing at the bar with a beer in his hand. He was looking around, too. Maybe they both had the same idea.

Linc had done some quick thinking on the drive to the ranch. He could care less about three years' worth of ribs. And he'd already planned on parting company with the bourbon. The one thing he couldn't risk was exposing Tracy to hurt and humiliation—which could happen if Chet opened his big mouth.

Linc felt his gut tighten as Chet made eye contact with him. He raised an eyebrow, a silent signal that he'd gotten the message. They would talk later.

He might have won the bet, but winning

wouldn't matter if he lost the woman of his dreams. As a sporting man, Linc took pride in never having made a dishonest wager. But tonight there was only one thing he could do.

Lie through his miserable teeth.

He and Tracy had agreed not to hang out together at the rehearsal dinner. Their rekindled romance was still too fragile and too private to parade in public. She had already left his side to greet some friends, who were exclaiming over the cast on her arm.

She was a sexy vision in the blue sundress he'd finally managed to zip her into. He loved the way it clung to her tiny waist and the way the skirt moved with her legs as she walked. Her auburn hair curled over her shoulders. Her silver earrings caught the light from the Mason jar chandelier above her head. If he could make her his again, he would never get tired of just looking at her.

He watched her until she disappeared, blending into the crowd. Then, with a careful glance around, he ambled across the room to stand a few feet away from Chet.

"You two looked pretty cozy coming in." Chet had moved close enough to speak in a low voice. "Are you here to tell me you've already won the bet?"

"Nope." Linc kept his gaze straight ahead. "I came to tell you that I've lost. It isn't going to happen. The lady isn't interested."

"No shit!"

"You heard me. I'd just as soon not drag this out any longer. I've got your Pappy Van Winkle in the trunk of my car. You can have it tonight—on two conditions."

"We didn't talk about conditions." Chet's voice had taken on a whine, like a dog begging for a treat held just out of reach.

"Maybe not," Linc said. "But if you want that bourbon tonight, give me your word you'll put it in your car, take it home, and not show it off. I don't want anybody to know where it came from or how you got it. Understand?"

"Hell, what's the fun of that?"

"This isn't about fun. It's about making sure Tracy doesn't know we made the damned bet." Linc lowered his voice. "Look, I don't have to pay off until Brady and Ellie leave tomorrow. You could still lose; you never know. I'm giving you a chance to collect now, in exchange for keeping your mouth shut."

Chet's mouth widened in a knowing grin. "Oh, I get it," he said. "All right, I'll play along. How do you want to work this?"

Linc spoke just above a whisper. "When you're ready, go out to the parking lot. Pull up alongside the red Mercedes convertible I drove here and wait in your vehicle. When I know the coast is clear, I'll come outside and give you the bourbon. You put it away and we go back inside separately, like nothing happened. Got it?"

"Got it."

"And not a word or I'll make you regret it."

"Don't worry." Chet made the *X* sign over his lips. "See you outside. Don't take too long." He finished his beer and sauntered toward the front door.

Linc took his time, sipping from a can of Mexican beer he'd picked up at the bar. Scanning the guests, he could see Tracy at one of the tables, eating and talking with a young couple. Her back was toward him. Now was as good a time as any.

Linc left the beer on one of the tables and meandered toward the exit. With a final glance to make sure Tracy wasn't watching, he slipped outside.

By now the evening sunset had faded to dusk. The barn cast a long shadow across the open ground that served as a parking lot for the event. There were about thirty vehicles, mostly pickups and SUVs, parked in loose rows. Linc had no trouble locating the red convertible, which he'd left on the far side of the lot, away from the entrance. A black pickup was parked next to it, in a spot that had been empty when he'd arrived with Tracy. That would be Chet.

Taking his time and humming along with the music that drifted from the barn, he walked toward the truck.

Tracy was enjoying the dinner and the company of her friends. But she'd overused her arm today. Beneath the cast, her wrist was throbbing, the pain was getting worse.

The over-the-counter meds she'd been taking were in her purse, which she'd left locked inside Linc's car. If she didn't take something for the pain in her wrist, she'd be miserable for the rest of the night.

There was nothing to do but find Linc, borrow his keys, and get her purse out of the car. Excusing herself, she got up from the table. She'd noticed him talking to Chet earlier, near the bar. He had to be somewhere close by. But after minutes of searching the room, she couldn't see him anywhere.

Maybe he was in the restroom. She glanced down the hallway toward the door to the barn's single unisex bathroom. The door opened. A middle-aged woman came out. There was no sign of Linc.

She decided to ask the young woman tending bar. "I'm looking for my friend," she said. "He's very tall, and—"

"Tall and drop-dead gorgeous? If that's the guy you mean, I haven't been able to take my eyes off him. He went outside a few minutes ago."

"Thanks." Tracy hurried toward the front door.

Maybe Linc had needed something out of the car, too. Whatever it was, she couldn't get her purse without his keys.

It was dark outside, but not too dark to see her way. When she didn't find Linc near the barn, she headed for the far corner of the lot, where he'd left the car.

She was partway there when she heard voices—one of them Linc's, the other familiar, though she couldn't place it. An instant later she saw a light—the kind that would come on when a car's trunk was opened.

What was going on? Had Linc caught somebody breaking into his car?

Heart pounding, she crept closer. A big SUV was parked near Linc's car. She ducked behind it and peered around the front end.

Linc was lifting a shoebox-sized wooden case out of the trunk. "Here you are." He held it out to a man who stood with his back toward Tracy. "You won the bet fair and square. Enjoy."

"Wow! All mine!" Tracy recognized Chet's voice and stocky frame. "I'm still amazed you couldn't get your ex-wife into the sack. I could've sworn you two had the hots for each other."

Tracy's jaw dropped. Was this what it sounded like? Had Linc really bet he could have sex with her? Or maybe that he couldn't?

Either way, she could feel her anger boiling up like hot lava in a volcano.

Chapter Six

Crouched behind the SUV, Tracy could scarcely believe her eyes and ears. She didn't understand everything that was going on, but she understood enough. She'd been the subject of an unthinkable wager—and she'd been cruelly played by the man she'd just begun to trust again.

"So we're done here." Linc closed the trunk. "The bet's paid off and I have your promise you won't say a word about it."

"Hold your horses a doggone minute." Chet hefted the box in his hands. He held it close to his ear and gave it a careful shake. "Before I let you off the hook, I want to make sure this is the real McCoy."

Setting the box on top of the trunk, he unfastened the catch and raised the lid. A satisfied grin spread across his homely face. "Oh, yeah . . . that looks like Pappy Van Winkle all right." He lifted the bottle from its packing and held it up to the little light that remained. "You wouldn't pull a fast one on me, would you? Maybe I ought to taste it just to make sure."

"I wouldn't advise that," Linc said. "If you drink out of the bottle, you're liable to backwash and contaminate the bourbon. It won't be worth much after that, except for you to drink."

"Hell, I was just gonna drink it anyway." Chet gripped the bottle with one hand. The other hand twisted the top, straining to break the tight seal. He was still trying when Tracy walked into the open.

Linc groaned at the sight of her. Right now, Tracy was the last person on earth he wanted to see.

She faced him like a warrior queen, fury in every inch of her posture and murder in her eyes.

"Tracy, I can explain—" he began.

"Don't bother." She cut him off. "I've heard enough to know what's been going on. You used me—*used me*—to make a bet! That's got to be a new low, even for you!"

"I was just—"

"I don't want to hear your excuse, Linc. I'm still in shock. But why should I be surprised? Everything's always been about you and the thrill of winning! And you never care who you hurt! I never want to see you again."

"Just listen to me, Tracy." He put out a calming hand, which she ignored. He was dimly aware of Chet watching, openmouthed. "It's true, I was stupid. I made a bet. But so help me, I lost! I was paying it off!"

"Here's what I think of you and your stupid bet!" With a lightning move, she snatched the bourbon from Chet's hands. Caught off guard, neither man had time to stop her as she hurled the bottle in an arc over the nearest line of parked vehicles. Coming down, it struck the bumper of a truck and shattered in an explosion of glass shards and 23 Reserve Pappy Van Winkle. Within seconds, the precious liquid had soaked into the earth.

Stunned speechless, Linc stared at his ex-wife. He'd seen some shocking things in his day, but this was in a class by itself. He didn't know whether to laugh or cry.

Chet was groaning. "That's not fair," he whined. "You owe me another bottle."

Linc found his voice. "I don't owe you a damned thing. You had the bottle. If you hadn't been so all-fired anxious to open it, this wouldn't have happened. We're done here."

Slinking away like a whipped dog, Chet took the empty box, climbed into his pickup, drove to a spot on the far side of the parking lot, and went back inside the barn. He would no doubt spread the story; it was too juicy to keep to himself. But that didn't matter anymore.

As Chet's taillights disappeared, Linc turned to face his ex-wife. Now that he'd found her again, the thought of losing her a second time was as bleak as a prison sentence. Watching her fling that bottle of near-priceless bourbon—damn it, that had been the perfect thing to do. She was magnificent.

He took a step toward her. "Tracy—"

Her icy expression stopped him. "I'd ask you how you could do something so despicable, but I really don't care to know. Get my purse out from under the seat. I'll be taking a cab home. Once Hero's donation is settled and the paperwork is signed, I never want to hear from you again."

Linc felt as if he were drowning and had lost his life preserver. Somehow he had to keep this woman from walking away.

"Be sensible," he said. "A cab would have to come from town. You'd have to wait for it and it would be a fifty-dollar ride back at least. Let me drive you. We can leave now and I won't say a word unless you want me to. I promise."

She sighed. "All right. I really don't want to go back in there. And I don't feel like talking. I just want to go home."

"Understood." He opened the door for her. "Come on, let's go."

Tracy pulled her purse from under the seat where she'd stuffed it. The bottle of extra strength ibuprofen was tucked into a side pocket. She shook two tablets into her hand and managed to swallow them dry.

"Are you all right?" he asked, starting the car.

"Just sore." She closed her purse and buckled her seat belt. She felt wretched. She'd let herself believe he'd changed. She'd even trusted him to make love to her. But she should have known better. He'd been playing her the whole time, just so he could win the bet he'd made.

Except that he hadn't won the bet. He'd lost. That was why he'd given Chet the bourbon. Something didn't make sense.

After a few miles of silent thought, she spoke. "It won't make any difference, understand, but as long as we're here, I'd like to know the story behind that bet."

She listened as he told her: the banter with Chet, his decision to make the bet.

"Those first few minutes at the shower, you treated me like something you'd scraped off your shoe," he said. "I wanted you even then, but I also wanted to put you in your place. I made that fool bet out of spite. By the time I realized it was a bad idea, it was too late."

"Why too late?"

"Because I always honor my bets. And because I knew that if I won, and you found out, I'd lose any chance of getting you back."

"Well, you were right about that," Tracy said.

"I know." He paused to pass a slow-moving truck. "So I decided I had to lose. I was doing a pretty good job of self-control. Then you asked me to help you into that dress . . ."

"So you really won the bet. But you told Chet you lost and gave him the bourbon."

"That's right. I didn't want you hurt, so I lied."

"That's insane."

"I know."

"You're a blithering idiot, Linc. I wouldn't have you back if you held a loaded gun to my head."

"I know that, too."

They didn't speak again until they were a few blocks from the condo. Linc slowed the car. "The wedding's tomorrow at three," he said. "You'll need a ride to the ranch. Let me drive you there and back. No strings attached."

"Why?"

"To help you," he said. "And to say good-bye at the end like two civilized adults."

"All right." She sighed. "You know I'll never trust you again, don't you?"

"Yes, I know. I blew it, Tracy."

He pulled up to her condo and stopped at the curb. She reached for the door, fumbling with her awkward left hand. Before she could raise the latch, he came around and opened the door.

"I'm fine," she said, climbing out. "I can let myself in."

"It's dark. I'll see you to the door."

Staying a little behind, he followed her the short distance to the stoop. Tracy already had her key in her hand. She shoved it into the lock, gave it a turn, and opened the door.

"Hold still." He touched her shoulder.

"What is it?" She imagined a spider crawling up her back.

"Just one last thing." His fingers found the zipper tab at the back of her dress. In one neat move, he pulled it downward, opening the zipper to the bottom. "Now you won't need help. Sleep tight, Tracy. I'll see you tomorrow."

By the time Tracy got inside and locked the door, he was back in his car. As the sound of the engine faded, she made her way into the dark living room and switched on the table lamp. Sinking onto the sofa, she buried her face in her left hand and cried her heart out.

At ten minutes after two the next day, Linc arrived at the condo to take Tracy to the wedding. He'd thought about bringing her flowers for their anniversary. But given the way she felt about him, she probably would have tossed them in the trash. He'd decided against it.

When he rang the bell she was at the door, ready to go. She looked amazing in a sleeveless, body-skimming knit peach dress, cinched at the waist with a gold belt. No zipper. He couldn't help checking as he opened the car door for her. He'd put the top up to save her hair and allow them to talk without wind and traffic noise.

"Happy anniversary," he said as he pulled away from the curb.

"Don't remind me." There was no warmth

in her voice. "When are you going back to Lexington?"

"My flight leaves tomorrow morning. I only came for the wedding." Small talk was better than no talk. At least she was speaking to him. But Linc knew how badly he must have hurt her last night. Little had he known, when he'd made that bet, that he was making the worst mistake of his life.

"You told me you did pro bono work on Saturdays," he said. "Did you have to miss that today?"

"I checked in with my clients by phone this morning," Tracy said. "Everything's up-to-date. But I'll need to make up for lost time next week. I suppose I'll have to hire a ride service until I get this cast off my hand."

"You know, I never understood this need of yours to make the world a better place. I even made fun of it. Saint Tracy, I called you."

"I remember. I remember how it hurt, and how hard I tried not to let it show."

"I was an insensitive jerk."

A ghost of a smile tugged at her mouth. "Yes, you were."

"When I went to check on that new place for Hero, I had to watch while I waited for the folks in charge. Some of the workers there were volunteers. I could see how much they enjoyed helping those wounded vets with the horses.

Their only pay was knowing they'd made a difference. But that seemed to be enough. I think I began to understand what makes you tick in a way I never had before."

"Congratulations." She didn't sound impressed.

Linc drove on in quiet desperation, battling the urge to pull off the road, grab her shoulders, and force her to face him while he told her exactly what was on his mind.

Can't you see that I love you, you mule-headed woman? I know I've made mistakes, stupid mistakes like that bet. But I'm not the man I was when we were married. I'll do anything to make you happy. Just don't shut me out like this. I can't stand it!

They drove on to the ranch and followed the beribboned signs to the little rustic chapel where the wedding was to be held. The grassy area marked off for parking was nearly full and guests were still arriving. "Looks like it might be standing room only," Linc said.

Tracy thought of the high-heeled gold sandals she'd worn and how her feet would feel after an hour of standing. "If you want to let me out by the door, I'll run in and try to find us seats," she said.

"Good idea." Linc stopped the car by the front steps. "If you can only find one seat, take it. I'll stand." He let her out and drove on to park.

Tracy hurried inside. She was in luck. The last row had room for two people on the side nearest the door. When no one appeared to be saving the space, she sat down and put her purse in the last empty spot for Linc.

The little chapel was beautifully decorated, the western theme perfect for Brady and his bride. The staging of this wedding had taken time and care. Tracy remembered her own small wedding on this very day of the year, hastily arranged because Linc needed to return to Lexington and he wanted to take her with him. Her parents had flown in from their retirement condo in Florida. They'd invited a few friends, found a justice of the peace, and rented the rooftop garden room of a hotel. Her strapless dress, hastily bought off the rack at a discount bridal shop, had nonetheless been beautiful. And she'd been so much in love. She'd felt like a princess, marrying her prince.

Where was Linc? He should have come in by now.

A glance out the open door told her the wedding procession was about to begin. But there was no sign of him.

At the first notes of Pachelbel's "Canon," from a country guitarist who was giving it his all, the guests stood. The two bridesmaids entered first; pretty girls, demurely dressed, with bouquets of daisies and ribbons. Tracy had had no bridesmaids at her wedding. There'd been no time to ask anyone. But the music—Fauré's "Pavane," which she loved—had been played by two of her friends, a flute and classical guitar duo. She'd seen tears in her father's eyes when she'd taken his arm to walk down the aisle. "Be happy, girl," he'd whispered, squeezing her hand. And she had been—for a while.

Where was Linc? Could something have happened to him?

Now the organ broke into "The Bridal March." Ellie was coming down the aisle on the arm of the handsome officer who was her best friend. She looked like a little doll in her white cowgirl hat and boots, paired with a sweet fluff of a dress and a veil. Even from the back of the chapel, Tracy could see Brady's adoring expression as she went toward him.

Brady had been Linc's last-minute best man at her own wedding. She remembered Linc, standing beside him as she came down the aisle—the smile on his face, the loving look in his eyes. She remembered the certainty in her heart that this was the man she wanted to be with for the rest of her life, for richer or poorer, for better or worse . . .

Why hadn't he come into the chapel? Surely he'd had time to park by now. What if he'd decided to make a clean break and just leave

473

her here? That would be like Linc, especially after the way she'd treated him. She could have laughed off that silly bet and his frantic efforts to put things right. Instead, she'd let it drive a wedge between them.

How could she have been such a fool?

Now Brady and Ellie were saying the vows they'd written, so sweet and sentimental that there was barely a dry eye in the chapel. Tears trickled down Tracy's face as she remembered the tender words she and Linc had spoken to each other at the altar. How could something so beautiful have gone so wrong?

Had she and Linc been given a second chance? Or was it already too late?

The ceremony was over. Brady and Ellie were kissing as man and wife. The organ music rose as they joined hands for the happy rush back down the aisle to begin their new lives. The guests rose, ready to follow them.

Tracy slipped out the door. Her eyes searched frantically, scanning the parking lot and the overflow of people who'd come too late to find a seat inside. She couldn't see Linc anywhere.

Please, please let him be here. Give me the chance to tell him that I'm sorry, that I love him. Give us the chance to try again . . .

She was about to give in to despair when she saw him. He was coming around the corner of the church with a very elderly couple. The old man was using a cane, his wife leaning on a walker. Linc followed them, almost protectively. His tie was loosened, his slacks were stained with grass and dirt, and he had a grease smudge on his cheek.

He caught sight of Tracy. "I can explain," he said as she hurried toward him.

"No, let me explain." It was the elderly woman who spoke. "Our car hit a rock and blew a tire coming into the parking lot. This good man took the time to change it for us. I don't know what we'd have done without him!"

"It looks like we all missed the ceremony," the old man said. "We'll have to catch Brady and his bride out here. He's our great-grandnephew, by the way." He turned to Linc and offered his hand. "Thanks again, young man," he said. "I owe you."

"You don't owe me a thing." Linc shook the arthritic hand. "It was a pleasure to be there for you."

The old woman gave Tracy a knowing wink. "If this handsome fellow is yours, I'd advise you to hang on to him. He's a keeper!"

"I plan to—if he'll let me," Tracy said.

"What was that all about?" Linc slipped an arm around Tracy as the elderly pair hobbled away. "If I'll let you what?"

Tracy nestled against him. "Stick around and

maybe I'll tell you. But only if you promise to behave."

"Behave? Me? Dream on, lady!" He nuzzled her hair, his gaze following the old couple as they made their way through the crowd. "Look how they take care of each other. All that love. Where do you suppose we'll be when we're their age?"

"I don't know. But as I was sitting in the chapel, wondering where you were and listening to those beautiful vows, I couldn't help remembering our wedding and the words we spoke. I realized then that I still meant those words."

His arm tightened around her. "I still mean them, too. Wherever this crazy journey takes us, I want to make it with you. So happy anniversary, girl. What do you say we celebrate?"

Tracy's throat was choked with tears. She could only wrap her arms around him and raise her face for his kiss. They would need time to sort things out—lots of snuggling and talking, maybe more than a few long-distance phone calls, even a few good, healthy arguments. But somehow, she knew, they would make this work.

Love had given them a chance—a second chance.

Epilogue

Mr. and Mrs. Brady Cutwright made their getaway from the wedding on horseback under the guide of a brilliant yellow moon.

They rode bareback, Ellie sitting sideways behind Brady because she was still in her wedding dress. The horse was a gentle old girl Brady had owned since he was a boy, and she loped carefully across the pasture toward the Cutwright ranch.

Ellie rested her head against her husband's back, heard the steady lub-dub of his heart, and tightened her arms around his waist.

It was the best night of her life.

A Cinderella story. A dream come true. She'd found her Prince Charming and he was a million times better than she'd ever imagined.

She savored the moment, breathing in his scent, realized how very lucky they were to have found each other.

"We're home, wife," Brady said, pronouncing *wife* like a caress.

Ellie slid gracefully off the back of the mare as if she'd been born to do it. Easy. It was so easy being here with Brady. Things went so much easier when you went with the flow of life, didn't fight against it.

A stable hand came out to take the horse to the stables.

Brady got off, turned to face her, pulled her into his arms, and gave her a magnificent kiss. "I'm dying to get you into bed."

She went up on her tiptoes, nibbled his earlobe, and whispered, "So what are you waiting for?"

He needed no more invitation than that. He swept her into his arms, into the ranch house, carried her to the master bedroom, and lay her carefully on the bed. Stood looking down at her with so much love in his eyes it took her breath away.

"Look what we started when we were brave enough to join that dating service," she said.

"In just a few short months the world has opened up so many possibilities. Did you see how many happy couples there were at our wedding? Love is in the air and you're at the center of it all," Brady said, sinking down on the mattress to ease off her cowgirl boots.

"*We're* at the center of it all. Not being afraid to trust is the key," Ellie whispered. "I told that to Shane and look what happened with him and Meg. Seems like our best friends are on *their* way to the altar."

"And they were so skeptical of us at first. We really turned them around."

"We won," Ellie giggled.

"Sweetheart, everyone wins." He dropped her boots to the floor and stretched out on the mattress beside her. "Because of you."

"Us. We're a team."

"God, how did I ever get so lucky." He traced a fingertip over her nose.

"When I stared into your eyes for those four beautiful minutes on the night we met, I felt as if I stepped through the looking glass and into a beautiful, magical world that I always hoped was true but couldn't quite believe in. It was like having everything I'd ever lost returned to me."

"I felt as if I'd found my life's mission," Brady said.

"And what's that?"

"Loving you."

And with that Brady kissed his happy, happy bride and sealed their spiritual union with their earthly bodies, loving each other with passion, hope, courage, and trust. Both of them knowing deep down inside it was a love that would last a lifetime.

Center Point Large Print
600 Brooks Road / PO Box 1
Thorndike, ME 04986-0001 USA

(207) 568-3717

**US & Canada:
1 800 929-9108**
www.centerpointlargeprint.com